Many Waters

Many Waters

by

William Woodall

Jeremiah Press · Antoine, Arkansas

Jeremiah Press
PO Box 3
Antoine, AR 71922

© *Copyright 2013 by William Woodall. All rights reserved.*
www.williamwoodall.org

This is a work of fiction. Any resemblance to actual persons, places, or events is purely coincidental.

No part of this book may be reproduced, stored in a retrieval system, or transmitted by any means without the written permission of Jeremiah Press.

Cover image copyright 2013 by William Woodall, with stock provided by Simon Carrasco.

First published by Jeremiah Press on 06/21/2013.

Printed in the United States of America.

This book is printed on acid-free paper.

ISBN 978-0-9819641-9-5

*For my dearest and only one,
Ma plus chére et ma seule.*

Books by William Woodall:

The Last Werewolf Hunter Series

Cry for the Moon
Behind Blue Eyes
More Golden than Day
Truesilver

Other Novels

Tycho
Many Waters
Unclouded Day
The Prophet of Rain

Collections

Beneath a Star-Blue Sky
(short story collection)

*Many waters cannot quench love,
 Neither can the floods drown it.*

-Song of Solomon 8:7

Cody
By Lisa Marie Stone

Sometimes at night I think I dream,
Of blossoms tossed by summer breeze,
While weaved amongst my flowing hair,
Beneath the rustling white-oak trees.

I watched you gather a blade of rye,
In June all soft and palest green,
To taste the sweet and loving earth,
So fresh and cool and misty-clean.

Your skin was warm as summer hay,
The sun had kissed all golden brown,
Your touch as soft as the breeze that day,
That curled your dampened hair around.

Oh, your love was all the world to me,
And the thought that you were mine,
More beautiful then than a shining star,
When only one is in the sky.

For who could ever take your place?
And who could touch my heart so deep?
And how could I ever count the ways,
Your love has meant so much to me?

Though storms may rage and dark may fall,
And heartache come for a year and a day,
I still feel the warmth of your hand in my own,
And your love washes sorrow forever away.

Contents

Part One
Goliad

Prologue – Cody.. 13
Chapter One – Lisa 19
Chapter Two – Cody 28
Chapter Three – Cody 37
Chapter Four – Lisa 44
Chapter Five – Cody 49
Chapter Six – Lisa 58
Chapter Seven – Lisa 67
Chapter Eight – Cody 73
Chapter Nine – Lisa 76
Chapter Ten – Cody 84
Chapter Eleven – Lisa 92
Chapter Twelve – Lisa 100
Chapter Thirteen – Cody 108
Chapter Fourteen – Lisa 112
Epilogue – Cody.. 119

Part Two
These White Silver Plains

Chapter Fifteen – Cody 125
Chapter Sixteen – Lisa 131
Chapter Seventeen – Cody 135
Chapter Eighteen – Lisa 142
Chapter Nineteen – Cody 148
Chapter Twenty – Lisa 155
Chapter Twenty-one – Lisa 164
Chapter Twenty-two – Lisa 173
Chapter Twenty-three – Lisa 181

Cont'd

Chapter Twenty-four – Cody *189*
Chapter Twenty-five – Lisa *192*
Chapter Twenty-six – Cody *196*
Chapter Twenty-seven – Lisa *201*
Chapter Twenty-eight – Lisa *210*
Chapter Twenty-nine – Lisa *216*
Chapter Thirty – Lisa *224*
Chapter Thirty-one – Cody *228*
Chapter Thirty-two – Lisa *236*

Part Three
In Beauty Be It Finished

Prologue – Lisa *243*
Chapter Thirty-three – Cody *244*
Chapter Thirty-four – Cody *258*
Chapter Thirty-five – Lisa *267*
Chapter Thirty-six – Cody *275*
Chapter Thirty-seven – Cody *283*
Chapter Thirty-eight – Lisa *291*
Chapter Thirty-nine – Cody *300*
Chapter Forty – Lisa *307*
Epilogue – Cody *314*

Author's Note *318*
Discussion Questions *320*

Quotable Quotes

"It's been said that love and beauty are linked forever in the soul of man, and that's why boys always yearn after beautiful things, and know not for what they wish, nor why." – **Lisa Stone**

"There's so much depth and richness to the world beyond what the eye first sees, if you only take the time to learn about it. A man could live his whole life awash in wonders, if he only knew." – **Cody McGrath**

"I loved him more in that moment that I ever had before. Whole entire orders of magnitude greater; it was like everything I'd ever felt for him before was no more than hints and trifles in comparison, like turning from the morning stars to the blazing sun at noon." – **Lisa Stone**

"I don't mind fighting when I need to, but I don't particularly like it. I'd rather be the sunshine and the rain that makes little things grow strong, a steady rock to shelter the weak." – **Cody McGrath**

"It's so easy to make promises, when nothing is at stake and you know they'll never be put to the test. Now I was staring Death in the face, and I wondered if I had the strength to keep my word." – **Lisa Stone**

"There's a thing called magnanimity, or greatness of heart, and to me it's the most beautiful thing that ever there was. It means courage, but it's more than that. It means to cast aside all thought of yourself for the sake of another, like Moses in Gilead or the martyrs who died with a smile on their face. In its own small way it's a reflection of the Lord Jesus at Calvary, and therefore of God, the Light so beautiful that no one who sees it can ever turn away." – **Cody McGrath**

"Love with strings attached is worthless." – **Lisa Stone**

"Few things are dearer to God's heart than a son or daughter who finds themselves forsaken and alone, who can see nothing but heartache as the result of obedience. . . and then obeys anyway." – **Cody McGrath**

"God is good that way; sometimes His love brushes your cheek like a gentle caress, at times when you need it desperately and in ways you never would have guessed." – **Lisa Stone**

"No one on this earth tastes near as much of Heaven as a man and woman who join hands to love the world as God does." – **Lisa Stone**

Part One

Goliad

Prologue
Cody

Love has a way of sneaking up on you sometimes, especially when you least expect it.

So does evil.

I certainly never expected to find both of those things in the space of a single summer, but sometimes life is really strange that way.

I was mucking out the horses' stalls when it all started. Every now and then I had to stop and wipe the sweat off my face with my shirt-tail, and I think I would have traded my firstborn child for a cold Dr. Pepper right then. If you've never shoveled horse manure for two or three hours under a blistering Texas sun, then you've missed out on one of life's truly memorable experiences, buddy.

I wasn't expecting visitors that morning, so when I saw a black truck come bouncing across the cattle guard I was understandably curious. Strangers can be good or bad, but they always have to be watched carefully till you know which kind they are. I put down my shovel and started walking toward the front drive to meet whoever-it-was, secretly glad for the chance to take a break for a few minutes.

When I got close enough I noticed that the truck had Louisiana tags, and even though that's not *such* an oddity, it was unusual enough to elevate my curiosity another notch.

I was just in time to see a young man getting out of the driver's seat. He looked to be about two or three years younger than me, maybe eighteen or so, but I'd never seen him before in my life. He was wearing ratty jeans and a chocolate colored t-shirt that matched his hair and eyes, and he had the athletic build of a dude who runs or swims a lot.

"Can I help you?" I asked, when he was near enough to use a normal voice.

"Yes, sir, I think you can. My name's Matthieu Doucet, and I'm looking for the owner of the Goliad Ranch," he said. He had an ever-so-slight Cajun accent that marked him as coming from somewhere a lot farther south than Shreveport, and I wondered again what he could possibly want.

"Well, that'd be me. Cody McGrath," I said, offering my hand. Matthieu nodded and shook it, with a surprisingly strong grip.

"Pleased to meet you, Mr. McGrath. I'm afraid my business might take a little bit of explaining. May I come in for a few minutes?" he asked politely. I couldn't think of any reason not to hear him out, so I took him inside to the kitchen table and sat down. It's the place I always gravitate whenever there's a serious conversation afoot.

"I know you're probably busy, Mr. McGrath, so I'll get right to the point. We think your family might be in danger," he said.

That put me instantly on guard, of course, just like it would anybody, but I didn't let it show on my face.

"What do you mean?" I asked carefully, and Matthieu looked at me for a second, like he was sizing me up. I hate it when people do that; it almost always means they're trying to figure out how to get me to do whatever it is they want. I braced myself to be even more wary than usual, but what he said next totally blew me away.

"Mr. McGrath, do you believe in magic?" he finally asked.

Well, now *that* was a question I wasn't expecting. I *did* believe in it, of course; the Scriptures are chock full of stories about real-life witches and sorcerers. But they're also full of warnings about how we're not supposed to have anything to do with those kinds of things, so Matthieu's question alarmed me to say the least. I don't mess with stuff like that, and I don't allow it in my house, either.

"I think it's real, if that's what you mean," I said carefully.

"Well, then, maybe you can also believe it when I tell you that my job is to track down evil things like that, and put a stop to them whenever I can. That's why I'm here. Your name happened to come up recently during a fight with some especially cruel and powerful sorcerers, and that could mean you're a target. I don't know that for *sure,* but I'd be careful with strangers for a while, if I were you. Evil may not always look like you think it will, so please keep your eyes open," he said, cool as a cucumber. He seemed absolutely earnest and serious, like it was the most ordinary thing in the world.

"I see," I said, unsure what else to say.

"I'm also here to offer you some help if you *are* attacked at some point, but that's entirely up to you. I hope you never need to call on me, but if you do, please feel free," he said, offering me a business card which I took without thinking. It was cream colored, with shiny dark blue upraised italics that said *Matthieu Doucet, Avenger,* with a phone number listed at the bottom. I didn't know quite what to say to that, either.

Matthieu saved me the trouble of having to think of an adequate answer, because he got up from the table with an air of finality.

"Anyway, that's what I came to tell you. I hope you'll take it to heart, Mr. McGrath. Good luck, and God be with you," he said, offering his hand. I shook it, and that was that.

I stared at the dust trail from the disappearing truck, thinking to myself that I'd just experienced one of the strangest conversations of my entire life. I slipped the business card inside my billfold just in case, but honestly I hoped never to see or hear from Matthieu Doucet the Cajun Avenger ever again.

I went back outside to finish mucking out the stalls while I still had time, uneasy and full of foreboding. Mostly because Matthieu's warning wasn't nearly as much of a surprise as he probably thought it was.

You see, for as long as I can remember, I've had dreams.

I don't mean the kind that everybody has. I'm talking about *true* dreams. Visions. Glimpses of things yet to come. Most of the time they're incomprehensible; strange, vivid, unbelievably realistic tales that leave me baffled as to what they mean. Only rarely do I get a clear look at the future. But you better believe I pay close attention either way, just in case. Mama has always told me they're a gift from God, like the prophets in olden days used to have. All I can say is, if that's really true, then sometimes gifts are hard to bear.

Oh, not always, of course. I remember one time when I was eight years old and Mama lost her wedding ring while she was cleaning. That night I dreamed I saw it up under the dryer, and sure enough, when we looked the next day, that's where it was. It was a little bit uncanny, maybe, but nothing exceptional. That's how things were for a long time. I rarely dreamed at all, and even when I did they were usually fairly ordinary things like that.

But lately my dreams had turned dark and grim, full of monsters and blood. I didn't know quite what to make of them, but it didn't take a genius to figure out that whatever they meant, it was nothing good.

That's why Matthieu's warning was no shock to me. He was a little more specific about it, maybe, but I'd already known for weeks that I had some kind of ominous danger hanging over my head.

And then purely aside from the spooky stuff, it hadn't rained a drop since March, and the drought was killing us. We were losing money hand over fist, in fact, and even though you can run a business at a loss for a little while and still have a chance to make it up later, you can't do that forever. If something didn't change soon, I didn't know what I might have to do. Thinking about all that was enough to keep me awake at night sometimes, even if I didn't dream at all.

So what with one thing and another, I guess you could say I was pretty stressed out and preoccupied right then, jumping at shadows and inclined to think there were monsters hiding behind every tree. When you don't feel safe even in your own bed at night and you're also teetering on the brink of financial disaster, you tend not to care too much about other things.

Including girls.

In fact, I can safely say that I needed romance right then just about as much as a rooster needs a pair of socks. Maybe even less.

Which I guess goes to show what a really strange sense of humor God must have sometimes.

Mama came outside about ten-thirty to bring me a glass of tea and to make sure I hadn't collapsed from manure inhalation, I guess. It wasn't quite a Dr. Pepper, to be sure, but I was way past caring about that.

I drank the whole thing at one pull, then used the cold glass to wipe my forehead.

"Thanks, Mama, that was really good," I said, handing the glass back to her.

"Well, I thought you might need something cool to drink, it's so hot out here. Are you just about done?" she asked.

"Yeah, I'm finished now. Fixing to go load up some cows to take to the sale barn, as soon as Marcus gets back with the trailer," I said.

"Oh, all right. I don't guess you'll be back in time for lunch, then, will you?" she asked.

"No. Marcus said something about going over to his sister's place, and I'll probably stop in Ore City and grab a burger at the Dairy Dip on the way home. Don't worry about cooking anything," I said.

"All right. I hope you do good with the cows," she said, and I nodded. I hoped so too; God knows we needed the money.

I crossed my fingers and prayed for a good day, and never had the faintest clue how that prayer would be answered.

Chapter One
Lisa

I didn't recognize Cody at first.

The lunch crowd had finally trickled out from the Dairy Dip, and I was sitting at the register for a while to rest my aching feet and read a little bit of my brand new Scarlett Blaze romance novel. It was only my third day on the job, and it takes a while to get used to standing up so much.

It had been one of those days when it's hot enough to make the devil sigh, when nothing wants to move but the flies against the window panes and the dirt devils on the empty highway. It was hot even with the air conditioner on full blast, and I remember hoping there wouldn't be any more customers to have to deal with before I went home at three. I was ready for a shower.

All that changed when Cody walked in. All I noticed at first was a particularly handsome young cowboy, with the broad shoulders and lean muscles that come from a lifetime of ranch work. He was wearing boots and dusty Wranglers, with a white straw hat and a horsehair belt with a silver buckle that had a golden letter C in the center of it. He had close-cropped dark brown hair and bright blue eyes like a Siberian Husky, and that's when I knew him; no one has eyes like Cody. . . bluer than gas flames or corn flowers, blue as the lupines that blossom in spring.

I hadn't seen him since I was twelve, but I'll never forget those eyes.

"Cody?" I asked, getting up so fast I almost dropped my book. He glanced at me carelessly for a second, and then his face lit up with recognition.

"Lisa!" he cried, and immediately swept me up in a ferocious bear-hug. He smelled like sweat and horse manure, but I was too glad to see him to care about that. I hugged him back, and then stood back and looked him up and down again.

"So where have you been, boy? You've changed a lot," I said. And he had, too; he was nothing like the thin, rangy kid I remembered.

"Oh, same old place, you know. But what about you? I bet it's been eight, ten years since I saw you last time," he said.

"Well, we just got back in town about three months ago. Mama dragged us off to South Carolina for a while, and then Florida. But we're back now, as far as I know. Jenny's working down in Tyler and I'm going to nursing school and working here part time," I said.

"That's awesome. Well, listen, why don't you give me a call sometime? We can catch a movie or somethin', catch up on old times," he said.

So we traded numbers, and after he left with his cheeseburger and coke, I thought to myself that the world can be a really small place sometimes.

There was a time when I used to think I was in love with Cody, back in seventh grade when we both thought the whole meaning of the word was to hold hands in the hallway and keep pictures of each other on our phones. But still, he was the first boy who ever kissed me, at the fall dance that year, and when we had to move away at Christmas I thought I was heartbroken forever.

But time passes and you tend to forget about such things after a while. My childhood love was long ago and far behind, and life tends to be a lot more complicated at twenty-one than it ever was at twelve. But the memory of loving him was still sweet, and I was unattached at the time, and I confess the thought did cross my mind that there might still be some lingering embers between us. Maybe it was silly to think so, but then again I'd never know unless we spent some time together.

So I went with him to the movies in Longview on Friday night, mostly just for fun but also out of curiosity to see if anything might develop. I don't remember what we watched; a forgettable creature feature with enough of a love story to make it interesting for me and enough explosions to make it interesting for him. We brushed fingers in the popcorn tub now and then, and I could almost-but-not-quite swear he lingered a fraction of a second longer than strictly necessary whenever we touched. I don't think he was even aware of doing it, but I smiled to myself.

He took me out for frozen yogurt afterwards, something I hadn't done in years. I got a single scoop of mint chocolate chip (my favorite), and he had two scoops of strawberry vanilla swirl.

"So what did you think of the movie?" he asked.

"Eh, it was pretty good. The monster looked fake, though," I said.

"Yeah, I agree. No real monster would look anything like that," he agreed, and I laughed.

"You know what I meant, silly," I said.

"Sorry, couldn't resist," he said, taking another bite of his strawberry vanilla.

"I bet not," I said.

"So what brings y'all back to town after all this time? Any special reason?" he asked.

"Well, yeah. Mama had a stroke a few months ago, and things got hard after that. Grandma's old house in Ore City was just sitting there empty, so we decided to move back home to be closer to family and cut down on expenses and things like that," I said.

"Oh, I'm sorry to hear that," he said.

"It's all right. She's doing a lot better now, but she still needs somebody to help her out with things," I said.

"Well that's good, at least. So you think you'll be around for a while, then?" he asked.

"Yeah, for the foreseeable future. It's good to be back home, though. No place else is ever quite the same," I said.

Cody smiled a little, and I knew what he was thinking. He's always been the kind of boy who had dirt in his blood, as they say; he loved the land almost the way you'd think a hickory tree might love it, with roots planted deep in one spot and limbs reached out to taste the sunshine and the rain beneath a sheltering sky. He was strong that way; full of life and sure of where home would always be. It was one of the main things my younger self had always loved him for, and I was glad to see it hadn't changed.

We talked for a long time that night about all kinds of things, sitting on the tailgate of his truck and eating our yogurt till it got too drippy to be any good. After that we just talked. I told him about how I liked to do landscape painting with oils and watercolors, and he told me about his calf-roping days on the high school rodeo team. But the most interesting thing I found out was that he had a band called the Mustangs along with two other boys.

"What kind of stuff do y'all play?" I asked, curious.

"Red-dirt mostly, sometimes southern rock or gospel," he said.

"That's so cool. You really get paid for it and everything?" I asked, suitably impressed.

Red dirt music is basically homegrown Texas country, just in case you never heard of it before. The kind of stuff local bands like to play on small-town summer evenings, mostly for love of music and home. There's nothing better than a good red dirt band and some spicy beef barbecue at a Friday night tailgate party, and a case of cold Dr. Pepper to wash it all down with. What's not to love? Maybe I'm letting my southern country girl roots show, but hey, that's who I am.

"Yeah, sometimes we get paid a little bit, but we mostly play for tips. We have to take whatever we can get, pretty much. Coffee houses, county fairs, things like that. Sometimes even bars and honky-tonks if that's all we can find. And then we do the music service at church every Sunday, but we don't get paid for that. You ought to come listen sometime," he said.

"Where at?" I asked.

"At the cowboy church in Avinger. Starts at eleven, if you want to come. Just wear jeans or whatever; it's not formal at all," he said.

"I'll see what I can do," I agreed.

And so it was that I found myself driving out to Avinger on Sunday morning, dressed in nothing fancier than a pair of jeans and a t-shirt. Mama would have died a thousand deaths before setting foot inside a church in anything but a dress, and I have to confess I was more than a little uneasy with the idea myself. I had to keep telling myself I'd been specifically told to wear jeans.

I'd never actually been to a cowboy church before, even though I'd seen them often enough. The one in Avinger looks more like a barn than a church, although I have to admit it's the only barn I've ever seen that had stained glass windows. It helped when I got there and saw that everybody else was wearing jeans and such, too, and when I got inside I soon found out the reason. The church was built like a barn on the inside, too. Everything was rough wood and bare concrete with sawdust sprinkled on the floor. People were sitting on bales of hay rather than pews, and the only modern-looking spot in the whole place was the podium and the altar. It was quite a sight, to me at least.

I spotted Cody and a few others up on the stage area behind the podium, setting up sound equipment and fiddling with instruments. I waved at him when he glanced my way, and he smiled and bounded down off the stage.

"Hey, Lisa. I'm glad you could make it," he said, giving me a quick hug.

"Aw, I wouldn't have missed it for anything," I said.

"So what do you think of the place?" he asked, sweeping his arm around at everything.

"It's definitely different," I admitted, and he laughed.

"Yeah, that's what everybody says at first. I guess it seems ordinary to me by now," he said.

"When are y'all playing?" I asked.

"In just a minute. We'll go first, and then preaching, and then some of us at least will go out on the trail ride for an hour or so. Want to come? I know you don't have a horse but I guess we could ride double if you want," he offered.

"Sure. Wore my jeans, didn't I?" I said.

"Yup, that you did," he agreed.

He had to get back up on stage after that, and then they played for about thirty minutes. They were pretty good, as far as I could tell. They played several songs I'd never heard before, and a couple of hymns straight out of the hymnal.

Cody came down and sat next to me on the hay bale when the music was over, and from then on out the service progressed more or less like I was used to.

After church he led me out the back exit doors to the corral; another anomaly. I'd never been to a church that had a corral before. It was full of horses, and Cody seemed to know exactly which one he was after.

"Be right back," he told me, climbing up and over the metal pipe fence and landing on his feet. It didn't take him long to catch a pretty brown-and-white splotched horse, which he led up to the fence by his halter.

"This is Buck," he said, as if introducing me to an old friend.

"Buck?" I asked.

"Yeah. Short for Buckwild. I named him that because he was so crazy when I first went to break him. Threw me in the dirt more times than I can remember. He's my buddy now, though," he said, stroking the horse's mane affectionately.

"How long have you had him?" I asked, reaching out to pet the horse's soft nose and being careful not to let him nip my fingers.

"I got him when I was fourteen. We went to a place where they let you adopt abused and neglected horses. He was an orphan so I had to bottle feed him for a little while," he said.

He led Buck outside the corral and quickly and expertly slipped his bridle on.

"I think we'll ride bareback, if that's okay. Not really good for his kidneys to ride double with a saddle on there. Just hold on tight to me and not him, and sit as far forward as you can, okay?" he said, and I nodded.

He got on first and helped me up behind him, and I laced my fingers together around his stomach and stayed as close to him as I could, just like he told me. I could feel his taut muscles and smell the clean scent of his skin through his t-shirt, and I won't deny that I enjoyed it very much.

We rode along a dirt track that wound through the wooded hills behind the church along with a group of several other people, and it was hot even with the breeze that day.

"Y'all played really nice today. I really liked that song about *Nebo's Crossing,*" I said after a while.

"Thanks. Me and Cyrus wrote that one, actually. I think I've got some demo disks out in the truck, if you'd like one. That song's on there," he said.

"I'd love one," I said.

"Okay. Just remind me about it when we get back so I don't forget," he said.

It wasn't all that much longer before we did get back, and he swung me down with one arm before dismounting himself. He took Buck's bridle off and turned him out in the corral while I waited beside the truck.

"So what about that disk you promised me?" I asked when he got back.

"Hold on a second and I'll see if I can find one," he said, rummaging through the console.

"Here you go," he finally said, handing me a disk in a paper sleeve. The name of the group was written on the disk itself with a black marker, along with a website address and a phone number.

"I'll listen to it later sometime. I'm fixing to have to get home and check on Mama, but you can stop by about one thirty and have lunch with me at work anytime you want to. That's my break time," I offered, and he nodded.

"We'll see what we can do," he said, with one of his little smiles, and then he gave me another hug before I left.

On the way home I found myself thinking a lot about the way his muscles felt under the thin cotton of his t-shirt, and the deep but musical drawl of his voice, and a dozen other things like that. He was no boy anymore, and I couldn't deny there was definitely still some chemistry there. I couldn't help wondering if he felt it too.

I suppose I've always had a certain romantic streak. My father was like that; he loved poetry and music, and I remember him telling me he hoped I might find such a love as that someday, so fiery and strong that naught on earth could ever break it. Those were the very words he used, too. He fed me on Marlowe and Coleridge from my earliest memories, and after that, how could I not be an idealistic dreamer?

Unfortunately he wasn't exactly the faithful type himself, and he finally disappeared completely when I was twelve; that was the main reason we moved away that year. I had a hard time with it for years, but Mama always told me to love the good in him and forgive the bad, and never to drink the poison of hating him. I've been grateful to her many times for that, for casting aside her own pain and showing me by example that we live for God and not for the world. She's my hero, and always will be.

Another thing she's always told me is that whenever I meet a man who seems interesting, the very first thing I should do is to pray about the situation. Cody was definitely appealing, so I murmured a silent prayer that God would touch his heart and inspire some interest in return, if that was something which would make both of us happy and if that was what He wanted for both of us.

No, I wasn't exactly thinking about running down to the church to get married before the sun set; I'm not that silly. But it's always something to consider, at least in an abstract, long-term kind of way. I certainly didn't want to end up as one of those frumpy, starchy old spinsters who talks to her tomato plants and lives in a run-down house with forty cats.

On the disk, Cyrus was singing *Nebo's Crossing*, a verse about how Moses stood up on top of Mount Nebo at the end of his life and saw the Promised Land across the Jordan River, and how

God is always faithful to keep His promises even though it might take longer than we like, sometimes. Very true, and good to remember.

As soon as I got home, I went out to the back yard to weed and water the garden, but my mind was a million miles away from such a mundane chore. We'd had a vegetable garden for as long as I could remember, no matter where we lived; mostly tomatoes and squash and a few other things, and cabbage and broccoli in the winter. It was a quiet and satisfying kind of hobby, even though I was having to keep a close eye on things to make sure the plants didn't burn up in the heat.

But the whole time I was busy digging and weeding, I kept thinking about Cody; the sound of his voice, the roughness of his hands, and perhaps what his lips might feel like, pressed up to mine. A little bit of bare skin contact on a hot afternoon goes an awfully long way, when it comes to putting thoughts like that in your head.

But in the meantime, I was content to wait and see.

Chapter Two
Cody

Old flames die hard, it seems.

I could tell Lisa still liked me, just from the way she held me a little closer than she really had to, and the way she put her face against the back of my neck once or twice. You can always tell about things like that, if you pay attention.

That was bad.

Even worse, I enjoyed it myself. She was pretty and sweet and fun to spend time with, and I swear the way she pressed the tips of her fingernails up against my stomach muscles that day was enough to make me forget my own name. If circumstances had been different, I might have taken the bait, so to speak. No, scratch that; I *know* I would have.

But as it was, I knew better than to take even the first step down *that* path. She didn't have a clue what she was getting herself into, but *I* did, and so I owed it to her to keep my distance, much as I might regret it. I had too much going on in my life to think about getting close to anybody.

Ominous dreams and business headaches were bad enough, but there was yet a third issue that bothered me when it came to forming any kind of potential relationship.

It so happens that I like to study my family history. A pretty harmless hobby, for the most part. But one of the things you start to notice after a while is what killed everybody. Not to sound morbid or anything, but you can't help seeing patterns if there happen to be any. I guess I was about sixteen when I first noticed an odd pattern in the way my father's family died. Not a single one of them ever lived to see his thirtieth birthday. It wasn't obvious at first because it didn't seem to affect people who married in; only the natural-born members. But once you *did* notice, it was plain as a pikestaff.

My father drowned at twenty-five. My Aunt Linda was killed in a car wreck at eighteen. Grandfather died of cancer at twenty-nine. And the list went on, and on, and depressingly on. It was always something different every time, but always something commonplace like that. Nothing you could put your finger on and say it was anything unusual.

At first I thought I was imagining things, that it was just a string of nasty coincidences which didn't really mean anything. But when the list gets as long as your arm and there are still no exceptions, then you have to start wondering if there might be something else at work.

In fact, in my darker moods I was almost certain the McGraths had our own private version of the Mummy's Curse, and I was the next one whose head was on the block. Sometimes I felt like I might as well have an expiration date stamped on the bottom of my foot, like a carton of milk.

Of course I didn't *know* that. I couldn't prove it, the way you'd prove something in a book. But I'd seen the dates on the tombstones. I watched my father drown. I drove past the spot where Aunt Linda died, every time I went to Longview. It was hard not to at least semi-believe it, after all that, and Matthieu's warning about evil sorcerers only inflamed my fears even more. I never talked about it much, but it was always there in the back of my mind, a dark suspicion that I didn't really want to think about too often.

But suffice it to say, I believed it enough to take it seriously. And that along with everything else made me hesitant to get involved with Lisa, or anybody else for that matter.

I've always believed it was cruel and selfish to knowingly drag another human being into danger and heartache, if you have any choice in the matter. Least of all a person you claim to love. I'm not that selfish, or at least I hope I'm not. There's such a thing as honor, you know, even when it hurts.

But still. . . I'd be lying if I said I never thought about love and family and all those things. I was always brought up to believe that family is everything, that I have an obligation to the past and to the future, to honor my parents and love my children. In my heart of hearts, nothing would have pleased me better than to find my one and only true love and then settle down to raise corn, kids, and tomatoes at Goliad and live happily ever after.

Sound funny, coming from a young guy? Well, maybe so. But that's who I am and I'm not ashamed of it, and I know well enough that I'm not the only boy who ever thought likewise. You might be surprised how many of us think that way, if you took the time to ask.

But they say you always wish the most for the things you know you can never have, and for that reason among others I could almost wish I'd never bumped into Lisa again at all. I liked her too much, and that made things hard.

I probably should have found something more productive to do when I got home, but I grabbed my guitar and went to sit under the hickory trees in the back yard to play a few songs. They say music soothes the savage beast, or I guess in my case the troubled spirit. I love all music, but besides red-dirt, my favorite is southern gospel, or blue-eyed soul as Mama always likes to call it. Her father, my Grandpa Tommy, used to play in a band called *Southern Psalms* when he was young, and when me and Marcus and Cyrus Clay decided to start up a band after high school, he gave me his original 1939 twelve-string Martin acoustic guitar as a graduation present. It's from him that I get my love of music, and my middle name, and the color of my hair. On a small bronze plate at the foot was the name *Tommy Lee Grey, Avinger, Texas* and below it the inscription:

> *To the Lord God Almighty, the Creator of all Music,*
> *May the Hands that play these strings give You glory.*

   I always liked that, although I've wondered many times why old folks always seem to want to capitalize every other word that way. Anyway, if you don't know anything about guitars, then I'll go ahead and tell you Martins are the best that money can buy, especially the old ones. At first I'd been so intimidated by such an awesome instrument that I'd been afraid to actually play it much, but Grandpa Tommy only laughed and told me to use it for what it was meant for instead of treating it like it was made of gold leaf. So that's what I did, and ever since then I've hauled that guitar around with me all over half of Texas and parts of three other states. It's one of my most prized possessions.

   So I played *His Life is an Open Book*, and then *Send the Fire* and *Nebo's Crossing*, singing the words when I felt like it and sometimes not. I can't sing quite as well as Cyrus, but I've been told I have a nice voice. And just like always, it gave me some peace in the midst of my troubles.

   We'd been up till two a.m. the night before, playing a hundred-dollar gig at the *Little Brown Jug* down on the Longview highway. That's a honky-tonk place where guys get busted over the head with pool cues and beer bottles pretty regularly, and the smoke is so thick it'll make your eyes water and it feels almost like walking through a big bowl of tapioca pudding. I don't much like to play at bars, but when money's tight then it sure does make it hard to turn down a paid gig. At least there hadn't been any fights, but I was still tired from the late night.

   So after a while I gave up playing and lay down on the ground instead, looking up at the hickory leaves dancing in the sunlight and using my guitar as a headrest. I pulled my hat down over my face to shade my eyes from the sun, and soon enough I dozed off in spite of myself.

   And dreamed.

I found myself standing on a rocky hill under a grove of enormous pine trees, disoriented and not sure where I was. Below me was a stony path under the light of a full moon, and presently I saw a girl in a white gown walking silently along. She was paler than usual, but I recognized her immediately as Lisa.

She passed by me, and I silently climbed down to follow her, till we came to the mouth of a cave in the side of the hill. It was dark inside once we passed beyond where the moon reached, but not quite. A faint gray glow seemed to come from everywhere, just enough to find our way. I followed her down a winding staircase cut out of the living rock, and at last the tunnel opened out into a huge cavern. And here was a wonder of wonders.

The path went on through a forest of trees, but not like the kind I knew. These were of crystal and glass, brittle and glittering even in the weak light. They were exquisitely beautiful, and as we passed by I broke off a twig from one of the crystal branches.

Then we came to a lake with troubled waters dark as soot, and far off on an island in the middle of the lake was a palace blazing with light. A bridge of silver filigree crossed over to the island, and when we arrived I saw a finely-dressed young man awaiting us.

Up till then I hadn't seen anything especially alarming, but when we got close enough I saw that the man was nothing but a skeleton dressed in fine clothes. Lisa seemed not to notice, and she laughed and joined hands with him. Then for several hours I watched them dance, till morning came and she climbed the stone stairway back to the outside world. I couldn't help but notice that she looked even paler then, weak and sickly, indeed almost at the very edge of death. It was only when we reached the sunlit world again that she seemed to revive a little, but somehow I knew the man in the blazing palace hadn't turned her loose for long.

I pulled the crystal twig from my pocket and watched it crumble to black dust in the morning sunlight, and then a voice from above me spoke.

"Save her from the evil one," it said.

Then I woke up, covered in sweat and gripping the grass with my fists. I hate the ones like that, when I know they mean something really important but I can't guess what it is. Who was the evil one, and what did all the rest of it signify? I couldn't tell, except that like all the others lately it was obviously something really bad. And worst of all, what was I supposed to do about it?

I did *not* need this. It wasn't like I didn't already have enough of my own problems to deal with.

"What's wrong with you, boy?" Marcus's voice cut through the haze of reverie, startling me.

"Huh?" I asked, still half-dozing. I pulled the hat from my face, shielding my eyes from the light. Marcus was looking down at me, and I yawned and sat up.

"You were twitching and talking to yourself, so I wondered what was wrong," he said.

"Oh. I was only dreaming, sort of. That's all. Sorry about that," I said.

"Dreaming about what? Hot mermaid babes in real estate jackets again?" he teased, and I laughed a little. Back when I was eighteen I had a dream about a mermaid who was also a real estate agent and came up out of the sea wearing an old-fashioned gold-colored Century 21 jacket. I never did figure out what that one was supposed to mean, although I have to admit she was a smokin' hot babe and it sure was entertaining. I told Marcus about it years ago, and he's never ceased to think it was hilarious.

"No, not this time. It was about a skeleton, mostly," I said.

"Dang, boy, you're weirder than I thought," Marcus said.

"Ha, ha, very funny," I said.

"So what do you think it means? Anything?" he asked, and I hesitated. Marcus knows all about my dreams, with good reason. But he also knows I don't like to talk about them much.

You see, on Christmas Eve my senior year, I dreamed I saw a boy about my age sitting in his bedclothes at the pole barn in the Ore City park, fifteen miles away. I never would have had any reason to go nosing around over there ordinarily, and especially not on Christmas morning. But to make a long story short, I went out there to check, and sure enough there he was, exactly like I saw him in my dream, shivering in the cold and wrapped in a blanket with nowhere to go.

You probably guessed by now it was Marcus. Turned out his dad got drunk and kicked him out of the house that morning, so he wandered over to the pole barn and tried to think what to do. Christmas Day is a bad time to be out on the streets; everything is closed, and nobody wants visitors. We didn't even know each other at the time; he went to school at Ore City and I went to Avinger, and we'd never had a reason to meet before then. He was already eighteen, barely, so I guess Mr. Cumby had a right to throw him out if he wanted to, but I thought then as I think now what a sorry thing it was to do.

So I offered him a place to stay for a while and a job helping out around the ranch. I guess I probably should have asked first, but when I brought him home that day Mama treated him like a long-lost son, just like she would have done with any other lost kid who needed a place to be loved. He's been here ever since, and in all that time I couldn't ask for a better friend.

Except when he gets some kind of bright idea in his head, and then he can be stubborn as a green-broke stallion. Like now.

"Cody, I've been thinking. I was listening to the radio the other day and there's a preacher down in Longview that was talking about dreams and visions. Why don't you go see him? Maybe he could help you figure somethin' out, you know?" he asked.

That was actually one of the more sensible suggestions Marcus had come up with lately, and I frowned, thinking about it. The simple and obvious dreams I never needed any help with, but what was I supposed to think about crystal forests and dancing skeletons? I'd tried most everything I could think of at one time or another to help figure out the obscure ones like that, from psychology textbooks on dream interpretation to simply praying for understanding, but so far nothing had ever worked. I knew in the old days there were people who could understand the meaning of dreams and visions, like Daniel did for the king of Babylon, and Joseph did for Pharaoh and others. I'd often wished I knew somebody like that; it would make the whole thing so much simpler. But since I didn't, I was ready to try just about anything.

"Who is he?" I asked.

Marcus gave me the name and address, and I decided it was worthwhile to go ahead down there and see the man.

It turned out to be a non-denominational church over on the east side of town, and of course those are always a gamble when it comes to what they teach and believe, but I figured I didn't have to listen if I didn't want to. It's not that I hadn't asked my own pastor about the dreams before; I had, several times. We'd even prayed together about it. But nothing had ever come of that, and I decided I had nothing to lose by asking somebody else.

So I went inside and sat down in one of the pews to think for a few minutes, not sure what I wanted to say or even who to say it to. The office was empty and there didn't seem to be anybody around, although I knew there had to be, since the building was open.

I hadn't been there five minutes when a janitor appeared from one of the doors beside the podium.

"Excuse me, sir, can you tell me where I can find the pastor?" I asked him, getting up from the pew. He gave me a long look, and then shook his head.

"Nobody here but me, son," he said.

"Oh, all right," I said, disappointed. I was just about to ask him what time I needed to come back, when he got close enough to hand me a folded-up sheet of notebook paper. I took it without thinking.

"What's this?" I asked, looking down at it.

"Go see him. He can tell you what you need to know," the man said.

I looked down at the paper, which had the name *Brandon Stone* written on it, along with an address in Ravanna, Arkansas. I didn't know who that was, but Ravanna is only about thirty miles from Goliad. I looked up to ask for clarification, but during the second when I glanced at the paper the janitor had already disappeared.

Well, I've had my share of odd experiences now and then, and I guess compared to some of them, a disappearing janitor doesn't amount to much. I looked at the paper again and figured I had nothing to lose by going to see Mr. Stone, whoever he was.

My first thought was to wonder if he might be some relation of Lisa's, unlikely as that seemed. I left the church mighty puzzled, but at least I had something concrete I could *do* for a change.

There were still a good three or four hours till it got dark, and I decided that was plenty of time to run over to Ravanna. It wouldn't take more than an hour or so to get out there and find the place.

Chapter Three
Cody

Ravanna sits right on the edge of the biggest cypress swamp in the world, in case you didn't know. It fills up all the wide valleys that drain down into Caddo Lake, but there's still quite a bit of high ground where the towns and things are.

Brandon Stone didn't live on high ground.

He lived in an old school bus at the end of a muddy track that barely deserved to be called a road, amongst a thicket of cypress trees at the edge of a blackwater bayou. A rusty stovepipe stuck out one of the windows near the back, and the yard was littered with trash and three or four rusty vehicles up on blocks. Three mongrel dogs lay curled up under the bus in the shade, watching me. Maybe they were too lazy to bark; it wouldn't have surprised me, if they took after their master.

I went up to knock on the door of the bus, only to find a double-barreled shotgun pushed right out into my face.

I really don't like having guns aimed at me; there's just something that really bothers me about that, you know? But I put my hands up where the dude could see them and backed up real slowly, making sure I didn't make any sudden moves.

The door opened, and there stood a young boy no more than fourteen at the most, barefoot and bare-chested, with nothing on but a pair of overalls that were way too big for him. He looked just like the boy on the Tennessee Pride sausage wrappers, red hair and all, and I might have laughed if he hadn't had a gun pointed right between my eyes. Somehow that killed all the humor in the situation.

"What do you want?" he asked, not even pretending to be friendly.

"I'm looking for Brandon Stone," I said.

"You found him. Now what do you want?" he asked again, and I decided this was no time to beat around the bush.

"I was told you could tell me what I need to know. I have dreams sometimes. True ones. But I don't always understand what they mean. I need your help," I said. I didn't know if he'd believe me or if he'd think I was crazy, but I couldn't think of anything else the janitor could have meant by telling me this kid could tell me what I needed to know.

The boy looked hard at me for a while longer, and then slowly lowered the shotgun to his side.

"I see. Don't know that I like that, much. Who told you where to find me?" he asked.

"A janitor at a church in Longview. I don't know his name," I said truthfully.

"Hmm. Well, you best come inside, then," he said.

I followed him inside, and when I got closer I caught a whiff of body odor so strong it could have gagged a maggot at thirty paces. Not just body odor, either, but *old* body odor. I wondered when the kid had last taken a bath.

The smell was even stronger inside the bus. Dried sweat, wood smoke, and mildew all combined in a way that made me wish I could stop breathing for at least an hour.

The bus seats had been ripped out and the place had been refitted into a one-room house, sort of. There was a stack of ancient mattresses in one corner which passed for a bed, a table and chairs, a potbellied wood stove, and some canned goods and such on a shelf. Not much else.

I sat down in one of the chairs, and Brandon took a seat on the bed.

"So spit it out. I can't tell you anything if you don't cough up the story," he finally said, with more than a hint of impatience in his voice.

So I told him the dream about Lisa, making sure not to leave out any details whether they seemed important or not. He listened without saying a thing, and when I was finished he did the last thing I would ever have expected. He got down on his knees beside the bed and prayed for at least five minutes, leaving me to sit there watching him.

When he was finished, he got up and sat back down on the bed again, watching me curiously.

"Well?" I finally asked.

"This is what God is saying to you. The cave means a time of doubt and uncertainty, and the crystal forest is a time of happiness that you and the girl will pass through. The silver bridge over dark waters means that you'll face a dangerous time which you'll need money to get through. But when you find it, that will lead you directly into the palace of the worst danger of all. The skeleton means death. Death to the girl, and to you too. But both of you will go willingly to meet it, because it'll be cloaked in beauty. Don't be fooled," the boy said.

"Is that all?" I asked, chilled.

"Not quite. In spite of the disguise, you'll still be able to see the evil underneath the surface, if you pay attention. The bones will still be visible underneath all those fine clothes, so to speak. The evil one will ask you to do something you know is wrong, just like the skeleton asked the girl to dance. Don't do that thing, no matter how minor and harmless it might seem. If you do, it'll cause you more grief than you could ever imagine. Once all is said and done, and final happiness seems to be in your hands, you'll find that it suddenly crumbles to dust before you can stop it. That's the meaning of the crystal twig falling to ashes in your hand," he said.

"It seems awfully gloomy," I muttered.

"I'm sorry to have to give you bad news," the kid said, softening a little bit.

"Yeah, well, I wish I knew what I'm supposed to do, that's all," I said.

"Follow her, just like you did in the dream. That's your job right now. Stick to her like glue. That's all I know," he said.

"Thanks, I guess," I said.

"You're welcome, maybe," Brandon said with a scowl.

"I'm sorry, I didn't mean it like that," I said.

"Yeah, whatever," he said.

"So how old are you, anyway?" I asked, changing the subject to something less disturbing. It had nothing to do with what we'd been talking about and it was really none of my business, but finding a kid living alone in the middle of a swamp *is* a little strange, you've got to admit.

"Thirteen and a half, and before you even ask, yeah, I live here alone, I take care of myself, my parents are gone, and that suits me just fine. Anything else you want to know?" he asked, hostile again.

"No, I guess not," I said.

"Good. And if you're thinkin' about telling anybody I'm here, you better think again. I *will* come after you," he promised. I stared at the dirty boy across from me, with his twelve-gauge shotgun still within easy reach if he needed it, and somehow I wasn't inclined to doubt he'd try his dead-level best to make good on that threat.

Well, I wouldn't rat him out. Not because I was scared he might hunt me down later, but just because he helped me and you don't betray people who do you a favor. He seemed to be surviving, at least, even though that was no way to live to my way of thinking.

I still had two hundred dollars left in my pocket from selling cows. We needed it, to be sure, but not as much as this strange kid did. Maybe I couldn't help him any other way, but money might buy him food and clothes for a while. Better than nothing. I took it out of my pocket and offered it to him.

"Please take this, so I can thank you," I told him. He eyed the cash, looking from it to me and then back again, like a coon watches a sweet plum in your hand while it decides whether it's safe to grab it or not. Slowly he reached out and took it, stuffing the money inside his dirty overalls without even counting it.

"Much obliged," he said.

"Least I could do," I said.

I left after that, trying not to let it show how sweet the air smelled after that fetid bus. I didn't want to offend Brandon; I might need his help again someday. Dream interpreters are hard to come by.

So I went home, thinking hard about what he'd told me and what all it might mean. I was supposed to stay close to Lisa; well, okay, I could handle that. The rest of it still seemed pretty murky, but if I kept my eyes open and paid attention, then there was a good chance I might spot the signs while there was still time to do something about them.

I hoped.

Lisa texted me later that evening while I was doctoring a cut on Buck's fetlock, and we talked for a while about horses and music and whatever else came to mind.

Over the next few days we took to calling or texting each other now and then throughout the day, and you know, she was really good at cheering me up whenever I was inclined to worry about how dry the fields were and how thin the cattle were getting or whether monsters or evil sorcerers or skeletons dressed in designer outfits were fixing to bash the doors in and kill us all.

I didn't tell Mama about any of it, at least not yet. Marcus I didn't have much choice about since he already knew I'd gone to check on things and he pestered me till he got the story. So I told him about what Brandon said the dream meant, confusing as that still was.

My conversations with Lisa were better. It's not that she talked about anything in particular. She really didn't say all that much at all, honestly. She just asked me what I was doing and thinking and it always seemed like she was interested to hear about anything I felt like telling her. It didn't matter if I was feeding the cows or working on the tractor or practicing music, she never seemed to get bored.

So we talked about herbicides and fertilizer and the best way to handle aphids and a dozen other farming-related topics, and other times we talked about red-dirt bands and playing music at tailgate parties and going mudding on back roads after the rain, when the clay is so thick and sticky you could spread it like crimson peanut butter. Ordinary stuff, sure, but I think sometimes it's that ordinary, everyday kind of conversation that really draws people closer.

I was working in the cotton fields one afternoon when she called me on her lunch break.

"Hey, Cody. What are you doing?" she asked.

"Just spraying the cotton, that's all. Trying to keep the bugs down," I said absently. I had my headset on so I could use my hands to drive the tractor, and that's where most of my attention was focused.

"Oh, I see. Should be close to ripe by now, huh?" she asked.

"Few more weeks. But I'm not sure if it'll make it, honestly. Been too hot lately. Once it gets over a hundred and five degrees outside then it starts killing things, even if they've got plenty of water. All the heat this summer is burning everything up, no matter what I do," I said.

"Maybe it'll break soon," she said sympathetically.

"Yeah, maybe," I agreed, without much enthusiasm. Short of a miracle or a hurricane, I didn't see much chance of a break till fall.

"My garden's doing real good. Got me some really nice watermelons coming on now," she said.

"That's cool. You like melons?" I asked.

"Oh, there's nothing better than a nice, sweet, lusciously succulent watermelon, ice cold and dripping with juice," she said, and I laughed a little.

"I don't think I ever heard anybody talk about a watermelon quite like that, Lisa. Have you got yellow ones or red ones?" I asked.

"Red, of course. I always thought the yellow ones looked funny," she said.

"I'm surprised you've still got any left, with the grasshoppers so bad this year. They pretty much destroyed everything in Mama's garden even before it got hot," I said, sliding back into my worried mood.

"Oh, I've got chickens to handle all that. They get rid of the 'hoppers real well. I'm surprised y'all don't have any," she said.

"We do, but the garden is always fenced off to keep them out because they like to eat the tomatoes," I said.

"Well, yeah, that they do," she admitted.

She was like that. Always keeping my mind on something cheerful when I needed it the most, but always subtle about it. She had this wonderful gift for making it seem like everything would be all right, no matter what. That's a powerful thing, when you stop to think about it. The more we talked the more I wanted to talk, and it got to the point that I looked forward to our conversations as one of the highlights of my day.

I might have worried more about how close we seemed to be getting, but she had that gift so strong that when we actually talked, I wasn't even worried about that either. She was like an addictive drug, and I just couldn't get enough of her.

I didn't totally lose my head, of course. I was careful never to hint that we were anything more than good friends, and she never seemed to expect anything more. As long as things stayed like that, I could handle it.

Chapter Four
Lisa

    I could tell there was something on Cody's mind, some kind of issue that kept him wary and distant sometimes, but I couldn't think what it might be to save my life. There didn't seem to be anything obvious.

    I couldn't have put a finger on exactly when my thoughts had changed over from curiosity into wishful daydreams, but at some point they certainly had. I wanted to be more than just friends, and I was almost certain he did, too. I caught him watching me sometimes when he didn't know I could see, and things like that. So his cool and detached behavior confused me, and I wondered if I was doing something wrong that he didn't like for some reason, or if he had some other girl he was interested in. He never complained and he never talked about anybody else, so all I could do was puzzle my brain till I went around in circles.

    I thought several times about flat out asking him what he was thinking and why he was being so standoffish. Most people do appreciate forthrightness, after all, even if it stings for a minute. But then I always ended up thinking uneasily about what he might say. What if he really didn't like me at all except as a friend and he was only enjoying having somebody to hang out with? I wasn't quite ready to face that possibility yet. I much preferred to wait a while and see what happened.

Mama always used to tell me that it's the patient girl who gets her man sooner or later, so I finally decided that was the best advice I knew of at the time. I was willing to let him go at his own pace, however much he mystified me sometimes. So I bit my tongue and pretended everything was fine, determined not to worry about it.

Jenny couldn't help but notice my blossoming semi-love affair, of course, and when I got home from church Sunday afternoon she pulled me aside for some serious dirt-digging. She had a new boyfriend who'd been taking up most of her time lately, which meant I hadn't seen her much since I bumped into Cody.

I might as well admit that I've always been a little envious of my sister. Jenny is tanned and blonde and outgoing and she has perfect legs and the guys are always drooling over her. As for me, on the other hand. . . my hair is a dull reddish-brown, and somehow I always look too pale even when I put on blush. Add to that a quiet personality and you get, well, blah. Sometimes I think my sister must have arrived in a gift box while I showed up later on in a paper sack. Everybody tells me I ought not to compare myself to her that way, but it's hard not to sometimes.

Mama always used to tell me I'm beautiful and that still waters run the deepest, but somehow I'd always had trouble believing all those things.

"Okay, spill it, sis. Who is he?" she asked.

"I don't know what you're talking about," I said innocently. I kind of wanted to tell her about him, honestly, but I wanted to make her work for it a little bit first.

"Who's this boy you've been talking to all the time? I've never seen you so ditzed out. So come on, give me the goods," she said.

"Well. . . you might not remember him, but his name's Cody McGrath," I said, drawing it out and relishing the suspense for as long as possible.

"You mean the one that lives out there on the way to Linden?" she asked, and I thought to myself dryly that I should have known Jenny would remember him. She knows everybody in three counties on a first-name basis, it seems.

"Yeah, he's the one," I agreed.

"Sis, I hate to bust your bubble, but Cody. . . he's a little weird, you know," she said, frowning.

"What are you talking about?" I asked.

"Well. . . he wouldn't go out with Sheila Jackson last month, even though she's the hottest girl in town," she said.

"So? Sheila's a tramp, and you know it as well as I do. I don't blame him a bit for not wanting to go out with somebody like her," I said. Not to mention she was a snotty, stuck-up diva who thought the world revolved around her just because her daddy was a bank president and they always had plenty of money. Any male with half a brain would've run from Sheila like she was the Thing from the Black Lagoon. Which I guess goes to show how few of them have that much sense, but I was certainly glad Cody did.

"Well, okay, point taken. But what about Janice Loving? He wouldn't go out with her, either," Jen said.

"I don't know her," I said, shrugging.

"Yes, you do. She was runner-up for Watermelon Queen last summer. Pretty girl, *definitely* not a tramp, and she's loads of fun to spend time with," she explained.

I did remember Janice, now that she mentioned it, and it was true, she was almost as pretty as Jenny was. Of course, Jenny's idea of "fun" sometimes differed from what a normal person would think, so her recommendation didn't carry much weight as far as I was concerned.

"I don't know what all he likes in a girl, sis. I've never asked him about who he's been out with before now," I complained. Mostly because I preferred not to know, if the truth be told. It was much nicer to imagine that he spent nine years yearning after me and never even looked at another girl, no matter how silly that was. Jenny likes to tell me I live a rich fantasy life sometimes.

"Well, I've got it on good authority that he's never had a steady girlfriend in his life, in spite of the fact that half the girls in the county would die just to go out with him. Now all of a sudden he's got a thing for *you?* What's the deal?" she asked.

"Thanks for that vote of confidence, sis," I said dryly, but I couldn't keep a tiny sliver of doubt from creeping into my mind in spite of myself. In spite of my private imaginings, I didn't *really* think Cody would have spent half his life pining over a seventh-grade crush. So why no girlfriend, then? It was kind of worrisome, and I was furious at Jenny for making me wonder.

"We're really more just friends right now, anyway. All we do is talk and go out together sometimes, that's all," I said.

"Uh-huh. You can never be just friends with a guy, honey. Trust me on this. Not unless you're blood kin or he thinks you're ugly as the back end of a gasoline truck. Sometimes not even then," Jenny said firmly.

"Well, we are, anyway," I insisted.

"No you're not. People don't float around in a dream world over somebody who's just a friend. Don't feed me that bull," Jenny said.

"Does it really have to have a label? We like each other a lot and we have fun together. Isn't that good enough?" I asked, not liking how peevish my own voice sounded.

"All right, then, whatever you say. I'm just telling you to be careful, that's all," Jenny said.

"I know. And I will. But you just don't know him like I do. If you did, you'd never think he was anything but the sweetest, kindest, bravest, most handsome and chivalrous man you ever met," I said, and Jenny snorted in disgust.

"Yeah, sure, whatever. I guess you better tell me all about Mr. Wonderful, then," she said, resigned.

"He plays guitar in a band, did you know that? And he runs that whole ranch all by himself, with just his mother and one other boy to help," I began.

"Great, so he's a mama's boy who thinks he can sing. It just keeps getting better and better," Jen said. I gritted my teeth, but plunged ahead doggedly.

"He likes my paintings, too, and he told me I'm different than all the other girls he ever met before," I told her.

"Well, the boy ain't lying about that part, at least," Jenny said.

"He told me I'm beautiful," I said softly, beginning to be hurt by Jenny's invincible cynicism. At first I thought she was about to make another snappy comment about that, too, but for once she didn't.

"Do you think he meant it?" she finally asked.

"What do you mean?" I asked.

"Has he asked you for anything? Does he mean it when he says all that stuff, or is he just buttering you up so he can take advantage of you?" she asked.

"Take advantage of me how? What's he got to gain? It's not like I'm rich or anything, and he's good looking enough that there's plenty of pretty girls who'd be glad to have a roll in the hay with him, if that's what he wanted. Why would he lie?" I asked. The very thought of it hurt more than I liked to admit.

"I don't know, sis. Some guys like a challenge, you know; a girl who's too easy to get is not worth having, that kind of thing. Maybe he likes a challenge. I'm not saying it's like that, just that it *might* be," she said.

The idea was plausible enough that it created another disturbing drop of doubt in my mind, and I wished I'd never said anything to Jenny to begin with. She was ruining everything, just like she always did.

"I don't think he's like that," I said, and I could hear how unconvincing my voice sounded.

"Well, maybe not. Maybe he really means every single word he said and he's every bit as wonderful as you think he is. Maybe you're really the one and only girl in Texas who ever won Cody McGrath's heart. Stranger things have happened, I guess," Jen finally said.

"Yeah. . . maybe I am," I said, half to myself, and in spite of all my sister's dark hints and conspiracy theories, the thought brought a smile to my face.

Chapter Five
Cody

I stopped by to see Lisa at lunchtime a few days after I visited Brandon.

I was already unhappy when I pulled in to the empty parking lot at the Dairy Dip, though I tried hard not to show it. The place was deserted after the lunch crowd, and I found her sitting in the corner booth just about to eat her own lunch. She smiled when she saw me, and in spite of my dark mood I couldn't help smiling back.

"Hey, stranger. What brings you to this neck of the woods?" she asked.

"Aw, I heard there was a pretty girl in here who didn't have a lunch date," I said, sliding into the booth across from her.

"Ha. Wrong on both counts," she said, smiling a little.

"So what's for lunch?" I asked.

"The special today was meatloaf and mashed potatoes; I saved you a plate over there if you're hungry," she said, nodding at the order window. I went to grab it and got myself a Coke before sitting back down at the booth.

"Looks good," I said appreciatively.

"Thanks. Cooked it myself this morning. Anyway, did you get Buck home all right after church the other day? I wondered later, since I didn't see a horse trailer hooked up to your truck," she said.

"Yeah, Cyrus took him home for me. He's got a two-horse trailer, so we didn't see any reason to haul them both out there separately," I said.

"That makes sense. It's good you've got some friends like that," she said.

"Yeah, they're the best. I don't know how I'd ever get all the work done at Goliad if they didn't pitch in sometimes. Me and Marcus usually manage to keep it all covered, but now and then we still need help, like when the peaches are ripe or things like that," I said.

"You never told me about the peaches before," she said, taking a bite of her meatloaf.

"Did I not? Yeah, twenty acres worth. It might not sound like a lot but believe me, it's enough to load you down," I said seriously.

"I bet it is," she agreed.

"Especially at harvest time. You can smell peaches everywhere, then. All through the house and the fields, all over your clothes, every time the breeze blows. I used to like it when I was younger, but nowadays it mostly reminds me how much work I've got to do," I said. That was really a half-truth; I love the smell of the peaches when they're ripe, and I've never minded the work that goes along with them. They're one of the things that means home in my mind, and I wouldn't change that even if I could.

"You sure do have a lot of different things going on out there," she said.

"Well, yeah, but you have to, you know. You can't stick to just one thing because you never know what'll happen with the prices every year. It's safer to diversify a little bit," I explained, and she laughed.

"What's funny?" I asked, mystified.

"Oh, nothing. It just sounded funny to hear you use the word 'diversify', that's all," she said, looking embarrassed. I guess I could have been insulted if I'd wanted to, but it only amused me.

"Is that so? Surely you're not saying you think I'm too much of a yokel to know how to use big words, are you?" I teased, and she dissolved in giggles.

"Nope, I'd *never* say that," she promised, smiling.

"Humph. Okay, then. Long as we got that straight," I nodded, with mock seriousness.

"Speaking of words, I listened to that disk you gave me. I meant to ask you if there was some special story behind *Nebo's Crossing*. It seemed so much deeper than the rest of them," she said.

That was more of a personal question than it might seem, and it always makes me a little uncomfortable to talk about things like that. I've had more than my fair share of sorrow and loss in life, and I don't relish the memories. But I figured it wouldn't kill me to share at least a little bit.

"Well. . . I wrote it for my dad. I got to thinking one day about how Moses never got to enter the Promised Land, but his people did. Sometimes you can't have the things you want the most, even if it breaks your heart to give them up, you know. Sometimes you have to spend your life like he did, and sacrifice everything so the people you love can have happiness later," I said, scuffing my boot on the floor.

I glanced at Lisa, wondering what her reaction to all that might be. But she only nodded, seemingly mute, and I laughed to lighten the mood.

"It's kind of a double meaning, I guess you could say. Mount Nebo is the tallest mountain in the Land of Gilead, and that's where Moses was buried after he looked out across the Jordan with his last sight. But if you think about it a little bit, Goliad sounds a lot like Gilead, doesn't it? I think my Grandpa Reuben must've thought the same thing when he first settled the place, because there's a big hill out there on the property that he named Mount Nebo, and that's where my father is buried," I said.

"So why didn't he just name the place Gilead, then? Seems like it would've been easier," she said.

"Oh, that. Well, he was a soldier in the Texas Revolution and fought at the battle of Goliad, way down there in south Texas. He was one of the only survivors, actually, so after the Republic was set up they granted him a thousand acres up here. We've still got a copy of the original land patent papers tucked away somewhere, I think. It's been in the family ever since," I said, with what I hoped was pardonable pride.

"That's awesome; I love things like that. Your family is so cool. I wish I knew some interesting stories like that to tell," she said, shaking her head and taking another bite of her meatloaf.

"Yeah, I guess so. I'm the last one, though," I said, and almost immediately regretted saying it. Lisa had a way of putting me at ease and loosening my tongue which nobody else could have matched. Much to my discomfiture, I might add.

"What do you mean?" she asked, and I figured if she knew that much then she might as well know a little more.

"I'm the last McGrath, and Grandpa Reuben set it up in such a way that the land could never be divided or sold outside the family. So if anything happens to me or I don't have any kids, then I'm not sure what'll happen. There's nobody else," I explained.

"That must be really hard for you," she said sympathetically, and I looked deep into her eyes for a minute, searching for. . . something. I couldn't decide what, exactly. Most people who hear that story tend to say something sarcastic like how they wish *they* had that kind of problem, or something like that. Not many people understand what a heavy responsibility it can be. I didn't used to think of it that way at first, but gradually I came to understand how much this place meant not just to me but to all the people who ever lived there, or ever would. I feel the burden keenly sometimes.

"Most people seem to think I'm a crybaby for mentioning it," I said in a deliberate tone, wanting to see what she'd say to that.

"I haven't seen you crying about it. You're doing what you have to do and trying your best to do what's expected of you, that's all. I know what it's like to have to carry a heavy load on your shoulders when you feel like you never had a chance to live your own life first," she said, poking at her mashed potatoes with a fork.

I looked at her wonderingly; that was *exactly* how I felt sometimes. I almost told her everything, then. . . dreams and curse and all. But I bit my tongue at the last second.

"How do you do it?" I asked instead.

"How do I do what?" she asked, looking mystified.

"How do you always know exactly what I think and how I feel?" I asked, and she laughed.

"Cody boy, I promise you, there are a lot of times when I don't have a *clue* what you're thinking or feeling," she said.

"It sure does seem like you do," I said.

"Sometimes I can guess pretty well, maybe, that's all," she said. I thought she was being overly modest, but I didn't argue about it.

"Well, you're one of a kind, Miss Lisa; I can say that much," I said.

"Why, naturally," she agreed, laughing it off.

"So what's your story, then? What's your burden to bear?" I asked, curious.

"What do you mean?' she asked.

"You said you knew what it was like to have to carry a heavy load. Surely you had something particular on your mind, didn't you?" I asked.

"Nothing as interesting as yours, I'm afraid," she demurred.

"No, really, tell me. I'm curious," I persisted, and she glanced around like she wanted to make sure nobody was close enough to overhear us.

"Well, I've always been the one who had to take care of everything, you know. It's been worse since Mama had her stroke, because now I have to take care of her, too. Jenny tries to help, I think, but she's kind of silly and irresponsible sometimes, to tell the truth. I don't mind doing it, really; Mama was my best friend and she always encouraged me and taught me everything I know. I'd never turn my back on her when she needs me like this, but. . . it's hard, sometimes," she admitted, looking down at her plate.

"I'm sorry," I said.

"Oh, it's all right. Just hard sometimes, that's all," she said, and then there was a long pause while we both pretended to eat our food.

"So. . . do you still like poetry?" I asked, grasping at memories. I knew she used to be a Shel Silverstein fanatic back in seventh grade, but it seemed like a good way to break the ice and keep the conversation going. She laughed.

"I can't believe you still remember that. Yeah, sometimes," she agreed.

"So what's your favorite poem these days?" I asked.

"Anything sweet and romantic, but I could never pick just one. I was reading Christopher Marlowe last night, if that tells you anything," she said.

"Never heard of him before," I admitted, and she laughed a little again.

"No, I didn't think you would have," she agreed.

Her lunch break was over not long after that, and I reluctantly let her get back to work. As usual, she had a way of making me wonder how I could ever have worried about anything, at least for a little while.

Later that evening I found myself alone in the barn for a while, working on the tractor and trying not to cuss the stupid thing. It had a short in the ignition system somewhere, and trying to trace down electrical shorts is hard, time-consuming work. It probably didn't help that I was still thinking about Lisa instead of focusing on the wires like I ought to have been doing. But when the phone rang and I saw that it was her, I can't deny I was glad for an excuse to get away from mechanicking and talk to her.

"Hey, Lisa, what's up?' I asked.

"Nothin' much, just fixing some beans and cornbread for supper," she said. I hadn't realized it was so late already, and almost on cue, my stomach rumbled.

Many Waters 55

"Well, hey, I'm glad you called. Are you busy tomorrow?" I asked.

"No, not that I know of. Why do you ask?" she said.

"Well, I thought it'd be cool if you came over for a while, if you want to. We could grill some brisket, hang out, things like that," I said, not letting it slip how unusual of a question it was. I didn't often have visitors, and certainly not girls.

"I'd love to. What time?" she asked.

"Um. . . maybe five or six would be good," I said.

"Yeah, that'll work. If I get Jenny to run me out there, do you think you can give me a ride back home?" she asked, and the thought actually pleased me very much.

"Sure," I said.

"How do you get out to y'alls place, exactly? I'll have to tell Jen, and I'm not real familiar with that area," she said.

"Well, you know how to get to Linden, right?" I asked.

"Yeah," she agreed.

"Head out that way, and then turn right on the third gravel road on the right after you get out of Avinger. Go down that road for a couple miles till you get to a white wood rail fence, and then you'll come to the gate. You can't miss it," I said.

"Sounds pretty easy," she agreed.

"If you happen to get lost, just call me and I'll come find you," I told her.

"Okay, see you then," she said, and that was that.

* * * * * * *

I got up earlier than usual the next morning, determined to get all my chores done and make sure things looked nice by the time Lisa got there.

The first order of business was to finish fixing the tractor, if possible. I threw myself into it with a will, and by the time the sun was well up I'd found that the ignition module itself was burned out. There was no way to fix that except to replace it, so I put it aside for the time being and climbed up on top of the barn to have a crack at replacing two pieces of sheet metal which had come partially loose. I definitely wanted to get done with that job while it was still early; it looked like it might turn out to be another scorching kind of day later on.

I spent most of the morning finishing the barn, and by noon I was done with that project, too. I climbed down with a sigh of relief and put away the ladder and the metal screws, and then went home to clean the house a bit and wash some clothes; something I normally do only when I run out of socks and underwear.

Mama noticed me unloading the dryer.

"What's the special occasion?" she asked, looking askance at the basket full of clean laundry.

"Do I have to have a special occasion to wash my clothes?" I asked innocently, and she only laughed.

"Yes you do, as a matter of fact. So what's going on? Unless I missed a news flash, I don't think the world is coming to an end today, is it?" she asked.

"Well. . . I kind of asked Lisa to come over for supper tonight," I admitted, knowing full well what kind of response I was inviting. But I couldn't exactly keep it a secret, now could I?

"Really?" she asked.

"Yeah, she'll be here about five or six," I said.

"Well, that's wonderful, Cody! You should have told me sooner. I'll have to put a brisket on the grill and make some fresh tea," she said. I think Mama worries sometimes that I'll end up an old bachelor one of these days, so she's always pleased when she thinks I might be going out with somebody. I couldn't help smiling at her enthusiasm, even if it was completely misplaced.

"We're just friends, Mama, that's all. You don't have to make a big production out of it," I told her.

"I can if I want to," she said, with a touch of asperity.

"All right, then. If that's what you want," I said, and kissed her cheek.

She immediately fired up the grill in the back yard with charcoal and hickory chips, not wasting a second. By the time I got back from taking my clothes home she'd already put the brisket inside to start cooking, and there were two jugs of tea already sitting on the picnic table to brew in the sunshine. Mama can be awfully efficient when she wants to be, and anything that involves my so-called love life is sure to get her energized like nothing else.

I had to get online to order a new ignition module for the tractor, which I did while I finished my lunch. When I was done with that, I idly looked up Christopher Marlowe out of curiosity. I only found a single poem of any importance, it seemed, and I read the words to myself quietly.

> *Come live with me and be my love,*
> *And we will all the pleasures prove,*
> *That hills and valleys, dale and field,*
> *And all the craggy mountains yield. . .*

It went on for a good bit longer, but I finished the whole thing. I don't normally read things like that, partly because poetry is not my thing and partly (if the truth be told) because it makes my heart ache. I don't like to be reminded of impossible wishes.

Mama came up behind me, and I quickly deleted the website so she wouldn't catch me reading such a thing. I'd never live it down in a million years.

"There's a tree limb down on the fence by the gate, son. You might want to go out there and fix it while you've got time, so the cows don't get loose," she said, and I nodded. One more thing to take care of.

I quickly cut up the branch and put it behind the house in the woodpile, and then grabbed a hammer and a bag of nails from the storage shed to get the fence rails put back up. It was blistering hot outside by then, but I consoled myself with the thought that at least I'd get to take a nice cold shower and put on some clean clothes before Lisa got there.

Chapter Six
Lisa

Ore City is a small enough place, but Avinger is even smaller, with nothing much there but a gas station and a little country school so tiny it doesn't even have a football team. In Texas, that's almost a crime. The McGraths lived several miles even farther out, *way* out in the country, and if Cody hadn't told me how to find the place I'm pretty sure me and Jenny never would have found it on our own. I'd never been out there before, and all I knew about the Goliad Ranch was what Cody had told me. It's bordered on the east by Black Cypress Bayou, but that's the only boundary I've ever understood well enough to remember.

It wasn't too long before we found the gravel road, and then the white wood rail fence that Cody had said to look for. That's when I first realized how much land a thousand acres really is; that fence seemed like it stretched along the road forever before we finally got to the gate, and there was no telling how far it went on the other side. Cody had mentioned that the road dead-ended at the river eventually, where there was a sandy beach and a swimming hole, but I wasn't sure how much farther that was.

The gate itself was made of wooden posts painted white like the rails, with black letters in an arch across the top that said

Goliad. When we got there, Cody was up front hammering at part of the fence. It looked like one of the rails might have come loose, but I couldn't tell exactly. He was wearing a plain old white t-shirt, grubby with sawdust and dirt and soaked in sweat from the heat.

"See you later, Jen," I said, waving to her as I got out of the car and shut the door. Then I walked up the graveled drive to where Cody was standing.

"Hey, Lisa. You're here early," he said, looking up to smile at me. He had three sixteen-penny nails in his mouth, which made his words come out a little garbled, but I understood him well enough.

He smelled like a boar hog from working, but I pretended not to notice. Mama had drummed it into my head for years that a gracious and well-mannered young lady should never say or do anything which might embarrass another person or hurt their feelings. And besides that, I knew I'd caught him off guard. No doubt he would have gone in to clean up before I got there if he'd known I was coming.

"Yeah, it was the only time Jenny could bring me. I'm sorry I interrupted you; I didn't know you'd be busy," I apologized.

"Nah, it's all good. Just let me finish this little bit of rail right quick, and then we'll go inside for some iced tea. What do you say?" he asked.

"Sounds good to me," I said.

"Okay. I'll be done in just a sec," he said. He took off his white straw hat, wiping the sweat from his forehead and scratching his buzzed-off hair, frowning just a little. Then he seemed to have a change of heart.

"You know what, I think the fence can hold off awhile. Let's go on in," he said, setting down his hammer and nails.

He offered me his arm, very gentleman-like, and in spite of his sweatiness I smiled and took it without so much as a second glance at how grimy it was. That was another thing I liked about Cody; he's so courtly without being a snob about it.

The house was a big old white Victorian-looking thing, with two stories and a verandah that wrapped all the way around. The driveway was edged on both sides with bright yellow rose bushes, most of them in full bloom. I noticed they were the scentless kind, no doubt to keep from attracting bees and wasps.

"Mama loves roses," Cody commented when we were about halfway up the drive.

"Yeah, I can tell. She must spend all her time weeding," I said.

"Well, no, not really. They're pretty tough little boogers," he said.

"Why so much yellow, though?" I asked, and he laughed.

"Oh, Lisa, please don't get her started on *that*. She'll tell you everything from how they're a symbol of joy and freedom to how they're a memorial of the Texas Revolution, and everything else in between. Believe me, I've heard it all a thousand times. She could go on about those roses all day," he said. I could tell he wasn't really complaining, though; he had a tolerant smile on his face.

Right in front of the steps, the driveway curved into a circle around one of the hugest pecan trees I'd ever seen, and Cody's old Chevy was parked at a rakish angle underneath its spreading branches. It was still hot even in the shade, and when we got to the verandah he opened the front door to usher me inside where it was cool. When my eyes adjusted, I saw that most of the house was done in polished hardwood and rough timber, which I thought was pretty even though it made things a little bit dark inside. There was a red-brick fireplace, and lots of photographs. It was nice, but nothing too fancy. Goliad was a working ranch, not one of those fake little ranchette things people build so they can say they've got a taste of the country.

His mother was washing dishes at the sink when we entered the kitchen, with her long brown hair tied back in a ponytail. She was singing something to herself, but I couldn't tell for sure what it was over the sound of running water. It sounded like *Leaning on the Everlasting Arms*.

"Hey, Mama. Lisa's here; she got dropped off a little early," he said. She turned around with a smile, drying the soap suds from her hands before she gave me a hug.

"I'm so glad to finally get to meet you, Lisa. Cody talks about you all the time," she declared.

"He does?" I asked, absurdly pleased with that idea.

"He surely does," she said.

"Aw, Mama, hush," he said. But she only laughed.

"Did you get the fence fixed, son?" she asked, turning to look at him.

"No, ma'am, not quite. I think it'll hold up till tomorrow, though. I didn't want to be working while we had company," he explained, and she nodded like that was the most obvious thing in the world.

"Of course not. Can I get y'all some sweet tea or maybe some lemonade?" she asked.

"Yes, ma'am, I'd love some tea, if it's not too much trouble," I said.

"No trouble at all," she said, and busied herself filling two glass tumblers with ice and then pouring the tea. Cody drank his whole glass in one long pull, but then I figured he was probably dying of thirst after being out in the hot sun for so long. I only sipped mine because I wasn't all that thirsty, but I did want to savor it. It tasted like homemade sun tea, the really good stuff you make by leaving it outside in a big one-gallon pickle jar to slow-brew in the sunshine. It must not have been ready for long, because it was still lukewarm when I took my first sip. That was all right, though; it wouldn't take long for the ice to cool it down.

"Thanks, Mama," Cody said when he finished the glass and wiped his mouth with the back of his sweaty hand. Then he poured himself a second glass and drank most of that one, too.

"Yes, thank you, Mrs. McGrath," I echoed.

"Now, honey, the only people who call me Mrs. McGrath are bill collectors and strangers. Call me Josie," she said.

"Thanks, Miss Josie," I said.

"You're surely welcome. Now y'all run along and let me finish this kitchen while I can. There's more tea in the icebox if you want some," she said. My glass was still almost full, but Cody took her up on the offer and refilled his for a third time.

"If you'll excuse me just a minute, ladies, I'll be right back," he said, ducking out of the kitchen.

It wasn't long before he came back, looking much fresher than when he left. He'd washed off as much sweat as he could in such a short amount of time; his ears were still wet from where he'd splashed his face and been in too much of a hurry to dry off completely. He had on a clean black t-shirt that read *Cowboy for Life* across the front, and I noticed that he'd even put on cologne; something that reminded me vaguely of Old Spice, even though I was pretty sure that wasn't what it was.

Miss Josie shooed both of us out of the kitchen as soon as he got back, and he led me outside again, through the back door this time.

"Where are we going?" I asked when we got outside.

"You'll see when we get there," he said, sounding very mysterious.

I noticed there were more roses in the back yard, not all of them yellow, and a picnic table beside an outdoor grill. Something must have been cooking, because there was smoke coming out of it. Whatever it was, it smelled delectable.

Cody didn't stop in the yard, though. He opened a gate in the fence and led me across a wide pasture that sloped down to a lake. There was fresh horse manure here and there and a half-full hay feeder next to the barn, but no horses to be seen. I guessed it was Buck's pen, but maybe he was staying inside out of the heat. I couldn't blame him.

"It's real pretty out here in the springtime, believe it or not. The whole pasture is full of bluebonnets, as far as you can see," Cody commented, kind of apologetically.

Maybe so, but you never would have guessed it by looking. There was nothing there now except a little bit of wispy dead grass, and the dirt was so dry it had cracked open in spots. The whole place looked deader than the surface of Mercury.

I think it was hotter than the surface of Mercury, too. I could feel sweat popping up on my skin after the first few seconds, and I was sure Cody's black shirt was soaking up the heat like a beach towel. But thankfully, we soon came to a shady grove of pecan trees at the edge of the lake, and I was glad when we got up under the canopy and out of the sun.

The lake was a little bit low from the drought, but not by much. There was a gazebo beside the water with a porch swing hung from the center of it, and I guessed that's where we were headed. Turned out I was right.

Cody sat down on the swing, and I joined him. There was a breeze coming in off the lake, which was a blessing of epic proportions by itself. On the far shore I could see what looked like a peach orchard on a rise that sloped upwards to a steep hill covered in pine trees, which I guessed was Mount Nebo. It was a pretty view.

"I like your mama," I finally said.

"Yeah, she's somethin' else, I tell you," he agreed, but I could hear the love in his voice when he said it.

"Has it always been just you and her?" I asked.

"Mostly. Daddy passed away when I was six years old, and she never dated or anything after that," he explained.

"I wonder why. She's still a fairly young woman, and she's so pretty and nice, it's a wonder the men didn't beat the doors down," I said.

"Aw, they did, believe me," he chuckled.

"So how come she never. . . " I asked, leaving the thought trailing.

"Well, it's a long story. They got together in junior high, you know, and neither one of them ever went with anybody else. She always says Daddy was the love of her life, and no other man could ever take his place. Life is short, but love is forever," he said.

He said that last part like he might be quoting somebody else, but he also had the kind of expression on his face that a man only has when he's speaking about something he believes with his whole heart and holds so dear that to give it up he'd have to unmake himself. He might ostensibly be talking about his mother, but I suspected I might have touched something deep in his own soul, too.

"Is that what you think, too?" I asked, curious. He didn't answer me right away, maybe considering how much he wanted to say, or maybe just choosing his words carefully.

"Yeah, deep down I guess I do. I want my one and only, someday," he finally said in an offhanded kind of way, looking down and rattling the ice in his glass.

"Really?" I asked, enthralled, and I saw the ghost of a smile on his lips.

"Yeah, if it ever happens. I have my doubts about that sometimes," he said cryptically. It seemed like an odd thing to say, and for once I indulged my curiosity.

"How come? I bet half the girls in the county would love to get their hands on you," I asked. I said it jokingly, even though the question was a serious one. But Cody only laughed.

"Do you, now?" he asked, amused.

"Yeah, I really do," I agreed.

"Hmm. . . well, I don't know. Maybe I never found the right one, yet. I've been out with a few girls now and then. Even kissed a few. But that's as far as it ever went. Never anything serious," he said, gazing out across the lake.

"Really?" I asked again, still finding it hard to believe. But he only laughed again.

"Yeah, really and truly. I've got my reasons, though," he said softly, and I didn't push him any more even though I was dying of curiosity. I was afraid he might clam up again. He rarely talked about things like that or showed his heart so openly, and I wished we could have a thousand talks like that.

"I want my one and only someday, too," I confessed, hoping I wasn't going too far.

"Yeah, I can tell. I read some Christopher Marlowe this morning," he admitted.

"No way," I said.

"Yeah. I was curious, after you mentioned him yesterday," he said, and it touched me that he cared enough to do such a thing.

"Which one did you read?" I asked.

"I don't know the name of it. Started out with *'Come live with me and be my love'*," he said.

"Oh. Yeah, I love that one. What did you think of it?" I asked, and again he took a while to answer, perhaps thinking.

"Sorrowful," he finally said, succinctly, surprising me. *Sorrowful* wasn't a word I normally would have picked to describe that particular poem, and I wondered if there was some private reason why it might have affected *him* that way. He was such a riddle sometimes.

"Not too many guys like poetry. Not even a little bit," I said, choosing once again not to push him too hard. He'd tell me when he got ready, if it was anything I needed to know.

"Well, now, I'm not your typical guy, am I?" he asked, with another one of his little half-smiles, and I had to laugh.

"No, sir, that you're most surely not," I agreed.

They say that a noble heart is more beautiful than the most brilliant of diamonds, and the way Cody talked about love that day touched a very deep place in my own heart. In so many ways, he was tough as nails on the surface and then sweet as peach pie when he didn't think anybody would ever know it.

I think it was then that I first realized I might really be starting to love this boy, or at least that the chance was definitely there. Not just a wash of nostalgia, or a weakness for handsome young cowboys, but the real thing. And that scared me, because so far he'd given me precious little reason to think he felt the same way. I was afraid of getting hurt.

"I don't usually bring girls home to meet Mama, either," he added in that same offhand tone, still gazing out across the lake.

I was quiet for a few seconds, dying to ask him what that meant and too scared of what his answer might be for me to get the words out.

"Thanks," I said, inanely, and he laughed, breaking the tension that had crept in between us.

"You want to see my place?" he asked suddenly, as if the thought had just occurred to him.

"I thought you lived here," I said, confused.

"Well, yes and no. I'm still here on the ranch, but I moved out to the bunk house a couple years ago, so I could be on my own and have friends over whenever I wanted to and stuff like that, without disturbing Mama," he explained.

"I'd love to," I said.

"All right, then. It's close enough to walk, if you don't mind a little exercise," he said.

"Not at all," I agreed.

Chapter Seven
Lisa

We left the gazebo, and instead of going back the way we'd come, Cody took me farther down the lake shore. He let us through a gate in a barbed-wire fence, and on the other side the pecan trees switched over to white oak and pine, dense and impossible to see through.

Finally we came to a clearing on a broad-shouldered hill above the lake, and a long, rambling white house with a wide porch. It reminded me of the big house in some ways, I think mostly in the way the eaves and windows were made. Probably built to match.

"This place has been here ever since I can remember. It's been used for everything from a guesthouse to a junk barn over the years, sometimes as a place for some of the ranch hands to live. We've got three more of them over there on the other side of the lake, but this is the one I always liked the best because it's got the most privacy. Me and Marcus shared it for a little while, till he moved into one of the other ones. So it's all mine now," he murmured, unlocking the door to let us in.

The second we stepped inside, I felt like I'd entered a scene straight out of *True Grit.* Cody had covered the couch with a whole skin from a Holstein dairy cow, with all the black-and-white-splotched hair still attached. It looked like he'd built most of the tables and furniture himself from rough plank lumber that matched the paneled walls of rough-cut white oak wood. He'd scrounged a few street signs to put on the walls, and there was a Texas flag in the window and a real bear-skin rug in the middle of the floor that still had the claws and teeth on it. It still had the eyes, too, and I almost felt like it was staring at me.

I glanced at Cody, and saw that he was watching me with a proud smile on his face, like he thought he'd done something really special. I laughed a little.

"Did you kill that?" I asked, nodding at the bear, which was still staring at me.

"Yeah, sure did. Way back in a holler up in the Ozarks a couple years ago," he said proudly, and I laughed again.

He gave me the quick tour, such as it was, ending at his bedroom. It didn't take long since the whole place was set up on a fairly simple plan; living room and kitchen combo in the middle, with four bedrooms surrounding it; two on each side. It was pretty obvious he didn't use the extra bedrooms very much, so there wasn't a lot to show me. One of them was full of cardboard boxes and bunk beds taken out of the other rooms and shoved in there for lack of anywhere else to put them. Another one had nothing in it but a forgotten scrap of sheet music on the floor, and the third one was empty. I paid attention to everything as we went along, but of course it was Cody's room itself that I most wanted to see.

It fit the same young-single-redneck-cowboy style as everything else, only more so. He had a big double bed built of rough-cut cedar logs, with a handmade red and blue quilt in a starburst pattern, neatly made. There was a matching dresser with a big mirror on top, and a silver bolo tie in the shape of a bull's head hanging from the corner of it. Another white straw hat was hung from the other corner. On the wall were a few pictures in wooden frames, and a Texas Rangers pennant.

There was a desk with a computer on it, and a handful of reference books about farm business management and soil conservation and veterinary medicine and so forth. The books looked like he used them pretty often.

Besides that, there wasn't much else in there except a little shelf of knickknacks nailed to the wall beside his closet door. A high school rodeo trophy buckle. A horse carved from cedar wood with a pocketknife. A glass ball from Zion National Park. A toy monster truck like somebody might build from a model kit, of all things.

"What do you think?" he asked.

"If I hadn't known you lived here, I think I could have guessed it after seeing this room," I said humorously.

"Yeah, it's me, huh?" he asked, obviously pleased with my reaction.

I walked over to the knickknack shelf to meddle with his things, and saw that he'd won the rodeo buckle his senior year for calf roping. Then I looked at the picture of his parents. Miss Josie didn't seem to have aged much in all those years, and they both seemed very much in love. Sometimes you can tell, even in a picture. It gave me a wistful feeling, to see them like that. Cody didn't really look much like either one of them, but then I guess sometimes kids don't.

"You like to whittle?" I asked, picking up the horse. It was a stallion reared up on its hind legs, eyes wide and nostrils flared. It was exquisitely carved, with amazing attention to detail. I could even see the hair.

"No, but Marcus does. He gave me that for Christmas a couple years ago. It's supposed to be Buck, but I think he flattered the old boy a little bit. He's real good, though, huh?" he said, and I had to agree.

The glass ball was about the size of an orange and solid all the way through, with some desert wildflowers preserved inside. I don't know what kind they were, but they reminded me of the little blue lupines that bloom in early spring. At the bottom was a caption that read *In Beauty be it finished.* A pretty thought, even though I wasn't quite sure what it was supposed to mean.

Then I picked up the monster truck and raised an eyebrow at him.

"Yeah, that's somethin' I built a long time ago. I used to like to go to truck rallies and stuff like that," he said sheepishly, like he was afraid I might think the truck was a stupid thing to have on his shelf. I didn't, really, and besides that I was much more interested in what he said about truck rallies.

"How come you don't go anymore?" I asked.

"No particular reason. Just busy, I guess, and Marcus doesn't really like that kind of stuff much. It's no fun to go by yourself," he said.

"I'd like to try one," I said.

"Would you, now?" he asked, curious.

"Sure. If I had anybody to go with," I added.

"Well, then, I might have to take you sometime, whenever one pops up anywhere close," he said.

"I might have to take you up on that," I agreed.

After that we went back to the gazebo for a while, but that was all we said about serious things for the rest of the day. He told me some funny stories about places where the Mustangs had played now and then; brawls he'd been in and things like that. He told me about a sweetheart gig when they got to play at the Four States Fair in Texarkana two years ago, which they only got because Cyrus's brother was going out with one of the board members' nieces at the time. The power of networking, I guess you could call it.

Anyway, he said the last song they played that night was *Dixie,* and half the crowd was half drunk by then, and all those rednecks and hillbillies got all teary-eyed and Southern-patriotic and sang half the song with them and gave them a standing ovation at the end and they collected almost nine hundred bucks in tips. We both laughed at that and I kind of wished I could've been there to see it.

He cracked open some of last year's pecans for us with his bare hands while we sat there and swung back and forth, which reminded me of something Daddy used to do when I was little. We always had a butter churn full of pecans and we'd sit around the fire to eat them on winter evenings while we watched TV. He always crunched them in his fists like that. Eating pecans all night is a surefire way to get fat, no doubt, but I was too young to know or care about such things back then.

But I certainly knew *now,* so I mostly just nibbled even though I enjoyed the memories it brought back. We were careful to throw the broken shells over the railing into the lake; pecan shells hurt when you step on them bare-footed.

When we finally got back to the house, Miss Josie was right in the middle of transferring a warm, steaming brisket from the grill to a serving platter, and it smelled wonderful. Cody hurried to open the back door for her, and together we all went back into the kitchen. She deftly put the brisket down on the dining room table, and I saw that she'd already set out the plates and silverware and everything.

"Miss Josie, you should have come and got us sooner; I would have been glad to help you with all this!" I said, feeling bad that she'd been slaving away in the hot kitchen all evening while me and Cody had been drinking iced tea in the gazebo.

"Aw, now, it was no trouble at all. Now, y'all come eat before it gets cold," she said.

We did, joining hands while Cody blessed the meal, and then Miss Josie served the food. She'd whipped up mashed potatoes and corn on the cob to go with it, and a key lime pie for later.

"Now, Cody, make sure you don't run off anywhere tomorrow till that fence is done, and then Mr. Jackson'll be here sometime in the morning, too. He said he'll need to talk to both of us," she said.

"Okay, Mama," he said, when he swallowed his food. It sounded like he didn't really want to talk about the subject, whatever it might be.

I wondered fleetingly who Mr. Jackson was; the only one I could think of offhand was Sheila's daddy, Howie, the president of Piney State Bank. But I kept my curiosity to myself.

I wanted to help clear the table after supper, but Miss Josie wouldn't hear of that, either. She sent Cody and me back outside to wait for her on the verandah while she finished up in the kitchen. Finally she came out with her camera, fiddling with the buttons.

"Now, y'all go stand against that pecan tree over yonder and let me get some pictures," she said, and Cody laughed.

"Aw, come on, Mama; you want to take pictures *now?'* he asked.

"Yes, I sure do. Now y'all get over there," she told him, and so we did, standing in between the tree and Cody's truck. He put his arm around my shoulders and we shot as many poses as it took to satisfy Miss Josie. Then we sat on the verandah for a while and drank some more tea and talked about nothing in particular until it got dark and the lightning bugs started to come out.

Chapter Eight
Cody

I don't know why, but I was happy that day, in a way I hadn't been for a long time. I felt whole and at peace, like I suddenly had something back that I'd never known was missing.

About ten o'clock, I grabbed my truck keys to take Lisa home before it got too late.

"I'm really glad you came today," I said while we walked out to the driveway. The air was full of the mingled scent of mimosa blossoms and wild honeysuckle, the sweet smells of a southern summer night, encouraging both of us to walk slowly.

"Yeah, we'll have to do it again sometime. But next time you'll have to come over to my house," she told me.

"Sure," I agreed, and then we were getting in the truck for the drive back to town.

I walked her up to the front porch when we got there, and then lingered for a few minutes in the darkness, not wanting the evening to end. I just stood there, looking down at her beautiful face while she gazed up at me. I noticed that her lips were slightly parted, and I thought to myself how amazingly kissable they looked.

So I did the most natural thing in the world at that moment. I leaned in and kissed her, soft and sweet and tender, just like it ought to be. I certainly hadn't meant to do it, but I found that for once temptation was irresistible. Almost without thinking, I slipped my hand around her back and pulled her closer, and she pressed up as close to me as she could. Before long, the kiss which had started out so sweet and soft had become considerably more passionate.

"I better go," I finally said, breaking the kiss reluctantly. I didn't want to, and I could tell she didn't want me to, either. But I had to be strong.

"I'll see you tomorrow," she said faintly, and I nodded, not trusting myself to speak.

Maybe it was just a moment of weakness, brought on by reading that sorrowful poem and spending the day talking about things I ought not to have talked about. But even so, whatever delusions I might have had that I could keep things safe and friendly between us were officially blown to pieces, never to be believed again. I was kidding myself if I tried to think otherwise.

I realized with a dull, hopeless kind of ache that I ought to have known better from the very beginning. I'd been flirting with disaster ever since the first time I ever laid eyes on the girl. I should have known there'd come a day of reckoning, sooner or later. Now it had, and I was snared no matter what I did. It didn't matter that I hadn't had much choice but to hang out with her. I still should have been stronger.

I made it home without wrecking the truck, a minor miracle in its own right considering the state I was in. But by the time I pulled in under the pecan tree I knew what I had to do.

The only honorable choice at that point was to tell her everything, to lay it all on the table and try to explain to her the situation I was in, and then see what she thought about it herself. There was no more middle ground and no more wiggle room.

Knowing what to do is not quite the same thing as doing it, though. I went through the motions of brushing my teeth and getting ready for bed, wishing I could bury my head in the sand like an ostrich and make the whole nasty mess somehow go away. But that was impossible, and I soon found that even sleep was beyond my reach. Even after lying in bed for almost an hour, I was still wide awake.

I got up and went to the computer for a while, looking for a monster truck rally like I promised her I would, hoping the distraction would help. But sleep still eluded me even after I found one, so finally I decided to take a walk and maybe think about something else for a while, if such a thing were possible.

I slipped on a t-shirt and some cut-off jeans before quietly making my way barefooted down by the lake and finally to the gazebo, where I sat on the swing and threw green pecans across the lake. The water was lit up by one of the biggest full moons I'd seen in a long time, an especially pretty one with a ring of blue around the outside edge. I lay down on the swing and wondered if maybe Lisa was looking at that same moon and thinking about me, too.

After a long time, I decided there was absolutely no way this could wait any longer, not even till morning. I'd be out of my mind by then.

It was well past midnight at that point, but I decided to give her a call anyway.

Chapter Nine
Lisa

Cody's kiss left me floating in a warm pool of something very much like love that night, to the point that I almost forgot to take my shoes off before I went to bed. It was exactly the way I'd always imagined it would be, sweeter than honeysuckle, softer than baby's breath. It was a million times better than that awkward smooch at the fall dance all those years ago. I kept replaying it over and over again in my mind, wanting to make sure I never forgot even the slightest detail.

I fell asleep still thinking about it, and my dreams picked up right where memory left off. No surprise, there. Somehow the two of us were somewhere far away; I knew that much, even though I couldn't have said *how* I knew. A full moon shone down on a sandy white beach, and I stood there barefoot with palm trees all around. It was just like a scene from *Scarlett's Hawaiian Nights*, one of my favorite stories of all time.

For a second I was confused as to how I got there; it was one of those dreams which seems so real it's hard to distinguish it from waking life. Then I saw Cody standing there in the shadows, watching me, and he put a finger to his lips to shush me when I startled. I saw the glint of a ring on his finger in the moonlight, and I thought with a flood of happiness that we must be married, though I couldn't remember when or how.

He wasn't wearing a shirt, and his smooth skin was pale in the moonlight. He came closer, and then I felt his arms around me, strong and sure, while I buried my fingers in his close-cropped hair and felt the muscles on his back rippling. He kissed me passionately, and then. . .

Suddenly I woke up, the taste of him still on my lips, the smell of him still in my nostrils, my body still warm from the memory of his touch. I cried out in frustration, trying to keep the dream from slipping away. But he was gone, and I was back in my old room, and the phone was ringing.

I thought to myself that if that caller was anywhere within a hundred mile radius, I was prepared to get in the car, drive to his house, and literally beat him to a bloody pulp.

"Hello?" I snarled.

"Hey, did I wake you?" Cody asked, sounding taken aback.

"Oh, no, I'm sorry. I mean, yes, I was asleep, but it's all right. I'd rather talk to you, anyway," I said, my anger evaporating. Dreams were awesome, but the real thing was even better. Even if all I could do was talk to him.

"Oh, okay. Go look outside," he said. It wasn't exactly what I expected him to say, but I was willing to go along with it.

"What am I looking for?" I asked.

"Never mind that. Just go look," he said. I got up and grabbed a robe from the closet, then quietly walked downstairs and out to the patio in the back yard. Just above the trees was the biggest full moon I'd ever seen, wrapped in a blue ring of wispy clouds and flooding the world with silver light.

"Do you see it?" he asked.

I did, and for a second I was reminded vividly of the moonlight through the palm trees reflecting off his smooth skin, and my whole body felt warm at the memory.

"You mean the moon? Yeah, it's beautiful tonight," I said.

"I couldn't sleep, so when I saw it I had to tell you," he said.

If one of Jenny's boyfriends had woken her up at midnight to ask her to go outside and look at the moon, I'm fairly sure she would have cussed him out and told him to call her back in the morning. But as for me, well, I think Cody could have asked me pretty much anything that night and I would have thought it was sweet and romantic.

I laughed a little.

"What is it?" he asked, and I guess my laugh probably made him think he'd stuck his foot in his mouth after all.

"It's nothing. I was thinking about something Jenny said, that's all. Where are you? At home?" I asked him.

"No, I took a walk down by the lake. I'm sitting on the swing at the gazebo," he said.

"Wish I was there with you," I said wistfully, unable to contain myself.

"Yeah, me too. I couldn't stop thinking about you tonight," he admitted.

"Yeah, you've been on my mind tonight, too," I agreed, and smiled to myself. I could tell him that much without seeming disreputable.

"Well, listen. . . I found a monster truck pull in Lufkin on Saturday, if you want to go," he said.

"Sure. What time do I need to be ready?" I asked.

"Um. . . maybe four o'clock? It's kind of a long drive, you know," he said.

"Perfect. I'll see you then," I agreed.

There was a pause, but he made no effort to hang up the phone.

"Was there something else on your mind?" I finally asked, pretty sure there was.

"Well. . . yeah, actually," he admitted, reluctantly.

"Mm-hmm, thought so. What's up?" I asked, and again there was a long pause.

"Do you think you could meet me somewhere for a little while, Lisa? I know it's late, but there's something I need to talk to you about," he said.

I furrowed my brows at that, wondering what could be so important that he'd feel compelled to ask me such a thing. Under the circumstances I wasn't inclined to say no, even though I wasn't particularly thrilled with the idea of going out so late, either.

"Sure, I guess. Where at?" I asked.

"What about the park?" he suggested.

"No, that won't do. If the sheriff comes by and sees us sitting there he'll wonder what we're up to and he'll come harass us. Do you know where Autograph Rock is?" I asked.

"Yeah, I know where it is," he agreed.

"Can you meet me there in fifteen, twenty minutes?" I asked.

"Sure," he agreed, and that was that.

I went back inside, wondering what other strange and fantastic things might happen before daylight. I threw on some clothes and quickly brushed my hair so it wouldn't look too ratty, and then grabbed the keys off the kitchen table. I slipped outside without a peep, letting the car roll downhill into the street before I started it. Then I drove away, still yawning.

Autograph Rock is maybe two miles out of town, on an old dirt road in the middle of nowhere. It's a big block of sandstone, covered in names which people have carved there for generations, some of them so old they're almost weathered away. It's kind of a tradition amongst the old folks that whenever you get married, you go out to Autograph Rock and carve your names in the stone. I guess it's supposed to symbolize that your love will last forever, or something like that. People don't do it quite as much as they used to, but I'd always thought it was a sweet idea and hoped I'd get to follow through with it someday myself. But in the meantime, it was a good landmark where we could meet up and talk about whatever it was that Cody was so tied up in knots about.

He was already there when I pulled in, sitting on his tailgate and looking at the moon. I killed the car and went to join him, trying not to yawn too much.

"So what's on your mind, bubba?" I asked, sitting down beside him. The moonlight softened his features, making him look younger than he really was, and for a fleeting moment I was reminded of my dream again. He seemed ill at ease, taut as a bowstring, and I wondered what could be wrong.

"Lisa. . . do you like me?" he asked.

"You know I do," I agreed, deciding maybe it wasn't the best time in the world for a joke. He didn't seem to be in the mood for light banter.

"I mean like more than just friends," he clarified. That confused me a little; after the way he kissed me earlier it seemed like that would have been obvious. If it wasn't, then something was wrong. So I hesitated, wondering what to say. For once I couldn't read him at all, and every answer I could think of seemed dangerously risky. All I could think to do was speak the truth and hope for the best.

"Yeah," I finally said, unable to think of any way to embellish or clarify it. Cody let out a deep breath.

"Me too. I guess you already know that, after earlier. But I need you to know some things, before we ever let it go any further. If it changes things then I'm okay with that, but I have to tell you," he said.

"What is it?" I asked, uneasy.

"Do you remember when I told you I was the last McGrath?" he asked.

"Yeah, I remember," I agreed.

"Well. . . there's a reason for that," he said.

"Go on," I finally said, when he didn't seem disposed to continue. He ran his fingers through his hair and sighed.

"None of us has ever lived past thirty. My father, my grandfather, my aunts and uncles, all of us. No exceptions," he said.

"So what is it, then? There's like a disease that runs in your family or something?" I asked.

"No, nothing like that. It's always something different. Accidents, diseases, wars; it's never the same thing twice. The only thing we've all got in common is that none of us ever lived to be older than twenty-nine," he said.

"But that's just a- " I began.

"Coincidence? Yeah, that's what everybody says. And maybe if it was only three or four times then I might believe it. But every single family member since 1861? Nope, don't buy it," he interrupted.

"But what else could it be, though?" I asked.

"Maybe it's a curse," he said, watching me carefully.

"I don't believe in stuff like that," I said automatically, and realized almost immediately that it was the wrong thing to say.

"No? Well, I guess it doesn't matter what you call it. I still might not be here much longer," he said.

I understood lots of things at that moment, and felt a gentle wash of compassion for him. I didn't know what to think about his theory of a family curse; I was still inclined to believe it was bosh, honestly. But then again I'll be the first to admit there are a lot of things in the world that I don't understand, and only a fool says 'there's no such thing' about anything. It didn't really matter whether I believed it or not, though. What mattered was that *Cody* believed it, and that explained a lot.

"That's why you never would get too close, isn't it?" I asked. All those times when he'd been so distant and cool made perfect sense now.

"Yeah. I didn't think it was fair to put somebody through that," he said.

I don't know how else to explain it other than the grace of God, but somehow I had the wisdom not to argue with him over whether the Curse was real or not. That would have ended badly. Cody didn't want a debate over the nature of reality; he wanted an answer for how I felt just in case it *did* turn out to be true. And that part was surprisingly easy.

"It doesn't matter," I said.

"What do you mean, it doesn't matter?" he asked.

"Well. . . maybe that's not exactly what I meant. I wasn't blowing you off. I only meant it doesn't change anything, that's all," I said.

"It doesn't?" he asked.

"No. Mama always used to tell me you're never guaranteed tomorrow and you can't buy back yesterday. Now is all that matters, cause it's all you'll ever have. Either one of us might die before we make it home tonight. Even if right now was all the time we ever had together, I'd never be sorry for that," I said.

"Really?" he asked, still looking like he didn't quite believe me.

"Yeah, really and truly. Never think of it again," I told him, and grasped his rough hands in my own. His blue eyes were soft and lambent in the moonlight, and for only the third time he kissed me then, holding me tight in his arms and making it last a long, long time.

Oh, I won't pretend his revelation didn't scare me a little bit. I'm not the superstitious type, but nobody is immune to a cold shiver of doubt now and then. No one wants to get caught up in that kind of heartache, either, and I'm no exception. But then on the other hand, the thought of abandoning him because I was afraid of what the future might hold seemed to me to be the most contemptible idea I'd ever imagined. I might not know what was coming, but I wasn't going to bolt and run, that was for certain.

"There's something else, too," he said, when the kiss was over.

"Worse than what you already told me?" I asked.

"Well, no. Not exactly, anyway," he said.

"I guess you better tell me, then," I said, resigned.

"Okay then. Sometimes I have dreams," he said.

"Well, yeah, so does everybody," I said.

"No, I don't mean like that. I mean real ones. True dreams," he clarified.

"I don't know what you mean," I said.

"I mean sometimes I see things that will happen in the future," he said.

"I see," I said. I remembered hearing about things like that at church now and then, so I couldn't exactly say it was impossible, but I'd never met anybody who said it was something that happened to them.

"I know it's a lot to swallow in one night," Cody said, sounding sad.

"I'm sorry. I'm not trying to doubt you or anything. What do you dream about?" I asked, feeling guilty for not believing him.

"You, among other things," he said, and I might have been pleased if I thought that was something good. But as it was, all it did was give me a deep sense of foreboding.

"What about me?" I whispered.

"You're in danger, that's what. Or you will be; I still don't quite understand that part," he said, and proceeded to tell me a crazy story about dancing with skeletons and I don't know what all else.

I think if it had been anybody else but Cody, I might have cut him loose right then. There's only so much insanity a person can deal with at one time. But he already held too big a piece of my heart, and I couldn't have let go even if I'd wanted to.

I remembered my prayer that God would touch his heart and find a way for us to be together, if that would make both of us happy. Now here he was, the untouchable Cody McGrath, spilling his guts and telling me he wanted to be mine. I could only believe that all this was God's gift to me and His will for my life, however crazy it might seem. I couldn't imagine Cody saying all those things otherwise.

I only hoped I was right about all that.

"Never mind. We'll figure it out together," I said.

Chapter Ten
Cody

From then on, there was no more talk about being just friends. We were officially a couple, and for a little while I think me and Lisa had our fill of happy days. I know I did. I didn't forget about all the things hanging over us, and I didn't forget about Brandon's warning, either, but I did come to think maybe this was our walk through the crystal forest, if you will. Our sweet taste of happiness before the bad times came.

The truck pull was loud and messy and muddy and mean, just like the best ones always are. . . so loud we couldn't hear a word the whole time. I could tell Lisa had never been to one before, because she obviously hadn't expected the noise level. She kept putting her hands over her ears during the especially loud parts, but the rest of the time she laughed and cheered with the best of them.

I took her horseback riding on the road that circled the lake the next afternoon, and we talked about it.

"It was really cool, the way you cheered at the truck pull last night," I told her. We were on a shady part of the road riding side by side beneath the pines and the white oaks, with her on Nikki and me on my trusty Buck. Nikki was Mama's old gray mare, a nice, sensible horse who didn't toss up too many surprises.

"What, you thought I was pulling your leg about wanting to go?" she asked.

"Well, you know, sometimes girls *have* told me a couple things just to impress me," I said. I was playing with her, of course, but she didn't take the bait.

"I'm sure they have. You're a pretty hot commodity, Coby," she said, and I laughed.

"Coby?" I asked skeptically, and she smiled a little.

"Sure, why not? Cody boy. Coby. See there, how good at nicknames I am? Buck likes it, I bet," she said, reaching over to pat the horse's neck. I rolled my eyes but didn't say anything. I couldn't remember anybody ever calling me Coby before, but all it did was amuse me. Mama used to call me Dock when I was little because I used to like Bugs Bunny cartoons, but that's about it as far as nicknames go. My name's too short to really need one. But I was still buoyed up by that conversation at Autograph Rock, and Lisa could have gotten by with calling me just about anything right then if she'd wanted to.

Words are not my specialty, but the silly nickname made me feel unexpectedly tender towards her, and when we came to a big mimosa tree beside the wooden bridge over Cadron Creek, I saw my chance to do something.

"Are you ready for lunch, yet?" I asked casually, like it didn't matter too much.

"I'm fine, but we can go ahead and eat if you want to," she said.

"Sure. This looks like a good place," I said, nodding at the tree.

Mimosas are also called Formosa trees sometimes, a name which means simply *the beautiful tree,* and that they surely are. Not only that, but Cadron Creek is named after the brook of the same name that flows near the Garden of Gethsemane, which they say is one of the most beautiful places in Jerusalem. So you might say I picked a sweet and symbolic kind of spot, if you care for things like that. I sure do. I love the way there's so much depth and richness to the world beyond what the eye first sees, if you only take the time to learn about it. A man could live his whole life awash in wonders, if he only knew.

So we got down and sat in the shade of the sweet-smelling blossoms, eating our sandwiches and drinking Dr. Pepper, and while we were sitting there I gathered up a double handful of mimosa blooms and started weaving them together. It was more or less like braiding a rope, and I'd had lots of practice with that. I picked a blade of rye grass from the edge of the water and chewed on it absently while I worked, like I usually do when I need to concentrate. Otherwise I tend to stick my tongue out without thinking, and that's undignified, you know.

"What are you doing?" she asked, watching me.

"Wait and see," I told her, and with that she had to be content. It took me a few minutes because the stems were so small, and I have to admit it was a bit lopsided, but when I was done I had a pink-and-white crown of fragrant powder puffs. I had her lean over, and I carefully pulled a few strands of her hair through to hold it in place.

"There. Now you look like a princess from back when the world was young," I said. It was my best stab at poetry, such as it was.

"I feel silly," she said, but I could tell from her eyes that she really didn't. She leaned over and kissed me then, one of those happy, innocent kisses with nothing behind it but simple love, and I felt warm from the tips of my toes to the ends of my ears.

I took a drink of Dr. Pepper and kissed her in return, my mouth still full of soda pop, cold and sweet. She always laughs when I do that and calls them monkey kisses, from the way monkeys feed each other with a mouthful of food or water. She tells me Dr. Pepper is fine, but if I ever try it with a mouthful of chewed-up broccoli, she swears she'll slap me.

She didn't take off the mimosa crown when we left the bridge, even though it soon wilted from the sun when we came back through open spots.

We passed in front of Marcus's house and came to the big aluminum gate where the lakeside track emerged onto the main haul road beside the peach orchard, and I had to get down so I could open it for us. Lisa rode through while I led Buck by the bridle so I could fasten the gate behind us again and keep the cows out of the peaches.

Then we headed back toward the barn. The haul road passes over the top of the earth dam that forms the lake, and below it the land drops off to the flats near the bayou; cow pasture down there, mostly. The herd was grazing under the cypress trees that grew near the bayou, too far away to see them very well. I rambled on for a while about how black cows were worth more money than any other color because of the fad for Black Angus meat, but I noticed she wasn't really paying much attention.

"We've got a gig coming up next weekend in Dallas," I mentioned after a while, changing the subject.

"Really? Where at?" she asked.

"Aw, just another honky-tonk joint, that's all. But we'll make better money than we do around here, that's for sure," I told her.

"Can I come?" she asked, and I glanced at her skeptically.

"You really want to? It's not a very nice place, you know," I reminded her.

"Sure. I think it'll be fun," she said.

So we took her with us, and she was good about helping to load up the sound equipment and such, and she didn't complain when the two of us had to squeeze into the tiny back seat of Cyrus's truck.

The place turned out to be rougher than I hoped; the kind that has chicken wire in front of the stage. That's always a bad sign. But nevertheless, the four of us quickly unpacked and set up the equipment, and Lisa found a stool so she could sit at the end of the bar and watch. I was afraid she'd be bored to tears, honestly, but if she was then she did a good job keeping it to herself.

She looked awfully nice, to be in such a place as that. Marcus used to joke around that all it takes to turn a bar fly into a beauty queen is if she's still got all her teeth, and after some of the women I've seen in places like that, I don't even think he was joking. But Lisa was pretty in a sweet, fresh kind of way; the kind of way that you don't often see in places like that. It worried me a little, and I hoped the guys left her alone.

Things went pretty well for the first couple of hours, but then sure enough a fight started and pretty soon the whole place was engulfed in it. People were throwing beer bottles and food and even handfuls of sawdust, and chicken wire won't stop all those things. I barely had time to stash Grandpa Tommy's Martin behind the drum set before two men came crashing through the chicken wire and knocked me off my stool, and before I knew it all three of us were sucked into the brawl.

I hate bar fights. There's nothing noble or attractive about them; they're ugly and senseless and mean, and people get hurt really badly sometimes, especially if somebody pulls a knife or a gun. Not to mention a lot of expensive equipment can get busted to pieces in the blink of an eye.

Normally I would've stayed up on stage to defend the equipment, but not with Lisa out there in the very thick of things. I could see her crouched down at the end of the bar, trying her best to stay out of the way. So I bulled my way through the melee and hustled her out the back door as fast as I could. That earned me a busted lip from somebody's flying fist in the process, but I've had worse.

"Are you all right?" I asked her as soon as we were safely out in the alley. My mouth was full of blood and I had nothing to wipe it away with, so I turned my head and spit it out on the pavement.

"Yeah, I'm fine," she said. She sounded fairly cool about the whole thing, actually.

"We'll be going home in a few minutes. As soon as the cops get here they'll shut the place down for the night," I told her.

"No doubt. I never knew you spent so much time in saloons," she said, shaking her head.

"I wouldn't, if I had my druthers. But I guess it grows on you after a while," I said dryly, and she actually laughed.

"Yeah, I can see how it would," she agreed.

"That was a joke, Lisa," I said, wondering if maybe she'd hit her head on something before I was able to get her outside.

"I know. Maybe it's being out here with you and the others that I like. Even if all we do is go to a bar fight," she said. I laughed and kissed her for that, forgetting my split lip until too late. A stab of pain reminded me, and I left bright red blood on her mouth, too, like she'd been kissing a vampire. Not a very pretty picture.

"Are *you* okay?" she asked, trying to see in the dim light.

"Yeah, it's only a busted lip, that's all. No big thing," I said.

"Okay, then," she said, and kissed me very softly right on my lower lip, not even hard enough to hurt.

Marcus and Cyrus came out the back door right about then, grumbling about how somebody had kicked in a speaker. Marcus had a black eye, but it didn't look like Cyrus had any obvious injuries. It could've been a lot worse.

The four of us loaded up the drums and the amp and I fetched my guitar from behind the stage, and then we collected our money from the owner and went home. Lisa actually seemed like she had a good time, hard as that was for me to believe.

She went with us to several other gigs after that, until we all started thinking of her as our semi-official roadie, and marveled that we were big-league enough to have a roadie in the first place. Marcus and Cyrus thought she was awesome, and never failed to tell me so. Marcus joked around about how if we ever broke up then he wanted first chance to pick up the pieces, and Cyrus asked if she had a sister. It was all good-natured fun, of course, but whenever anybody said something like that she always put her hand on my arm or hugged me or some such thing, just to show the whole world she didn't give a fig about anybody except me.

I couldn't help myself. . . I gloried in it. I'd never tasted that kind of love in my whole life even though I'd wished and longed for it ever since I was old enough to know I wanted anything at all. It's all the sweeter, when you're suddenly handed something you wanted that much and always thought you could never have. The more time passed, the more certain I was that I loved her and she really was my one and only; incredibly, unbelievably, right there by my side. But I never said so, because in spite of everything I still kept worrying that it was all too good to be true, and sooner or later the other shoe would drop and everything would fall to pieces.

"Why don't you sing with us sometime, Lisa? We could always use a girl's part, you know," I asked her one day, after we'd finished a gig in Tyler. It was one of the more upscale places we'd been to; a trendy little coffee house named Sufficient Grounds, where the manager served us complimentary espresso and strawberry cheesecake when we took our break.

"Oh, I could never do that," she demurred, although I could tell she was flattered to be asked.

"Sure you could. I bet you could even help me write some song lyrics, if you wanted to. They're just poetry, after all," I suggested.

"Well. . . sure, why not?" she said.

So we sat down and tried it, scribbling verses and musical notations for hours on the front porch at Goliad. I played the tune to see what she thought of it every now and then, and I'd try to sing the words she wrote. Cyrus could have done that part a lot better, of course, but at least she didn't laugh too much.

"So let me hear *you* sing something, darlin'. I was serious about needing a girl's part," I finally told her.

"You promise you won't laugh?" she asked shyly.

"Cross my heart," I said, and after hesitating another few seconds she started to sing.

> *Sleep, my love, and peace attend thee,*
> *All through the night*
> *Guardian angels God will send thee,*
> *All through the night. . .*

She started out soft and uncertain, but after a while she seemed to forget about that and became more confident. She grasped my hands, and looked into my eyes, and I couldn't have torn myself away even if I'd wanted to.

If you've never seen love in someone's eyes, you might be tempted to think it's only a figure of speech. I'm here to tell you it's not. I saw it that day, and I knew what it was immediately. I was startled, but not unbelieving. I've always heard that the eyes are the windows of the soul, and I guess I never really understood that before. I think now I do.

"That's beautiful," I finally managed to say, and she smiled.

"My mother used to sing it for me when I was little. It's an old Welsh song. Mama's grandmother was from Caerleon, which they say used to be Camelot, where King Arthur lived," she murmured.

"See, I knew you had some interesting stories to tell. Maybe you're secretly a princess after all," I said, and she laughed.

"Maybe to you, Coby," she said, amused.

"Yeah, definitely to me," I said softly.

Chapter Eleven
Lisa

I was really nervous the first time Cody came to my house. Going to see him at Goliad was one thing, but having him right there on my own turf was nerve-wracking.

He took his hat off when he came indoors and nodded his head when I introduced him to Mama, proper as could be, and I think that impressed her. She couldn't smile very well anymore, but I saw the light in her eyes that meant the same thing. I don't think he ever knew how much that meant to me.

I showed him the vegetable garden and then took him upstairs to show him my room. I think that was probably the hardest part of all. Your personal space is, well, *personal,* you know. Nobody had ever set foot in there except me and Mama and Jenny. No guys, ever.

Cody didn't know that, of course, and I didn't particularly feel like telling him.

He came inside and glanced around, his eyes pausing briefly on the seven teddy bears on my bed and no doubt noticing how much I liked pink and white things. Then he saw something that interested him.

"What's that about?" he asked curiously, looking at the painting above my desk. It was a portrait of Queen Victoria on her wedding day, with flowers in her hair and a long white dress.

"That's Queen Victoria. Haven't you heard about her?" I asked.

"No, can't say that I have, honestly," he admitted.

"I've always admired her so much. She liked to paint watercolors, you know, and she loved her husband so much that after he died she still had his clothes laid out for supper every night for the rest of her life, and she was buried in her wedding veil," I said. Cody gave me one of his little half-smiles, and I couldn't tell whether he thought the story was silly or sweet.

"She does sound like a beautiful lady," he agreed.

"Oh, she was. She's my hero," I said.

He didn't seem to think the portrait called for any more comment, so I don't actually know what he thought of it himself. Instead, he went over to the bookshelf and ran his finger along a few of the paperbacks. They were mostly my collection of Scarlett Blaze romances, but not all.

He pulled a book from the shelf and I came closer to see what he was looking at. *Tristan and Isolde,* by Joseph Bédier. One of my favorite stories of all time, even if it was kind of obscure nowadays.

"What's this one about?" he asked, looking at the back cover.

"Oh, surely you've heard *that* story before, haven't you?" I asked.

"I've heard of Tristan before, but I don't know anything about him," he said.

"Hmm. Well, it's fairly long in the original but I can tell you the gist of it, anyway, if you like," I said.

"Sure," he agreed.

"Okay, then. A long time ago, there was a young man named Tristan, and he was the most handsome and noble of all the knights in Tintagel. Now it so happened that his uncle, the King Mark, had been at war with another kingdom for many years, and at last they made peace by agreeing that King Mark would marry the daughter of his enemy. But since the ocean was wild and the way was treacherous, Mark sent his beloved nephew Tristan to escort the young lady home. The Princess Isolde was unhappy with the idea of leaving her home, and of having to marry an old man like King Mark, but the herbalist of the king's court had given her a drink which would cause the two people who shared it to fall in love forever. It was meant to be a comfort to her, to help her find some happiness in her new life, and she was told to drink it with Mark when she arrived in Tintagel. The Princess had finally given up and accepted her fate, but on the way across the sea she spoke to Tristan often, and fell in love with his brave and noble heart. Therefore she took the potion that was meant for King Mark, and poured it into a golden cup, and asked him to share a drink with her, as people sometimes did in those days. So then he fell in love with the Princess forever, and he could never take back his heart, nor she hers," I said, speaking with what I thought was the proper storytelling flair.

"I bet King Mark didn't like that very much," Cody said sardonically.

"No, I'm afraid things didn't go so well for them. I'm sure it must have been awful, to be always in love with someone you knew you could never have," I said sadly.

"So what finally happened?" Cody asked. He was trying hard to pretend he wasn't interested, but I knew him too well by then.

"People say different things, so I guess it depends on who you choose to believe," I said.

"What do you think happened?" he asked, and I laughed a little.

"I think somehow or other Tristan found a way to be with his princess, and they lived happily ever after, of course," I said, and he smiled.

"I like that story," he said.

"Yeah, me too. It's one of my favorites," I agreed.

I think sometimes Cody has a certain streak of Tristan in his own heart; a love for honor and chivalry, for glorious last stands and victories won against impossible odds in the very jaws of defeat, and yes, even for the kind of love that lasts forever. It's one more thing I love about him.

In fact, the only thing that marred the whole summer from my point of view was that he never said he loved me. I was pretty sure he did, deep down, but he never would *say* it, and I was too afraid to be the one who said it first.

Oh, I know how I *felt*. I really loved him, or at least I thought I did. Things might have started out as a sweet memory, colored with daydreams and romanticism, but it was way beyond all that, now. He was all I could think about; all I *wanted* to think about. If I let myself go there, I'd be lost all the time in gooey dreams about fairytale weddings and babies that looked just like Cody, and the kind of happily ever after stuff that hardly ever comes true in real life.

He was my treasure and the very heart of my heart, whether he knew it or not. I wanted to join together with him like two drops of rain on a window glass. I wanted to become one body with two hearts, like Albert and Victoria, like Tristan and Isolde, and a hundred other couples I'd read and dreamed about all my life.

There was nobody I could talk to, though. Jenny would have thought I'd lost my mind from reading too many Scarlett Blaze novels, and Mama couldn't answer me. I had to keep it all to myself, like it or not.

I would have given my left kidney to be able to read Cody's mind right then, but I didn't dare come right out and ask him if he felt the same way about me. Because if he didn't, then my heart was going to break right in two, and nothing would ever be the same. They say the first cut is always the deepest, and you better believe it's the truth, too. Cody was the first one I'd ever felt that way about in my whole life, and it terrified me to even think about the possibility of losing him.

So I dithered and worried and daydreamed and hoped and prayed and generally lived on an emotional roller-coaster of uncertainty for a while. Then came the night when my life changed forever.

It started out like any other day. We went fishing at the gazebo for an hour or two, and I listened to him talk about how he might have to sell off the rest of the cows if it didn't rain soon. He'd got to where he talked to me a little more about things like that than he used to. I could tell how much it worried him, but short of becoming an expert in cattle futures and commodities trading, or learning how to change the weather with a snap of my fingers, I didn't know of anything I could do to help him or to make things better. All I could do was listen if he felt like talking, and hope that it would take his mind off things.

Miss Josie made supper that night as usual, and when the sun started to go down, I thought we'd probably watch TV for a while or do something ordinary like that. But Cody had something else in mind.

"Come on, Lisa; let's go for a walk," he told me, and I was glad to join him. I thought at first he might be taking me to the bunk house for some reason, since that's the way he headed. But no, he went right on past that, around the back side of the lake and over the wooden bridge where the big mimosa tree grew.

"Where are we going?" I finally asked, when he still didn't slow down.

"Just wait; you'll see," he said, with a smile in his voice.

Back behind the orchard and the lake there was the steep sandstone knob of Mount Nebo, which I'd seen from a distance many times but never climbed, and when Cody turned off the main road onto a narrow track that ran sharply uphill, I began to get some idea of where we might be headed.

Nebo is easily the highest point within several miles, and in spite of the cool air I started to get a little sweaty and breathless on the steep slope. We finally came out onto the flat top of the hill, and immediately found ourselves face to face with a cemetery. It had a wrought iron fence around it and tall, massive headstones with lichen growing on them, and three gnarled old cedar trees that looked like they'd been there since dinosaurs walked the earth. The arch over the gate said *Nebo*.

I stopped.

"You wanted to bring me to the cemetery?" I asked, staring at it skeptically. As much as I loved Cody, I couldn't help thinking taking me on a date to a graveyard was more than a little creepy.

"No, not *that*," he said, laughing.

"Then what?" I asked.

"This," he said, leading me past the cemetery and up onto a little bit higher piece of ground not far past it, at the very summit of the hill. There was a rocky outcrop, more or less flat, and he sat down on top of it, looking west. The sun was just setting in a blaze of glory, golden and red across the rolling landscape. The bare top of the hill left the view wide open, giving us a breathtaking vista.

"It feels like you can see forever from up here, when the weather's nice. I used to climb up here a lot when I was a kid, whenever I wanted to be alone. It always seemed like I had the whole world down there at my feet," he murmured.

"It's beautiful," I agreed.

"It's my most favorite place in the whole world. I thought you might like it up here, since you love landscapes so much. Maybe you could paint it sometime," he said, and I laughed, because that was exactly what I'd been thinking.

"You know me way too well, boy; you're starting to read my mind," I told him, and for a little while we sat in companionable silence. Neither of us was in any special hurry to leave, so we sat there and watched until the light faded away and the stars came out, thick as diamond dust across the sky.

It's been said that love and beauty are linked forever in the soul of man, and that's why boys always yearn after beautiful things, and know not for what they wish, nor why. Maybe that's truer for some than for others, but I think for Cody it's always been so. I may never know for sure, but I believe that sitting there beside me in that high place under a canopy of shining stars is what finally opened his heart.

"I love you, Lisa," he said after a while, in his quiet, offhanded kind of way.

I almost thought I'd misheard him at first, it was so unexpected. Then I decided that yes, he'd really said it.

"I love you too, Cody," I said, very tenderly. I felt like I'd waited forever to hear those words from him for the first time, and to be able to say them myself.

"Do you really? Not just saying it cause I did?" he asked, half jokingly.

His voice was teasing, but I could sense how serious the question was and how desperate he must have felt at that moment to know that I really meant it. I would have felt the same way myself, if the shoe had been on the other foot.

"I love you more than anything in the world, Cody Lee McGrath, my dearest and only one," I told him, and squeezed his hand. I heard him sigh with a mixture of relief and happiness, and then he kissed me.

"I want you to have something, Lisa," he said, taking his Avinger High ring off his finger and slipping it onto mine. It was too big to fit, of course, but I figured I could put tape around the band or maybe wear it on a necklace if I had to.

It might be only his high school ring, but in some ways a ring is always a ring, poignant with symbolism. I knew Cody knew that just as well as I did. It was an implied promise, of a sort, even if it was a very dim and shadowy one. I knew *that* wasn't lost on him, either. He could be awfully subtle when he wanted to be.

"I'll never take it off," I whispered, and that was another oblique hint of a promise yet to come. I knew it was a kind of game we were playing, and that in some ways it wasn't a game at all. But the Great Romance always feels like a game, even when the end in view is very serious indeed.

We didn't say much on the way back down the hill, and as soon as we got back to the house, I found some tape in the bathroom and thickened the band enough so I could wear his ring without it slipping off. It was gold, with a dark red garnet; Cody's birthstone. On one of the side panels was a cowboy holding the reins of a horse while he knelt in front of a cross, and on the other side was a Texas flag and a Confederate flag with the poles crossed, and below them the caption *Texas Rebel.* And so he was, in so many, many ways, I thought to myself.

I'm sure Miss Josie couldn't have kept from noticing the ring on my finger, but she was the soul of discretion and said nothing at all about it.

Chapter Twelve
Lisa

Jenny, on the other hand, was another matter.

"How cute," she said, as soon as she saw my ring the next morning. We were supposed to be going to the mall in Longview together, and true to my promise to Cody, I was determined never to take that ring off my finger.

"Yeah, he gave it to me last night," I said, and Jenny rolled her eyes.

"Come on, Lisa; are we still in high school? Don't you think you're a little bit too old to wear a guy's class ring? Much less with *tape* on it?" she asked, looking at the band in horror.

"I can wear anything I want to. What are you now, anyway, the fashion police? You're just jealous, that's all," I told her.

"Jealous? Of what?" she asked.

"You're jealous because I've got a boyfriend who really loves me and all you ever end up with are dirtballs, that's what," I said. It was harsh, but there was a grain of truth in it, too.

"You think he loves you, huh?" she asked, ignoring the comment.

"I *know* he does," I said firmly.

"How do you know?" she asked, and in spite of her attitude I thought I detected a note of something deeper in her question, like maybe she really did want to know. Which might make sense, if she was even half as jealous as she seemed to be.

But on the other hand, what could I tell her that she'd believe? A hundred things came to mind, but I knew Jenny could shoot them all down if she wanted to. Any one of them might be a lie, or a hoax, or whatever the case might be.

"It's no one single thing, Jen. I know he loves me because he shows it in all kinds of different ways, even when he thinks I don't notice. Sometimes you just know," I told her, knowing she wouldn't be satisfied with that.

"Yeah, maybe so. We'll see," she said.

"Yup, we sure will," I said firmly.

"Well in the meantime will you at least take that ridiculous thing off your finger? People are laughing," she complained.

"No, I won't. I haven't heard anybody laughing, and honestly I don't care if they do," I said.

"You're impossible," Jen said.

"You better believe it," I said smugly.

But in spite of Jenny's insinuations that I was being juvenile, I never had anybody else laugh or complain about the ring on my finger.

It was just me and Mama for supper that night, so I showed her the ring and for a long time I sat there telling her all about Cody and the things we'd done together and all the hopes and dreams I had for the future. She couldn't answer me, of course, but sitting there talking to her was almost like old times.

I hauled my canvas and brushes up to Mount Nebo to give it a try, and soon took a real liking to the place. It was an awesome spot to paint. Early mornings were best, when it was cooler. There was something about the way the light struck the trees and the lake, and the color of the sky. Sometimes in really dry years, the dust comes up and fills the sky with brilliant colors at sunrise and sunset, so maybe the drought did have one or two minor good points about it, too. It still hadn't rained a drop, and there was no prospect of it anytime soon.

Sometimes Cody would come up there to watch me work when he could get away from his own chores for a while. He said I had a way of capturing the exact way the light fell and making the picture look almost *more* than real, which of course pleased me to no end.

He was up there with me one morning when I finished a particularly nice pink and gold sunrise scene with a blue, blue sky, and when I put the final touch on my signature he clapped his hands.

"Beautiful work!" he said.

"You think so?" I asked, flattered.

"Absolutely," he agreed.

"Then it's yours, baby. My first commission," I said, laughing self-consciously.

"That's perfect. I'll get Marcus to make a frame for it and then we'll put it up in the house somewhere," he said.

"It's nowhere near good enough for *that,*" I objected.

"You're right, it's better," he said, and I could have kissed him for saying it. In fact I *did* kiss him, but not too lingeringly.

"Well, I guess I'm done up here for today. Want to help me take all this stuff back down?" I asked.

"Sure," he agreed. We gathered up the canvas and the paints and all the other stuff, and slowly made our way towards the path. But when we got to the cemetery I stopped.

"Your dad is buried up here, isn't he?" I asked, glancing at the stones.

"Yeah, back there in the corner," he agreed.

"Can we see his grave?" I said. It was partly just an impulse, for no particular reason that I knew of, but I'd also been thinking about painting a scene with those magnificent cedar trees, and I wanted to walk around the cemetery a little bit and see where I could get the best view of them.

"Uh. . . sure, I guess," Cody agreed dubiously, setting down the canvas. He opened the wrought iron gate and led me way back to a double headstone of pink Texas granite, with the name *Blake McGrath* on one side and *Josie Grey* on the other, and below them this epigram:

> *Many waters cannot quench love,*
> *Neither can the floods drown it.*

I noticed there were fresh yellow roses on Blake's side of the grave, and wondered how they'd gotten there.

"Mama brings them up here, every Sunday afternoon," Cody said quietly, watching where my eyes had rested.

"What happened to him, anyway?" I asked, unsure what to say in the face of such steadfast devotion. *Love* seemed almost too tepid a word for it. Cody had already told me how she felt about him, of course, but I guess seeing it in person makes a lot bigger impression than just hearing about it.

"He drowned. We went camping on the Brazos River one spring at Possum Kingdom, because he always liked to fish for rainbow trout below the dam out there. Anyway, the water level was high and some kids were out messing around in the edge of the river even though you're not supposed to do that because of the undertow. A girl got swept away, and he went in after her. Never made it out," Cody said.

"What about the girl?" I asked.

"Yeah, she made it. We think Daddy might have hit his head on a rock and that's what kept him from swimming, but nobody knows for sure. It was a pretty bad scene, I hear, but they didn't let me see that part, thankfully," he said softly, running his hand along the top of the stone.

"I'm sorry," I said.

"It's all right. Mama always says he died the way he would have wanted to, saving somebody else, and that now he's safe in the arms of God. I know that's why she picked that verse on here, though," he said.

"The one about many waters?" I asked.

"Yeah. . . because he drowned in the river, you know. That verse was her way of promising him one last time that she'd love him forever, no matter what. So she tells me, anyway," he said.

When I thought about the unswerving way that Miss Josie had kept that promise for all those years, it was enough to bring tears to my eyes.

"That's a beautiful story," I said.

"Yeah. . . I always thought so, too," he admitted.

"I don't know how it keeps from breaking her heart," I said.

"Sometimes I think it still does. You know that song she always likes to sing?" he asked.

"Leaning on the Everlasting Arms?" I asked.

"Yeah, that one. Whenever you hear her singing that, she's thinking about him," he said.

"How do you know that?" I asked.

"Because that's what the name of the river means. *Brazos de Dios,* the Arms of God. She says things like that are never a coincidence, and part of the reason why he died in that particular place was to always remind her that God is love and would never forsake either one of them, even when something terrible happens. She says whenever she thinks of that, it reminds her that everything happens for a reason. So she's loved that song ever since, even though it still makes her cry now and then," he said.

I wondered if I could have had the courage to see things the way Miss Josie did, if Cody had been the one who drowned on a fishing trip and left me a widow at the age of twenty-five with a young child to raise and a ranch to manage all on my own. I honestly didn't know the answer.

All this talk about death and tragedy reminded me uneasily of all that stuff Cody believed about having a curse on his family, and I felt a chill in the pit of my stomach. Yeah, I know I said I'd never let it matter, and to be honest it was easy to blow it off as an old wives' tale most of the time, but standing there in front of Blake McGrath's grave and hearing that story about how he died. . . it suddenly made the whole thing seem a lot more credible.

"So who all else is buried up here?" I asked, not liking the subject anymore.

"Oh, lots of people. My grandparents, great-grandparents, aunts, uncles, cousins, you name it. All family, though," he said.

"What's the oldest one?" I asked.

"Um. . . My Grandpa Reuben is buried up here. You remember him, don't you; the one who fought at Goliad and first settled here? His stone's over here," Cody said, walking across to another part of the cemetery. I couldn't help noticing how young so many of the people were when they died, and that made me even more uneasy. Try visiting a cemetery chock full of twenty-somethings and see how it makes *you* feel. I guarantee you won't like it.

The headstone turned out to be another double one, with *Reuben McGrath* on one side and *Hannah Trewick* on the other. It was marble instead of granite, though, and in the middle between the two halves was a tapering column about four feet high, with a quartz crystal about the size of a peach pit cemented on the very tip of it like a diamond. It was clear and perfect, with no cracks or inclusions, and someone had polished it so the facets were clean and smooth as a jewel.

"Where'd *that* come from?" I asked, staring at it.

"It's cool, huh? It was Grandma Hannah's. She used to wear it as a brooch, or so I've heard, and she loved it so much she had it put up here on her tombstone. I tried to pull it loose a few times when I was little, because it was so bright and shiny," he said.

"He sure was a lot older than her," I commented, reading the dates on the stone. Reuben was almost thirty years older than his wife.

"Yeah, people did that kind of stuff back then, I guess. I don't think she got along with her family very well, so maybe that was part of it," he shrugged.

"Was Reuben really the only one who survived at Goliad?" I asked, nodding at the monument. I knew Cody wouldn't be able to resist an invitation like that.

"Oh, no, he wasn't the *only* one," he quickly corrected me, and then he was off to the races.

So I listened while he waxed enthusiastic about Reuben McGrath's adventures in the Texas Revolution and elsewhere, with a smile on my face. Who ever knew that a visit to a cemetery could be so educational?

We did lots of other things, of course. We spent evenings together on the beach at the end of the road, sometimes with Marcus and Cyrus, and sometimes just the two of us. There were several big sycamore trees that leaned way out over the water, filling the air with their strong scent. The boys had nailed little pieces of plank all the way up the biggest trunk to make a ladder to reach the top, and once you got all the way up there, you were nearly thirty feet over the coffee-brown water of the bayou.

Me and Cody jumped off that tree more times than I could count, hitting the water so hard it stung the bottoms of our bare feet. It was a deep enough hole that we didn't have to worry about hitting the bottom, and we'd come up gasping and sputtering after what seemed like ten years down under. Sometimes he'd kiss me right there in the water, still too blurry-eyed to see a thing. I loved it when he did that.

Other times, we'd light a bonfire on the sand and he'd play guitar while we sat on the tailgate till one o'clock in the morning. Cody could play almost anything, I think, and sometimes did. Everything from *Lily of the Valley* (his favorite hymn) to old Buddy Holly songs, and everything imaginable in between. He particularly liked the ones that took a lot of fast chord changes like *I Fought the Law,* I guess so he could show off a little.

I remember one night he sang me Jake Owen's *Barefoot Blue Jean Night,* a wild song about sitting barefoot on the riverbank to watch pretty auburn-headed girls drinking iced tea with their ruby red lips, among other things, and that was close enough to describing *me* that I laughed and turned a little red.

I think those nights at the river are some of my sweetest memories, actually, full of music and warm kisses and talks that went on for hours. Every time I catch the scent of a sycamore tree, that's always what I think of.

We gradually formed a habit of going to the Dairy Dip for lunch every Saturday afternoon, and before long the corner booth was always "ours" whenever we went there. One day when the place was empty and there was nobody to see, Cody slipped out his pocketknife and quickly carved our initials into the surface of the table.

"What are you *doing,* you nut?" I asked, watching him in mixed horror and amusement and glancing around nervously. If word ever got back to old Mrs. Gillespie, I'd probably get a good cussing at best and maybe even fired.

"Hush. Nobody's looking," he told me, as he finished the last letter. He carved them deep, too; as long as that table stayed in the Dairy Dip, there was no way those initials were going anywhere either.

Whatever my objections to his vandalism might have been, I relaxed when he was finished with it and finally even laughed.

"You're truly crazy, you know that?" I asked him.

"Yeah, I know, but you love me anyway, don't you?" he asked.

"Yup. Can't help myself," I agreed.

I was so happy that summer I think I could have floated on air. I had the man of my dreams and everything (well, almost) that I'd ever wanted. Yeah, there might have been some clouds on the horizon, but they were faint and far away.

Things were sweeter than honeysuckle dew, for a little while.

Chapter Thirteen
Cody

On a night in late July, I dreamed again for the first time in weeks.

This time was nothing like the crystal cave I saw before. I saw a pitiless desert scene, harsh and bright, and a white silver plain writhing with copperhead snakes. One of them was larger than the rest and devoured the smaller ones until none were left. Then it looked at me with glittering eyes and would have devoured me too, but in my hand was a shining star which held it back.

The next morning I told Lisa about it.

"I had another dream last night," I said.

"A true one?" she asked.

"I think so. It was weird, but then I guess they always are," I said.

"So tell me about it," she said.

"It was horrible. There was a sandy desert full of copperheads, and one of them ate all the rest and then tried to eat me, but it couldn't because I had a star in my hand. Then I woke up," I said.

"What's that supposed to mean?" she asked.

"I'm not sure, but I know who we can ask," I said.

"Who's that?" she asked.

"His name's Brandon Stone; he lives over there in Ravanna," I said.

"Brandon *Stone?*" she asked.

"That's his name. I wondered if he was some kin of yours, but I didn't think to ask," I said.

"I don't know of anybody with that name, but you never can tell. My father had more girlfriends than Carter's got liver pills. He might even be my brother for all I know," she said, and I was sure I detected an edge to her voice which wasn't usually there. Not that I could blame her, if that's how things had been.

"You don't have to go, if you don't want to," I said gently, and she sighed.

"Yeah, I know. But I might as well bite the bullet. Mama always told me not to be a mouse," she said.

"All right, then. We'll go see him tomorrow," I said.

So that's what we did, and I don't think Brandon expected to see me again so soon. But at least he didn't stick a shotgun in my face this time when we showed up.

He was still wearing those same dirty overalls he'd had on the last time. He was sitting on a cypress log next to one of those decrepit old wrecks, doing something up under the fender well with a wrench. I couldn't help thinking he was crazy if he thought he'd ever get any of those vehicles running again, but I kept my opinion to myself.

He set down his wrench on the log and watched me come closer, nodding when I got within earshot. I did notice that he smelled a little nicer than before, so maybe he'd had a bath since we last met.

"Cody," he said, a simple acknowledgement and no more. He didn't get up to shake hands or even wave at Lisa, still waiting in the truck.

"Brandon, I need your help again," I said.

"Yeah, I'm sure you do. You wouldn't be here if you didn't. Spill it," he said.

From then on out the ritual went pretty much like before. I told him my dream, he prayed, and then told me what it meant.

"This is what God is saying to you. The snake is the same person as the skeleton you dreamed about before. A deceitful enemy who will destroy you if possible. You'll meet on a white silver plain, empty and lifeless, where your enemy has already destroyed many others before you. Be faithful and true, and your enemy will flee from you for a while," he said.

"But-" I said.

"That's all I know," Brandon interrupted, waving his hand dismissively.

"Thanks," I said, not sure what else to say.

"Uh-huh," Brandon said, picking up his wrench and going back to whatever he was doing to that old truck. I left him some money on the end of his log, held down with a rusty brake rotor to keep it from blowing away. I don't even know how much it was; whatever was left over in my pocket.

"Not a very friendly kid, is he?" Lisa said while we bumped and splashed our way back out of Brandon's driveway.

"Oh, he was an angel compared to how things went the last time I was here. I thought he was fixing to blow my head off with a twelve-gauge," I said.

"Really?" she asked.

"Yeah, really. He's tough as nails," I said.

"What's a kid that young doing living out here in the middle of nowhere like this, though? Where are his parents?" she asked.

"He said they were gone. As to what he's doing here, I couldn't tell you. He seems happy, though," I said. Well, maybe *happy* was a bit much; Brandon never seemed exactly *happy,* but satisfied anyway.

"So what did he tell you?" she asked.

"He said the snake was a deceitful enemy that I'll meet on a white silver plain where many others have been destroyed before me, but if I'm faithful and true then he'll flee from me for a while," I said, shaking my head.

"Well, that shouldn't be too hard for you," she said.

"So you think. I just wish he could speak plainly, you know, instead of giving me all these puzzles and riddles," I said.

"I'm sure he gives you what you need to hear," she said, and I guess maybe she had a point about that. Sometimes the simplest answer is not the most useful one, even if it might seem that way at first.

We got to play at a high school chili supper in Linden that night, which was nice since we didn't have to go far. They only paid us fifty bucks, but at least we did get to eat as much free chili as we wanted. So we played them some country dance music since that's what the kids had asked for, and I even had time to dance a few songs with Lisa myself. Those are my favorite kinds of gigs, I think, even if we don't really make all that much. When the crowd cheers and claps and loves what you're doing, that's really an awesome feeling, you know. It reminds me of why I started playing music in the first place.

We finished up with *Lord Have Mercy on a Country Boy,* one of those old songs everybody and their hound dog knows the words to, so the kids could sing along and end the whole shebang on a high note, so to speak.

We left the parking lot in pretty high spirits not long after that, happy that things had gone so well. I wish every day could be that good.

But things don't work that way, of course, and if the dreams were to be believed then I knew we had to be drawing near to the end of our happy times, and therefore I should expect some kind of trouble with money pretty soon.

Oh, joy, I thought to myself, wondering how things could possibly get any worse in that respect than they already were.

No doubt I'd find out soon enough.

Chapter Fourteen
Lisa

It might seem like I already had enough on my mind not to need or want anything else right then.

But somehow I kept thinking about that boy out there in the swamp, and no matter what I did the thought kept nagging at me. I kept wondering who he was and how he got there and I had an almost irresistible urge to go see him and find out all those things.

I've learned that sometimes that's God's way of telling you to do something, so finally I broke down and went.

I wasn't sure if I'd be able to find the place at first. There's a big black oak tree with a red X carved into the bark, right next to the Three State Stone where Texas, Arkansas, and Louisiana all come together, and I remembered having to turn off the highway right past that. But then things got tricky, because there are a lot of snaky little gravel roads back in those woods, and not too many landmarks to help you remember the way.

It took me a while, and I made a few wrong turns along the way, but eventually I found the mouth of a certain muddy track winding its way back into a cypress bog. I hesitated, not sure whether Mama's car would make it in there and back without getting stuck. It was a lot lower to the ground that Cody's truck was.

I decided it was better to be safe than sorry, so I parked on the side of the road and walked it, just in case.

A cypress swamp is a surprisingly pretty place, believe it or not. Black water, still as a mirror under the big gray trunks and feathery leaves. It was awfully quiet, except for a bird or two, and the sound of my shoes squelching on the wet ground. It wasn't quite mud, but it wasn't far from it.

The only really bad thing was the mosquitoes. They came out of the trees in clouds, and I stayed pretty busy killing them. I'd probably be covered in bites head to toe by the time I got out of there.

It was only about a fifteen minute walk, even with the bugs and having to pick my way around several mud holes big enough to swallow a cow. But finally I glimpsed the old rusty yellow bus through the cypress trunks, and soon came out onto somewhat firmer ground again.

There didn't seem to be anybody around, but as soon as I got within sight the dogs started barking their heads off. I'm not really afraid of dogs, but I know better than to get too close. So I stopped right where I was and let them bark, waiting to see if anybody would come to see what was going on.

In a minute the door opened, and Brandon stuck his head out. He had his gun with him, I noticed, but when he saw me he set it down.

"Hush, Cut!" he yelled, throwing a stick at one of the dogs. She stopped barking and retreated under the bus, still growling at me now and then. Brandon paid her no mind. He came a step or two closer, then crossed his arms.

"What do you want?" he asked.

I took the chance to really look at him this time; he'd been too far away when I was sitting in the truck. He was tall for his age, and broad and heavy-set, but it was all bone and muscle, not fat. He had a snub nose and pale skin like me, and an almost invisible dusting of freckles across his cheekbones like Jenny has. He was even handsome, in a youngish kind of way. He reminded me very much of what my dad might have looked like at that age, even down to the red hair and blue eyes.

"What do you keep staring at?" he asked.

"I want to know what your father's name is," I told him, just as brusquely. If he wanted to be blunt then so could I. I must have surprised him, because he took a minute to answer me.

"Why?" he finally asked, and since there was no way to sugarcoat it, I didn't try.

"Because I think you're my brother, that's why," I said. It was a leap in the dark, and I wasn't totally sure I was right, but I had a strong enough suspicion to want to know the truth.

"No, I don't have any sisters," he said, shaking his head.

"Your dad was gone a lot when you were little, wasn't he?" I asked.

"Yeah, so?" he said.

"Did he like poetry a lot? Tall and red-headed?" I asked.

"Maybe," he said, still not willing to commit himself.

"Is his name Crush?" I asked, losing patience. I know I always used to think Daddy had the stupidest name on Earth, on a par with those poor unfortunate souls with names like Dusty Rhodes or Virginia Hamm, but now I was perversely glad for it. I was ninety-nine percent sure there couldn't possibly be more than one Crush Stone in the world. One was more than plenty.

"Yeah, so what if it is?" Brandon said.

"That's my dad, too," I told him.

"How do I know you're not lying?" he asked coolly, and that infuriated me.

"Oh, for pity's sake! Why would I lie?" I demanded.

"I don't know; you tell me," he said, not ruffled a bit.

"Look, either believe me or don't. I can't force you," I said.

"Why do you care, anyway?" he asked. He seemed to genuinely want to know, so I reluctantly sat down on one of the logs nearby and tried to think what to tell him. I knew well enough what he meant by asking. What he really meant was why should *he* care, and that was hard to answer.

"Because I want my brother to be part of my life, that's why. I want us to know each other. I want our kids to be able to play together someday. I want all those things families do," I finally said.

"Why?" he asked.

"Bran, you can keep asking why till the cows come home. All I want is to have my brother back. Is that really so hard to understand?" I asked.

"No, I guess not," he said softly.

"So tell me, how'd you end up *here?*" I asked him.

"That's a long story," he said, shrugging.

"I've got plenty of time," I said.

"Okay, then, fine. You won't like some of it, though," he said.

"Try me," I said.

"Well, everything was fine till last winter. Then Mama got drunk and hit a tree one night, and they said I couldn't live by myself. Nobody could find Daddy or Brian, and my aunt didn't want me. She said I was too much trouble. So they put me in a shelter for a while till they could find somewhere else to send me, but I hated that place. I kept getting in trouble and they finally said they'd have to lock me up if I didn't settle down. So I got tired of being pushed around and I left one day," he said. Then he hesitated, like he didn't want to go on.

"I'm sorry," I said.

"Yeah, well, things happen. I didn't know where to go at first. I knew I couldn't go home. So I figured I'd have to take care of myself," he said.

"So what did you do?" I asked.

"Whatever I had to. I took things. I went to parking lots and swiped the change out of cars that people left unlocked. I went to grocery stores and ate food and then left without paying for it. Got in a few fights, had to run from the cops a time or two, stuff like that. I headed south cause I figured it'd be warmer in the winter, so I walked and hitchhiked till I got this far, maybe three months ago. That's when I found this old place, and it seemed like a good place to set up camp for a while. Nobody's bothered me since then," he said.

"But how do you live?" I asked.

"I fish and hunt, and sometimes I pick up cans for money. It's hard, but I wouldn't change it. I figure I'll be grown in a few years and then nobody can tell me what to do. Just have to slug it out till then," he said.

"That's brave," I said.

"What else could I do?" he asked, shrugging.

"Nothing. I would have done exactly the same thing," I said, wondering if I would have. I guess you never really know what you'll do until you're tested, but that's one test I truly hope I never have to face.

"So, you still want a brother who's such a screw-up?" he asked.

"Yeah, I do," I said softly.

He got a little teary-eyed then, and I saw the misery and exhaustion in his face; he was still only a kid, after all, under a lot of pressure and stress. Exactly how much pressure and stress I was just now beginning to understand. I didn't try to hold him; guys don't always like that, and I didn't want to make him mad. He wiped his eyes and got himself back together again pretty quickly, and I pretended I hadn't noticed.

"Sorry," he said apologetically.

"It's okay. You know, Bran, I really don't think you should stay here. Especially not in the wintertime," I told him.

"I'll be fine," he said fiercely.

"I'm sure you would, but it'd be a lot harder than it has to be. I don't want you to have to go through that anymore," I said.

"What else would I do?" he asked.

"I bet Cody and Miss Josie would probably let you stay at Goliad, if I asked them. You could work a little bit, and you could even go back to school. You might not think you want to right now, but it'll make life a lot easier later on, I promise," I told him. I was pretty sure what Cody and Josie would say, knowing them as I did. And if they didn't, then I'd find some other solution. Either way, I had no intention of letting him spend the winter out there.

"No. I don't need any help," he said.

"Yes you do, Bran. There's no shame in that. It's not like we're strangers, anyway. You're my brother. That's what family is for," I urged. I could tell how much he hated the idea, but his face softened a little. Finally, reluctantly, he met my eyes.

"I'll think about it," he said at last. I could tell that was the best I'd wring out of him that day, so I let it be. He was stubborn as a boot, whatever else he might be.

"All right, then. Think about it. In the meantime I want you to keep this," I said, handing him my phone number on a piece of paper. I would have bought him a phone, but of course there was no way for him to keep the battery charged out there.

"What's that for?" he asked.

"If you decide you want to give it a try, call me and I'll come get you. Or if anything goes wrong, you know. I don't want you out here with no way to reach anybody," I said.

"Thanks," he said.

"I'll come check on you now and then, either way," I said. He nodded.

I gave him a hug and a kiss on the cheek before I left, wishing he didn't stink quite so much. I guess it's hard to stay clean when you don't have any running water, but it's still nasty.

I walked back to the car not even paying attention to the mosquitoes and the mud anymore. I hoped Bran would decide to let me help him, after he thought about it for a while. But even if he didn't, I promised myself I'd go check on him as often as I could and make sure he didn't need anything. I had an uneasy feeling that come winter he'd have a harder time than he thought. But I knew better than to try to force him. He'd just run away again if I did that, and then he'd never trust me again. There are times when you have to use the gentle treatment, like it or not. He was like a wild dog that you had to tame down slowly.

I debated with myself about whether to tell Jenny or not. I didn't know what she'd think, and I certainly didn't want her spilling the beans to Mama. It's not that it was Bran's fault what Daddy did, of course, but he looked so much like him I was afraid he'd be a constant reminder to her.

But on the other hand, did I really have the right to keep something like this a secret?

By the time I got back to the car I decided there was no reason to say anything immediately. I could always tell Jenny later, but there was no putting the cat back in the bag once I let it out.

I just hoped I was doing the right thing.

Epilogue
Cody

Brandon showed up about week later, walking up the dusty driveway in his bare feet and dirty overalls. I don't know how he got here from Ravanna; hitchhiked I guess, and walked the rest of the way. Lisa had already told me what she said to him, so I guessed why he was there even before he said anything.

"Lisa said you might need an extra ranch hand," he said gruffly when he got within earshot. I didn't smile or let on like it was anything unusual for a not-quite-fourteen-year-old kid to ask such a question. If that's the way we needed to play it for a while, then that was fine.

"Yeah, as a matter of fact we do. Are you interested?" I asked casually.

"I might be," he said.

"Well, you'd have to help with the animals and the crops, and do some carpentry and mechanical stuff now and then, and whatever else we need you to do. And go to school and church, of course. But it comes with room and board and fifty bucks a week," I said.

"That's not much," he said, and I almost did laugh then.

"Put in some overtime and you might get a little more," I said.

"I'll take it," he said.

"Good. Glad to have you," I said, and stuck out my hand. He shook it, and that was that.

I took him up to the main house and turned him over to my mother, who gave him the spare room and sent him immediately to take a shower and put on some clean clothes for a change. She already knew all about the situation too, of course.

"Be careful how you talk to him for a while. Supposedly I gave him a job with room and board and fifty dollars a week to help out around here, so make sure you go along with that. Don't baby him," I warned her in a low voice as soon as he was safely out of range.

"Pshaw. I'll make sure he makes himself useful, no worries about that. There's no shortage of things he can do around here to earn his keep. But he's only a kid, and kids need loving, and if he doesn't like that then he'll just have to get used to it," she said.

"I'm sure he will," I agreed, amused, and then hugged her.

Two years ago, Mama took me and Marcus on a trip out west, mostly to visit the Grand Canyon but also anything else nearby. We ended up going to Zion, Bryce Canyon, and Petrified Forest, and a few other places I don't remember the names of, all around southern Utah and northern Arizona.

But even though the Grand Canyon is amazing and Bryce is like nothing you've ever seen before, we all agreed that Zion is the most beautiful. To stand there staring up at the Great White Throne at sunrise is one of those images that will live in my mind forever. When you first see it, you really could almost imagine that God Himself might sit there at the end of days while heaven and earth fled away at the fire of His eyes and all mankind who ever lived stood silently at His feet while the Book of Life is read. Zion is full of places like that.

Those kinds of thoughts are what led me to buy the only souvenir I picked up during the whole trip. It was a solid glass ball about the size of an apple, with a sprig of preserved wildflowers inside and a caption that read *In Beauty be it finished.* Proverbs are notoriously slippery things, of course, but I'll tell you what that one means to me.

There's a thing called magnanimity, or greatness of heart, and to me it's the most beautiful thing that ever there was. It means courage, but it's more than that. It means to cast aside all thought of yourself for the sake of another, like Moses in Gilead or the martyrs who died with a smile on their face. In its own small way it's a reflection of the Lord Jesus at Calvary, and therefore of God, the Light so beautiful that no one who sees it can ever turn away.

That's how I've always thought of it, at least, and that's why I keep that glass ball on my shelf where I can see it whenever I go by. To remind me to love without ceasing. Whatever else I may do with my life, I hope I can live it as a light in the darkness, and that Goliad will always be a place of peace for the lost and a refuge for the hurting. In the beauty of love may life be finished; to the glory of God may all things come to completion. That's my dearest and deepest wish. I don't talk about it much, and God knows I don't always live up to it, but it's still the one thing that I want most of all.

That's why it was never in doubt that we'd give Brandon a place to live, and in my heart of hearts I loved Lisa all the more for asking me. I don't think she ever knew how irresistibly beautiful she seemed at that moment, and how it was all I could do not to sweep her up laughing into my arms and kiss her till she melted. In fact that's exactly what I *did* do after we finished talking that day, and never in my life has a kiss ever tasted so sweet.

I still don't know for sure what the future holds. There are times when I lie awake at night and wonder how long it'll be till the next catastrophe strikes. I haven't forgotten what Brandon said, and I don't doubt my dreams. I know there's a storm coming, sooner or later. Probably sooner, if I had to guess.

But for now, the one thing I do know is that I'll always have Lisa to stand by my side, and I'm certain that no matter what happens, we'll both be all right as long as we face it together.

And for now, that's all I need to know.

End of Part One

Part Two

These White Silver Plains

Chapter Fifteen
Cody

The trouble came not long after Brandon arrived, in the exact way he'd warned us it would. On the second day of August I got a letter from Piney State Bank, with the news that no rancher ever wants to hear.

Foreclosure.

Like a lot of farmers and ranchers, we usually took out a business loan every spring, to cover planting and operating costs for the coming year, and then paid it back at harvest time. It's nothing unusual, and most of the time it works out pretty well. But this year, with no harvest to speak of and a huge loss even from the cattle. . . it was bad.

I'd seen trouble coming ever since the rain dried up in March, and I'd been meeting with Howie Jackson off and on for months, trying to work something out to pay the debts we already owed and get us enough capital to try again next spring. For a while it seemed like he might go along with it.

But I guess he must have changed his mind, because the letter politely informed us there was nothing else he could do. The bank couldn't loan us any more cash, not till we paid back at least part of what we owed. And furthermore, if we didn't bring our account current within thirty days, then they'd have no choice but to seize the property and sell it.

That was the straw that broke the camel's back. I think I could have found a way to cope with the drought and all the other things nature had thrown at us, if only the bank had been willing to work with us a little bit longer. But they weren't, and that left us high and dry with nowhere to turn, pretty much. We had no money to plant next year, no money to rebuild the cattle herd, and soon enough not even a place to live. There was no way I could make enough playing music; there just weren't enough gigs out there, and they didn't pay enough.

The only thing I could do was to find another job that paid better money, but I knew it would have to be a really good one if I was to have any hope of collecting enough cash to save the farm, so to speak. I crunched the numbers a dozen times, in every variation that I could think of, and the results always came out the same. It was either find a high-paying job or lose the place. Numbers don't lie, and a job at the gas station or the hardware store wasn't going to cut it.

The thought that I might actually be the one who lost the homeplace after all these generations broke my heart and made me feel like a complete failure in life. Oh, I knew it wasn't my fault the weather was bad, honestly I did, but knowing something in your head and feeling it in your heart are two completely different things, I promise you.

I didn't say anything to Lisa yet, not wanting to worry her. But I knew what I had to do and I resolutely started looking around to see what kind of work I could find.

That's when I thought about Alaska.

My cousin Troy was up there working in the oil fields, and he told me they paid really high wages, much better than anything I could find in Texas. That sounded promising, but even better was the timetable. Normally they worked a schedule of two weeks on and two weeks off, but I soon figured out that if I got two jobs and arranged them in such a way that they didn't overlap, then I could work every day and make twice as much money. When I sat down and worked it all out, I figured I could pay off the bank and get everything back on firm footing in a little less than a year. It was almost a miracle.

The thought of working twelve hour shifts every single day for a whole year with never a break was exhausting even to think about, but then again you can handle a lot of things when you know you have to. And I had to, apparently. Troy told me he knew the lady who did the hiring and he could probably put in a good word for me, if I was interested. A week later he called back and said I had a job, if I wanted it. All I had to do was get myself to Anchorage, and the company would take care of everything else.

At first I was thrilled, and my first impulse was to think I could pay for Lisa to come visit me for a few days every month or so. It wasn't an ideal arrangement, but I guess I could have been content with it for a while. But when I found out there was no housing available for anyone but the workers themselves, and not even any motels except during the summer, then my joy started to cloud over.

In fact, I found myself in an impossible fix. Could I really go away for almost a solid year and never see Lisa at all? Even worse, could I truly expect her to wait for me all that time till I could get back? Long distance relationships are notorious for not working out. I think if she ever traded me in for another guy, it'd probably kill me. Go ahead and laugh if you want to, but I don't think I'm joking. She was my one and only, hoped for beyond all hope, and when I told her I loved her that night on Mount Nebo, I gave myself up and bound my heart forever.

I flirted with the thought of telling Troy I couldn't come, after all. But then again I knew what that would mean, too. And if I lost the ranch and found myself broke and soon enough homeless, then what did I have to offer Lisa except my heart and my hands, let alone all my other issues? She might say it was enough; love has a way of making people think that way sometimes. But was it really?

And that wasn't even counting what might happen to Mama and Brandon and Marcus. I had so many people depending on me for so many things.

I wrestled with myself for days, heartsick over having to make any such choice at all. I tried to ask myself what the kindest and most loving thing I could do might be. I reminded myself that sometimes we have to make sacrifices for the ones we love, and sometimes we have to break our own hearts so that theirs can be whole. I prayed, I agonized, I tied myself in endless knots over the subject. I even went up to Mount Nebo to sit beside Daddy's grave and try to imagine what *he* would have done.

I don't remember my father very well. One of my clearest memories of him is how he used to lay his hands on my head before bedtime and pray over me, that someday I would find both love and peace. But other than his love and the blessing he gave me, I couldn't remember him well enough to find much guidance there. I missed him more right then than I ever had since I was a kid, and I felt more alone than I ever had in my life, I think.

But time was running short, and as much as I dreaded it, I couldn't put off telling Lisa any longer.

I asked her to meet me at the Dairy Dip for lunch the next day, exactly like we'd done a thousand times before. That was nothing unusual, but she could read my moods too well by then. From the second I walked in, she knew something was up.

"What's wrong?" she asked immediately.

"It's nothing," I told her hastily. I wanted to enjoy one last meal with her, if possible. So I pretended everything was fine, even though I was pretty sure she wasn't fooled.

But the weight of what I had to do was killing me inside, and I couldn't even eat my food. Finally I spilled the beans, after she asked me about it for the third time.

"There's something we need to talk about, Lisa," I said, reluctantly.

"What do you mean?" she asked.

"Come on, let's go walk down to the park, okay?" I suggested. It was only two blocks away, and at least then we'd be somewhat alone. Things would be hard enough without a room full of witnesses.

She nodded, and after I paid for our uneaten food, we walked down the street to the park together. The park in Ore City isn't much more than a pasture with a pole barn, honestly, but that was all to the good at the moment; it meant we had the place all to ourselves. We sat under a pine tree by the pole barn, holding hands. I wasn't eager to get started, but she finally prodded me again.

"So what is it?" she asked, sounding worried.

"Well, the thing is. . . I think I might have to go away for a while," I said.

"What do you mean?" she asked again.

"Look, I know I haven't talked about it much, but the ranch is in trouble," I said, wishing I'd explained more of this all along instead of having to bring it all up now.

"Because of the drought, you mean?" she asked.

"Yeah, mostly. It's come to a point where there's nothing left to work with. We lost a lot of money on the cows and the crops this year. The bank won't work with us any more. I can't even pay them back what we owe them, much less borrow anything for next spring. So now I'm kind of between a rock and a hard place. I can either go find work somewhere else, or we can lose Goliad. There are no other choices," I said heavily.

"Where would you go?" she asked calmly, like we were discussing the weather. I was amazed she was taking things so well.

"My cousin Troy got me a job as a roughneck up in Alaska, at Prudhoe Bay. It's the only place I know of where I can make enough money to do us any good. They want me up there by Monday," I said.

"How long?" she asked.

"A year, if all goes well. Just till I can make enough to get us out of debt and get the ranch back on solid ground. It shouldn't take longer than that. Long as we get a little rain between now and then," I added. It was a pretty good bet we'd get some good soaking rain when winter came, but if not then I honestly didn't know what I might have to do. I might even end up stuck in Alaska for another year or two.

"So what happens with the ranch while you're gone?" she asked.

"Mama knows what has to be done, and she's got Marcus and Brandon to help her. She can handle everything down here, till I get back home," I said.

"Will you be back to visit, at all?" she asked. We were edging ever closer to the moment I dreaded, but there was nothing to be done about it.

"Maybe at Christmas for a little while if I can swing it, but I'm not sure yet. Other than that, no," I said.

I don't know what I expected her to say to all that, but it certainly wasn't what she said next.

Chapter Sixteen
Lisa

"Then I'll come with you," I said immediately, not caring at that moment about school, or how Jenny would manage with Mama, or anything else for that matter. But Cody was already shaking his head.

"They won't let you, Lisa. They only provide housing for workers, not family. I already asked," he said. For a second I was comforted that he'd thought to ask, but then the full impact of what he was saying hit me.

"But you *can't* go," I said, anguished.

"I have to. I'm supposed to leave Friday. I just. . . I wanted to let you know," he said, and I knew he was hurting, too. I could hear it in his voice.

Mama always used to tell me not to fall to pieces when something bad happens. She said it never helps and it'll just make things harder in the long run. However tempting it was, I knew I couldn't let it happen. I needed to pull things together and be strong, for me and Cody both.

"Well, I guess we can slug it out for a year if we have to. We can talk on the phone, and write letters maybe. It really stinks, but we'll be okay," I finally said, resigned.

"I'm not so sure about that," he said, and my heart froze inside my chest.

"What do you mean?" I asked.

"I mean if you found somebody else in the meantime while I'm gone, I wouldn't hold it against you," he clarified, scuffing his boot on the dirt in that way he always did when he was uncomfortable.

"No. Don't you *ever* think like that. I don't care if you have to be gone for a year. I wouldn't even care if it was *ten* years. Nobody could *ever* take your place," I said fiercely, desperate to make him see.

"You say that now. But what about six months down the road, when we haven't seen each other for all that time and you meet somebody else you like?" he asked. That stung, and I felt tears begin to well up in my eyes.

"I never would!" I declared hotly.

"It happens all the time, Lisa. You know that as well as I do," he pointed out, and the fact that I knew he was partly right only made it worse.

"Cody. . . don't you love me?" I asked. It had the expected result; he immediately put his arms around me and held me tight.

"More than anything," he said, kissing the top of my head.

"Then how could you even think such a thing?" I asked, muffled against his chest.

He was silent for a minute.

"I'm sorry. I didn't mean for it to sound cruel. I only meant-" he began, but I cut him off.

"Yeah, I know what you meant. You thought you were being all noble and gallant and self-sacrificing. But that's not how it works. We stick together, no matter what," I said.

"Really?" he finally asked, like he still didn't quite believe it.

"Yeah, really," I promised, wiping my eyes on his shirt but not letting go of him.

"I don't deserve you," he said softly, and I hugged him a little tighter.

"Well, you're stuck with me anyway, bubba. So you better get used to it," I said, through the last of my tears. He kissed me again, and I think he wasn't quite sure what to say. He finally sighed.

"What is it?" I asked.

"Nothing. Just thinking how much I'm gonna miss you, that's all," he said.

"Me too," I agreed.

"Maybe I'll get to come home at Christmas. I sure do hope so," he said.

"We'll be all right, somehow or other," I said with conviction.

He still seemed doubtful, but he didn't say anything else.

* * * * * * *

I cried when he left, of course, even though I told myself a dozen times I wouldn't.

I rode home from the airport with Miss Josie in silence, too miserable to talk much. I glanced at myself in the mirror when I got home and realized I looked awful from crying, but I didn't care. I washed my face and brushed my hair so maybe Jenny wouldn't notice the condition I was in, and then lay down on my bed to stare bleakly at the ceiling, hugging the biggest bear I could find. However much I might promise that even ten years apart wouldn't matter, it was still hard.

I thought about lots of things, the next few days. I thought about going after him to Alaska, in spite of the rules against it. I thought about ways to get money so he could come back home sooner. I thought about all kinds of crazy plans. I even thought about trying to get a job with the oil company myself. One by one I realized how impossible and hopeless they all were. Leaving Mama with no one to take care of her except Jenny would be unforgivable, and as for money, well, I'm no trust-fund girl, that's for sure.

I finally came to the conclusion that all I could do was hunker down and wait it out till he came back home next summer, no matter how hard that might be. I meant what I said when I told him he was my one and only, and I wasn't going to give him up no matter what it might cost me.

I knew he was right about how people tended to get wandering eyes after a while, when they were apart for so long. That was no lie. I was determined never even to look at another man, but I guess somewhere in the back of my mind I couldn't help wondering what if *Cody* was the one who found someone else? What if he met some hot little chick up there in Alaska and decided he didn't want me anymore, and I ended up waiting for him for nothing? It wasn't like he wouldn't have his pick of them, if he wanted to. I could see it happening in my mind's eye, clear and sharp as on a movie screen.

The mere thought of Cody being with some other girl brought up a red-hot surge of loss and grief, and fresh tears spilled out to soak my pillowcase. I told myself to get a grip and not to be ridiculous, but that was hard, too.

My year of desolation had started.

Chapter Seventeen
Cody

I didn't take much with me except some clothes and razors and such, stuffed in an old duffel bag left over from my high school rodeo days.

"Don't lose yourself while you're up there, son. Come back whole," was the last thing Mama said to me before I left, and at the time I nodded, even though I didn't really understand what she was talking about.

Lisa cried, and that upset me, too, but all I could do was hold her for a while and promise her it wouldn't be as long as it seemed. I hoped that was true.

But soon enough I was in the air, and even though the flight was a long one it really didn't seem like very much time at all before we landed in Anchorage, and then Prudhoe Bay. Troy met me at the airport and helped me get settled in or I would have been completely lost, but still, even with him there I felt cold and small and awfully far from home.

I got used to Alaska soon enough, though, or at least as much as anybody ever gets used to a place like that who wasn't born and raised there. It's always cold, always windy, and always lonesome, and I would have added always boring to the list, too. I had nothing to do except work, eat, and sleep, for the most part.

I was on the six am to six pm shift, day in and day out with not the slightest variation. No days off, no changes in the schedule, nothing. It was monotonous to say the least.

I had maybe an hour's worth of daylight left after work, and if I wasn't too tired I usually went jogging for a few miles down the Dalton Highway toward Fairbanks. It kept me in shape, and it was more productive than sitting in my room watching television. I knew I'd get my fill of that soon enough anyway, as the days got shorter and colder when winter moved in.

But in the meantime, I kind of enjoyed the solitude out on the tundra. It was already chilly even in late August, but running kept me fairly warm. Now and then I saw a reindeer or a fox, and once in a long while even a vehicle of some kind. But for the most part, I had the road all to myself. The sound of the wind blowing across all those hundreds of miles of emptiness is soothing, in a strange and lonesome kind of way. The land is flatter than western Kansas as far as the eye can see, with not a single tree or even a bush or a rock to break the monotony. Nothing grows except a little bit of brown mossy stuff on the ground, and it's always wet and soggy when it's not frozen.

It's better than town, though. Almost all the buildings in Prudhoe Bay are prefab trailers built on cinderblocks to keep them up off the ground so the heat won't melt the permafrost. There's exactly one store, with prices three or four times what I was used to paying for similar stuff in Texas, a post office, and the living quarters for the workers which now and then moonlighted as motels for the occasional tourist during the summertime. I had my own private room at a place called the Arctic Caribou Inn, which on the inside looked more or less like any other motel room, maybe a little small. But at least I didn't have to share it with anybody. I was one of the lucky ones when it came to my room assignment; a good number of the guys I worked with had to share space with a roommate.

Troy took me up to the coast not long after I got there, to see the Arctic Ocean and do the traditional Polar Bear Plunge, as they call it. I had to strip down to my underwear and go swimming in the ocean for at least ten minutes. I'm game to try most anything at least once, so I gave it a shot. Even though it was still summer, the water was so icy cold it stung like red hot needles and snatched my breath away. I could literally feel it sucking the life out of my body the whole time I was in there. I hurt in all the places where I wasn't numb, and when I came running back out onto the gravelly beach even the wintry air felt warm. I threw a towel around my shoulders as soon as I could grab one, shivering violently and feeling ten times more alive than I ever had before. I relished the feeling, and I could see how people might get to like it; sort of in the same way as the man who kept hitting himself over the head with a hammer because it felt so good when he stopped, I suppose.

Troy took a picture of me when I first came out of the water, freezing and blue and a newbie member of the Polar Bear Club, and I told him he better save it because that was the last time I was ever setting foot in that water ever again. He only laughed and said he knew exactly how I felt.

I usually called Lisa and Mama every night for a few minutes and sometimes Marcus or Cyrus and even Brandon, partly to check on things back home and partly for lack of anything else to do. It got lonely after a while with nobody to talk to, and I was more than a little homesick, if the truth be told. Troy had his own job to do, and since his schedule wasn't the same as mine that meant we didn't see each other near as much as you might think.

About two weeks after I got there, I ran into Layla Martin during my evening run.

Encountering a woman of any kind in Prudhoe Bay is unusual enough; I soon discovered that men outnumbered women by at least ten to one or more. But Layla wasn't just female, she was young and beautiful, too. That's a combination which is almost unheard of on the North Slope.

It was chillier than usual that evening, even for northern Alaska. There was a dusting of snow across the tundra, turning everything cold and white. But the girl was jogging in nothing but a set of gray sweats. She looked vaguely familiar for some reason, but I couldn't think where I might have seen her before. Prudhoe Bay is a small enough place that I might have caught a glimpse of her a dozen times and never paid attention, I suppose. I couldn't help gaping at her a little bit in spite of myself, and I guess she must have noticed. She stopped running when she came even with me, breathing hard and taking a drink from the water bottle she carried.

"A little cold for sweats, don't you think?" I asked, for lack of anything better to say.

"A little late in the day to be headed south, don't you think?" she asked right back, with a smile.

"Yeah, probably. I was just fixing to turn around in a minute, though," I shrugged.

"Yeah? Do you run much? I think you're the only person besides me that I ever saw out here. I'm Layla, by the way," she said.

"Cody," I said.

"Nice to meet you, Cody. You work here, or are you only a tourist?" she asked.

"Yeah, I'm a roughneck," I said.

"You must be new, then," she commented, and I couldn't help thinking that was an odd thing to say. Prudhoe Bay isn't the biggest town on earth, to be sure, but there are still thousands of people who work in those oil fields. There was no way she'd met all of them. But then again, maybe she only meant she hadn't seen me on the highway before; that would make more sense.

"I just got here two weeks ago," I agreed.

"Well, listen. Why don't you come have supper with me? I always like to meet all the new guys that come in, and I think it's steak night at the cafeteria," she said.

"Are you like a welcome committee or something?" I asked, but she only laughed.

"No, honey, I just like to talk, that's all. And I don't meet too many runners, so when I do I'm always hoping it's somebody worth talking to. It can be awful dull out here, you know," she said.

I thought to myself that truer words had never been spoken.

"Sure, why not?" I agreed.

So we did, and I have to admit the sirloin steak was at least as good as anything I've ever had in Texas. Whatever shortcomings it might have as a place to live, Prudhoe Bay definitely has the best food I've ever tasted, bar none. But I guess if you want to run an oil rig hundreds of miles above the Arctic Circle, then probably the least you can do is to make sure you feed your workers well.

Layla was really nice, and I think I smiled more often that evening than I'd done ever since I first got to Alaska.

"So listen. I've been looking for a running partner for a long time and I never could find one. Want to go jogging with me after work? It sure does make things a lot nicer if you've got a buddy, I promise," she asked.

I thought about it for a while, and decided it might do me good.

"Absolutely. That'd be great," I agreed.

"Cool. I'll meet you at six fifteen out there by the mileage sign on the highway. How about that?" she asked.

"Sounds good to me," I said.

So that's what we did, and I can't deny having a partner made my jog a lot more fun. Layla always had something interesting to talk about, and she was the kind of bubbly, happy person that makes you smile to hang out with. When the days got too cold and too short for running (which happened within weeks), we moved indoors to the gym and used the exercise equipment instead.

Things were fine for several weeks, but after a while I couldn't help noticing that Layla was gradually getting a lot friendlier than I liked. She was always touching my arm or patting my back or things like that. Once in a while at the gym she'd make comments about how handsome I was or how nice my muscles looked. It made me a little uneasy, but at the same time I didn't really take it all that seriously, either. Some people are just flirty like that, and nine times out of ten they don't really mean it. And even if she did mean it, there was zero chance it was going anywhere. So I smiled and nodded, not giving her any encouragement but tolerating it in the meantime till she caught the drift that I wasn't interested and gave up.

Everything came to a head one day when I went to the washateria to get some laundry done. I usually did laundry on weekday evenings, when the place was deserted. There's just something about looking at a complete stranger's dirty underwear which is kind of disturbing, you know? So I went when I wasn't likely to have company, and sometimes I took a pen and paper with me to jot down some musical notations to help pass the time while the clothes washed and dried.

I hadn't done much songwriting since I got to Alaska, but that particular day I happened to overhear one of the guys at work humming an old Buck Owens tune. That got me to thinking about home and red-dirt music again, and after work I went to the store to have them order me a cheap guitar. I hadn't wanted to bring Grandpa Tommy's Martin up there, but I didn't want to get out of practice, either.

So I sat there on the hard plastic seat, scribbling some chords and looking forward to when the guitar would arrive in a few days. I'd barely put my second load of clothes in and shut the lid on the washer when Layla walked in, carrying a laundry basket under her arm, with a bottle of liquid detergent balanced on top.

She was dressed for wash day; old t-shirt and sweat pants. Just about the most unglamorous outfit you could possibly imagine, but she was pretty enough to look nice no matter what she had on.

"Hey, Cody," she said, waving at me when she came in.

"Hey, Layla," I said absently, barely looking up from my notebook.

She got her clothes going, and then came to sit down a couple of chairs away from me. She smelled like soap and dryer sheets, but then so did everything else in the place. We chatted about this and that for a while, and eventually I happened to mention Lisa for some reason. Layla got a faraway look in her eyes, and when she spoke again her tone was different.

"Cody, I was thinking about something today," she finally said.

"Yeah? What's that?" I asked.

"Well, you said you wouldn't be going home till next August, right? That's a pretty long time, you know," she pointed out.

"Yeah, I know," I agreed neutrally, not sure I liked this.

"I guess what I'm saying is, you're a real nice man. There's a lot of girls who'd love to get to know you a little better, if you'd give them a chance," she said.

I'm not stupid. I knew what she was hinting at, and I decided it was time to lay down some firm rules about the way things had to be.

"Layla, I know what you're trying to say, here, and I'm flattered, but I'm not looking for anything like that right now. Let's be friends and leave it at that," I said.

"You mean you wouldn't even think about it? Not even just to grab a Coke and talk for a while?" she pressed.

"Nope, 'fraid not," I said, trying to be kind about it.

Then, before I knew it, she was kissing me. A deep, passionate kiss that tasted like warm vanilla. For a split second I was too startled even to think, and then I gently but firmly pushed her away. I was tempted to say something downright nasty at that point since kindness hadn't seemed to cut the mustard, but the harsh words died when I saw the ashen look on her face.

"What's wrong?" I asked instead. She looked like she might faint from terror at any second. I glanced over my shoulder to see if I had a vampire creeping up on me or something else that might explain her weird reaction, but there was nothing there.

And soon as my face was turned, she jumped up and ran from the washateria like it was an Egyptian snake pit.

Chapter Eighteen
Lisa

Two weeks after Cody left, I got a call from the school to come pick up Brandon for fighting. That was nothing new, unfortunately. The school year had barely started and he'd already been in trouble three times.

He was sitting there in the office with a tight-lipped scowl on his face when I went to pick him up, but I pretended not to notice.

"Here, Lisa, just sign him out and he can come back in a week. Five day suspension," the secretary said. I wordlessly signed the papers and left, wondering what it would take to knock some sense into the kid's hard head. I don't think I was ever that stubborn when I was fourteen; God knows I hope I wasn't. If I was, then I wouldn't have blamed Mama for killing me.

"What happened?" I asked, as soon as we left. I was casual about it, being careful not to raise my voice or seem upset. I'd already learned from past experience that that didn't help.

"Got in a fight," he muttered.

"Yeah, so I heard. Are you all right?" I asked.

"Yeah, I'm fine. Broke Brayden's nose, though," he said, and I was sure I detected more than a trace of pride in his voice.

"Hmm. That must have really hurt him," I said.

"Maybe. I hope so," he said.

"Why is that? How come y'all got into it anyway?" I asked.

"He was running his mouth, that's all. Talking trash about Lana," he said. I'd been too preoccupied with my own issues lately to pay much attention to Bran's crushes, and it's never been his nature to volunteer much unless you pry it out of him. But I knew Lana was a Russian exchange student who lived with one of the families at church. Just your typical flash-in-the-pan junior high relationship, no doubt; short, sweet, and intense while it lasted. But if he felt compelled to defend her honor then I guessed they must still be together, if you wanted to call it that.

"I see. And do you think breaking his nose will make him change his mind?" I asked gently.

"I don't care if he changes his mind. He can think whatever he wants to. But I bet you he'll learn not to say stuff like that," he said with conviction. I gave up; there are times when you can't reason with somebody, and this was obviously one of those times.

We rode home in silence, and I guess he must have been thinking about what I said. At least *that* was a definite improvement.

"You're not mad at me?" he asked after a while.

"No, Bran, I'm not mad at you," I said.

"How come?" he asked. Most people wouldn't have asked such a question, but my brother is nothing if not blunt. I wanted to tell him it was because I knew it wouldn't do any good, but that would have been unkind, I guess. So I chose my words carefully.

"Because I know you meant well, by defending her. I just think you could have picked a better way to handle it, that's all," I said.

"Like how?" he asked.

"Well, you know how in chat rooms and stuff there are always people who like to start trouble by saying nasty things?" I asked.

"Yeah, trolls. What about them?" he asked.

"What do you do with people like that?" I asked.

"You block them," he replied promptly, and I mentally sighed. Of course.

"And if you can't do that?" I asked.

"Then you don't pay them any attention and sooner or later they'll go bother somebody else," he said.

"Right. Never feed the trolls. It sounds to me like Brayden is a troll in the real world, and he runs his mouth just like the others do. So handle him exactly the same way," I said.

"You think I should just ignore him?" he asked.

"I think you might be better off. You can't pay attention to what stupid people say or you'll never have time for anything else," I said.

"Maybe," he said, sounding unconvinced.

I left it at that. He could think about it for a while and maybe he'd decide to give it a try or maybe he wouldn't, but that was the best I could do.

Still, there would have to be some consequences put in place, too. I'd have to talk to Miss Josie about that since she'd be the one who mostly had to enforce them, but extra chores would probably be part of it at the very least. I'd probably have to spend most of the week at Goliad to make sure he did them and didn't go anywhere, even though he'd probably drive me crazy talking about how bored he was.

I really don't know what to do with him sometimes, and over the past few weeks I've come to see very clearly why his aunt didn't want to deal with him. I don't agree with her, mind you, but I do understand. He's a handful if ever there was one. I sent him outside to mow the grass when we got to Goliad; that was something to keep him occupied.

Nobody else was there, and I prepared myself to hang around until Miss Josie got back from wherever she'd gone.

Cody rarely calls except during the evenings, but now and then he'll surprise me at lunchtime. Well, lunchtime for him, anyway; it's three hours earlier in Alaska than it is in Texas. But I was happy to hear his ringtone just then.

"Hey, Lisa, what's up?" he asked.

"Nothin' much, just now had to pick up Brandon from school again," I said, letting a little bit of my frustration show.

"Fighting again?" he asked.

"Yeah, he broke another kid's nose for talking trash about this girl he likes," I said, and Cody laughed a little. He really seems to love Brandon and calls him his little scrapper, which doesn't help things at all, I'm quite sure. I guess I should be thankful those two get along so well, but sometimes they both aggravate me to no end.

"It's not funny. He got suspended for five days," I scolded him.

"Yeah, I know it's not funny. I'll talk to him later, okay?" he said.

"You can try. Maybe he'll listen to you. Where are you, anyway?" I asked.

"Fixing to eat some steak, my love," he said, and as usual that melted me. He knew that, and probably did it on purpose for that very reason, but even though I knew all that the words never failed to make me smile.

"Okay, babe, I guess I'll let you eat, then. I'm glad you called, though," I said, and that was that.

I still didn't hear the mower running, so I went outside to check on what Brandon was up to. He was nowhere to be seen, which irritated me. The mower might have been over at the bunk house or something like that, but it still shouldn't have taken him so long to go get it. I was determined to say something to him about it as soon as he showed up again. He was already on thin ice. But when he still didn't show up for fifteen minutes or so, I decided to go looking for him.

There's a flowing well on the back side of Mount Nebo, where Cadron Creek comes up from underground and flows down to fill the lake. It's always clear and cool, and I suspect that stable source of water is one of the reasons why Reuben McGrath picked this place to homestead. At some point in time, one of the family members had built a rock wall around it to form a pool about thirty feet across. The water spilled out over a low spot in the ledge to flow away down the creek bed like it always had, but on most days the pool itself was smooth as glass and reflected the sky like a mirror. There were a couple of benches in the clearing, and for some reason or other Brandon had loved that place ever since the first time he laid eyes on it. That's where I decided to look for him first.

Sure enough, that's where he was, staring at the water like he might find some wonderful secret there.

"What are you doing, Bran?" I asked, not even trying to hide my annoyance.

"God loves reflections," he said absently, still so intent on the water that I doubt you could have torn his eyes loose with a pry bar. I didn't see anything but clouds and sky.

"What do you mean by that?" I asked, nonplussed. Brandon has his moments like that, when he says things that utterly confuse me and I'm not sure whether he's saying something deep and profound or whether he's lost his mind. Interpreting dreams is one thing; I could accept that as at least semi-normal, if only because I had to. But there are other times when he gets that faraway look in his eyes, like he's seeing something nobody else could ever see, and then he's liable to spout out some weird stuff about how God loves reflections, or something equally bizarre.

"He loves reflections. Hints and images. Things that remind us of something bigger than themselves," he said.

I pondered that for a minute, and finally decided it was probably true. God is indeed fond of things that remind us of something greater than themselves. I've seen it in the way that we love people who remind us of Him, in the way that the moon reflects the sun and the lakes reflect the sky. It's a theme written across the whole face of the world, in letters so large that sometimes we miss them completely.

Which might make an excellent starting point for a sermon, I guess, but I still couldn't fathom why Brandon had said it.

"So what's your point?" I finally asked.

"Nothing," he said.

"All that, to say nothing?" I asked skeptically.

"Well, maybe not nothing. This pool reminds me of something, but I can't remember what it is or why it matters. So I was just thinking out loud, I guess," he said, shrugging.

"I see. Well, you still owe me some mowed grass, kid," I reminded him.

"Yeah, I know. I'll be up there in a minute," he said, and with that I had to be content.

Chapter Nineteen
Cody

"Hey, Layla! Wait!" I called, running after her.

I barely caught sight of her turning the corner at the end of the hall, and then I was just in time to see the front doors slamming behind her. I ran outside without even stopping to grab a jacket, but by the time I got there she was nowhere to be seen.

I cussed under my breath. It was useless to go searching for her amongst the buildings in the dark. She could be anywhere, and I was already shivering. I kicked the frozen ground in frustration and retreated to the warmth of the building. There hadn't been anyone around to see what happened, so I was able to get back to the washateria without having to explain things to anybody, at least.

Which was good, since I couldn't think of any remotely sensible explanation for it.

Layla's purse and clothes were still sitting on the seat where she'd left them, and at first I thought she'd come back for them in a few minutes.

But time dragged by, and she never showed. By the time my clothes were dried and folded she still hadn't returned, even though at that point it had been over an hour since she left.

I drummed my fingers against the cold steel of the washer, trying to think what to do. I couldn't very well leave the purse unattended, and I didn't feel like staying there to guard it all night either. I finally decided to take it with me; she knew where my room was, and she could go there just as easily as she could go to the lost and found. Maybe that way I'd have a chance to get some answers.

I actually started to worry about her a little bit when she still hadn't showed up by the time I got off work the next day. Yeah, I might have been irritated with her for kissing me, but that didn't mean I wanted her to get chomped by a grizzly bear or freeze to death out on the tundra. I went to her room and got no answer when I knocked on the door, and when I asked around a little bit it turned out nobody could remember seeing her since the day before.

Nobody, that is, until I thought to ask the ticket office at the airport. The man didn't know Layla by name, but like I said there are precious few pretty young women in Prudhoe Bay. A girl matching Layla's description had left that very morning on the first flight to Fairbanks. I didn't doubt it was her, but that only left me even more confused than ever. I started to wonder if she'd lost her mind.

I know it wasn't proper, but I decided that under the circumstances I didn't have much choice but to go through her things and try to find some kind of clue as to what was going on.

With that thought in mind, I went home and quietly dumped her purse out onto my bed, rummaging through it to see if there was anything worth paying attention to. There didn't really seem to be, other than the usual things. Credit cards, lipstick, an expired New Mexico driver's license for Layla Martin, things like that.

Then I noticed an anomaly. The picture on the driver's license was most definitely Layla, but the birth date seemed to be saying she was thirty-two years old. I moved the plastic into the light from the lamp, sure I must have misread the year. But no, there it was, plain as day.

There was absolutely no way the girl I knew was thirty-two years old. Not unless she'd had some incredible plastic surgery in the meantime. She didn't even look twenty. I frowned again and set the license aside, digging deeper into the junk from the bag. But there was nothing else I could find that seemed to shed any light on the mystery.

I stuffed everything back into the purse, keeping only the driver's license. I didn't know what I might need it for, but it was the only proof I had that something weird was going on, even if I didn't have a clue what it was, yet.

That was before I talked to Troy. It was the first chance we'd had to socialize in weeks, and I was glad to see him.

"So what's up, lil cuz?" he asked, sitting next to me at the cafeteria table.

"Not much, really. Somethin' kinda weird happened last week," I said.

"Oh, yeah? What's that?" he asked, shoveling down his steak and mashed potatoes.

"Well, there's this girl named Layla Martin that I met not long after I got here, and she used to run with me down there on the highway after work, you know. But-" I said, and that was as far as I got.

"Bubba, I'm not gettin' in your business or nothin', but you're not, like, *with* that girl, are you?" Troy interrupted, looking anxious.

"No, but why do you ask?" I asked, curious.

"Oh, nothin', nothin'. Never mind I said anything," he said.

"Yeah, well, you *did* say something, so now you better tell me," I demanded.

"It's nothin', Cody. Really. I just heard some stuff about that girl, that's all. She's bad news," he admitted reluctantly.

"What are you talking about?" I asked.

"All I know is, she's had a lot of boyfriends, and some way or other they all end up goin' home sick after a while. It's only rumors, you know," he said hastily.

"She really seemed like she had a thing for me," I admitted, hoping that little tidbit might pry some more information out of him.

"Don't, bubba," Troy said, looking dead serious.

"Don't what?" I asked.

"Don't even *think* about goin' out with that girl. Please promise me you won't," he said.

"You're kinda creeping me out, dude," I said.

"Cody, I used to know one of the boys she went out with. He was younger than you, and healthy as a horse. When he left he looked *bad,* like an old man. I'm tellin' you, that girl is bad news," he repeated earnestly.

"Well, see, that's the weird thing. I didn't want to go out with her, but I liked her all right as a friend, you know. So I was sitting there in the washateria last week, just talking to her, and she comes right out and kisses me, totally out of the blue. So I push her away, not mean or anything, and she looks at me like she's seen a ghost and runs out of the building so fast I couldn't even catch her to ask what was wrong. Didn't even take her purse with her, and when I asked around a little bit I found out she left town on the first plane she could catch. I don't know what to think," I admitted.

"I think you should thank God she's gone, that's what I think," Troy said solemnly.

"I just wish I knew what was going on, that's all. What's the name of that boy you said you knew, the one that used to go out with Layla who ended up sick? Maybe he might know something," I said, thinking out loud.

"Um. . . Fitch, I think. James Fitch. He was from Memphis, or somewhere close to there. I don't know his number or anything but you might could find him if you dig a little. Give him a call, see what he says," Troy shrugged.

"Yeah, maybe I'll do that," I agreed, and that was that.

It took a little bit of work to find James Fitch's number, mainly because it turned out he was from Memphis, Nebraska, instead of Memphis, Tennessee. But there was no doubt I'd found the right person. I confirmed it with the personnel department at the oil company, and now all that was left was to call him.

I sat beside the phone uneasily, with the number written down on a slip of notebook paper on the table. Then I slowly punched in the buttons, not sure what to say even if I got hold of the man.

"Hello?" the voice on the other end said. He had a strong Midwestern accent, and he sounded awfully old to be the age Troy said he was.

"Hi. Is this James Fitch?" I asked.

"Yes, who's this?" the man said.

"Uh, my name's Cody. I'm Troy Carter's cousin; he said he knew you when you used to work in Prudhoe Bay," I explained.

"Yeah, I remember Troy. What do you need?" James asked. He didn't seem very friendly, but I plunged ahead.

"I need to ask you a few questions about a girl named Layla Martin," I said.

"I suggest you stay as far away from that woman as you can, if you value your life," James Fitch said immediately.

"Why?" I asked.

"Look. I don't know what she did to me, or how she did it. All I can say is that I was nineteen years old when I went to Alaska, and since I got back home the doctors tell me I've got the body of a sixty year old man. My hair's turned gray, and I have to wear glasses when I read. I look like my grandfather, and I feel like him, too. I know it was her that did this. I *know* it was. But nobody believes me," he said.

"I believe you," I said, and for some reason I really did.

"Do you? Then do yourself a favor and stay away from her," James said bitterly, and hung up. I tried to call back twice, but no matter how many times I let the phone ring, it was never answered again.

The conversation disturbed me, to say the least. I meant it when I said I believed James Fitch's story. I of all people had good reason not to doubt such things, and Troy wasn't the type to get scared over nothing. Quite the opposite, in fact. Evil is very real, and there are times when it can be deceptively beautiful on the surface, like a gorgeous carnivorous flower that will eat you alive if you get too close.

It didn't take too much thought to come to the conclusion that Layla had probably had the same fate in mind for me that she'd already dealt out to all those other young men. It was obviously some kind of sorcery, and in that case it puzzled me why it hadn't worked. By all rights, I should have been on a one-way flight to the nearest nursing home by then, but for some unknown reason it hadn't happened. Maybe that's what freaked her out, if she tried to use her magic on me and it didn't work.

I couldn't figure out what was so special about *me*, though. Why did I get an exception to the rules, when nobody else did? I was in favor of it, but I sure would have liked to know the reason why.

The thing that really scared me was that I'd never suspected a thing, and I *should* have. It had all been right there in my dream, plain as day in hindsight. I met her on a white silver plain (that is, the snow-covered tundra), she was beautiful and deceptive, she'd destroyed many others before me, and she'd asked me to do something I knew was wrong (that is, go out with her behind Lisa's back). I hadn't done it, and then she'd run away from me. It all fit the dream, right down to the last jot and tittle, and I'd been too thick-headed even to recognize the signs because a pretty girl wasn't what I expected.

But as soon as I figured all *that* out, I remembered that Lisa was also supposed to have an encounter with this same evil person, and hers might not turn out so well as mine did.

It was already evening by then, so I called her immediately to let her know who to watch out for. Her cell phone wouldn't ring, but I finally got Jenny to answer the house phone.

"Where's Lisa?" I asked instantly.

"Oh, she went to see a movie. She probably won't be back till late," Jenny said.

"She did?" I asked, frowning. It seemed like an odd thing for her to do, if only because she would have known it would cause us to miss our nightly phone call. But it would've sounded vain to say *that*, of course.

"Well. . . .listen. Would you tell her to call me whenever she gets home? I don't care if it's late or if she wakes me up. It's kind of important," I said. I was reluctant to say much more than that to Jenny.

"Sure thing, sugar," Jenny said.

The only good thing about the whole situation was that Layla had completely disappeared from Prudhoe Bay. If nothing else, then at least she wouldn't be stalking my friends and co-workers anymore. I didn't doubt she'd probably turn up soon enough in some other obscure place and start working her evil there instead; people like that almost always do. But I was blessed if I could think of a single thing to do about that. The world is a very big haystack, to find a single person in. Layla Martin might not even be her real name for all I knew, and unless she was an idiot then the address on the driver's license was almost certainly bogus, too.

I thought seriously about quitting my job to go home and defend Lisa. But then again, I knew what the consequences would be if I did that, not just for me but for her and everybody else, too.

There was Matthieu Doucet, of course; he'd warned me about this very type of situation and specifically offered to help. But he was several hours away from where the action would be if Layla showed up, so that didn't seem like such an ideal solution, either. Besides the fact that I didn't know him from Adam and he'd told me with his own mouth to be careful about strangers.

I finally decided this was a time when all I could do was depend on Marcus to fill in for me and make sure everybody was protected. He was close, and I knew I could trust him. I didn't like having to lean on him so hard, but under the circumstances I didn't have much choice. Sometimes every option you've got is a bad one and all you can do is pick the one which is least awful.

Chapter Twenty
Lisa

I spent a lot of time at Goliad during those first few weeks after Cody left. Hard as it was to be apart from him for so long, it made me feel a little bit better to be near the people and the places that he loved. I took to stopping by after work when I could, and sometimes went to the cowboy church with them on Sundays. Marcus and Cyrus still played the music service even without Cody, and I'd usually sit with Miss Josie on our regular hay-bale on the third row. Sometimes Brandon was with us and sometimes he sat with Lana and her host-family. She was short and slight, with longish brown hair and not much of an accent, but I can't say that we ever talked all that much.

Some folks like their hymns, so Marcus and Cyrus always played a few of those every Sunday, and it so happened that one morning they got a request for *Unclouded Day.* Nothing particularly unusual about that. But after a while, I noticed that Bran was crying, and that shocked me. I would have had an easier time believing the government is run by lizard people than that Brandon Stone could cry in public. Let alone over a song.

"What's wrong?" I asked in a low voice, not wanting to embarrass him.

"Nothing," he said, wiping his eyes and trying to hide his face. He didn't do a very good job of it, of course, and I decided this wasn't the right place to talk about it, whatever it was.

We were close to the back door that led out to the corral, and I grasped his hand.

"Come outside with me," I said. He didn't seem enthusiastic, but he didn't argue. We both got up and slipped outdoors without too many people noticing that anything was wrong, and once we were out there I sat down with him on the tailgate of Marcus's truck.

"Now what's wrong? Don't tell me nothing, either. You don't cry over nothing. So tell me," I said.

"Nothing," he insisted, wiping his eyes again. I wanted to either cry myself or choke him.

"Bran, I can't help you if you won't talk to me," I pleaded.

"I told you it's nothing," he repeated.

"So why'd it make you cry, then?" I asked. He was calmed down again now, stoic and iron-faced as always. He looked at me, weighing his words.

"You wouldn't understand," he finally said, looking away. And that, apparently, was all I was going to get out of him.

"Well, I love you, kid. Don't you ever forget that," I told him. He nodded, but I couldn't tell what he was thinking.

Miss Josie came outside right about then, looking uncertain.

"Is everything okay?" she asked when she got close enough.

"Yeah, it's all right. He's fine now," I said. Times like that make me wonder just how true that is, and how deep Bran's cuts really go. I worry about him sometimes, especially when he does strange things like that and won't explain. But there's no way to force it out of him, if he won't talk. All I could do was love him and pray for him and keep my fingers crossed that he'd somehow come out of it one of these days.

But things like that were an oddity, and most times we had fun when I was there. Sometimes on Sunday afternoons I helped Miss Josie cut and weed all those beautiful roses, and I soon found out Cody was right about how much she loved to talk about her flowers. She knew more history and folklore about roses than I'd ever dreamed existed in the world. But it was fun to listen to her because she was so enthusiastic about it.

I found myself talking to Marcus a lot more than I used to, also. He reminded me of Cody in a lot of ways; they were the same age, and he wore the same kinds of clothes and had the same deep voice and rough hands. Other than that I don't guess they really look much of anything alike; Marcus has longer hair and paler blue eyes, and he's a good bit taller and stockier, too. Not a bad looking boy, but still, not nearly as handsome as Cody.

We reminisced about the good old days of running all over East Texas to sing at hokey little street fairs and supper clubs till three am, and laughed about some of the things we'd seen along the way. People are funny, sometimes even when they don't mean to be. All that was a thing of the past, at least till Cody got back. Cyrus had talked about maybe finding another guitarist to fill in for a few months, but so far it was nothing but talk.

"So what's the deal with you and Cody, anyway?" Marcus asked me one day. He was brushing the horses and cleaning the tack out in the barn, and I was sitting on an upended water bucket to keep him company. It was mid October by then, and it was the first time he'd ever come right out and asked me about me relationship status.

I immediately remembered all that loose talk over the summer about how he'd like to pick up the pieces if I ever broke up with Cody, and wondered if Jenny was right after all about how you can never really be just friends with a guy.

So I hesitated, choosing my words carefully.

"We're doing pretty good. I miss him a lot, but I figure we'll take it one day at a time," I finally said.

"But you don't want anybody else, right?" he guessed, looking at me keenly. That made me even more uneasy, to tell the truth. I didn't want to get into a clash with Marcus, especially not over something like *that*.

"No. He's my one and only," I said firmly. But Marcus seemed not to notice. He just kept brushing Buck's mane, and it was several minutes before he said anything else.

"You know Cody's got some issues, right?" he finally asked, clearing his throat.

"What do you mean?" I asked.

"Well. . . he thinks he's got a one-way ticket to the boneyard, you know," Marcus said. It sounded unkind, but I couldn't decide if he was being snarky or if he simply had a strange way of putting things.

"Yeah, he told me about the Curse and everything, if that's what you mean," I agreed, deciding to give him the benefit of the doubt for the time being.

"Did you believe him?" he asked offhandedly. That was a hard question to answer, honestly. I still hadn't quite decided what I thought about the Curse yet, and Cody hadn't said a word about it since that night when he first told me. It had been easy to sweep it under the rug and not think about it much, what with everything else we'd been through since then. I frowned, but Marcus seemed to be absolutely serious about the question.

"Do *you* believe him?" I asked instead, playing it safe.

"Yeah, I really do," he said.

"I still don't know what I think about that," I admitted.

"I didn't believe it at first, but then I got to thinking, you know. He's been right about everything else he ever said. There might be some truth to that, too," Marcus said.

"Maybe. He never said much about it, except that nobody in his family ever makes it past thirty. I don't think he likes to talk about it much, so I haven't pushed him. Life's been too crazy lately to worry about something like that, anyway," I said.

"Well, you know about his Grandpa Reuben, right?" he asked.

"Yeah, a little bit. He named this place and fought at Goliad and all that," I agreed.

"Okay, so you know he was a soldier most of his life, right? He fought down there at Goliad and then later on at Mesilla and Glorieta Pass out in New Mexico during the Civil War," he said.

"Yeah, I know all that. Fought under Baylor, captured a platoon of drunk and dehydrated Yanks who tried to cross the White Sands Desert after filling up their canteens with whiskey instead of water. Cody goes on about that stuff all the time. But what's your point?" I asked.

"Well, they *say* Reuben picked up that curse from a witch in Mesilla. He killed her son in battle, so she cursed him and said none of his sons would ever live longer than hers did. And ever since then, none of them ever have," he said, sounding very spooky and mysterious.

"Oh, come on, Marcus. Really?" I scoffed. It sounded like a lurid campfire story that kids told to scare each other before they scampered back to hide in their tents.

"That's what I heard. Honest," he said.

"Heard from who? Cody never said anything like that," I said.

"No, it wasn't from Cody. My grandmother told me," he said.

"And how did *she* know anything about it?" I asked.

"It's a small town, Lisa. People notice things, even if they don't talk much. There's always been a rumor amongst the old folks about a curse on the McGraths. It's nothing new. They'd never say anything to Cody or Miss Josie, of course, not in a million years. But Granny told *me* about it when she found out I was working here, because she was worried about me. She made me promise never to tell anybody, though," he said.

"You're telling me," I pointed out.

"Anybody at Goliad is what she meant, so I never said anything to Cody about it. I didn't see any point in passing along gossip, anyway. Especially when it's nothing but a little snippet like that which might not even be true. It may only be a wild rumor, for all I know," he said.

"Okay, fine. But you still haven't said what the point is," I reminded him.

"Well, I got to thinking. If Cody's really got this death curse on him, then don't you think we should try to find a way to break it? He's my best friend and I owe him a lot. I'd save him if there was any way I could," he said, and that softened my heart. He loved Cody too, in his own brotherly kind of way, and I could relate to that.

"What did you have in mind?" I asked.

"I thought I might go out there to Mesilla and see what I could dig up. It's a little town, too. Surely if there was ever a real live witch in a place like that, somebody'd remember something, wouldn't they? Or if not that, then maybe there'd be some records of her somewhere, at least. Seems like it'd be worth a try," he said, shrugging.

"I'm not sure Cody would like that idea much," I said, surprising myself. I was actually toying with the thought of running off on a wild goose chase to some dusty little Podunk town in the middle of nowhere, all so I could find out about a witch who might not exist and a Curse I still wasn't even entirely sure I believed in.

"Nope, I can tell you right now, he wouldn't like it at all. He'd think I was either wasting my time and money or maybe even putting myself in danger for his sake, and that wouldn't set well. That's why I'm talking about doing it now, while he's not here," he countered.

"So I'm guessing there's something you want me to do, right?" I asked.

"Well... yeah. You never know what you might run into when you're out there on your own like that. It's best to be careful. So I thought I might text you, maybe once an hour, and if I don't then you'll know something's wrong and you'll know exactly where to find me," he said.

"What if you get a dead battery on your phone or something?" I asked.

"I won't let that happen. I'll call you from a pay phone, if I have to. I *won't* lose touch, no matter what," he said.

I considered all the various things that might go wrong, and finally admitted that it might be a halfway decent plan. If he dropped out of contact then I'd immediately know it was time to call for help. It remained to be seen whether he'd find anything useful or not, of course, but I figured it was worth a shot.

So Marcus went, and we both agreed that it was a secret to be kept strictly between the two of us. No one could know; not Miss Josie, or Cyrus, or anybody else. And most especially and emphatically not Cody.

That was the hardest part, I think. I usually wrote Cody a letter every night, sometimes pouring my heart out for ten or twelve pages when I missed him especially much. Now and then I rose to such lyric heights that it was almost a kind of poetry, and I never considered the fact that all this might be too much for the poor boy. Thankfully it only seemed to leave him faintly bemused, and maybe a little amused. I could read between the lines of his (much shorter) letters well enough to tell what kind of look he must have had on his face while he wrote them. Once in a while he joked about the post office having to deliver his mail with a forklift, but I knew he was only playing with me.

In his first letter he sent me a picture of him standing on a gravelly beach in nothing but his boxer shorts, soaking wet from the ocean. Somehow it never crossed my mind that they might have beaches in Alaska; it's just not the kind of place you normally think of when swimming comes to mind, you know.

He sent me another picture of him sitting at a metal table holding his lifetime membership certificate to the Polar Bear Club, but at least he was smiling in that one even though he looked tired. He never wrote much, but then he'd always been a man of few words.

We talked on the phone for about an hour or so before bed most every night, and I would have talked longer if I could have. But he was usually tired and his phone service wasn't always that great, especially when the weather was bad. I've always heard that letter writing is a dying art, but there are still times even nowadays when it has its special appeal. When I couldn't reach him any other way, then the most ancient method of all was sometimes the best.

But all this back-and-forth did make it awfully hard to keep secrets. Several times I had to bite my tongue to keep from letting something slip, but somehow I managed to keep a lid on it all.

Things were sweet as soda pop, for a little while.

The first hint of trouble came when Marcus stopped answering my texts.

The hourly text plan worked fine for several days. He made it to Las Cruces with no problems, and found a cheap motel right outside of Old Mesilla. He told me there didn't seem to be anything sinister about the place, so he'd been busily digging up tons of interesting folklore ever since; most of it completely irrelevant.

But then he'd found a book of oral histories at the library and come across something really useful for a change. According to the article he read, a lady named Selena Garza had supposedly been an infamous witch in the area during the middle of the nineteenth century. The most interesting tidbit of information about her seemed to be that she'd been present at the Battle of Mesilla in 1861, which was definitely an oddity for a woman in those days. The book didn't say anything about curses, but it did mention that the information had been provided by a certain Miss Layla Latimer, a lady who lived in White Sands, right outside Las Cruces.

Marcus had decided it was worth going to visit Miss Latimer himself, to see if she might know anything else besides what was in the book. He texted me again right before he headed over to the woman's house, and that was the last I ever heard from him.

At first it didn't worry me too much. In spite of what we said, I didn't want to fly off the handle just because he was thirty minutes late texting me. But after several hours of no word, I started to worry. A *lot*. There was no reason I could think of why Marcus wouldn't have been able to get in touch with me within *that* amount of time, unless he was in serious trouble.

I fought down a rising sense of dread and tried to grasp at straws. I hadn't really expected much from Marcus's expedition except that he'd find out a lot of useless trivia and then come home empty handed after a few days. Now he was missing, and he was depending on *me* to do something about it.

I still didn't dare tell Cody. I knew him too well; he'd feel like he had to come running home from Alaska to look for Marcus, and I knew exactly what that would mean. He'd lose his job, and then soon enough he'd lose Goliad. Cody was the last person on earth who needed to know.

But who else could I ask for help? I didn't feel like I knew Cyrus well enough to confide in him, and I wasn't even sure if he knew about the Curse in the first place. The only other person I could think of was Miss Josie, and that was hardly any better.

What I needed was a schemer, and as soon as that thought crossed my mind, I knew the perfect person to help me, if she would.

Chapter Twenty-One
Lisa

"Jenny, I need your help," I said, sitting down on my sister's bed.

"Oh, really? For what?" she asked, looking skeptical.

"I need you to cover for me a few days, while I go look for Marcus," I said.

"What's wrong with Marcus? And why do you care who knows what you're doing?" she asked. I didn't want to tell her anything, but I knew she'd have to have *some* kind of explanation or she wouldn't lift a finger to help me.

"He went out to New Mexico for a few days, and he was supposed to keep in touch no matter what, and now I haven't heard from him in hours. Something's wrong," I explained, too distracted to come up with any kind of elaborate story.

"Excuse me, did I hear you right? You're worried 'cause you haven't heard from him in *hours?* What are you, hung up on *him,* now?" she asked scornfully.

"You don't understand. It was maybe dangerous, what he was doing. That's why we said he'd text me every single hour, unless he was asleep. No matter what he had to do to make it happen. It's been close to four hours, already. I'm telling you, something's wrong," I repeated.

"What's he doing, drug running?" she asked, and that was enough to break my last nerve.

"I don't know why I even bother to talk to you about anything," I said in disgust, getting up to leave the room. Jenny let me get almost to the door before she called me back.

"Hey, sis. . . I'm sorry. I didn't mean that," she finally said, when she saw I really did mean to leave the room. I stopped in the doorway, hesitating, and then finally turned around and came back to the bed.

"Look. This is no stupid little game. It's *serious,* and if you don't want to help me then just say so and I'll find somebody else who will. I don't have time to mess around with you today," I said.

"Sure, I'll help. Really. Just tell me what you need," she said meekly.

"Okay. This is what I need you to do. If anybody calls or shows up wanting to talk to me or asking where I'm at, then make something up to put them off. Tell them I'm sick, or I'm in the shower, or whatever you want. Just don't let anybody find out that I went to New Mexico, and don't give them any reason to be suspicious. All you have to do is put them off for a while, till I can get back. That's it," I said.

"What about Cody?" she asked.

"Especially not Cody," I said.

"But how long am I supposed to keep this up?" she asked, and I had to think about that for a minute.

"I'll be back in five days. If I can't find Marcus by then, I might as well come on home, anyway," I sighed.

"Why don't you just call the police?" Jen asked.

"Because I don't know if anything's really wrong or not, and I don't want to make a scene, and I don't want Cody to find out. If I can't find him myself then I *will* call them, but I hope I don't have to," I said.

"Whatever you say," she said.

"And one other thing. The last place Marcus went was to see a woman named Layla Latimer; she lives in White Sands, which is kind of a suburb of Las Cruces. So that's the first place I'll check. If anything happens to me for some reason, call the cops," I said.

For once in her life, Jenny actually looked a little bit worried, which might have been funny if things hadn't been so serious.

"Don't sit there looking like you swallowed a frog. Will you do it or not?" I asked.

"I said I'll do it," she said.

It was a chancy thing whether Mama's old Ford would make it all the way to New Mexico or not. It's an eight hundred mile drive, and that's hard on any vehicle. I had no choice but to try, though. I wasn't old enough to rent a car, and I didn't have a credit card in the first place. But I babied it along, stopping only for gas, and as soon as I got to Las Cruces I found a cheap motel and collapsed into bed absolutely exhausted.

In the morning I slept in until nine, and then got up with the express purpose of going to see the mysterious Layla Latimer. I had to drive across the dry Organ Mountains to get there, and when I reached the top of the pass I found myself looking out across the broad plain of the White Sands Desert, blindingly bright in the sun. It crossed my mind that Reuben McGrath must have walked on the very road where I was driving, all those many years ago. I couldn't help praying my journey would turn out better than his did.

I found Miss Latimer's address easily enough, and for a little while I stood outside on the porch, trying to control my breathing so I wouldn't seem nervous. When I finally thought I could speak in a normal voice, I determinedly knocked on the door.

"Just a minute," came a muffled voice from inside. It sounded remarkably normal, and that reassured me somewhat. A second later the door opened to reveal a young girl who looked to be maybe nineteen or twenty, and I found myself wondering what on earth I'd been so scared of.

"Can I help you?" she asked, with a pleasant smile.

"Uh. . . yes, I think so. I'm looking for a friend of mine who was supposed to come see you yesterday morning. His name's Marcus Cumby, and he was interested in the article about the

Battle of Mesilla that you wrote for the historical society a few years ago," I explained, and the girl laughed.

"Oh, yeah, I know who you're talking about. He did stop by, and we talked for a while. Please come in," she said, and so I did. There was a strong smell of burning incense in the house and a few oddities sitting around; a crystal ball on the coffee table and a dark red dyed-rice curtain dividing the living room from the kitchen. Nothing super weird, though. We sat down across from each other with the coffee table between us, and made ourselves comfortable.

"Do you know where Marcus is now?" I asked, disarmed by how helpful and accommodating the girl seemed to be.

"He's still doing his research, as far as I know," she said.

"He is?" I echoed, unsure what that was supposed to mean and why Marcus hadn't contacted me, if that was the case.

"Yeah. He wanted to know about some things the article didn't mention, so I told him I had all kinds of stuff stored at my brother's house," she explained. Which, needless to say, didn't seem to explain much.

"But is that where he is now? Where does your brother live?" I asked.

"Well, before we get into that, let's talk a little more about why you're really here. Then I'm sure we can work something out," she said.

"What are you talking about?" I asked, even more confused.

"Now, Lisa, let's not beat around the bush. People who come here asking the kinds of questions you and Marcus ask always want something which they can't get anywhere else. And I can almost always give it to them. For the right price, of course. So what is it y'all are really after? Like I said, I'm sure we could work something out. I love to make deals," she said, with another bright smile.

I never told her my name. I was absolutely sure of it, and Layla Latimer was definitely beginning to creep me out again. But it was no time to be a mouse.

"Can you break a curse?" I asked boldly.

"It depends. What kind?" she asked, without so much as a blink.

"My boyfriend has a curse on him that he'll die before he's thirty years old. Can you break it?" I asked, and the girl actually laughed.

"Oh, *that* old thing. You're talking about Cody McGrath, right? I can see why you'd want to keep him around a little longer; he's a sweet chunk of meat," she said, making it sound like he was a juicy steak she couldn't wait to sink her teeth into.

If any other woman had said something like that to me, I would've had some choice words to give her and they wouldn't have been pretty, either. But it was scary how much this girl knew, and I was afraid if I said something nasty she might not deal with me at all.

"Yeah, that's him," I said tightly, ignoring the rest of her words. If Jenny ever taught me anything, it's how to have a thick skin when I need to.

"Well, I have to say that particular curse has been awfully entertaining over the years, but it does seem to have reached the point of diminishing returns. I tell you what; I'm willing to break it," she agreed.

I felt my heart lift, but I was still wary. I hadn't heard the price, yet.

"What's your price?" I asked carefully.

"Hmm, now that's a good question. I think I'd like to see you break up with him. A really nasty scene that makes him feel terrible and ruins his life. Let's see, maybe we could have you hook up with Marcus, too; that's his best friend, I do believe. A little extra betrayal to spice things up a bit. Yes. That's *wonderful*. Let's do it that way," she smiled, looking pleased with herself.

I sat there on the couch with my mouth hung open and eyes wide, utterly at a loss for words.

"Let's not attract flies, my dear. Will you take the deal or not?" she asked, like it was the most reasonable thing in the world.

"You. . . that's. . ." I sputtered, horrified. She seemed to be enjoying the sight.

"Now, if you do decide to take me up on the offer, I'll want you to wear this little hi-def camera on your lapel, of course, so I can see and hear the whole thing when you break up with him. Just make sure you don't block the lens, you know," she said calmly, pulling a small device from her purse and placing it on the coffee table within easy reach.

"Why would you want something like that?" I whispered, staring at the camera like it was a rattlesnake. Layla smiled broadly.

"Oh, my dear. Pain is sweet. It's beautiful, really. The only truly beautiful thing there is. You're asking me to give up a certain amount of it, if I break that curse for you. I'm willing to do it, but only if you give me some other pain to replace it. Something fresh and new and flavorful. Yours, and Cody's, and Marcus's. It's not so hard to understand, is it?" she asked reasonably.

It made a kind of horrifying sense, I suppose. . . if you had the heart of Satan. I realized that up till then I'd never in my life met anyone who was truly evil. And this pretty, fresh-faced girl with her sweet smile and colorful blouse was the stuff that nightmares were made of. Real ones.

"I can't do that," I finally said, gripping the edge of the couch cushions tightly to keep from shaking.

"No? Maybe if I let Marcus go, too? Although I have to admit, he does look pretty tasty himself," she laughed, and that was enough to make me shudder in spite of my grip on the couch. Whatever this devil meant by "tasty" I devoutly didn't want to know. I could think of a dozen possibilities, each one more horrifying than the last.

"How do I know you'll keep your word?" I asked, and she smiled again, seemingly not offended at all.

"Tsk, tsk. I always keep my word. If I didn't, I'd never get any customers, you know," she said reprovingly.

I still couldn't bring myself to agree to such a thing. How could I tell such a horrible lie to all the people I loved? How could I tell my mother? How could I tell Miss Josie? How could I tell Brandon, or Marcus, let alone Cody? Besides the way it affected me, it had the potential to bust up everybody else's lives in all kinds of ways. It could easily end up costing Marcus his job, his best friend, his home, and even his most favorite hobby as the Mustangs' drummer, all at one whack. Miss Josie would think I was no better than trash, and how could I blame her? And then when it came to Cody. . . my heart broke when I thought about how much it would cost *him,* no matter what happened. I knew him too well. It would wreck every ideal about love that he'd ever believed in.

Which was exactly what Miss Latimer had in mind, no doubt. I looked at the woman with loathing, wondering how it was possible for any human being to be so cruel or so filthy.

"I'll have to talk to Marcus, first," I said, temporizing, and for the first time Layla frowned slightly.

"You don't have much room for negotiation, you know," she reminded me, and then she seemed to have a change of heart.

"But nevertheless, I'm feeling generous this morning. Let's go talk to Marcus, and then you can make up your mind," she said. I doubted whether Layla Latimer ever had a generous impulse in her entire life; most likely she hoped to witness some more grief and heartache out of the deal. Probably mine, when I got a glimpse of whatever she'd done to Marcus.

And so it was. I followed Layla's little brown Subaru wagon back up into the mountains again, until we arrived at a fancy mobile home hidden away in a dusty and very secluded valley surrounded by rugged peaks.

I killed my engine, not wanting to get out. But I was the one who'd asked to go there, after all, so I nerved myself and opened the door.

Layla was waiting for me at the door.

"Hurry up, slowpoke. I've got things to do, you know," she said, tapping her watch.

She led me to one of the back bedrooms, and my hand flew to my mouth when I saw Marcus hanging from the ceiling by his wrists. He looked up when the door opened, his eyes full of pain, and his face clouded over with fresh misery when he recognized me. He probably thought I was Layla's next captive. My tongue stuck in my throat, and Layla herself seemed to be enjoying the sight of all this horror like a cool drink on a hot day.

"Cut him down!" I demanded, when I could find the strength to speak.

"Certainly," she agreed, and slashed the rope that held Marcus to the ceiling. She did nothing to break his fall, though, and Marcus crashed to the floor in a heap, groaning. I ran to him and threw my arms around his body, trying to comfort him.

"We're going home, Marcus. Get up if you can," I whispered in his ear, almost in tears. Only the thought of how much Layla would enjoy it if I started to cry gave me the strength to hold it back.

"I'll try," Marcus croaked, and he made a valiant effort. But even with my help he wasn't able to stand, much less walk. All I could do was help him crawl, dragging him in places. Layla followed, watching us.

I finally got Marcus out to the car and into the passenger seat, and then found Layla close beside me.

"I assume we have a deal, since you're taking him with you?" she asked, gesturing toward Marcus.

"Yes," I whispered, hardly able to choke out the word.

"Good. Now, here's your camera. Make sure to get some good footage, please. I'll give you a few days to work out all the details, of course, but I'll expect to see you again no later than. . . hmm, let's call it two weeks from today? I'll break the curse when I see you then, as long as you keep up your end of the deal in the meantime," she said, placing the small camera in my palm and squeezing my fingers around it. Her skin was cool and dry like lizard scales. It was all I could do not to shudder again.

I couldn't have said another word right then to save my life, so I only nodded. Then I fled from that horrible place as fast as I could safely go.

My first impulse was to hit the gas and fly back home as fast as the car would take us. But Marcus needed attention, so I stopped at a convenience store in Las Cruces to get some bottled water and some ointment for his wrists. They were raw and bloody from the chafing of the rope, and I wondered how long he'd been hanging there before I arrived.

He'd passed out in the car seat almost as soon as I got him in there, and he was still deeply asleep when I came back out of the store. I washed the sweat from his face and cleaned his wrists, and in spite of my gentleness the pain must have woken him.

He jerked back violently and tried to hit me, and if he hadn't been so weak then he might easily have given me a black eye.

"Marcus! It's me," I told him, and then he came to his senses. He stared at me with wild eyes, and then gradually relaxed.

"I'm sorry, Lisa. I wasn't thinking," he said hoarsely.

"It's all right. Here, drink some water. You look like you need some," I told him, and he didn't need to be asked twice for that. He grabbed the bottle and drank all of it, hardly slowing down to breathe.

"I haven't had anything to drink since yesterday morning," he said, as soon as he could talk.

"What happened? What did she do to you up there?" I asked.

"Not now, Lisa. Please. I'll tell you when we get home, but I can't do it yet. Just get us out of here," he said.

"All right. Go back to sleep, Marcus," I said, smoothing the hair back from his face.

Chapter Twenty-Two
Lisa

I drove in silence, leaving the radio turned off for Marcus's sake, and when we got back to Goliad late that evening I was exhausted all over again. I drove across the dam and past the peach orchard to his house, not knowing where else to take him, and I guess he'd started to recover a little bit by then. He was able to walk inside, at least, and lie down on the bed by himself.

I stayed with him that night, worried that he didn't need to be left alone just yet. I slept on the couch, and in the morning we talked.

He was already more or less back to normal by then, except for his wrists. But still, there were shadows under his eyes and a haunted look on his face that I'd never seen there before.

"So what happened?" I asked.

"You really don't want to know, Lisa," he said darkly.

"No, but I probably ought to," I said.

"Well, I went to see her that morning, like I told you. She seemed friendly enough, told me a few things about Selena Garza, and then said she had some more stuff back at her brother's house if I wanted to go see it. And me, like an idiot, I fell for it. She seemed so dadgummed sweet and innocent, you know. Anyway, once she got me out there alone in the middle of nowhere, it was all over. She sneaked up and hit me on the head from behind, and next thing I knew I woke up tied to the ceiling," he said.

"Did she hurt you?" I asked.

"No, not really. Not the way you think, at least. All she did was let me hang there. No food, no water, no nothing. It wasn't too bad at first, but then my wrists and my shoulders started to hurt something awful. She came in now and then just to stand there and watch me suffer, like she was enjoying it or something," he said bitterly.

"Yeah, I think she does," I agreed.

"I don't think she cared if I died or not. I think she wanted me to. I think I *would* have, if it'd been much longer. She said I'd probably taste good, whatever *that* means. She seemed to think it was funny," he said.

"You don't think she, like, *eats* people, do you?" I asked, feeling sick.

"I don't know. I wouldn't put it past her," he said.

"I'm sorry, Marcus," I said.

"Wasn't your fault. You saved me from that nutball," he pointed out.

"It's not over, yet," I said, and his head snapped up.

"What do you mean?" he asked.

"She said she'd break the curse on Cody's family, but only if I hurt him really bad and break up with him. She even wants video," I said.

"That's crazy!" he said.

"It gets worse, I'm afraid. She wants me to tell Cody that you and me hooked up and we're together now, to make it hurt more," I said, forcing myself to say the words. Marcus just stared at me.

"We can't do that," he said.

"That's what I said. But if we don't, then the deal's off. Cody's back under the curse and I'm not sure what she'd do to you and me. Probably have us both hanging from the ceiling till we die of thirst. I'm afraid all three of us are on the block, here," I said.

"You don't think we could just tell Cody the truth, and try to figure something out?" Marcus said.

I hesitated; the same thought had crossed my own mind, but there was one stubborn problem with that idea.

"I want to. But if we do, then what'll happen? Layla will never break that curse unless we do this. I want to give Cody his life back, and the only way to do that is to give the monster what she wants," I said.

"You believe in the Curse now?" he asked.

"Yeah, I guess I do," I agreed.

Marcus is no fool; he recognized reality when he heard it, no matter how much he hated the idea.

"So what's the plan, then?" he asked, defeated.

"I guess I'll have to go to Alaska and do what I have to do. Then we'll see," I said, surprised that I could be so steely-eyed about it.

"Do you think you can make Cody believe it?" he asked.

"I have to. Maybe I can tell him we went to a party and got drunk, or something like that," I said.

"You know he'd never believe that. He knows neither one of us is a boozer," he said.

"Well. . . I don't know. What if I tell him it was supposed to be a fish fry or a wiener roast or something innocent like that, and somebody spiked the punch? He might believe that," I said.

"Yeah, he might. Tell him it was at Tommy Jones's house; he's a meth-head from way back," he suggested.

"I don't know Tommy that well," I said. I remembered him slightly, since Jenny had dated him for a while a couple months ago. He was exactly her type; a good-looking, muscular ex-football player who loved to party and run wild.

"He lives over there on Redbud Street in Ore City. I used to run around with him a little bit, before I moved out to Goliad my senior year. He didn't used to be quite as much of a doper as he is now. Anyway, Cody knows all that, so maybe he'd believe it if you told him we went over there," he said.

"I guess so," I agreed, thinking how unreal it was that I was actually sitting there having a serious discussion about how best to deceive Cody.

There was nothing left to say, and waiting would only prolong the agony. I figured if the thing had to be done, then it was best done quickly. But there was still one more conversation I needed to have before I hit the road.

I wasn't sure if Miss Josie would be home or not, but after leaving Marcus's place I pulled in at the main house just in case. There was a slight chill in the air as I headed up the steps, and I pulled my sweater a little closer around my shoulders. Miss Josie must have seen me coming, because she opened the door with a smile before I even had time to knock. Then she saw the look on my face, and her smile faded.

"Is something wrong, Lisa?" she asked, looking concerned.

"No, ma'am. I just came to talk to you about something, that's all," I said, nervously fiddling with my keys.

"Oh, all right. Well, come on inside, then, before you catch your death of cold out there," she said, stepping aside to let me in. I followed her to the kitchen, shutting the door behind us.

"Can I get you some coffee, maybe some hot chocolate?" she asked, in her usual hospitable way.

"I'd love some hot chocolate," I admitted, knowing how much she liked to be a good hostess.

"Sit down, then, and we'll talk awhile. I was fixing to go wash some clothes, but that's nothing that can't wait," she said.

She proceeded to busy herself at the stove, pulling out milk and chocolate and this and that and the other thing. I knew her well enough by then to know that she would have been horrified if you'd suggested using instant hot chocolate, or anything else instant, for that matter. She always made everything from scratch. But practice makes perfect, I guess, because it didn't take her long to get the chocolate done, and then she sat down across the table from me while we sipped the warm drinks. The cup felt good on my cold fingers.

"So what is it, sweetie?" she asked, taking a sip of her own chocolate.

"I don't want you to think badly of me," I began, me palms beginning to sweat with nervousness. Telling Miss Josie was a major risk, but I just *had* to.

"Oh, honey, no. I could never think badly of you. You can tell me, whatever it is," she promised me.

"All right, then. Just promise you'll hear me out to the end, okay?" I asked, and she nodded.

"A few months ago, Cody told me he thought there might be a curse on y'alls family, that everybody would die young," I said.

"I see," she said.

"I didn't really believe it at first. Not then. But then several days ago Marcus told me some rumors he heard about how the curse came from a witch in New Mexico, and we finally decided it was worth having Marcus go out there to see if he could find out anything, since it seems to bother Cody so much," I told her reluctantly, my nervousness increasing to the point that my throat was getting dry and making it hard to talk. I took another swallow of hot chocolate to moisten it.

"I see," Miss Josie said again.

"We didn't tell Cody anything. You know how he is; he would've worried, and maybe even come running back down here, if he couldn't talk us out of it," I said, pausing to take another drink.

"Go on," she said.

"Some bad stuff happened. I had to go out there and bring Marcus back. That curse is not just a fairy tale, Miss Josie. It's real. I believe that now. But I think... I *hope*, we found a way to get rid of it," I said, forcing myself to say the words. There was a thick pause in the room, and I wondered if the woman thought I was crazy.

"How would you do that?" she finally asked.

"It won't be easy. I don't know what all I might have to do, yet. I might be gone for a while. I might. . . I might have to tell Cody some things that are not true. Even some really bad things. I just want you to know that I love him and I always will, no matter what. He's everything to me. Whatever you hear and whatever happens, please believe me when I say that," I said.

"I believe you, Lisa. But I can't lie to him, if that's what you're asking," she said sternly.

"I'm not asking you to do that. Only to keep all this to yourself, and please remember what I said, that I love him more than anything in the world. That's all," I said.

"I don't understand," she said.

"Do you think if I told him a lie that really hurt him, that he'd forgive me later on? If he knows I only did it for his own sake?" I asked.

"I honestly don't know what he might say in a situation like that," she admitted.

"Me neither," I said.

"I do know this much. You'd be a lot better off if you told him the truth," she said.

"Not about this," I said bleakly, and Miss Josie shook her head.

"Lisa, I've been around for a good many years, and I've never yet seen a time when deceit was the right choice. Not even to protect someone. It always comes back to haunt you later on. Cody has the right to make his own choices about what he wants to do with his life, just like you do. You can't make them for him, no matter how well-intentioned you think it is. Believe me, he won't thank you for that," she said.

"Even if we're talking about saving his life?" I asked, my voice cracking. Miss Josie took a long time to answer that one.

"I don't know. I guess it's possible there might be exceptions to every rule. I can't tell you for sure what you should do. But I would think long and hard before lying to him, no matter how good you think the reason might be," she said.

"But if I *have* to. Do you think he'd forgive me?" I insisted.

"I think if it was a case where you really, truly had no choice in the matter, then yes, I'm sure he would. He's not unkind, you know," she said.

"Yeah, I know that," I agreed.

"So have some faith in him, and trust God that things will work out the way that they should," she said.

I left not long after that, heavy-hearted as ever. I drove slowly, trying to count up in my mind how much money I had. I didn't know how much it might cost for a plane ticket to Prudhoe Bay, but I was willing to bet it wouldn't be cheap.

It turned out I had a little over a thousand dollars saved up. It was supposed to be set aside for emergencies, but I figured this surely had to count as one if anything did.

The cheapest flight I could find turned out to be thirteen hundred dollars, which left me about two hundred dollars short. I didn't know where I might get the rest, let alone have anything left over for food or anything else. I finally scraped it up, though; I pawned whatever jewelry I could find and sold my computer and my textbooks. All together, it was barely enough.

I bought the ticket for Thursday so I'd get there on Friday afternoon, and then I was supposed to come back on Monday evening. Even though I didn't really expect to stay that long, I'd already decided I had to make it seem like this whole thing was a legitimate attempt to win his forgiveness. Layla wanted her footage up close and personal, and there was no way Cody would believe I'd come all the way to Alaska to break up with him. I could do that much by phone or letter and spare us both an ugly scene. But he might believe it if he thought I'd come to make up with him. I was going to have to hurt him so much that *he'd* be the one to break up with *me;* that was the only way it would ever work, and I was terrified that I wouldn't be able to pull it off.

I hoped they'd change my ticket and let me come home early after it was all over, because if not then I didn't know what I might have to do. I wouldn't have enough money left over to rent a hotel room, that was for sure. But that was all right; I was grimly determined to do whatever it took, even if I had to sleep on the floor at the airport.

I'd have to tell Jenny and Mama where I was going, of course, and I braced myself for the argument *that* would cause. Jenny would have to drive me to the airport and come pick me up when I got back, and I could just imagine some of the choice words *she* might have for the whole adventure.

I could have asked Marcus to take me, I guess, but considering what I was fixing to have to tell Cody, I think that would have been unbearably awkward at the time. What do you talk about for two hours with a guy you're pretending to have a fling with? Celebrities? The weather? Out of all the convoluted stories I'd ever read, there was nothing to cover a situation like this one.

All I could do was cross my fingers and pray it all worked.

Chapter Twenty-Three
Lisa

"You're going *where?*" Jenny asked, as soon as the words left my mouth.

"Prudhoe Bay," I said, knowing perfectly well that she'd heard me the first time.

"And your reason for this is. . . ?" she asked, raising an eyebrow.

"My own business. I need to talk to Cody," I said.

"Um. . . sis, they do make envelopes and telephones, just in case you hadn't heard," she told me.

"No, I need to see him in person," I said, shaking my head.

"Why?" she asked.

"I told you, that's between me and him. You'll know soon enough, I'm sure, but not till I get back," I said.

"Has it got something to do with your little vacation to New Mexico?" she asked.

While I was gone, Jenny had somehow come up with the notion that I'd cooked up the whole trip to Las Cruces as a scheme for arranging a romantic getaway with Marcus without anybody finding out about it. It seemed like the stupidest plan anybody would ever have thought of, let alone the fact that New

Mexico is hardly the first place that comes to mind when I think about romantic getaways. So I don't know where she got that idea, unless it was the simple fact that it was easier for her to think that I was a tramp than to accept the scary story I'd told her at first. Sometimes it's easier not to believe, when you don't want the truth to be true.

And as much as it galled me, I had to let her keep thinking so. It made things much easier (in a way) if she thought the whole thing was all bosh and melodrama. The only bad part about the situation was that Jenny-the-Cynic had returned with a vengeance.

"Nope, it's got nothing to do with New Mexico at all," I lied.

"Hmm. . . sounds like a kiss-and-make-up kind of trip to me. You know, sis, playing both ends against the middle like that never works for long. One of them always finds out sooner or later, I promise," she said, like she was sharing some great piece of wisdom.

"Oh, for pity's sake! That's not what I'm doing at all," I said in exasperation. The fact that she was so close to guessing the gist of my little story only infuriated me all the more.

"Sure, sure. Just saying, that's all. The whole thing still sounds pretty fishy to me," she said.

"Maybe so, but will you take me to the airport or not? If you won't then just say so, and I'll find somebody else," I said, tired of arguing with her.

"Yeah, sure, I'll take you. What time do you have to be there?" she asked.

"I have to leave from Dallas at six o'clock tomorrow night," I told her.

"And you'll be back when?" she asked.

"One-thirty on Tuesday afternoon," I told her.

"Well, I don't care what you do. I might go to the beach for the weekend with Janice and Sheila," she said.

"At Galveston?" I asked.

"Yeah, probably. It'll be too cold before much longer. Might as well have one last hoot before winter gets here," she said.

"What about Mama?" I asked.

"I'll see if she can stay with Aunt Michelle for the weekend," she said, and I nodded. Michelle lived in Lufkin, which was right on the way if she was headed down to the coast. I had my doubts that she'd agree to keep Mama if she thought it was only to let Jenny kick up her heels at the beach for a couple of days, but I couldn't worry about that. Putting a crimp in my sister's social life was the least of my concerns at the moment.

By the next afternoon I'd already packed and repacked my travel case at least five times, and I was so nervous I could barely remember to breathe. I hadn't talked to Cody very much since the encounter with Layla for fear I'd break down and blow everything, and I knew he probably wondered about that. I could only hope he hadn't started to guess that something was up.

When he told me to watch out for an evil woman named Layla I almost wanted to laugh hysterically. But I didn't dare tell him that his warning came too late.

I didn't particularly care to talk to Jenny much on the way to the airport, and I didn't particularly care for the plane ride, either. I had two layovers, in Phoenix and in Anchorage, and since I didn't sleep very well on planes that meant I was awake pretty much all night long.

I got to Prudhoe Bay in the gray half-light not long before the sun came up, about 9:15 in the morning. My first sight of the place wasn't very encouraging; it looked like a jumble of beat-up trailers and industrial buildings, some ice and snow scattered here and there, and the rest of it pretty much bare gravel.

It was also frigid. The pilot told us the high for the day was supposed to be ten degrees, right about normal for late October. I shivered just hearing the number; I'd never been so cold in my entire life.

I knew Cody would be at work till six o'clock that evening, so I sat in the airport and tried to keep warm by imagining tropical beaches and mountain vistas and pretty much anything other than the barren, empty landscape I found myself in and the horrible encounter that lay ahead. I read for a while and caught a few snatches of sleep when I could, wondering how anybody could stand to actually live in such a place.

I took the camera out of my purse and attached it to the collar of my blouse. It was made to look like a button or some innocuous clip-on decoration, so that no one would be likely to pay any attention to it. All I had to do was touch it to activate the recording.

I felt like a ghoul, feeding off the misery and suffering of others. I had to keep reminding myself I was doing this to save his life. To save *all* our lives, most likely, and however filthy and loathsome it made me feel, I didn't dare cave in.

It got dark again about five-thirty, and by the time it was safe to call Cody, there was nothing outside but the almost-full moon. At six fifteen I called him, and he answered on the third ring.

"Hey, Lisa, what's up?" he asked, sounding tired. As well he might, after a twelve hour shift.

"Oh, nothing much. Got a surprise for you, though," I said, with fake enthusiasm.

"Yeah? What's that?" he asked.

"Are you anywhere close to the airport?" I asked. Cody isn't stupid; I knew he'd put two and two together the second he heard that word.

"Um. . . Lisa, at the risk of sounding dumb, you wouldn't happen to be *at* the airport, would you?" he asked.

"You better believe it," I told him, happily. For a second he seemed stunned.

"Hold on; I'll be there in five minutes," he said.

He was as good as his word, and five minutes later he came walking into the airport, still dressed in his dirty work clothes and with his face red from the cold.

As soon as he saw me he stopped in his tracks, like he thought he might be imagining things. He looked thinner than I remembered, and tired and worn, but he was still my dear, handsome Cody, and for a second I could pretend nothing was wrong. I ran to him and threw my arms around his midsection, and he swept me up in a bear hug and kissed me long and tenderly. Two and a half months might not seem like such a very long time to most people, but to me it felt like an eternity had passed since the last time he'd kissed me.

"You're really a sight for sore eyes, babe; I can't believe you're really here," he said, shaking his head.

"I couldn't take it any longer; I just had to see you," I explained. Lie number one, I thought sadly.

"How long are you here for?" he asked.

"Only a day or two," I said.

"Um, you do know there's nowhere to stay up here except in the work camps, don't you?" he asked.

"I found a website that said there are supposed to be two or three hotels," I said, not mentioning the fact that I knew they were closed for the winter and didn't expect to need one anyway. After the initial joy of seeing him again, my fear of the upcoming encounter was beginning to creep back again in full force. No, *fear* is too mild a word. Holy terror is more like it. I was going to have to give the performance of a lifetime and break his heart in the process. Even though none of it was real, it was already killing me inside.

"Well, yeah, technically. But only in the summertime. It's way past tourist season now. I guess you can stay with me in my room for a couple days, if you don't mind hiding out. It'll get me in trouble if anybody finds out you're here," he explained.

"Sure," I agreed.

"Okay, then. Let's see if we can sneak back in there," he said.

When we got to the Arctic Caribou Inn, I found that it was a collection of trailers which had been modified to house the oilfield workers, and anybody else was more or less an afterthought. But I decided if Cody had been living there for months already, then I could surely make do for a few hours. He seemed uneasy and kept glancing around to make sure nobody had seen us.

He took me to one of the doors and unlocked it, letting us into a fairly small but decent bedroom. There was a bed, a nightstand table with a lamp and a telephone, a closet, a desk, and a wooden shelf. The only other feature was a door which presumably led to the bathroom.

It was chilly for my taste, but Cody didn't seem to notice. Maybe he'd been used to the cold for so long he didn't even pay attention to it anymore. He pulled off his jacket and coveralls and pretty much everything else he was wearing, till he was stripped down to his shorts and t-shirt. He didn't even shiver.

"Let me take a shower real quick so I can get the sweat and the grime off me, and then we'll talk, okay?" he said, and I nodded. He had all kinds of grease and dirt and ground-in grime all over him, especially on his hands. I couldn't blame him for wanting to clean up a little bit before bedtime. He grabbed some fresh clothes from the closet and I soon heard him scrubbing in the shower.

As soon as he disappeared into the bathroom, I sat down on the bed to wait. I was trying hard to have faith in him and to believe what Miss Josie had told me about how things always worked out for the best, but my heart was beating fast and I felt sick and scared. I took deep breaths to calm myself.

I couldn't resist snooping a little bit, while he was gone. He had a picture of me that I'd sent him, parked right there on his night table, and when I slipped the drawer open I found a thick stack of envelopes that must have contained every letter I'd ever sent him.

I didn't have time to look anywhere else, because it wasn't long till he came padding back out in his skivvies, still drying his hair with a towel. It had grown out a lot longer than I remembered, and yeah, he was definitely thinner.

He noticed me looking at his body, and did a slow twirl with his arms raised to show off, obviously enjoying my appreciation of the view. I thought he might even have built up a little more muscle since he'd been there, even if he'd lost some weight in the process.

"Do I look like myself?" he asked, smiling a little.

"Yeah, just a little thinner, that's all," I said.

"I can believe that. They work us to death up here," he nodded, sitting down beside me on the bed.

"I'm sorry, baby," I told him, wishing there was something I could do to make things easier on him. A solid year of twelve hour days with never a break or a single day off had to wear a man out after a while.

"It's all right. I'll survive. I've got some good news, though; I'll be home at Christmas for two weeks. My alternate wanted the extra days and I wanted the time off, so he's filling in for me. Then I'll be done up here for good on August fifteenth. I'm counting down the days; I promise you that," he said.

I could tell he was more tired than he liked to admit, so I slid over to make room for him to lie down on the mattress instead of having to sit up. He did, and then scrunched up close to the wall to make room for me, too.

"Come lay next to me, Lisa," he said, and I was happy to comply. I quickly snuggled up close to him with my head on his chest so I could listen to his heartbeat, and he put his arms around me.

"I'm glad you're here, darlin', but surely there had to be some reason besides just missing me, why you came all this way," he said. He was right, of course, but I was reluctant to get into all that yet. I wanted to savor the closeness of him, the warmth of his skin and the feel of his rough hands, if only for a little while. God only knew when I'd be able to do it again after all this.

"Yeah, but right now I just want to be close to you for a while. I'm starved to death for Cody time," I said.

"Hmm... makes me feel like a big bottle of apple juice you've been saving for a special occasion," he said.

"Hey, that's a good comparison. Sweet, healthy, and completely natural. There you go. I could write some poetry about my apple-juice boy when I get home. No wonder I'm starved for you," I said, and he laughed.

"You're such a nut, babe. Well, enjoy me all you want to, then," he teased, obviously amused. So for a while I was quiet, putting off breaking the news to him for as long as possible.

But I could tell he was fighting sleep, and as much as I hated to break the peaceful mood, I knew it was time to tell him. I brushed the camera to activate it, and then it was show time.

Chapter Twenty-Four
Cody

"Cody, do you love me?" Lisa said, tracing circles on my belly with her forefinger. Her nail was just sharp enough to tickle, and made my whole body tingle drowsily. I could feel sleep nibbling at the edges of my mind, and no matter how hard I fought it off, I couldn't help worrying that I might fall asleep right in the middle of talking to her. I was really that dead beat.

"You know I do. More than anything in the world," I said, yawning and making an effort to shake myself awake again.

"What if I did something that hurt you really bad; would you still love me then?" she asked.

That was enough to wake me up completely and make me forget all about her fingernails on my stomach. People don't usually say things like that unless they have a good reason, especially not when they travel thousands of miles to say it. But I knew the answer, anyway.

"There's nothing you could say or do that would make me not love you anymore, I promise," I said.

"Nothing at all?" she persisted.

"Nope, not a thing," I said, nervous about where she was headed with all this.

"What if I got totally wasted on meth and ecstasy at a party and hooked up with your best friend? Would you still love me then?" she asked jokingly, and then all my worries dissolved in a quiet explosion of mirth.

"That's a good one, Lisa," I laughed. She'd really had me going there for a few seconds.

"Well, would you?" she asked. I couldn't understand what her sudden obsession was, but I tried to consider the question seriously, since she seemed so concerned about it. I ran my fingers through her hair absentmindedly, thinking. It was soft and silky, like a baby calf in the springtime. I don't know if she would've liked that comparison or not, but I've noticed that occasionally random thoughts like that will pop into your head at the strangest possible times.

"I guess nobody ever knows for sure what he'd do till he's tested, but I hope I'd still feel just the same. Love is a cheap thing if it won't stand up under pressure," I said thoughtfully, choosing my words carefully.

"Fair enough answer, I guess," she said, sounding moody.

"Oh, come on, Lisa, lighten up; it's not like you'd ever do anything like that in the first place," I said, laughing again.

I didn't know where this dark mood had come from all of a sudden, and I wanted to get rid of it and enjoy the rest of the evening and fall asleep with her in my arms.

Then came the plunger.

"But I did, though," she said softly, and for a second I felt like the ground had suddenly opened up at my feet.

"Huh?" I asked, thinking I must have misheard her.

"I went to a fish fry with Marcus, only it turned out to be more of a party. Somebody spiked the punch and we both drank it. I got so stoned I couldn't think straight, and so did he. I never would have done something like that if I hadn't been high, Cody, I swear to you. I don't think Marcus would have, either. I'm so sorry. If you don't want to be with me anymore then I understand, but I hope you can find it in your heart to forgive me," she said, the words tumbling out in a rush.

At first I couldn't comprehend what she was saying, and even when I did comprehend it I still couldn't believe it. Lisa and *Marcus?* There haven't been too many times in my life when I've been struck totally speechless, but that was one of them. In fact, the only thing even more unbelievable than the idea of her doing such a thing in the first place was the notion that she'd tell me a story like that if it wasn't true.

"I see," I finally said, when I finally got my voice back. I think I was still in shock; the words sounded dry and factual, almost clinical, even to me. But it was all I could manage to say.

"What are you thinking?" she finally asked, after a long time had passed. At that I started to feel just a little bit of emotion coming back for the first time.

"I'm thinking. . . life really bites right now, if you want me to be honest," I said bitterly. *Bites* was a gentle word for it, actually. I felt like my whole life and everything I ever believed and wanted and dreamed of was falling to dust and ashes right around my ears.

"I'm sorry, Cody. I swear I never meant to hurt you. I never meant for any of this to happen," she said, starting to cry.

I sighed.

"I'm sure you didn't, Lisa. But now we have to deal with it all the same, don't we?" I said.

"Yeah," she whispered.

"I ought to *beat* Marcus when I get home," I said venomously, grasping desperately at the only other person I could blame, even though that was hardly any better. Marcus was supposed to be my best friend, the one who always had my back no matter what; even my brother, almost. The fact that it was *him* of all people hurt almost as much as the fact that it was Lisa. I wanted to kill both of them and I wanted to cry while I did it, and what kind of screwy thinking is that? But what do you do, when suddenly trust can't be trusted, and you find out that love isn't love after all?

Chapter Twenty-Five
Lisa

I could see Cody's agony, and hated myself for it. I felt lower than a wad of used gum on the bottom of a hooker's second-best shoes. It was all I could do not to break down and tell him the truth. Instead, I bit my lip hard enough to bring blood and made sure the camera had a good view.

"Don't blame Marcus either; he was just as messed up as I was. He wouldn't have done it either, if he'd been sober," I told him.

Any other time I knew he would have respected me for that, for not letting Marcus take all the blame. But as it was, I guess he must have been too torn up inside to care anymore.

"Well, what were y'all doing at a party like that, anyway?" he demanded, with real anger in his voice.

"I thought it was only a fish fry. Just somethin' fun to do and get out of the house for a little while because me and Jenny haven't been getting along too well here lately. It was at Tommy Jones's house," I told him.

"Well, that was your first mistake, darlin'. Everybody in town knows Tommy Jones is a meth head. All you have to do is look at his rotten teeth," he said.

"I didn't know. I don't keep up with the town gossip, and I didn't even see Tommy at the party at all," I said.

"Well, maybe not," he admitted, "but Marcus should have known; they used to be friends."

"He said Tommy told him it was only a fish fry, nothing else," I said.

"Then he's stupid, too, for believing it," he said savagely, fury filling his voice. I winced; he was basically (if obliquely) calling me stupid right along with Marcus, but I couldn't get mad about it or I'd blow my cover. Oh, I hated this.

"But I don't care who knew what, when. When y'all got to the house and saw for sure what the deal was, then you should have turned around and left right then," he went on, not finished yet.

"I know," I said softly.

"So how come you didn't, then?" he demanded.

"I don't know, Cody. I guess I didn't want to seem like a prude, you know. I didn't want to get ready and go all the way over there just to turn around and go home. I didn't want Marcus to think I was scared; stuff like that. I kept telling myself we could always leave if it seemed like it was too rowdy. What can I tell you, so you won't be mad at me for the rest of my life? Yeah, I know it was stupid, I totally and completely admit it. But haven't you ever talked yourself into doing something even though you knew better, and then regretted it later?" I asked him.

"Yeah, you got me there," he admitted, and for a second the question broke his anger and he sounded utterly lost again.

"I'm sorry, Cody," I said, for what felt like the fortieth time.

"Do you love Marcus?" he asked me, with an edge to his voice. It was the question I'd been dreading to hear, and I'd already made up my mind that I ought to hesitate just long enough to make him think I had feelings for Marcus that I wasn't willing to admit. But when push came right down to shove, I couldn't do it. Even at the risk of wrecking the whole plan, I couldn't bring myself to answer him with anything but the truth.

"No, Cody. I never loved anybody in my whole life except you," I said, knowing what a deep place in his heart those words would touch. They touched him, all right; I could see it on his face. They probably hurt him more than anything else I could have said, too.

"I never loved anybody but you, either, Lisa. That's what makes this so hard, you know. I wanted. . . I always thought. . . " he said, struggling to keep the tears out of his eyes. That shocked me almost more than anything; in all the years I'd known him, I'd never seen Cody crack like that.

I could hear the pain and the grief of loss in his voice, and it was all I could do not to cry out that it was all a horrible lie, to make it not to be. A part of me was dying inside; I could feel it happening. . . some small part of me which had been innocent and pure right up till that moment had winked out like a candle in a winter's draft, and I wondered if I'd ever in my life feel clean again after doing this to him, even to save his life.

"Go home, Lisa," he finally said, thickly.

"What?" I asked.

"Go home. You shouldn't have come here. You and me, we're just not right for each other," he said, and I could tell that he believed it. It was victory, of a sort; the kind of victory that left me with nothing but the taste of blood and a heart full of cold ashes.

"Cody, no. . . don't say that," I said, my voice cracking. But his heart was shut and his mind was made up.

"Come on, I'll take you back to the airport. They ought to change your ticket and let you go back home tonight. I'll pay the fee for you," he said, ignoring me as he got up to put his dirty clothes back on.

"You and me both are better off apart. Wait and see; you'll thank me someday," he added, and I could hear the desolation in his voice when he said it.

I didn't say a word the whole time while we drove back to the airport and changed my ticket, no matter how badly I wanted to speak. If I'd kept talking to him, I don't know but what he might not have broken down and forgiven me, even then, and I didn't dare risk that. We barely made it in time to catch the last flight out for the day, and when it was time to get on board the plane I swallowed hard, but my eyes were dry.

"It's better this way, Lisa, for both of us," he repeated, and then with one last little nod, he turned and walked away.

There was nothing I could do except get on the plane and leave. I did cry then, like I never have in my whole life, but nobody asked me what was wrong or even offered me a tissue. There were only a handful of people on the flight, and the others simply pretended not to notice the girl who was crying her heart out on the third row.

I got myself back together again a little bit by the time we landed in Anchorage, where I had an all-night layover. I'd done Layla Latimer's dirty work for her, and I felt like filth.

Chapter Twenty-Six
Cody

I don't know how, but some way or other I managed to make it back to the motel before I crumbled, and then for the first time since I was a kid, I wept. I cried myself to sleep that night, only to find that my dreams were no better than reality.

I felt like everything I'd ever believed in was nothing but a pipe dream, like I'd been a fool for ever thinking there was such a thing as true love. I should have known better all along. It made me wonder if my whole life up till then had been a naïve delusion.

When I was little, I used to have night terrors. . . those kinds of bad dreams where you wake up breathing hard with your heart racing, thrashing the covers and knowing something horrible was happening, but you can't remember a bit of it. That night I had another one like that for the first time in years, and woke up with fresh tears on my cheeks. God only knows what I was dreaming about. I can't remember, and I'm pretty sure I don't want to.

I went on for days like that, mopey and sad and touchy and apt to drive my fist into the wall at odd times for the stupidest of reasons, and I'm *never* like that. About the third time I busted my knuckles at work, I got written up for having anger problems and they told me if it happened again then I'd get suspended for three days.

I forced myself to get a grip after that. No matter how miserable I was, I still had responsibilities.

Nevertheless, the next few days were torture. I hated my job, I hated life, and I was surly and bad-tempered with everybody. I didn't hit the wall or show it on the surface anymore; I had more self-control than that, but it didn't keep me from wanting to. I was so curt that people started keeping their distance after a while, which only made me feel worse.

Eventually Troy caught up with me in the break room one day with a serious look on his face. I was sitting alone at one of the metal tables (a given, by then), and I had to force myself not to scowl when he sat down across the table from me. Company was the last thing I wanted, even from him.

"Hey, buddy boy. How you been?" he asked.

"Fine," I said automatically, in a tone that probably could have curdled milk. Troy ignored it, like he always does. He's never been the type to take a hint, by any means.

"Cody, I'm worried about you, buddy. You've been down in the mouth for days now, and you snap at anybody who says hi to you. What's up?" he asked.

"Nothing," I said.

"Don't tell me it's nothing. I know better than that. Talk to me, boy," he said, and I could tell he probably wasn't going to leave me alone until he got some kind of explanation.

"It's only a bad break-up, that's all. I'll get over it," I said, trying my best to smile and not doing such a great job of it.

"Yeah, that's bad. Do you want to talk about it?" he asked, and I hesitated. I really didn't, to tell the truth, but I suspected he wasn't going to leave me alone until he found out what the story was. So I told him what happened, more or less, and he nodded sympathetically.

"Anyway, I'll be all right. Just takes a little while, okay?" I finished.

"Yeah, okay. I know how it is," he agreed. I seriously doubted he did, honestly; Troy is the kind of dude who flirts and jokes and plays with all the girls but never takes any of it seriously. It's all just fun and games to him, and I strongly suspect he's never been in love before in his entire life. I always used to think it was kind of a shallow way of looking at things, but now I almost couldn't help but wonder if he was right after all. Love was a joke, and as for all that one-and-only honor-and-faithfulness junk I always said I believed in, well, we see how *that* turned out.

"I'll be fine, Troy. I promise. I just need a little time, that's all," I repeated, trying to make it sound as earnest and convincing as possible.

"Okay, buddy. I'm here if you need me; you know that, right?" he asked.

"Yeah, I know that," I said, relieved to be done with him that easily. There are certain people you can talk to about stuff like that, and there are others. . . well, let's just say they're not very good listeners. Lisa had been really good at that, but Troy was another story completely. He's fun to hang out with, but he's not such a good shoulder to cry on.

Thinking about Lisa didn't help my mood at all, but Troy wouldn't have understood any of that even if I'd tried to explain it.

After a week or so I did manage to get semi-collected again, at least enough not to snap at people when they tried to be friendly.

Once I had a cooler head and was able to think a little more rationally, I started to realize how much of a sacrifice that trip had probably been for Lisa, and how much she must have loved me to go to such lengths to ask my forgiveness. I hadn't handled the situation very well, and I thought several times about maybe giving her a call and saying I was sorry for the way I acted. I remembered what I said about how love is cheap if it won't stand up under pressure, and wondered if I was really such a hypocrite that I couldn't take the heat the very first time I got tested.

But before I could find the right words to say to her, it all turned out to be a moot point when I got the news from Cyrus that she was definitely going out with Marcus. She must have had some feelings for him after all, in spite of what she said before.

That knocked me back all over again, and all the hurt and anger I'd been feeling before came surging right back again for a day or two. But it didn't last near as long this time, mostly replaced by a kind of fatalistic hope that maybe things would work out better this way in the long run. I told myself I'd known all along that she was better off with somebody else, no matter how hard it was for me personally. In fact I ought to be happy for her, if I loved her even half as much as I said I did.

I kept repeating all that until I mostly convinced myself. Deep down in my heart I'm not sure I ever quite managed to make myself believe it, but nobody ever knew about that except me.

Weeks passed, and after a while I managed to come to some kind of terms with the fact that my life would never turn out the way I always thought it would. I felt hollow and empty inside, like I didn't know who I was or what I wanted anymore. I remembered what Mama told me about not losing myself and coming home whole, and for the first time I thought I understood what she meant. I felt like I'd lost entire masses and chunks of myself, my whole heart and half my mind.

In a moment of weakness, I even slipped up and said something about it to her.

"I don't guess you've heard anything from Lisa, have you?" I asked wistfully.

"Not for a while. Why don't you give her a call? You could probably still work things out, if you talked about it for a while," she said. I'd already told her about everything that happened, of course.

"No, that's all right. I just wondered, that's all," I said hastily, afraid she might take matters into her own hands and call Lisa herself. Mama could be bold as brass when she thought the occasion called for it. I didn't want to give her any ideas.

But that was pretty much the only time I slipped up, and for the most part I suffered in silence. I used to like to watch old Westerns sometimes where the cowboy had to bite down on a bullet while they cut an arrow out of him with no anesthesia, and most times he never even let out so much as a whimper. I wonder what he felt when that sharp knife cut down through his flesh, and whether he ever felt like screaming. I guess I'll never know. All I can say is, sometimes you can seem tough as nails on the surface even while you're slowly dying inside.

Chapter Twenty-Seven
Lisa

They routed me through Seattle and Denver before I landed in El Paso. Las Cruces is only about an hour's drive from there, and I didn't want to put off dealing with Layla for a second longer than necessary. The sooner I was done with that scumbag, the sooner I could call Cody and start trying to explain things. I didn't look forward to that conversation either, but I was sure we could work things out if I gave him a little time to think.

I took the shuttle bus from the airport, alighting in the parking lot of the Ramada Palms de Las Cruces. I had to take a taxi from there out to White Sands, and that just about wiped out the last of my cash. But at long last I found myself standing in Layla's living room again, less than a week after the last time I'd been there.

"Ah, there you are, Lisa!" she said, with what seemed to be genuine pleasure.

"Yeah, here I am. Did you break the Curse yet?" I asked, getting right to the point. I had no intention of pretending I liked the girl when I hated her guts.

"Not so fast, hon. Have you got the footage?" she asked. I reluctantly pulled the camera out of my purse and handed it over, waiting while she played back the recording in some little device beside her TV. She seemed to be awfully tech-savvy.

She watched the entire video right there in front of me in her living room, to my intense shame. I never wanted to think about that scene again for the rest of my life. But at last she seemed satisfied.

"Ah, that was beautiful. Truly beautiful," she said dreamily, as if she'd just witnessed something of exceptional power and delight.

"Can you break the Curse now, please?" I asked, almost frantic to be done so I could leave the place.

"Sure, no hurry. Here you go," she said, handing me a small tube of green liquid. It reminded me of antifreeze.

"What am I supposed to do with it?" I asked tightly.

"Just have him drink it, that's all. Might be a little bitter, but mind he doesn't spit it out," she said.

"Thanks," I said, and then started to get up from my seat.

"Just one more thing, sweetie," she said, and my heart filled with dread.

"What's that?" I asked.

"You might be thinking you can make things up with Cody at some point in the future. I'm afraid I'd have no choice but to see that as a deliberate breach of our agreement. If that ever happened, I think I might have to reinstate the curse, among other things," she said mildly.

"But you can't. . . " I began, and then trailed off. She *could,* and there was nothing I could do about it.

"Yes?" she asked, with one brow raised and a hateful smirk on her face. One last twist of the knife, the final cherry on top of her delectable feast.

"Nothing," I whispered.

"Good. I'm so glad we understand each other. It's been a real pleasure doing business with you, Lisa. And remember, I'll be watching!" she said pleasantly, and I couldn't think of a single word to answer her.

So I said nothing at all, and fled.

* * * * * * *

By the time I got back to Ore City, I'd had ample time to think about Layla's parting shot and what it might mean. Part of me wanted to scream and cuss in despair, and part of me whispered that maybe all this was a sign that I wasn't supposed to be with Cody, after all.

I didn't know what to do, honestly. I'd hoped that sooner or later Cody would come to understand why I had to lie to him and we'd be able to put the whole episode behind us and live happily ever after. But now. . . well, *that* was never going to happen, that was for sure. I didn't know what else Layla might do, but I seriously doubted she'd be content just to reinstate the curse. She'd come up with something even worse than that next time, if only for the pleasure of tormenting us.

I told myself I could live with the consolation that at least Cody would live a long life, even if it turned out to be with some other girl, and that his children and grandchildren would never again have to worry about the Curse hanging over their heads. It was cold comfort, but better than none at all. It reminded me of what he said when he talked about why he wrote *Nebo's Crossing*, about how sometimes you can't always have the things you want the most, even if it breaks your heart to give them up, so the people you love can have them later.

Ever since I was little, I always thought I'd have a fairytale wedding to my one true love, my Tristan, my Albert. . . my Cody. Never in my worst nightmares had I imagined anything like the situation I found myself in, making serious plans to give up everything I ever dreamed of in life, because it would kill him if I didn't.

I cried till my eyes hurt and there were no more tears left to cry, and I told myself it was worth the price of giving him up; it *was*.

It was a shame my heart didn't believe it.

I called Marcus when I got back home, and told him what happened.

"Do you think you can handle all that?" he asked.

"I have to. I'm fixing to go give the serum to Miss Josie, so she can have him drink it when he comes home for Christmas," I said.

"Why don't you just wait and do it yourself?" he asked.

"Because then I'd have to explain everything to him, and I'm already afraid he might change his mind about wanting to break up. You know how he is. He'll cool off and start feeling bad after a while, and then there's no telling what he might do. I can't let that happen or it'll all be for nothing," I said. I wasn't entirely sure that's how things would play out; Cody had seemed pretty firm when I left Prudhoe Bay. He might never speak to me again for the rest of my life, for all I knew. But I had to be sure.

"Well, yeah, true. I guess he might," Marcus agreed.

"That's why I think you and me should pretend we're really together for a while, till he decides to give up," I said, hoping he'd agree.

"I don't like that, Lisa. It was bad enough having to lie to him in the first place, without keeping on and on with it. It makes things really awkward out here. I might even lose my job, and they're too hard to come by," he said.

"It's not for long, Marcus. Only till I can think of something better," I explained, and he sighed.

"Okay. For a little while," he agreed.

"Thanks, Marcus. You're the best," I said, gratefully.

It was a little bit late to head over to the big house, but I didn't think Miss Josie would mind. She'd probably be watching TV, or some other quiet, domestic kind of thing like that.

I knocked on the door, and Miss Josie looked considerably less happy to see me than usual. That saddened me, but it was hardly unexpected.

"What is it, Lisa?" she asked, not unkindly. No doubt she'd already heard the whole story about what happened in Alaska, but she probably also remembered what I told her ahead of time about having to tell Cody some things that weren't true. She probably didn't know what to think, at this point.

"I came to bring you something. For Cody," I clarified, and she wordlessly stepped aside to let me in.

"I talked to Cody last night. I didn't tell him what you said about having to lie to him, but I want you to know I don't approve. I don't think you realize how badly you hurt him the other day," she said, frowning.

"Yes, ma'am, I do know. It was the only way to get this," I said, pulling the tube of liquid out of my purse.

"What's that?" she asked.

"It's the cure for the Curse. You need to have him drink it. I was told it might be a little bitter, but he needs to finish it all," I said, offering the tube. Miss Josie took it, holding it up to the light.

"But what is it? Where did it come from?" she asked.

"All I know is that it's supposed to break the Curse. I got it from a woman named Layla Latimer, out in New Mexico. Breaking up with Cody was her price for giving it to me," I said flatly.

"That doesn't make any sense," Miss Josie said.

"It would if you knew the woman. She's the most evil person I ever heard of. She likes to see people suffer. She made me wear a camera when I went up to Alaska, so she could watch me and Cody break up and enjoy how hurtful it was. I *had* to do it, Miss Josie; it was the only way she'd work with me," I explained.

"I can't believe you'd agree to such a thing," she said, shaking her head.

"I did it for Cody's sake. There was no other way," I said. I couldn't tell what she thought about that; maybe she thought I'd lost my mind.

"So have you called to tell him all this, at least?" she asked.

"I can't. Miss Latimer told me if I ever got back together with Cody that she'd put the curse back on him. Kind of like if I undo the breakup then she'll undo the cure. He can never know. Me and Marcus are gonna pretend to be together for a while, so he won't wonder why I won't talk to him. That's why I brought this to you. I'm sure you can think of a reason why he should drink it. It's not safe for me to see him," I said.

"Sweetie. . . I'm so sorry," Miss Josie said, putting a hand on my arm.

"Yeah, me too. I love him so much. It's hard to believe it's got to end like this," I said.

Miss Josie looked at me, like she was thinking about something.

"Lisa, can I tell you a story?" she finally asked.

"Yeah, I guess," I said.

"Do you know how Marcus ended up coming here to live with us?" she asked.

"Well. . . no, now that you mention it, I guess I don't," I admitted.

"It's because his father is an alcoholic. When Marcus was eighteen, his father got drunk and beat him up pretty badly and threw him out of the house. On Christmas Day, no less. I gather it wasn't the first time, from what Marcus has told me. But it so happened that Cody had a dream about it the night before, and found him sitting in the park that afternoon in his bedclothes with nowhere to go. Thank God it was fairly warm outside that year. But we brought him back here, and gave him some clothes, and we fed him and gave him a job on the ranch, and a place to live. He's been here ever since," she said.

"I never knew that," I said.

"No, he never talks about it very much. But the point is, it all came right in the end. Sometimes when things seem like they couldn't possibly get any worse, that's exactly when God has something good up His sleeve," she said.

"I wish I could be as sure as you are," I said.

"I know it may not look that way right now. I know you can't see how any of this could ever turn out for the good. But it will, I promise you. Marcus was a lost boy once, with nowhere to go and not much to hope for, pretty much like you're probably feeling right this minute. But sometimes the lost can be found, in the most unlikely ways. Now he has a place of his own, and work that he enjoys, and he's probably happier than he ever would have been if his father had never kicked him out. Have faith that everything will work out for the best. Things will be all right, for you and Cody both," she said.

I thought about that, and I guess she had a point. I didn't see how things could ever be right again, but it's true that God can do wonderful things. I believe in miracles, here and now. But short of a miracle, I didn't see how Cody and I could ever be together again, let alone how I could ever be happy apart from him. Miss Josie's story gave me the barest glimmer of hope, but not much more than that.

"Do you think Cody would even want me back, after all this?" I asked. What rich irony it would be if somehow Layla ended up getting eaten alive by a miraculous swarm of vicious fire ants, but then Cody decided he didn't want to get back together again anyway. I was ninety percent sure I could win him back if I ever had the chance, but ten percent doubt is plenty enough for your nerves to dance on, believe me.

"Cody is hurting right now, Lisa. Put yourself in his shoes and imagine how he must feel. But give him time. He can be stubborn and even foolish sometimes, but he does have a gentle heart when he's put to the test that way. He's not the type to hold a grudge," she said.

That was true, as far as it went. I don't think I ever really doubted that, or I wouldn't have felt like I needed to pretend to be going out with Marcus. The thought made me relax a little bit.

"He reminds me so much of Blake, sometimes. He was always noble like that, too. Even before we got married, he always told me he wanted our house to be a refuge for the hurting and a place of peace. . . a place where the lost could be found and the brokenhearted find happiness, as much as it lay within our power to give it to them. That was his dream, and the thing I always loved most about him. I've tried to live up to that, and to teach Cody the same. It hasn't always been easy," she said, and I saw that her eyes were full. I'd never seen Miss Josie get teary-eyed before, and I thought to myself how much pain this woman must have been through, and how incredibly strong she must be to have lived the life she'd chosen for herself.

I'd never heard any of those stories before, and they touched my heart. I hadn't known that Marcus had been a throwaway kid, or that Cody had rescued him, or why. I'd never known that there was any vision for Goliad except an ordinary horse and cattle ranch. I hadn't known so many things.

Suddenly I understood a little better Cody's fierce love for this place. It wasn't just the dirt in his blood, although that was part of it. It was also part and parcel with his greatness of heart, the very thing which (I now realized) was what I'd always loved most about him from the very beginning. I'd seen it when he talked about love that day by the lake. I'd seen it when he laughed and kissed me for asking him to give Brandon a place to stay, almost like I was the one doing *him* a favor. I saw it now in what he'd done for Marcus. Even that story about bottle-feeding Buck when he was a colt; it was all of a piece.

I heard a sermon on the radio once, about finding the things your mate treasures and learning how to bask in the reflected glory of his heart. On some level I think I always knew that. Maybe deep down everybody knows it. But I'd never thought of how it should apply to my own life. Right then, for just a moment, it was clear as crystal in my mind. Cody was a giver, one who poured out his life for others, and that kind of man never falls in love at all unless it's with a girl whose heart is just as great as his own.

The fact that Cody must have believed I was that kind of girl humbled and thrilled me at the same time, and I loved him more in that moment that I ever had before. Whole entire orders of magnitude greater; it was like everything I'd ever felt for him in the past was no more than hints and trifles in comparison, like turning from the morning stars to the blazing sun at noon. I caught a glimpse, for just a moment, of the kind of life we might have had together, for no one on this earth tastes near as much of Heaven as a man and woman who join hands to love the world as God does. Even the glimpse of it was enough to take my breath away, and I could truly understand for the first time exactly how Miss Josie must have felt about Blake.

Then I remembered why I was sitting there in Miss Josie's kitchen right then, and I felt more loss and hurt than I could ever have thought possible. In spite of my determination to be strong, I found myself crying, and none of her attempts to comfort me were any use.

Chapter Twenty-Eight
Lisa

"You've got to get ahold of yourself, sis," Jenny told me one day, after about a week of moping and crying.

"You just don't know what it's like," I said bleakly, hugging my knees while we sat on my bed.

"Yeah. . . actually I do. Believe me, you're not the first girl who ever had a broken heart, and I'm pretty sure you won't be the last one, either," Jenny said.

"But-" I said.

"No buts, sister. You can't keep wallowing like this. It's not healthy, and besides that it doesn't help. Cry over him for a few days, sure, and then let him go," Jenny said.

She didn't understand, of course; it was absolutely impossible that she'd ever felt anything like this. How could she possibly know what I was going through?

"You don't understand," I repeated.

"What do I not understand?" Jenny asked, and I hesitated. There was no way I could explain things to her, even if I'd wanted to.

"Let it alone, sis. I'll be all right," I told her, making an effort to smile. Jenny looked at me doubtfully, and then nodded.

"All right, then. But if I ever see that scumbag again, I'm giving him a piece of my mind!" she said, and in spite of everything I almost had to laugh. Jenny would probably do it, too, and Cody would probably listen respectfully with his hat in his hand and then never pay it another bit of attention.

"Whatever you say," I told her.

"What you need to do is get up out of this bed, get gussied up a little bit, and go out on the town tonight," Jenny declared.

"Go out on the town? In Ore City?" I asked skeptically.

"Sure, why not? It doesn't matter where, as long as you get out of this stuffy house and live a little. Even if all we do is go to the Dairy Dip and have a double chocolate sundae," she suggested.

The thought was appalling; I didn't know if I'd ever be able to set foot in the Dairy Dip again.

"No, not there," I said quickly.

"Yeah, you're right. Over-rated, anyway. We'll go to the soda fountain at the drug store in Gilmer instead," she said.

I considered it, and decided maybe Jenny was right. I had to stop wallowing, and maybe getting out a little bit would help take my mind off Cody for a while. Heaven knows I was ready to think about something else for a change. And honestly, how often does a good excuse for eating a double chocolate sundae come along?

I took a deep breath and got up from the bed.

"Atta girl!" Jenny said approvingly.

I took a shower for the first time in days and fixed my hair, and decided I really did feel better. Then we told Mama where we were going and headed downtown.

We had our sundae, and then took a walk downtown and browsed in some of the shops for a while. It was a sunny, breezy day, not nearly as chilly as usual, and a good day for outdoorsy things. I found a pair of silver spangled shoes that looked very nice, I thought, and a bracelet that matched them perfectly.

For a little while, I really did manage to forget about Cody, or at least to think about him less. That is, till I saw a young man with his girlfriend on the sidewalk in front of us, wearing a white straw hat just like the one Cody liked to wear. That undid me. I started crying again, and had to get Jenny to take me home.

I gradually got better over the next two or three weeks, but now and then little things like that white straw hat kept tripping me up. I'd see a boy with a horsehair belt, or pass some place where I'd talked to Cody on the phone, or some other trivial thing like that, and it would set me off again. It was awful.

And even though I slowly seemed to be getting better on the surface, down deep I really wasn't. True enough, I finally got to the point that I didn't cry anymore, and I could go to work and function pretty normally for a change. I could pass by the table at the Dairy Dip where he'd carved our names and not fall to pieces, for example. So yeah, things went back to normal in some ways. But way down deep, in the very heart of my heart so to speak, Cody was still there just as much as he always had been. I was beginning to think he always would be.

I made an effort to go out with Marcus once in a while and be seen in public, but that was fake and empty and I hated the pretense.

Jenny knew I still had Cody on my mind, and I think she found the whole situation incomprehensible. She kept telling me I ought to be happy with Marcus, or if not him then I ought to go out and meet some new guys till I found one ten times better than Cody ever was. She kept telling me there are plenty of fish in the sea. And maybe there were, for her. Maybe even for most people. But for me, there'd never be anyone at all but Cody McGrath. I knew it as surely as I knew my own name.

Maybe I *would* end up an eccentric old spinster who talked to her tomato plants, I thought to myself. It was supposed to be a joke, but it wasn't funny. I still clung tenaciously to the forlorn hope that somehow, someday we'd find a way to be together and put this whole horrible experience behind us, however unlikely that seemed. Tristan the Brave may have gotten his princess sooner or later, but I wasn't at all sure my own Tristan would ever get his.

I still had his high school ring. He'd forgotten to ask for it back. I took it off my finger and put it on a chain around my neck instead, so it would always rest right next to my heart. I didn't think that was too over-the-top; it's not like anyone could see it there. No one even knew about it except me. And maybe it was stupid, but every night before I went to sleep I kissed that ring and blew it toward the window, and imagined my kiss traveling all the way up there to Alaska, and slipping through his window, and landing right on his lips while he slept. And when it did, I hoped he thought of me, and smiled in his sleep.

Yeah, fantasy life big-time. I knew it even then. But that was all right, because I kept it all to myself and didn't breathe a word of how I really felt to anyone. It was simply my own little private sorrow.

I tried to keep busy. I took refuge in painting or gardening or writing poetry or anything else I could think of; anything to keep me from brooding too much. It helped a little, at least as much as anything did.

Which is to say, not much at all.

I did talk to Brandon sometimes, since nobody else seemed to understand. I had to go out there to Goliad occasionally for appearances' sake, ostensibly to visit Marcus. But there were times when I couldn't bear to actually see him, let alone Miss Josie. So on days like that I'd sit with Bran in the barn to keep him company while he did his chores after school. He was the only one who didn't make me feel guilty. Not that the others did it on purpose, you know; it was just the way I felt.

We never talked about Cody very much, but he knew at least part of what was going on, even if he didn't understand exactly why. We were sitting in the hayloft one day when he finally said something to me about it. The window faced north across the pasture, and many thousands of miles away that's where Cody was. I guess Bran must have noticed my glances in that direction, however surreptitious I thought they were.

"Everything will be fine. Don't worry," he said.

"Yeah, I'm sure it will. But when you love somebody then your heart is wherever they are, no matter what. That's the way it works. You'll meet somebody special one of these days and then you'll know what I mean," I said. I could say all that to

Bran because I knew he wouldn't repeat it, but the thought made me sad.

"Lana's pretty special," he said, and that was a welcome distraction from thinking about Cody.

"So tell me about her, then," I said.

"She's really smart. She got a scholarship to come here because she did such a good job in school where she's from," he said.

"Where is she from, anyway?" I asked.

"Vyborg. Close to Saint Petersburg. That's where she grew up all her life," he said.

"Really? What do her parents do?" I asked.

"Her dad's a dentist and her mom is a secretary, and she's got one brother and one sister but she's the oldest," he said.

"Sounds nice. How long will she be here? Just a year, right?" I asked.

"Maybe two. She said she might convince her dad to pay for another year so she can learn English better, 'cause he thinks it'll help her get into a better college and find a better job someday. He's got plenty of money so it's all good," he said.

"Maybe so," I agreed.

"I hope she gets to stay another year. I really like her," he said.

"It sounds like it," I said.

"She said she likes my muscles," he confided, striking a pose to show me his biceps. I couldn't help laughing.

"I'm sure she does, Bran. You're an awfully good-looking boy," I said, still smiling.

"Yup," he agreed, smiling himself.

"Hey, now, you're not supposed to agree with that. You're supposed to blow it off and mumble something under your breath about why it's not really true," I said.

"Why should I lie, though?" he asked. He was joking, of course, but I was glad to see it. When he first came here, Bran never smiled or laughed at all. Ever. Even now it's like a ray of sunshine in some gray and overcast land where the clouds never fade. But when he does, you can't help but smile back.

"Aw, shut up before you get yourself slapped, boy," I said. He could be a pain sometimes, but I was really glad to have him around at times like that.

It crossed my mind that he wouldn't have been, if Daddy hadn't abandoned my mother and Jenny and me. That was the worst thing that ever happened in my whole life, I think. But now I was getting an unexpected reminder that God can and will turn even the most hurtful things into a blessing. I had living proof of it, sitting right there beside me.

God is good that way; sometimes His love brushes your cheek like a gentle caress, at times when you need it desperately and in ways you never would have guessed. It gave me hope that even this whole horrible mess with Cody would turn out well, even if I couldn't see how.

I hoped I could manage to remember that.

Chapter Twenty-Nine
Lisa

Three weeks later there came a day I went out to Goliad and found Brandon and Marcus both gone for some reason. I found myself all alone for the first time in a while, and, not surprisingly, missing Cody more than usual.

It was only an impulse, but I decided for some reason to go talk to Miss Josie again. I couldn't have said exactly why; a melancholy, self-torturing wish to hear a little bit about how he was doing, maybe, or a wistful desire to be near some of his things and the places he loved. It made me feel closer to him, if only for a little while. Goes to show how well I was doing apart from him, doesn't it?

I hadn't been back to the main house ever since I gave her the serum, mostly because I was afraid it would seem awkward at best and probably hurtful, too. But now; well, I decided I didn't really care about all that anymore. If it turned out to be awkward and painful then so be it. I'd been through worse things lately.

So I circled back around, and as I drove through the main arch I couldn't help remembering the first time I ever set foot on that place, with Cody fixing the fence in his sweaty white t-shirt under the hot summer sun. I knew the very spot where he'd been standing, and if I closed my eyes I could almost imagine he was right there, close enough to touch. I could see the dark stubble on his chin, the nails he'd been holding in his mouth to leave his hands free, even the sawdust on his jeans. But most of all the light in his eyes when he saw me and smiled. It was all there in memory, even though it seemed like centuries ago.

I needed to quit thinking like that or I'd be an emotional wreck before I ever even set foot on the porch.

The place was quiet, and when I parked the car under the pecan tree in the circle drive and headed up the steps, I wondered if maybe nobody was home. I had no particular plan in mind, and found myself wondering what in the world I'd say to Miss Josie even if she was there.

She was, though, and when she opened the door it turned out I didn't have to think of anything to say, because she smiled warmly and beat me to it.

"Lisa! Come on in here, girl. How have you been?" she asked, stepping aside and inviting me in. I hesitated for a second, unsure, but then decided it would have been stupid to back out at that point. Talking to Miss Josie was exactly what I'd come for, after all. I stepped inside the foyer, and she shut the door behind us.

"Come on back to the kitchen and let's have some coffee; what do you say?" she said.

"I'd love some," I said automatically, following her to the kitchen. She started fixing the drinks while I sat down at the table, and all the while she kept talking.

"So tell me, what have you been up to? Haven't seen you since... oh, it's been *weeks* now, hasn't it?" she asked.

"I've been fine. Just working, mostly. How's Cody?" I asked. I'd meant to be a little more discreet and indirect than that, but somehow I couldn't help myself.

"Well, pretty good, I guess. He said it's dark almost all the time now, so he mostly holes up in his room and watches TV when he's off work. He said the food is pretty good but he misses Goliad something fierce. He asked about you the other day," she said, and my heart skipped a beat at that news.

"He did?" I asked, trying not to let it show how much that idea thrilled me and terrified me at the same time.

"He did. He asked if I'd heard from you lately, but of course at that time I hadn't," she said, coming back to the table with a cup of coffee for both of us.

"Did you tell him about the serum?" I asked.

"No. I thought it was best to wait till he gets home," she said.

"I really miss him," I admitted, and then wished I hadn't said it. It threatened to unleash more tears, and I didn't want that. Miss Josie looked at me sympathetically, and I couldn't help wondering what was going through her mind at that moment. I was afraid to guess.

I noticed for the first time that she still wore a wedding band even after all these years, and since talking about Cody was unbearable right then, I snatched at the chance to change the subject.

"Could you tell me some more about Blake?" I asked, nodding my head at the ring.

"Well, there's not much to tell, really. We knew each other forever, of course. We both grew up here in Avinger, him at Goliad and me down the road a little way. He gave me my first kiss when we were in kindergarten, I'm told. I don't even remember it, honestly, but my mother told me the story so many times it almost seems like a memory. Then we got together officially when we were in seventh grade, as soon as our parents would let us have anything even resembling a date. Nobody thought it would amount to anything; just puppy love, they thought. And I'm sure they were right. But sometimes puppy love grows into something more as the years go by. It did for us. He always had a silly side; I remember he kissed me for probably thirty minutes one time, right by the highway down there on the corner where everybody in town could see us and honk when they went by. He just laughed, and since he did, why shouldn't I? But it was always his heart that I loved the most, the way he loved God and tried to do what he could to make the world a better place. He was special. Oh, I know everybody always says that, but Blake really was. We got married the day after we graduated high school, and nobody thought that would last, either. But here I am, almost twenty-three years later, still just as much in love as I ever was. And if Blake were still here, I know he would be, too. People ask me sometimes why I don't go out after all this time, but how could I ever be satisfied with steel after I've once held gold? I'm spoiled forever," she said, with a little laugh.

"That's an awesome story," I said.

"I never used to think it was anything unusual, but maybe so," Miss Josie agreed.

We sat there and talked for at least an hour, and I wondered to myself why I'd put off visiting for so long. It was exactly what I needed. . . red meat and strong drink after all those weeks of nothing.

"Do you think it'd be all right if we went down to the bunk house for a little while?" I asked presently. I was calm enough by then that I thought I could hold things together. Cody's things weren't Cody, but they were as close as I could get at the moment, and that was better than nothing. Miss Josie must have understood, because she didn't start asking me all kinds of questions about why.

"I don't think Cody would mind if we took a sneak peek," she agreed, and together we crossed the pasture and the woods to the bunk house.

The moment I stepped inside his room, I felt enveloped in memory.

I could tell no one had been in there for a while, but there was still a faint scent of that knock-off Old Spice he liked. He still had the same quilt on the bed, and everything else was pretty much the same, too.

I noticed he'd left his boots standing beside the dresser, and his horsehair belt was still hung up on a nail right above them. The golden letter C on his buckle looked dull and forlorn, abandoned by its owner. His body might be in Alaska, but his heart was still in Texas. I could see that just from looking at everything he'd left behind.

Above his bed was the painting I made of that sunrise scene at Mount Nebo, and right there in the middle of his knickknack shelf, in a red cedar frame, was a picture of me.

Well, a picture of both of us, anyway. I recognized it immediately; it was one of the snapshots Miss Josie had taken when I came over for supper that first night. We were leaning against the pecan tree in the center of the circle drive, with his arm around my shoulder. He had one knee bent, with his boot planted flat against the tree behind us. We were both smiling, and I was overcome with emotion again. Miss Josie was watching me.

"Why don't you take that with you, sweetie? I can always have another one printed, next time I make it to town. The frame, too; I know where he got it," she suggested.

"You don't think he'd mind?" I asked.

"No, I don't think so," she promised.

"Thanks," I said simply, resisting the urge to hug the picture close to my chest.

"Don't mention it," she said.

We headed back up to the big house not long after that, and I lingered for a while longer, not wanting to go home.

"Now, Lisa, I want you to come back and see me as much as you want to. No need to call ahead or anything; just poke your head in the door and give me a yell whenever you come to see your brother. I'm almost always here, unless I'm outside somewhere," she told me, right before I left.

"I'll do that," I agreed, liking the idea.

"Good," she said.

I put the picture of me and Cody beside my bed when I got home, subjecting myself to withering scorn from Jenny as soon as she saw it. For once I guess it was hard to blame her, since supposedly I was still going out with Marcus. I don't know what she thought, honestly. All I know is that for a while she wasted no opportunity to mock me about it, calling me a cheap dime-store floozie and telling me I was no better than Sheila Jackson or any of those other girls I used to think were so trashy, and on, and on, and unendingly on. I couldn't explain what was really going on without blowing my cover, but I refused to take down Cody's picture even if it hare-lipped every cow in Texas. All I could do was try to ignore her for a while, but after a few days it really started to tick me off.

We had some harsh words. I told her she was jealous because she wanted him herself and couldn't have him, to which she said it didn't look like I had him either, and things deteriorated from there. She ended up storming off to her room and slamming the door hard enough to rattle the windows, while I tried to suppress an overpowering urge to choke her to death with my bare hands as soon as she showed her face again.

It never actually came to blows, but we barely spoke to each other for days after that, and the atmosphere in the house was so icy you could have made popsicles by leaving them out on the coffee table when both of us were in the room.

Sometimes I wish life didn't have to be so complicated.

Brandon must have been thinking about what I said about Cody, because next time I talked to him he had an idea for me.

"Why don't you ask for a dream to show you what to do?" he finally said one day.

"What do you mean?" I asked.

"I mean I can see you're chewed to pieces inside, like a pit bull got ahold of your heart and tore it up like a cheap rug. You've been that way for weeks. So why don't you pray about it? Lots of people have dreams and visions, you know, not just Cody," he pointed out. Comparing my heart to a cheap rug wasn't the most flattering statement he could have made, but at least it was brutally honest.

"Well, yeah, I guess they do," I admitted. I hadn't thought about it much, honestly, but I couldn't deny that what Bran said was true. But he wasn't finished yet.

"Did I ever tell you how I started reading dreams?" he asked.

"No, I don't think so," I said.

"A long time ago, when I was four years old, I died for a while," he said calmly.

"Really?" I asked, not sure what to think about such a statement.

"Yeah, really. No breathing, no heartbeat, cold as ice, for almost two hours," he said.

"So, what, did you fall through some ice or something like that?" I asked. Everybody has heard of little kids surviving cold-water drownings and such, so that wouldn't have been so shocking.

"No, I had pneumonia. They knew I was dead; they already took me to the morgue and everything. I don't remember very much about it, honestly, but from what I heard later my brother and his wife prayed over me and I came back to life. The only thing I remember for sure is that God told me I had a job to do, and He sent me back. Ever since then, I've been able to see what dreams mean, if I ask Him," he said.

It was the first time Bran had ever confided that story in me, and I guess I was still a little speechless.

"Well, I'm glad you're still alive," I said.

"Yeah, me too. But I'm telling you that for a reason. I can't tell you what dreams mean because there's anything special about *me*. It's only because I ask. Sometimes you have to ask for things or you won't get them. So maybe if you ask, you might get," he said.

There was some truth in that, too, so I went home and prayed hard that night. But just because you ask doesn't *always* mean you get what you want, and certainly not always right away. That was one of those times for me. All my prayers were to no avail, it seemed. No dreams came, and there was nothing but the quiet night to lie wakeful and sad in.

Sometimes it's easy to feel paralyzed when there's absolutely nothing you can think of to do. So I did my work and thought and prayed constantly that somehow, some way, I could have Cody back, no matter what I had to do. I prayed till I thought my mind was exhausted. I believe if it had gone on much longer, the stress would have turned me gray-headed.

But sometimes prayers get answered in ways you don't expect, and that's the way this one turned out.

Chapter Thirty
Lisa

    I tried to make it look good with Marcus. I really did. Whenever we went out we held hands, and I kissed him now and then even though that part was awfully hard, and we mouthed all the words that people expected to hear. The only time we could drop the pretense was when we got back to Goliad and there were no witnesses. Miss Josie knew the truth, and in spite of her disapproval we both knew she wouldn't say anything. We had to put on an especially good show whenever Cyrus was around, because he told Cody everything. I hated those episodes even worse than the ones in public, and I'm pretty sure Marcus did too. But I smiled and nodded and let everybody think we were a perfect couple, even though my heart was a thousand miles away.

    Christmas put me in a bad mood, mostly because I knew Cody was in town. It was easy enough to stay away from Goliad for a while, but the thought of accidentally bumping into him somewhere else was always on my mind. I couldn't imagine what we might say to each other if that happened. Poor Marcus didn't have a choice in the matter, and that only made me feel worse.

    I tried to take my mind off things by painting, and reading, or mulching the cabbages and broccoli that were still left in the garden. The weather report was calling for a strong cold front to sweep through sometime within the next week, with snow and ice and killing frost, so I had to make sure my vegetables were protected. It helped to while away the time, but unfortunately it didn't do a thing to help me forget the fact that Cody was only fifteen miles away. Nothing could do that, apparently.

I wondered if Miss Josie had given him the green vial yet. I hoped so, but I was reluctant to ask Marcus to find out.

We ended up having a very subdued celebration on Christmas Day, with no one there except me and Jenny and Mama. Jenny was in between boyfriends at the time, and even though I thought about asking Marcus over, I simply couldn't face the thought of any more intrigue and deception at the moment. So it was just the three of us, and I guess that was all right. Mama seemed more tired than usual and only picked at her food, even though I'd baked a ham and made all her favorite things to entice her.

The next morning I was supposed to go to work at the Dairy Dip, since they always needed extra staff over the holidays and God knows I needed the cash. But when the next day rolled around I woke up feeling awful, almost like I was coming down with the flu; my head hurt, my body ached, and I had a fever and swollen lymph nodes. I popped a few Tylenols and went on to work anyway, taking it easy because I still felt terrible even with the medicine. Somehow I managed to make it through the day.

A few days later I felt worse, and I finally succumbed to misery and took refuge in my bed, hoping the fever and aches would go away in a day or two. I thought about going to the doctor, but I strongly suspected they wouldn't do anything anyway except tell me to get some rest and drink plenty of fluids. If you already know what they'll say then why waste your time or money?

Three days after Christmas, the threatened front finally swept through, turning things bitterly cold and snowy and nasty for several days, which did nothing to help me feel better. I talked to Marcus or Brandon occasionally, and sometimes that cheered me up a little bit before bedtime, but there was really nothing anybody could do except let me suffer through it.

Then, on the morning of New Year's Eve, Mama had another stroke.

Naturally it was a holiday weekend and there was no doctor I could get hold of, and Jenny was gone to an early party with her friends and had her phone turned off. In desperation, I called Marcus.

"Marcus, get over here, *now!*" I screamed into the phone.

"What's wrong?" he asked, sounding scared. But then, I guess I would have been, too, if somebody called me up screaming.

"Mama's had another stroke. I need to get her to the hospital," I said.

"I'll be right there," he said, and I spent the next few minutes trying to get Mama ready to go. It was hard, with no help and still being as sick as I was, but somehow I managed it.

When Marcus finally got there and saw the condition I was in, it must have shocked him.

"You look awful, Lisa," he said, staring at me.

"Yeah, I feel like it, too. But that's not important right now. Come on, let's get Mama out to the truck," I said.

I was weaker than I thought, and eventually Marcus literally had to carry my mother out to the truck and put her in the seat wrapped in an old quilt to keep her warm, and then drive all the way into Longview to the nearest emergency room.

To make things worse it was snowing hard again, and he had to drive slower than a snail even on the highway.

It was over before we got even halfway there; Mama slumped over and stopped breathing, and there was no way I could reach her to do artificial respiration. Not unless we stopped and got out so I'd have more room.

"Stop!" I yelled at Marcus in a panic, and he hit the brakes, sliding on patchy ice before he came to a halt on the shoulder. He pulled off the road as much as possible, switching the flashers on. But before I even had a chance to get my door open, a car came out of nowhere in the snow and t-boned Marcus's truck as we sat there. It happened so fast it was over even before I realized what was going on. For a few seconds there was nothing but noise and cold and the truck flipping over and glass smashing, and then silence.

It didn't knock me out, but it dazed me; the truck was sitting at a crazy angle against the embankment, with shattered glass and blood everywhere; whether mine or Marcus's or Mama's, I had no idea. I looked over and saw Marcus lying very still, whether dead or unconscious I didn't know and honestly couldn't summon the energy to care. Icy cold wind was blowing in through the smashed windshield, showering me with snow. The foul smell of hot antifreeze was everywhere. I had an idle thought that we must be close to the same place where Linda McGrath had died all those years ago. I wondered if this was how her last minutes had passed, and what Cody would think when he heard about it.

I don't remember much after that, except in fits and starts. I vaguely realized I was bleeding a lot from a deep gash in my thigh, and I was light-headed and drifted in and out of awareness. I dimly remember somebody pulling me out of the truck and putting me in an ambulance, and when they got me to the hospital they wheeled me off for some kind of procedure to stop me from bleeding. I got hysterical again when they wouldn't tell me anything about Mama, and they had to knock me out before they could even do what they needed to do.

Chapter Thirty-One
Cody

I had a quiet vacation, for the most part. My last day at work was the twenty-first of December, and I got back to Goliad late the next afternoon.

I was glad to be home, gladder than I'd ever felt in my life, to tell the truth, but I can't deny that things were different. I felt like an empty shell of myself, nothing at all like the kid who left Texas four months ago. I didn't see the world in the same way anymore, and I didn't think I ever would.

Mama could see it the second I walked in, of course, but, being Mama, she only hugged me and fussed over me for a while without mentioning it. But after things settled down, she pulled me aside for a talk.

"You look sad, son. What's wrong?" she asked. I knew better than to tell her it was nothing; she'd shoot that down without blinking an eye.

"I guess I'm still a little messed up about Lisa, that's all," I said, truthfully.

"Yeah, I thought that's what it might be," she said.

"Can't blame me, can you? I mean, after everything that happened," I added, and she looked troubled.

"No, I don't blame you for anything. But if you're still missing her so much, why don't you give her a call?" she finally suggested.

"I don't know if she'd even talk to me, after the way things went last time. Besides, she's with Marcus now," I said, scandalized.

"She's not married, is she?" she asked.

"Well... no," I admitted.

"So call her, then. Even better, go see her. You know where she lives. If you tell her how you feel and apologize for some things, you might get her back, you know," she said.

I toyed with the idea for a minute, but the wave of pain and sadness that came over me when I thought about Lisa was more than I wanted to deal with.

"It's better if I leave it alone, I think," I said.

"Why is it better?" she asked.

"Because it is," I said, and realized that was no explanation at all. I didn't really have an explanation, other than the fact that after you've finally managed to close the covers on a painful and messy episode in your life, you're not usually eager to reopen that book all over again, not even for the sake of improving the outcome.

She searched my face, and she must have seen that my mind was made up.

"I can't make you talk to her if you don't want to, Cody. But I think you'll be sorry someday if you don't at least try," she said.

"I'll think about it," I finally said, just to get away from the uncomfortable topic.

And I did think about it now and then, sort of, but I couldn't decide what I wanted to do or whether to talk to her or not. It wasn't that I thought we'd have a big, nasty fight or anything. Quite the opposite. I was sure we'd both be perfectly civil to each other. We'd probably say all the proper things, telling each other that everything was just fine and burying the hatchet at least in words. But even though we might *say* all that, I didn't really believe it. I was inclined to think nothing could ever be right again, after all that had happened.

I didn't have much choice but to talk to Marcus occasionally, awkward as that was. But we kept it brief and strictly businesslike; two coworkers who didn't much like each other. I didn't think *that* relationship could ever be the same again, either. Losing my best friend made me sad, too, and there were times when I got the feeling Marcus was hurt almost as much as I was. But what else did he expect?

It turned cold a few days after Christmas, with snow flurries off and on for most of the next week or so. Everybody kept moaning and groaning about freezing to death, and I sort of smiled patronizingly. After you've lived in Alaska for a few months, even the harshest and most frigid weather Texas ever gets seems balmy and tropical in comparison.

I was out in the barn fiddling with the tractor on New Year's Eve, wearing nothing but jeans and a t-shirt in spite of the fact that it was snowing again outside, when Mama showed up in the doorway.

"What is it, Mama?" I asked, looking up.

"I just heard on the radio there's been a wreck out on the Longview highway, down by the river. It sounds like a bad one. Two cars flipped over in the ditch, blood everywhere," she said.

"Yeah, it's probably because of the ice," I agreed, wondering why she felt compelled to come out there just to tell me that. She usually wouldn't have, unless there was something else on her mind.

"I don't mean to upset you, son, but I think it's Lisa," she said, and I dropped my wrench on the ground.

"Huh?" I asked stupidly.

"I heard them mention some names. Not all of them because there was a lot of static, but I know I heard Lisa Stone. I thought you might want to know," she said.

"Is she all right?" I asked, surprising myself at how anxious I was.

"I don't know. It said they were taking everybody to the hospital in Longview. You might call them," she suggested.

I tried, but of course she wasn't there yet and they probably wouldn't have told me anything even if she had been.

Sitting at home wondering would have been unbearable, so I got in the truck and drove down to Longview myself, quite a bit faster than it was really safe to drive on the icy roads. I passed the place where the wreck had been and recognized Marcus's truck immediately, even though it was crushed gruesomely. I saw a blood stain on the back glass, and that only scared me even more.

I finally got there not long after the ambulance did, apparently, because they were still trying to deal with a hysterical Lisa who was fighting them tooth and nail. I ran back there without asking, and even though her eyes were open I could tell she didn't recognize me. She was covered in blood and so far out of it she probably didn't even know what planet she was on.

"Can't you knock her out?" I yelled.

"Who are you?" one of the nurses demanded, and that stopped me cold for a second. Who was I, after all, that they should pay any attention to what I thought?

"I'm her brother," I lied through my teeth, knowing they'd kick me out if I said anything else.

"She won't stop fighting us, but we've got to get her into surgery so we can stop her from losing any more blood," the nurse said.

"Then hold her down and knock her out!" I said, exasperated. They were in the middle of doing that very thing anyway, and as soon as they had her out they immediately hustled her off to the operating room to do whatever it was she had to have done.

I knew better than to follow them. Even family members aren't allowed into operating rooms. I soon found myself standing alone in the hallway, at a loss for what to do.

I bought a Dr. Pepper that I didn't really want, and went back to sit in the waiting room for almost two hours until eventually a nurse came out to tell me that Lisa would be okay. She just needed to sleep for a couple hours, but I could go sit with her if I liked. That was a huge relief, but there were a couple of other things I needed to know.

"What about Marcus Cumby, the boy who came in with my sister? Can you tell me anything about him?" I asked.

"He'll be fine. Cuts and bruises, mostly, and a ruptured spleen. We had to take that out, but he'll be okay. He's in room 326 if you want to go see him, too. Do you have any preference about which funeral home you'd like to use? For your mother, I mean?" she asked, and for a second my mind skidded. Then I remembered I was supposed to be Lisa's brother.

"Uh. . . we should probably wait and ask Lisa about that when she wakes up. We've got different mothers," I said wryly.

"All right. But make sure to ask her. We need to know as soon as we can," she said.

"Thanks," I said.

There was nothing I could do for Lisa at the moment, but nevertheless I made my way up to the third floor to sit with her. She looked pale and sick when I got there, and she had cuts and bruises in several places. I pulled up a chair beside the bed to wait.

"Are you sure she'll be all right? She looks awful," I asked again when another nurse came into the room. She sure didn't look like she'd be all right anytime soon.

"She'll be okay. She's had a pretty rough time, I'm afraid. Do you know if she's been in contact with any cats, lately?" the nurse asked.

"Cats?" I asked, mystified.

"Yes. She's got a severe case of toxoplasmosis. Kind of rare, but it usually comes from cats," she explained.

"Not that I know of," I said, baffled.

"Has she done any gardening work or anything like that recently?" she asked.

"Well, yeah, she does raise vegetables," I agreed.

"That's probably it, then. Stray cats like to use gardens as litter boxes because the ground is soft," she said.

"She'll be okay, though, right?" I repeated.

"Yes. She probably won't feel too good for a few days, though. She'll need to take it easy for a while, and y'all need to make sure she finishes her antibiotics. We'll probably let her go home tomorrow sometime, if everything goes all right," she said, and I nodded.

They left me alone with her again after that, and for a while I simply watched her sleeping. She looked fragile and weak, and all kinds of thoughts went through my mind as I sat there. I let my mind drift back to the summer, to mimosa crowns and passionate kisses, and to wordless promises on a mountain beneath the stars. I hadn't been all that wise since then, and maybe she hadn't either, but whatever might have happened in the past, I knew in that moment that I still loved her. I didn't know what she'd say to that or if she still felt the same way about me, but I wanted to give it a try if she did.

But there was someone else to be considered in all this, and since Lisa was still sleeping, I decided it was a good time to go see him. I leaned over and kissed her on the cheek, knowing she'd never know, and then slipped three doors down to Marcus's room.

He was awake, not-watching a game show on TV and looking like he was in a good bit of pain.

"Hey, Marcus," I said softly, and he smiled, more or less.

"Hey, Cody. Didn't expect to see anybody today, with the roads so bad," he said.

"Yeah. . . I had to come check on y'all," I said, sitting down in the chair beside his bed.

"How's Lisa?" he asked, and I quickly gave him a rundown on her condition, finishing up with the words I'd mostly come to say.

"I don't know what she'll say, but I'm fixing to ask her if she wants to get back together, Marcus. Just so you know," I told him.

Marcus didn't say anything about that at first, but finally he gave me a crooked little smile. A tired and pained one, to be sure, but still a smile.

"Yeah. . . I think you should, honestly," he said.

"I'm surprised you'd say that," I said, raising an eyebrow at him.

"I've been thinking about it for a long time, in the back of my mind. Me and Lisa never really had anything together except just friends, you know. I'm tired of pretending. We both almost died out there today, and I guess maybe that has a way of making you see things a little different. So yeah, go talk to her. I think y'all are better off together, no matter what happens. I always did think so," he explained, sounding sad.

The speech didn't seem to make a whole lot of sense, but I decided it wasn't the time to grill Marcus about what it all meant. I had my answer about Lisa, and that was all I really cared about at the moment.

"Well, good, cause if you didn't say it was okay, then I was gonna have to pound you as soon as you got home," I told him jokingly, and Marcus laughed.

"Aw, don't make me laugh, Cody. It hurts too much," he said, putting a hand on his left side, presumably where they took his ruptured spleen out.

"Sorry," I said.

"It's okay. They say they'll let me go home in a couple days, hopefully," he said.

"That's good. But I guess I better get back down there and check on Lisa. I'll come back in a little while, okay?" I said.

"Thanks," he said, and I gave him a rough hug, or at least the best one I could manage without hurting him.

"Get well, boy," I told him.

"I'll do my best," Marcus agreed.

I went back down to Lisa's room after that, to see if she was awake yet. She wasn't, and for a long time I sat there in the chair looking out at the snow and watching her breathe. I didn't know how to get hold of Jenny, so there was nothing I could do except keep watch while she slept.

Chapter Thirty-Two
Lisa

When I finally woke up, I was lying in a hospital bed in a quiet room, hurting in every way imaginable. Mind, body, and heart were all shattered. My world was nothing but the depths of bleak devastation, black as the bitterest night.

It was still snowing a little bit, but it was the big flakes that always come near the end, when the storm is almost over. From what I could see, there was only maybe an inch or two on the ground.

Then I turned my head away from the window, and to my utter shock, Cody was there, sitting in the chair beside my bed. He looked careworn and sad, and he was wearing that same old *Cowboy for Life* t-shirt that he'd worn the first day I went out to see him at Goliad, all those eons and centuries ago. It reminded me of happier days, or at least it would have if Cody hadn't seemed so sorrowful, like he thought I might never open my eyes again. In a way I think that comforted me just a little bit; when your heart is broken, it's a comfort to know that your pain isn't yours alone.

"Cody," I said, and I was surprised how weak my voice sounded. He stirred, and reached out to clasp my hand. Any other time I wouldn't have let him do it, but at the moment I needed the touch.

"Hey, Lisa," he said.

"How did you get here?" I asked.

"Well. . . Mama heard about the wreck on the radio, so I decided to come down here and see if you were all right. It sounded pretty bad, the way they talked about it," he said, not quite looking at me.

"I'm so sorry," I told him. I don't even know why I said it or what I was supposed to be sorry for, but I was such an emotional basket case right then, I might have said just about anything and it would have felt logical. Sorry for lying to him? Sorry for making him have to drive to Longview in the snow? I really had no idea. All I knew was that I felt like I'd let him down, like I'd let everybody down, and Mama most of all. Tears started to run from the corners of my eyes, and he quietly wiped them away with a tissue from the bedside table.

He must have guessed my apology had something to do with the wreck.

"It's nobody's fault. The road was bad, and there was nothing anybody could have done different. But the nurse said you lost a lot of blood and they've got you on some pretty strong antibiotics, too. You've got a bad case of toxoplasmosis. But they say you'll be fine in a couple days," he told me.

I'd never heard of toxoplasmosis. I didn't know where it came from, or how I could have gotten such a thing. But it didn't matter, anyway.

"What did they do with Mama?" I asked dully.

"Nothing, yet. They wanted me to ask you which funeral home you'd like to use. If you want to, I thought we could bury her at Nebo. Maybe keep y'all from having so many arrangements to make," he said.

It didn't surprise me that he'd make such an offer. He was always like that, when he thought nobody was paying attention. But still, I was grateful beyond words for that small act of kindness.

"Thanks," I said.

"It's the least I could do," he said.

"Where's Marcus?" I asked.

"He got banged up pretty bad, but they think he'll be okay. He's down the hall, there," he said, nodding his head in that direction.

"I'm glad you came," I told him, truthfully.

"Well. . . I couldn't pretend I didn't know," he said, scuffing his boot on the floor a little bit.

"I've really missed you," I told him, not stopping to think or care how that might sound. He raised an eyebrow at me.

"Still?" he asked.

"Always," I admitted. It says in Proverbs than an honest answer is like a kiss on the lips, and I guess that's how my words must have felt for Cody. He was silent for a few minutes, maybe thinking, and then cleared his throat.

"Lisa, I know this is maybe not the time or the place, but I've been thinking an awful lot. I really didn't mean all that stuff I said when you came up to Alaska. I was mostly just mad and hurt, and then later when I found out about you and Marcus getting together, I don't know, it seemed like it was better to let it alone. Anyway, I know me and you both have done some stupid stuff, but I'd like to try to maybe work things out, if we can," he finally said.

I wanted to say no. I knew what the price would be if I didn't. But I was sick and weak and my heart was already broken, and I didn't have the strength to turn him away. I knew it might be the last chance we ever had together. No matter how hard I tried, I couldn't make myself do it.

"Yeah, me too," I agreed softly, and squeezed his hand.

"What about Marcus?" he asked.

I thought about that, but the prospect of explaining to him that I'd never really been with Marcus in the first place was more than I could handle right then. It would drag in the whole mess with Layla and the fake breakup in Alaska and who knew what else, and all of it together was too much.

"Marcus knows how I feel about you. He always has. I'd like to think he'd be happy for me," I said instead, which was as much of the truth as I knew how to give him at the moment.

"He said he was glad, when I talked to him earlier," he said.

"You talked to Marcus?" I asked. I couldn't help wondering what they might have said to each other, and how much information Marcus had let slip.

"Well, yeah. He's still my best friend, you know. But I told him I was fixin' to ask you if we could work things out, even if I had to beat him bloody if he didn't like it, so he gave me his blessing," he said. I laughed a little, even though it hurt.

"He's a good man," I said.

"Yeah, he is," Cody agreed.

We didn't say anything else for a while, but at last he took a deep breath and ran his fingers through his hair.

"I probably better go, Lisa, unless you need me to stay. There are some things I need to do, to get ready for the funeral, you know. I'll try to call Jenny to come sit with you, if you'll give me her number," he said.

"Sure, go ahead. I'll be all right," I said, giving him the number. I would have liked him to stay, honestly, but I didn't feel like I had a right to ask him for anything, yet. Our relationship was still in the eggshell stage, tenuous and fragile.

"Okay, then," he agreed. Then he kissed me goodbye, just a quick peck, and left the hospital to do what needed to be done.

I watched him leave, and for a little while I slept again until Jenny showed up. I almost would rather have been alone, if the truth be told, but I smiled tiredly and prepared myself for whatever the encounter might bring.

"How are you feeling, sis?" Jenny asked, in a subdued tone.

"I've been better. What about you?" I asked.

"I'll be all right. Mama wouldn't have liked it if we fell apart, you know," Jenny said, and in spite of my exhaustion and desolation, I had to smile a little. It was true; that's exactly what Mama would have said. To be strong and hold it together, no matter what. It surprised me that Jenny had ever paid attention.

"Cody told me not to worry about anything, cause he was taking care of all the funeral arrangements. He said y'all already talked about it. Now, it's not like I'm not grateful, you know, but what's he doing here at all?" she asked. I thought wryly that my sister was the same yesterday, today, and tomorrow; always nosy.

"He heard about the wreck, so he came down here to see me, that's all. He's only being the way he always is. He didn't want me to have to deal with all that from a hospital bed," I said. I didn't mention the fact that we both knew Jenny couldn't have handled it period; there was no need to hurt her feelings by saying so.

"Well. . . okay. Just seemed strange that *he* was the one calling me, that's all," she said.

"We're gonna try to work things out one more time, I think. See what happens. And I don't want to hear a word about it from you or anybody else," I said, a touch severely.

"I won't. I'm glad for you, that you got him back. I think he really loves you," she said, and that surprised me almost as much as anything Jenny had ever said.

"You do?" I asked skeptically.

"Yeah. He wouldn't still be here after all this, if he didn't. I hope y'all work out this time," she said.

"Yeah, me too," I agreed.

This time, in my heart of hearts, I really believed it would.

End of Part Two

Part Three

In Beauty Be It Finished

Prologue
Lisa

The next person who walked into my room was Layla Latimer.

It was morning by then; I could see it from the way the light fell on the trees outside my window. I wanted to scream when I saw her, but I found that my tongue was stuck in my throat, and I couldn't make a sound.

"Now, Lisa, really; I told you I'd be watching," she scolded when she got close enough. I noticed she had a syringe in her hand, but I seemed frozen, unable to lift a finger as she came up beside the bed and inserted it into my IV line.

"This'll just knock you out for a little while, so there's no fuss. We'll be headed back to New Mexico in a few minutes; you and me and Marcus. Then we'll wait for Cody to come along, which I'm sure he will, shortly," Layla said soothingly, as if comforting a recalcitrant child.

Then the darkness took me, and I knew no more.

Chapter Thirty-Three
Cody

I got most of the funeral arrangements done by the time evening came, and then went home tired and wet to take a hot shower and eat supper with Mama. It was just the two of us, for once; Brandon was spending the night with one of his friends. It was a lot quieter with him and Marcus both gone, but that was all right. She fixed spaghetti and garlic bread, one of my favorites, and the quiet was soothing after such a rough day.

"I talked to Lisa today. I think maybe we might work things out, after all," I mentioned between bites of food, knowing she'd be pleased at that news.

"I'm glad," she nodded.

"Hmm. . . would've thought you'd been more excited," I said jokingly.

"Did she get a chance to tell you?" she asked.

"Tell me what?" I asked.

"Obviously she didn't," she said.

"I guess not. So what's the big secret?" I asked.

"I'm not sure if I should be the one to tell you or not," she fretted.

"Well, since you already mentioned it, you might as well tell me. If you don't then I'll have to worry about it all night long till I see Lisa again. Come on, Mama; I promise I won't be mad at her for not telling me. I know she was in pretty bad shape this afternoon," I said.

"All right, then. But don't judge, till you hear the whole story," she warned.

"Do I ever?" I asked, frowning.

So she proceeded to tell me the whole story about New Mexico and Miss Latimer and the fake breakup, and I couldn't decide whether to be shocked or sad or numb. I'd finally struggled my way through all that garbage till I reached some kind of understanding and acceptance of reality, to forgiveness and peace, and the revelation that things had never been quite what they seemed to be knocked me flat in the dirt all over again.

I really hate to be manipulated, and the idea that everybody I loved and trusted was secretly maneuvering behind my back was a hard pill to swallow. It stung almost as much as that whole incredible story about Lisa and Marcus hooking up at a party. In hindsight, I couldn't believe I'd ever swallowed such a whopper as that in the first place. She must have been really desperate, to come up with something that stupid. I ought to have known better. I ought to have demanded more answers when she tried to feed me that line of bull. If I had, then things might have turned out different.

My face flushed red when I thought about what a fool I'd been.

"Why didn't you tell me all this sooner, if you knew?" I asked, accusingly.

"Because I knew y'all would work things out sooner or later, if I stayed out of the way. It wasn't my place to meddle in the meantime," she told me, and I grudgingly decided maybe she had a point.

I was still struggling to adjust myself to the idea that Lisa had been lying to me this whole time. I couldn't decide whether to be furious or whether to feel sorry for her, let alone Marcus. Knowing they did it for my own sake and no other reason made it easier to forgive, I guess, but that didn't mean I was okay with it, either. As soon as things settled down a little, we all three needed to sit down and have a serious talk about what it means to trust somebody.

"Here. This is the stuff that's supposed to break the curse. Lisa dropped it off awhile back, and told me to have you drink it," Mama said, holding up a tube of green liquid. I stared at it, and reached to take it into my own hand.

I looked at the vial, watching it glitter in the soft light, and my heart softened. I could only imagine how much it had cost Lisa to get that little tube, all the fear and humiliation she must have suffered. All for me, and not even any thanks. That was greatness of heart if anything ever was.

I think I've said before how irresistible that trait has always been in my eyes; that reflection of the Light that illuminates the world and makes everything beautiful that it touches. I think I would have fallen in love with Lisa all over again, just from hearing that she'd done such a thing for a complete stranger. It was the deed itself which was beautiful, not the fact that she did it for me.

But it *had* been for me, and there was no way I could thank her, nor ever repay the gift she'd given me, except to love her forever with my whole heart. And that I had every intention of doing.

But there was still the issue of what to do about Layla, because there wasn't a shred of doubt in my mind that she was the same person as this so-called Miss Latimer. According to the dreams, we were both still in danger of death if I understood things right. Layla had practically said as much, if and when she found out Lisa and I were back together again. Therefore I didn't drink the liquid right away, and handed it back to Mama.

"What's wrong?" she asked.

"I think I'll let you hold on to that little gem for a while before I use it," I said, my mind already working far ahead.

"How come?" she asked.

"Well, it seems to me Layla can't curse me twice, and I think it's about time I paid her a visit. I might need that cure more when I get back," I said.

"Back from where?" she asked.

"I think it's about time I went out there to New Mexico and busted some heads," I said. Yeah, I know, it sounded like pure bravado. But I was dead serious, too. If anybody thought they could get away with hurting my family and the people I loved, then they'd find out otherwise real quick. That was a lesson already burned deep into my soul by a hundred generations of history.

My family is from Cumberland, you see, right on the border between England and Scotland. That was always a land of conflict and strife, of raids between the two kingdoms and governments who did nothing to protect their people. For thousands of years it was like that, ever since the Picts and Romans fought over the same ground; maybe even earlier. People had no one to depend on but family, and that was a bond you never, ever forsook. So maybe somewhere back in the misty depths of time there's still a Borderland warrior who looks out of my Texan eyes and sees a world very different, yes, but in some ways no different at all. I like to think so.

For all I know, one of them might even have been a knight in shining armor back in the old, old days, a man of honor who not only knew how to fight but also how to care for the sick and the hurting, how to build things of beauty and to humble himself before God. I'd like to believe that, too. True, I have my own battles to fight and my own courage to find, but it surely does help to remember those things.

Mama didn't say anything right away, but she looked unhappy.

"Before you do anything like that, I guess there's something else I need to tell you," she finally said.

"Well, this sure is turning out to be a night for secrets, isn't it?" I said dryly.

"It's just some things your father told me when you were a baby, that's all. I don't know how much of it is true, or even if any of it is," she said.

"Mother, just *tell* me, for pity's sake!" I said, exasperated.

"Well, for one thing he told me that story Marcus heard, about the curse and where it came from. I never realized other people in town knew anything about it. He also told me those bright blue eyes of yours are the mark of a curse-breaker, but I guess I'm getting ahead of myself a little bit. Do you know that crystal up there on your Grandpa Reuben's tombstone?" she asked.

"Yeah, what about it?" I asked.

"Your daddy always told me that crystal is tied to you. As long as it's up there on the mountain, in that very spot, then it'll guide and protect you no matter what. It'll give you true dreams to show you which way God would have you to go, and no kind of magic can touch you. Not even the curse. He said your Grandma Hannah dedicated it to you when she first put it there. But you still have a hard choice to make," she said.

"What kind of a choice?" I asked.

"Well, you can decide to live out your own life just like a normal person if you want to. The crystal will protect you from the curse for as long as you live. You'd be skipped over, you might say, but in that case the curse would pick back up again with any kids you might have," she said.

"And what's my other choice?" I asked.

"Well, he also said you could choose to take that crystal loose and use it to make an end of the curse forever. He never said how, but he did say it'd be dangerous and you might even die. He personally never doubted which choice you'd end up making, though, and that's why he told me not to say anything about it till you turned twenty-five, so you'd have time to come to your full strength before you put yourself in danger. That's why I never told you anything," she said.

I sat there with my mouth open, reeling from yet another shattering of everything I ever thought was true. Mama knew about the Curse? I was immune to magic? That was incredible. My mind jumped instantly to that night Layla tried to kiss me, and the fear in her eyes. Suddenly finding out she couldn't hurt me might have been why she turned tail and ran off like a scalded dog. Not knowing why her magic didn't work *would* have been scary, I guess.

There was something else that bothered me about the whole thing, though.

"But how can *any* of that be true? I wasn't even born yet when Grandma Hannah put that crystal up there. How could it have anything to do with me one way or the other?" I objected.

"Maybe she had a dream about you," Mama said.

There was always *that* possibility, of course. Hannah had owned that crystal for a long time before she ever put it up there on the tombstone, so if it could really give visions of the future then it was entirely possible she might have had a few. I certainly couldn't think of any *other* way for her to know all those things.

"But why *me*, though?" I asked, and Mama shook her head.

"That I don't know, son. I'm sure there's a good reason, but sometimes we have to be content not to know what it is," she said.

I decided she was probably right about that. Sometimes you simply have to accept reality for what it is and let that be the end of the matter, no matter how unsatisfying that may be. As the saying goes, it is what it is. That might sound like the kind of frivolous and flippant thing only a high school kid would ever say, but it actually contains a grain of very good sense when you think about it for a while.

Well, all right, then. I could accept the fact that I might never know why God chose me instead of somebody else, but I couldn't help wondering how Hannah must have felt about that. She and Reuben only ever had one child, my Grandpa Nicholas, and I suppose she would've liked to use the crystal to protect *him*, if she had her own way. From her point of view, it must have seemed that God was asking her to condemn her own son to an early death to save me instead, her grandson's great-grandson, and it must have seemed utterly irrational since the crystal could have been passed down to me eventually anyway. That's what I would have been thinking, at least. She must have wondered why God would ever ask her to do such a thing, and for her to actually go through with it must have taken a kind of faith I could barely imagine.

I guess it's possible that that in itself was part of the reason why He asked, of course. Greatness of heart in one person is an inspiration to all others who see it, and the ripples may wash ashore in far times and places and in ways the original doer of the deed knows nothing about. But then again, there might also have been some very practical reason why He asked; that crystal might have saved me from death a dozen times already, for all I knew, in some odd way that never could have happened otherwise. Nobody ever knows what *might* have happened.

Or maybe it was both.

I loved her a little bit then, this old woman I never knew who sacrificed so much for me, and for a fleeting moment I wished I could have met Hannah Trewick McGrath, if only just once, to thank her for having the courage to believe. As it was, I could only bless her silently, and pray that her dreams gave her comfort, and promise her that I'd never let her sacrifice be in vain.

I guess Daddy was right about what choice I'd make, after all.

But my head hurt from trying to digest too much new information, and I was so confused about everything by then that I didn't know what to think anymore.

"But what am I supposed to *do?*" I finally asked.

"I've told you all I know, Cody. If you don't know what to do then maybe it's not the right time to do anything yet. Wait for a dream. You might have to be patient," she said.

"I've got to think about all this for a while," I finally said, shaking my head.

"Yes, you do. Whatever you're supposed to do, I can't help but think it's something more than just busting some heads, as you put it," she said.

"So what changed your mind? Why are you telling me all this *now,* all of a sudden?" I asked.

"Because I don't want you to do anything foolish, that's why. You can't make wise decisions if you don't know everything, and if things like this are happening then I think it's time I told you," she said.

"Well. . . thanks," I said.

"You're welcome. Just think about what you need to do, and I'll support you whatever you decide. But don't do anything hasty, all right?" she asked.

"I won't," I said automatically.

That night, I dreamed again.

At first it seemed ordinary and even dull, because it started out in a place that I knew quite well; the cemetery at Nebo. The only odd thing was that it seemed to be almost empty of tombstones. The only one in sight was my Grandpa Reuben's, and the dirt seemed fresh on that grave. I wondered if I was seeing something from long ago instead of the future, and if so I wondered why.

In front of the grave was a lady in a black dress, praying, and somehow I knew it was Hannah. Then I saw her lift up her hands to Heaven, and she spoke *my* name, and I glimpsed a shining crystal in her hands. She said some words from Scripture that I vaguely remembered hearing before, kissed the jewel, and then attached it firmly to the top of her husband's tomb.

Then she turned around, and I could have sworn she looked right at me. I don't know if it's possible to communicate across time that way, but I know for just a second we locked eyes, and she smiled. But only for a second, because then the whole scene vanished and I found myself reeling into utter insanity again.

I was in the midst of a howling storm on a mountaintop at night, with lightning bolts striking the boulders all around me and splintering the stone. I wanted to cower down under the rocks to keep from getting burnt to cinders, but my other self in the dream did no such thing. He climbed on top of a boulder, then reached out and grabbed one of the bolts in his bare hand. Then he threw it back at the clouds, for all the world like Thor in a cheap Viking movie. Then the storm hushed, and there was rain.

Only rain, quiet and still.

* * * * * * *

I would have dearly liked to talk to Brandon the next morning, but since he wasn't there I didn't have much choice except to wait till he got home from school. I consoled myself with the thought that quiet rain is a comforting kind of thing, so whatever the dream portended, it seemed to be mostly good. I sure did hope so.

I did look up those words that Hannah said, and found the place in the Book of Numbers where they came from. They were the specific words of blessing that God told the priests to speak over the people, and the concordance noted that they'd also been commonly used over the centuries by a parent or grandparent as a blessing for a child. That seemed fitting, coming from my far-distant grandmother. Whether they always had to be spoken when setting the crystal or whether that was something she meant only for me, I couldn't have said.

The meaning of the lightning storm on the mountain was just as obscure as ever, but as it turned out, I never got a chance to ask Brandon what the rest of it meant.

Around mid-morning I got a call from Jenny, of all people, letting me know that Lisa and Marcus had disappeared from the hospital sometime before breakfast. No one knew where they'd gone or how they could have left the building without being noticed, but I didn't have the slightest doubt where they were.

That little tidbit of news settled all my doubts in a hurry, and so it was that I found myself packing Daddy's 30-30 Model 94 Winchester deer rifle behind my truck seat. It was old, true, but still well-oiled and ready for use. Under good conditions it could kill at two hundred yards or more, and with a little luck I expected to have excellent conditions in the desert. I'm a pretty crack shot, if I do say so myself.

I didn't have much of a plan, other than hunting Layla down and putting a bullet between her eyes if I had to. I was none too sure things would work out the way I hoped, though. She might not be able to use any magic against me, but there are plenty of other ways to kill a man without resorting to sorcery. I'm not immortal, not by a long stretch.

And then again, even if I succeeded, shooting someone is murder, after all. She was a cruel and evil person who'd done plenty of wrong, but the law wouldn't look kindly on killing her.

They tend not to believe in magic and curses, and I didn't particularly want to go to prison for life in New Mexico for killing the woman.

But what other choices did I have? The police were a waste of time; Layla was surely a respectable member of society, and I had no proof she'd done anything wrong. By the time the police were willing to do anything, she would've had time to get rid of Lisa and Marcus in a way so that nobody would ever find them. I didn't dare give her the chance.

I needed help in a major way, and that's when I thought about Matthieu again. True, I barely knew him, but when you're grasping at straws, sometimes you have to take a chance on the unknown. I fished out his number and called, praying he hadn't changed phones.

"Hello?" someone asked, and I recognized the voice.

"Hey, Matthieu, I know it's been a while, but how've you been?" I asked, not sure what else to say.

"Mr. McGrath! I'm glad to hear from you. What's up?" he asked. So I gave him a quick sketch of all the spooky events of the past few months, including Lisa and Marcus's disappearance.

"You should have called me sooner, Cody. That girl in Alaska sounds just like Layla Garza to me, and so does the one in New Mexico. She switches names all the time to make herself harder to track, but she's always got the same angle. She's a dangerous sorceress," he said.

"Yeah, I figured out that much on my own," I said.

"Well, never mind. The only thing that matters right now is to get Lisa and Marcus back, and then hopefully to deal with Layla once and for all. I'll meet you at Goliad in about three or four hours, okay? I'll have to get some stuff together and that plus the drive will take me about that long," he said.

"I'll be waiting," I said, wishing it wasn't so long. I couldn't imagine what Lisa and Marcus might be going through in the meantime while I twiddled my thumbs doing nothing.

"Back so soon?" Mama asked, when I walked in the door.

"I never left yet. I decided I can't tackle Layla alone. I've got to have some help," I admitted, and she nodded.

It seemed like an eternity, but eventually Matthieu showed up in the same big black truck he'd been driving the first time, only now it was fitted with a mean-looking iron brush guard across the grille. He was dressed in black combat fatigues, of all things, and he'd brought an extra set for me.

"We can't underestimate Layla. I don't doubt she's expecting us, so we have to be as careful as we can," he said, handing me the extra fatigues.

"Do you think she's got backup?" I asked.

"Possibly. But even if she does, she's still the most dangerous one, anyway," he said.

"How much do you know about her?" I asked.

"She drinks the life from a young man and turns him old, while she stays young forever. All she has to do is kiss him," he said, and I thought instantly of James Fitch.

"Is that all?" I asked.

"No, it's not. She can also change her appearance so you wouldn't recognize her. Her brother was a lot more powerful than she is, but we finally nailed *him* a few months ago. Layla might still have some of his items that she can use, though; one of his crystal balls at the very least and maybe some other things, too," he said.

"So if you got him then why didn't you get her, too?" I asked.

"She wasn't with him, then. She never stays in one place long enough for us to track. She likes places where there are not many women, and lots of young guys but not many locals. College towns, army bases, things like that. Prudhoe Bay sounds like a perfect hunting ground for her. Bet it freaked her out when her magic didn't work on you," he said, laughing a little. I didn't think it was all that funny, myself; even the memory of it was enough to send a chill down my spine.

"Do you think she was there after me personally, or was I just in the wrong place at the wrong time?" I asked.

"Who knows? We found your name in a list on her brother's hard drive, so I'm inclined to think she probably knew about you, at least. But I couldn't say whether she had her eye on you specifically or not. Especially when that's a place she would've liked anyway," Matthieu shrugged.

"So what's the plan for tonight, exactly?" I asked, changing the subject.

"Well, it's about a twelve hour drive to Las Cruces. We should get there about two or three o'clock in the morning, if all goes well. That'll be a perfect time to hit the place; the moon will be down by then and it'll be as dark as it gets. Catching her asleep is probably too much to hope for, but I'll be content with surprise," Matthieu said.

"Won't we be tired, at that time of night?" I pointed out.

"Yeah, no doubt, but we can take turns sleeping on the way out there. That'll help some," he said.

"What about when we get there?" I asked.

"I remember the place well enough, if she's really using her brother's old place like you said. There's a steel gate about a mile from the house with a lock on it. I can get us through that. Then we'll drive up to the house, real slow so we don't make any noise. I've got a set of night-vision goggles for both of us, so we can run with no lights on. We absolutely can't let her have a chance to get prepared. I think our best option is to do a direct frontal assault on the place. Ram the truck right through the front doors, come crashing in on her before she knows what happened. That's what the brush guard is for. Do you think you can drive, Cody, so I can be ready to jump out immediately?" he asked.

"Sure. I ram trucks through walls every day," I said dryly. Matthieu didn't laugh.

"I'm serious. Can you do it or not?" he asked.

"I can do it," I agreed.

"All right, then. I'll take care of Layla, and anybody else who's there. You just make sure to find Marcus and Lisa, and watch out for zombies. It's possible there might still be a few of *them* left up there, too," Matthieu said.

"Zombies?" I asked.

"Andrew Garza was a necromancer, among other things. He killed people and turned them into soldiers. Layla can't make them herself but I'm sure she wouldn't hesitate to use one if it was available. Let's hope they're all gone by now and then it won't be a problem," Matthieu said, without a trace of a smile.

"Can you kill them?" I asked.

"Well. . . you can't really kill something that's already dead. You mostly want to destroy their eyes and ears so they can't find you, or their arms and legs so they can't reach you. It's best to knock their heads off, if you can. Then they're useless," he said.

I swallowed hard, my mind giving me a hideous image of knocking the head off a dead man with a baseball bat. No game, this. But if that's what it took to save Lisa and Marcus, then that's what I'd do.

But there was one other thing that had to be done before we left. I had no idea yet what I was supposed to do with the crystal, but I did know I was supposed to carry it with me. Cutting that stone loose from its place would mean the end of my special exemption from the Curse, and it was no sure thing I'd survive the coming battle. But in spite of all that, when it came right down to it, the choice wasn't so hard at all.

Matthieu knew about it, of course; I'd told him that part along with everything else. But when I got back to the house holding it in my hand, he couldn't seem to tear his eyes away from it.

"You don't have any idea what that is, do you?" he asked.

"Uh, no, I guess I don't," I said.

"It's a Guardian Stone. They're very precious, and very holy, and there are only three of them in the whole world. Make sure you never lose it," he said, very solemnly.

I looked at my crystal with new respect, and carefully zipped it up in my chest pocket, where it couldn't possibly get lost. Then I thought better of it.

"You know what, I think you need this more than I do for now. You're the one who'll have to deal with Layla," I said, offering him the Stone. It wasn't the time for false humility, so he simply nodded and took it.

Matthieu liked to talk and he ended up telling me quite a few things during that long, long trip. He told me about fighting giant octopuses on the bottom of the sea, and hunting monsters in Kazakhstan, and other things even harder to believe than that. He was (he said) an Avenger, sworn to fight evil wherever it reared its ugly head. He made my own life seem tame and ordinary by comparison.

I suppose there's a certain thirst for adventure in the heart of every young man, me included, and therefore a certain admiration that wells up unasked, for those who live such a rough and tumble life as Matthieu talked about. I can't deny it. But all the same, if I had to choose, I think I'd rather be at Goliad with my hands in the dirt. I don't mind fighting when I need to, but I don't particularly like it. I'd rather be the sunshine and the rain that makes little things grow strong, a steady rock to shelter the weak. There are different kinds of strength, and different kinds of courage. So even though I admired Matthieu and enjoyed his tales, I'm glad his life is not mine.

Chapter Thirty-Four
Cody

So it was that, many hours later, we found ourselves parked in front of a steel gate on a dirt road in the Organ Mountains, with the lights of Las Cruces shining barely ten miles away. It seemed unreal, that such a dark and deadly operation should be going on within sight of the modern, ordinary world, right down there in the valley. We'd already been to the house down in White Sands, and found it dark and empty.

Matthieu was picking the lock while I stood there and watched him. We both had our night-vision goggles on, which I'd never used before. They painted the whole world in shades of ghostly green, spooky and mysterious. Still, I could see almost like it was broad daylight, and that was all that mattered. We were practically invisible in our combat fatigues, and as soon as he finished picking the lock, I silently swung the gate open and returned to the truck.

"Ready?" Matthieu asked. He was wearing a helmet with a face visor, to keep Layla from kissing him I suppose. He had the Guardian Stone to protect him, of course, but there's nothing wrong with taking extra precautions. My own head was bare, but I dearly hoped I never had to see Layla at all.

"Ready as I'll ever be," I muttered. I got behind the wheel and snapped my seat belt, knowing the sudden impact of hitting the house would throw me forward if I wasn't buckled in. I couldn't afford to get knocked out against the windshield, or worse, punch through it.

We crept forward with no headlights, as quietly as we could on the gravel road. When we came in sight of the house itself, I saw that it was a doublewide mobile home with French doors in front that led onto a concrete patio.

"Ram right through those doors," Matthieu whispered, nodding towards the front of the house, quickly buckling himself in for the impact.

"Here we go, then," I said, and hit the gas. The truck's powerful engine picked up speed quickly, and in spite of the goggles I shut my eyes reflexively at the last second.

The impact was incredible. I was thrown forward against my buckle with enough force that I was sure there'd be bruises there in the morning. There was a massive sound of shattering glass and snapping wood and squealing metal, and the truck's windshield blew out, showering us with bits of glass. Then we were through, and found ourselves sitting in the middle of what looked like it might have been a fairly ordinary living room before the wall came crashing down. Showers of sparks from ripped-out electrical wires lit up the room.

"Go!" Matthieu cried, and the two of us quickly scrambled out to head for opposite ends of the house.

I stumbled through rubble almost knee-deep, doing my best not to step on the live wires that were still sparking and shorting in places. My boots were supposed to be shock-proof, but I didn't want to test that theory. I remembered something about how Lisa had found Marcus hung up in one of the back bedrooms, so that was where I headed first.

Then I found myself tackled from behind and knocked hard to the floor, and before I could come to my senses I felt something *biting* me on my left shoulder, dangerously close to my neck. I instinctively punched at the thing, and my hand encountered dry, leathery skin barely clinging to bone. One of the zombies. It couldn't bite me very well through my clothes, but I can promise you it hurt plenty, and the thing was trying to get its stringy hands around my throat at the same time.

I fought the thing in a wave of revulsion and horror, and I found that every time I punched or ripped it, chunks would come loose in my hands, foul and greasy. None of that seemed to be hurting the thing, though, and we rolled and grappled on the floor for several minutes with neither of us able to get the upper hand. I was terrified that another one would pile on at any second, and if that happened then I was lost.

I vaguely heard gunfire and Matthieu yelling and the room was suddenly lit up by an explosion that threw both me and the zombie against the wall so hard that it felt like it might have cracked ribs. But at least it knocked loose the thing's hold on my neck, and before it could get up I scrambled to my feet and kicked it in the head as hard as I could with my steel toed boots. The thing's head came loose from its body and sailed across the room like a football, and then it was still.

I was still shaking from the fight, but there was no time for that. I quickly got a grip on myself and ran for the bedroom again, sliding along the wall to keep my back covered this time.

I kicked in the bedroom door without a second thought, and inside was a scene that broke my heart. In spite of the adrenaline rush of fighting off the monster and the blood and sweat and smoke of battle that was all around me, the sight in front of me was enough to stop me cold.

Marcus and Lisa were hanging from the ceiling by their wrists, just like Marcus must have been that other time. A long steel rod had been built into the ceiling, maybe for that very purpose, and both of them were almost naked except for whatever they'd been wearing at the hospital. The green glow of the goggles made it hard to see exactly what the situation was, but I could tell that Marcus's bandages across his stomach were soaked dark with blood, and neither he nor Lisa lifted their heads nor made a sound when I burst inside.

The battle was still raging outside the bedroom, and then all of a sudden there was silence. I almost dreaded to see what the outcome had been, but I was afraid to cut the prisoners loose without help. It might do more harm than good.

I crept back outside to the living room, where I found Matthieu sitting on the overturned couch while he put pressure on a bloody wound in his thigh as best he could.

"What happened?" I asked, staring at the blood.

"Got shot in the leg, that's what. Layla's pretty good with a pistol, turns out. But not as good as I am, though," he said with satisfaction.

"You got her?" I asked, hardly daring to hope.

"Yeah, I'm pretty sure I did. I know I got her better than she got me, but you better go after her and make sure, though," he said, handing me his pistol. It was a Glock .45, heavy and lethal. It still had several rounds left.

"Which way did she go?" I asked.

"She busted the bedroom window out and ran off up the valley, but she wasn't moving too fast. You better hurry, and take this, too," he said, handing me back the Guardian Stone.

I quickly zipped it up in my pocket where it couldn't get lost, then ran outside and picked up Layla's trail right where Matthieu had said I would. She must have been moving faster than he thought, though, because I lost her trail about a hundred yards from the house. I don't know if she went to ground or if she was still running, but either way she was gone.

I cussed and kicked the ground, but there was nothing to do except go back to the house and try to do what I could for the others.

Matthieu was still bleeding when I got back inside, and it was obvious there was no way he could help me with Marcus and Lisa.

"Was there anybody else?" I asked when I got back indoors.

"No, it was just Layla and two zombies, fortunately," Matthieu said.

"Are they both dead?" I asked, vividly remembering my brush with the one in the living room.

"Yeah. Well, 'deactivated' is maybe a better word, but you know what I mean," he said.

I went back to the bedroom, and found a chair to climb up and cut the ropes that held Marcus and Lisa to the ceiling, trying not to let them fall.

It didn't look good. They hadn't been in good shape to start with, and I was sure Layla hadn't given them any food or water ever since she hung them up in there. I had to get them to a hospital, and Matthieu too, for that matter.

"We've got to get y'all to the hospital," I told him, as soon as I carried Marcus and Lisa out to the living room.

"Yeah, but not in Las Cruces. None of us can be associated with what happened here tonight, not even remotely. In fact I'd like to get out of New Mexico completely, if we can. El Paso's only about forty-five minutes; I think it'll be best if we go there. But we can't leave the house like this, either. We've got to bury what's left of those zombies somewhere nobody will find them, and then we need to set this place on fire," he said.

"Can't we come back and deal with that later? Marcus and Lisa might not make it that long. You might not either, if you keep bleeding like that," I said severely. He gazed at the others, and finally nodded.

"Yeah, you're right. We'll come back later and finish up. Let's go. We can take Layla's car," he agreed.

I had to carry all three of them out to Layla's brown station wagon, laying Marcus and Lisa in the back seat as comfortably as possible, while Matthieu rode in front.

"You know, Cody, I've been thinking. You might ought to hold off a while before you drink that serum Layla gave you," Matthieu said after a while.

"How come?" I asked.

"Well...Curses are usually made to last forever, unless the one who cast them specifically breaks them. I'm not quite sure Layla had the power to break it in the first place. In fact, I wouldn't put it past her to give you a vial of poison, just for the pleasure of causing more heartache. You better let me stop by and test it, before you try to use it," Matthieu said.

I hadn't thought of that possibility, but I decided it was definitely a good idea to find out what was in that vial before I drank it.

"Okay, no problem," I said.

"I'll try to stop by on our way home. It's not too far out of the way. Just wait till then before you touch that liquid. I've got to get my uncle Rob and some of the others out here to take care of that scene in Las Cruces before somebody else finds it, so that might take a few days," he said.

"No worries; you know where to find me," I said.

We got to El Paso with no trouble, and then had to wait for an hour or more while the nurses decided what to do with us. Matthieu had to have surgery to get the bullet out of his leg, and the others were admitted to the hospital, too.

I called Mama to come get us, but El Paso is an awfully long way from Avinger. There was no way she could get there before late afternoon at the earliest. I wasn't sure yet when Marcus and Lisa would be released; hanging from a bar for several hours hadn't been good for them. Marcus had had his stitches torn open, and both of them were dehydrated.

But by late afternoon they were both awake at least, and the hospital was nice enough to let them have next-door rooms. Lisa was able to sit up in a wheelchair and let me push her into Marcus's room so we could talk, after he woke up from having his stitches redone.

"What happened?" he asked thickly, and I told both of them the story, with comments and interruptions along the way.

The hospital grudgingly let them go home the next morning (against medical advice), with a long list of home-care guidelines and strict orders to check back with a doctor if they took a turn for the worse. We probably would have stayed longer in El Paso, if it hadn't been for the need to get back home and take care of Mrs. Stone's funeral.

Mama left Brandon at home so he wouldn't miss school, even though he wanted to come. But it was better that way, since it left a lot more room in the car. We only drove partway that first day, taking it easy and spending the night at a motel in Sweetwater before finishing the trip the next morning.

Early that same afternoon, Matthieu stopped by on his way home as he'd promised he would. He had a white rat in a wire cage, which I could only guess was for testing the vial that Layla had given us. I was kind of disappointed, honestly; I could have done that much myself, if I'd known *that* was all he had in mind. Marcus was at home resting, but Lisa and I were sitting at the kitchen table with Mama, drinking hot chocolate.

"Are you all by yourself?" I asked, when he showed up alone.

"Yeah. The others are still in Las Cruces, getting the truck fixed and stuff. But they told me to go on home so I could rest," he said.

"Did you get everything taken care of at the house?" I asked.

"Mostly, I think. We buried those poor people out in the White Sands Desert where nobody will ever look; it was the best we could do for them. We pulled the truck out and got rid of all the evidence we could find. I think it'll be all right," he explained.

"Sounds like y'all are pretty thorough," I said dryly.

"We have to be. Now, do you still have that vial Layla gave you?" Matthieu asked.

"Yeah, Mama has it in her purse, I think," I said.

"May I see it?" Matthieu asked.

"Sure. Let him see it, Mama," I said, and she wordlessly handed him the vial. Matthieu held it up to the light and watched it sparkle.

"I see. And you've never tasted it yet, right?" he asked.

"Nope," I said.

"Do you have an eyedropper we could use, maybe?" he asked.

"Sure," Mama agreed, getting up to fetch one from the medicine cabinet.

"Now, let's see what happens to Mr. Rat when we feed him a drop of this," Matthieu said.

As soon as Mama got back with the medicine dropper and handed it to him, Matthieu took some of the green liquid from the vial, then poked the dropper through the bars of the cage. The rat came up to it curiously, sniffed the offering, and then licked it twice.

Nothing seemed to happen at first, but Matthieu kept watching intently, and sure enough, five minutes after tasting the liquid, the rat started jerking and twitching and fell to the floor of the cage curled up in a ball with a thin trickle of blood running from his mouth.

"That's what I was afraid of. That vial is nothing but poison. If you'd swallowed it, I don't think you would have been alive for long," Matthieu said calmly.

I don't guess I was all that surprised by this turn of events, but for Lisa it was a shock.

"But. . . " she said, looking stricken. I knew immediately what she was thinking; that all that suffering had been for nothing, and how close it had come to being even worse than nothing. Layla Garza's whole deal had been a cheat from the very beginning. It would have been one last twist of the knife; one last method of extracting a final bitter drop of agony, after all the rest. And worst of all, Lisa herself would have been a willing part of it. Without a word, I took her in my arms.

"Never think of it again," I whispered in her ear, too low for anyone else to hear; the same words she'd whispered to me on that night at Autograph Rock when I first told her about the Curse. I knew she'd remember, and I wanted her to know it didn't matter. She laughed through her tears, and then kissed me fiercely right there in front of company.

Matthieu discreetly pretended not to notice, and when Lisa had pulled herself together he went on as if nothing had ever happened.

"I'd get rid of this, if I were you," he said, holding up the vial.

"Is it safe to pour it on the ground?" I asked.

"I'm not sure about that, honestly. I can take it with me and get rid of it for you, if you like," he offered.

"Yeah, maybe you should. I'd really appreciate that," I nodded.

"No problem," he agreed.

"But what about the Curse?" I asked, and Matthieu seemed uncomfortable.

"It's still there, Cody. I don't know what to say. You'll still be okay as long as you keep the Guardian Stone somewhere on your body at all times``. But if it ever gets lost or stolen, I don't guess I need to tell you what happens then. I suggest getting it attached to a chain, to make it easier to keep up with. Maybe you should come over to Natchitoches sometime and we'll see if we can find out any more possibilities for how to break that curse. My parents have a library bigger than some small countries, all about things like that," he offered, and I let out a deep breath. If I'd lived with the curse this long, then surely I could live with it a while longer.

Hopefully.

Not long after Matthieu left, Brandon got home from school and I was finally able to ask him what my dream of the lightning on the mountain might mean.

"The lightning bolts mean that for a while you'll be surrounded by danger and evil and there won't be any place to hide. You'll have something to do which seems insane, like climbing up on that boulder. Throwing the lightning back at the sky means you'll have to take your enemy's greatest weapon and turn it against her. The rain means peace, but only if you have the courage to do the other things first," he said.

"You sure are obscure sometimes, Scrapper," I said with a sigh.

"I only know what I know," he shrugged.

And with that I had to be content.

Chapter Thirty-Five
Lisa

We buried Mama late the same evening at Mount Nebo, not far from the largest of the cedar trees.

It was a brief and simple service, partly because of the cold and partly because me and Marcus were in no condition to stay out there for very long. Cody prayed, and we sang a hymn, and then in the last of the failing light, we laid her to rest in the pale Texas ground. I guess that little plot has seen a lot of such burials over the years.

Not many people were there; just Cody and Miss Josie, and me and Jenny and Aunt Michelle, and Brandon, and Marcus and his sister.

I cried almost the whole time, and Miss Josie did her best to try to comfort me, with whispered words about how we shouldn't weep like those who have no hope. I knew that she of all people knew what loss felt like, and I was comforted at least a little bit.

Cody quickly filled in the grave before we all went back down to the house. Miss Josie had cooked a somber dinner, barbecued beef and pecan pie and various other things, and for a while we all gathered in the kitchen and the living room to talk in low voices. I only picked at my food and couldn't find the heart to socialize much, even though I knew it would have been worse to be alone. I just sat beside Cody the whole time, and he held me when I seemed to need it, and that was good enough.

After a while Marcus left with his sister, and Jenny seemed to be getting ready to leave with Aunt Michelle also. But I had something else in mind, and when I was alone on the couch with Cody for a few minutes, I brought it up.

"Cody, would it be okay if I stayed here with you for a few days, till you go back to Alaska?" I asked wistfully, with my head on his shoulder. I could imagine lots of reasons why he might not think that was such a great idea, but I hoped he'd say yes in spite of it all.

"You don't think it might make you look bad?" he asked, only half jokingly.

"I don't care what the gossips think anymore. You and me both know that nothing improper will happen, and so does God. I just need you right now, that's all," I said, and he nodded.

"All right, then. I'll only be here till Friday, though," he reminded me.

"I know. But it's better than nothing," I said.

We walked home together through the pecan trees, holding hands but not saying anything. It was hard to walk on my wounded leg, and I had to lean on his arm most of the way and stop several times to rest. But eventually we got to the bunkhouse, and he silently opened the door for me. Once inside, we quietly lay down together on Cody's big cedar bed, and then he held me while I cried myself to sleep.

That's how it was for a few days. I had my good times, when the sun was out and I felt a little better and it seemed like life might actually go on someday. Then I'd slide off another cliff's edge of black depression for a few hours.

Cody was always there, to hold me when I needed it, to make sure I ate and remembered to brush my teeth, to remind me not to give up on living. He took me outside when the weather was nice and tried to talk to me and make me smile, even though it didn't work too often. Still, I thought then as I think now; it's the quiet, loving angels of this world who ought to inspire more awe than any other kind of hero.

I still felt awful from the toxoplasmosis and the wreck and everything else, but I gradually healed, both in body and in heart.

Cody ended up taking an extra two weeks off from work to stay with me a little longer, although I suspect he probably got himself in trouble for that. He never said so, but I could read between the lines well enough to guess.

A week after the funeral, I could even smile again now and then, and by the time Cody's birthday rolled around on the eleventh, I'd gotten to the point that I could even laugh occasionally and felt almost like my old self sometimes. There was still a shadow of pain in my heart, but nothing like what it was before.

But a fresh parting was looming ahead, when Cody had to go back to Alaska for seven more months. Two extra weeks was as much as he could manage without quitting his job completely. I was about to lose my steady rock, and I still wasn't sure how I'd handle things with him gone.

He must have wondered about that very thing, because he asked me about it that day while we were sitting in the gazebo by the lake. We'd just come back from having birthday cake and burgers with Miss Josie and Marcus and Brandon, which had buoyed me up more than usual. It had warmed up again after all the recent nastiness, although nobody expected it to last very long. There were already dark clouds piled up to the north beyond the lake, and little gusts of wind that hinted at another storm. But in the meantime, it was nice outside.

"Do you think you'll be okay, if I head back up north?" he asked quietly, gazing out across the lake while he played with my hair.

"I'm sure I'll survive. I won't like it, but I know we're on the downhill slide, now," I told him.

"Yeah, but seven months is still a long time. If you need me to stay, I'll stay," he said.

Heaven knows I was tempted. But I knew what it would mean if I said yes, and I couldn't let him do that.

"It's all right. Go do what you need to do. Get the ranch back in shape, and then everything will be better for all of us. You're not doing it just for yourself; it's for me, too. I know that. I'll be fine; I've got Miss Josie to watch out for me, and Jenny, and Marcus and Bran. I won't fall apart, I promise. It's time I learned how to stand on my own two feet, anyway," I said.

"You always could," he said.

"You think so, maybe. Boy, are *you* ever wrong," I said.

"No, I know so. The way you handled Layla, and Brandon, and everything else, it's pretty amazing, you know," he said.

"No, not really. I just did what I had to do," I said.

"That's the whole point. You always did what you had to, no matter how sick and scared you might have been at the time. You're one of the bravest girls I ever met, and it's one of the things I love about you the most," he said.

I'd never known that Cody felt that way about me, or that he thought I was so courageous. I certainly didn't feel that way. But if he believed it, then maybe there might be a grain of truth to it after all. I smiled.

"Then don't worry about me, Coby. I'll stick it out, and then when you get home we'll all live happily ever after," I told him.

"Amen to that," he agreed.

It stormed again that night, heavy and hard, with a freezing cold wind howling down the plains from Canada. Sometimes people like to say there's nothing between Texas and the North Pole but a barbed-wire fence, and nights like that I can surely believe it. It was chilly even inside the house, and we burrowed under the covers in bed to keep warm. I snuggled up against Cody's side and laid my head on his chest, with both his arms around me, just like I had on that other cold night in Alaska. I could hear his heart beat, and I felt warm and safe and right where I wanted to be.

"Marry me, Lisa," he said quietly, when I was right on the edge of sleep.

"What?" I asked, not sure I'd heard him right.

"Marry me. I love you, and you're the only one I want, for now and always. Let's make it official," he said. I knew those weren't cheap words for Cody McGrath, and I was overcome with a surge of love for him.

"That's all I've wanted ever since the beginning. Of course I will," I told him, and he hugged me close.

I think that night was one of the happiest times of my life, no matter how odd the circumstances of his proposal might be. I was tucked away in a little house in the middle of a freezing storm on the Texas plains, and outside I could hear the wind whistling and howling all night long. But I was safe and warm, held close in the arms of my beautiful boy. It was bliss. In a lot of ways I felt like he was already my husband; he was so very much the heart of my world. In some ways, it felt like he always had been.

* * * * * * *

As soon as we got up the next morning, he took me down to Longview to Ambrose's Jewelers. The streets and sidewalks were full of melting slush, and it was hard to walk without getting our feet soaked.

"Do you know what kind of ring you'd like?" Cody asked.

"Just something simple, that's all. White gold, I think, maybe one stone," I said, thinking out loud.

"We'll see what he's got, then," he said.

But as soon as we got inside, the first thing he did was to pull the Guardian Stone out of his shirt pocket and ask if it could be put on a chain. Apparently it could, so while he and Mr. Ambrose haggled out the details of all that, I browsed the ring case.

After a few minutes he came up beside me.

"Did you get that all worked out?" I asked, still looking at rings.

"Yeah, it'll be ready on Tuesday. I know it's a little bit of a risk to be without it, but it's only three days, and I figure it's better than the risk of losing it if it's not attached to anything," he said.

He scanned the ring box, and then shocked me by immediately picking out the biggest diamond in the case, a round cut solitaire on a white gold band. When he slipped it on my finger, it fit perfectly.

"You like it?" he asked, grinning.

"It's beautiful, but I'm sure it's much too expensive," I said in a low voice which Mr. Ambrose pretended not to hear.

"Well, not so much. So happens I'm rolling in dough right at the minute; might as well spend some of it," he said. Nothing I could say would deter him.

When he paid for my diamond and matching bands for both of us, I almost fainted. It didn't seem to faze Cody a bit, though, and five minutes later I left the store wearing a diamond big enough to cut logs with. Well, really it was only one carat, but that was still bigger than anything I'd ever seen in my life. I was almost afraid to wear something that expensive, for fear I might lose it or have it stolen.

"I can't believe you did that," I told him when we got back to the truck.

"Well. . . I wanted you to have somethin' special, you know. It's a one-time thing; might as well make you happy," he said.

"Aw, I would've been happy with a ring from a gumball machine, as long as it came from you, Cody," I told him, and he laughed.

"Okay, then. Should we take the ring back in there and get a refund and go get you a really nice cubic zirconia for thirty bucks?" he teased.

"Don't you dare," I told him, and he laughed again.

"Uh-huh, didn't think so. I'm glad you like it, though," he said.

"I absolutely love it. I can't wait to show it to everybody," I said.

"Good," he said, sounding pleased as punch.

We drove for a while in silence, while I admired the diamond by moving it back and forth in the sun. It was the most beautiful thing I'd ever owned.

"Any idea what day you'd like to get married?" he finally asked.

"What about today?" I asked immediately, and he laughed.

"We can't do it today, Lisa. There's no way," he said.

"I don't care if it's fancy or not. I don't even really want anybody there except family and a few friends, anyway. It's for us, not for the whole world," I said.

"But it's Saturday. The courthouse is closed, and anyway you don't even have a dress," he objected. I considered that idea, and decided he might have a point.

"Well, okay, maybe we can't do it today, then. What about the day before you leave? That'll give us a week to get everything ready," I said.

"Are you sure? You wouldn't rather wait till I get back home?" he asked.

"No, I definitely want it to happen before you leave again," I said. I was firm on that point; I didn't want to take a chance on anything splitting us up ever again.

"Well. . . okay, then," he said.

"Are you sure? You don't sound real enthusiastic," I said.

"No, it's not that. I just always thought a wedding was something special for a lady, you know. I want you to have a nice one, that's all," he said.

"It'll be nice. This is what I want, Cody; I promise," I told him, and finally he smiled.

"Then that's the way it'll be. But I want you to have a pretty ring and a long white dress and all that stuff, too, even if it costs a little more. You can tell me you don't care about that stuff all day long if you want to, but I know better," he said, and all I could do was laugh. He had me pegged, and I couldn't deny any of it.

So he took me into Tyler that afternoon to go shopping, and I found the perfect dress in a bridal shop down there. It was white and lacy and beautiful, with a ten-foot train and little silver horseshoes embroidered into the hem with metallic thread; a very old custom, they said. I'd already decided I wanted Cody to wear a royal blue western shirt and black wranglers instead of a tux, with his silver dress-buckle and cowboy boots. He said that was fine with him; he never liked monkey suits in the first place.

Monday morning he surprised me with a real silver sixpence to wear in my left shoe; a very old one from 1897, from Queen Victoria's Diamond Jubilee.

"Where'd you get that?" I asked, holding the coin in my hand and staring at it.

"Ordered it online from a coin shop, had it shipped overnight. It wasn't all that hard to find, honestly. I remembered how much you loved Queen Victoria, so I thought you'd like to have it," he said.

I kissed him for that, and tucked the sixpence safely away inside my purse until it was time to use it. I already had my new dress, an old necklace that Mama had loved to wear, some shoes borrowed from Jenny, and a long blue ribbon for my hair. Something old, something new, something borrowed, something blue, and a silver sixpence to wear in me shoe. Now I had it all.

I didn't plan on a very big reception since I wanted something a little smaller and more intimate. . . only about two dozen people. Miss Josie was more than happy to have an excuse to cook and to bake us a cake, and I meant to serve the traditional red ginger ale punch out of my grandmother's crystal punch bowl.

We decided to have it in the living room at Goliad, since we couldn't find a church on such short notice. But that was all right.

In saner moments, I realized I might have been a little too optimistic about being able to get everything done in only a week. Well, okay, I'd been a *lot* too optimistic, actually. It made things hectic, trying to organize and arrange and make plans and run here and there to take care of all the various things. But nevertheless, I was too happy to care about minor inconveniences.

Chapter Thirty-Six
Cody

On Monday afternoon, I got home whistling under my breath. I'd gone into town to pick up a pizza for supper, and Lisa had stayed behind, saying she was tired.

I was glad to be back; it was blustery and wet outside, with showers of cold rain blowing in the wind. My mind was full of warm food and a warm fire, and maybe a few warm kisses if Lisa happened to be awake. But not much else.

I trotted to the porch hunched over from the rain, fishing my house key out with one hand. The front door was already unlocked when I got there, which might have seemed a bit strange if I'd thought about it; Lisa usually kept the door locked if she was home alone. But at the time I didn't think much of it, and went inside without a care in the world, but quietly in case Lisa was still asleep.

The first thing I noticed was that the drapes were pulled tightly shut to block out the light, which didn't particularly bother me except that it made things almost pitch dark inside. Then I flipped the light switch and discovered that the power was out.

That was nothing unusual when it stormed, so I put down my keys and the pizza on the table and shut the door to keep the cold air out, feeling my way forward in the darkness to open the curtains. I almost stumbled over the bear-skin rug, and then I was startled when I felt Lisa's arms encircle me. I jumped a little, and then laughed and hugged her back.

"You shouldn't do stuff like that in the dark, Lisa; you startled m-" I began, and then she cut me off with a passionate kiss. One hand began to play with the hair on the back of my head and the other lay flat against my chest. She was warm, and the taste of her lips was sweet and smooth as vanilla. I wondered fleetingly if she'd found some new gloss or some such thing. It seemed so unlike-

That was as far as I got, because a second later she kneed me right between the legs, hard. I went down in agony, and hardly felt the kicks and blows she rained on my body thereafter. I couldn't even breathe to ask her what she was thinking.

Nor did I have to wonder for long. Seconds later she ripped the curtains open, and through a haze of pain and utter astonishment I saw none other than Layla Garza standing there, with a smile of triumph on her face.

I couldn't lift a finger to fight her; not right then, and she obviously knew it.

"There now, Cody. I've been wanting to do that forever," she said, and I wondered whether she meant the kiss or the kick. I would have much preferred the kiss, if I got to choose.

"Well, you got it," I gasped.

"Yes, I did. Just as good as I always thought, too. See you around, sweet stuff," she said cheerfully, and aimed another sharp kick at my face before she headed out the door. I managed to duck that one, but it didn't seem to faze her. She simply walked out and slammed the door hard enough to knock picture frames off the wall. There was no way I could chase her, so I didn't even try. That could come later.

As soon as I was able to get my breath, I hobbled painfully to the bedroom to check on Lisa. She wasn't there, and for a second I was terrified that Layla might have done something to her. I found her in the junk room, though, tied up with a big bruise on the side of her face. I untied the nylon rope she was bound with, and she soon woke up when I started rubbing her wrists and ankles.

"What happened?" I asked, as soon as she was able to sit up.

"I don't know. A girl wearing a scarf came to the door, and the second I opened it she punched me. That's the last thing I remember till you woke me up. Who was she? What did she want?" Lisa asked.

"It was Layla. I guess she must have survived after all," I said reluctantly.

"Yeah? So why didn't she finish us off, then?" she asked.

I started to answer her, but then I was overcome with a sudden wash of sick horror. Layla's power was to take the life from a young man with her kisses, like she'd done with James Fitch. . . and the Guardian Stone was still at the jeweler's.

I felt ill.

"She kissed me when I first came inside. It was dark and I never thought about anybody else being in the house. I thought she was you at first," I said.

"At first?" Lisa asked, and I couldn't tell if the question was a joke or serious.

"Yeah, for about two seconds or so. Right up till the point when she kneed me. That kinda spoiled the whole illusion, you know," I reminded her.

"I'm sorry. I didn't mean it to sound like that," she said.

"It doesn't matter. Let's find her, before she gets away. You didn't happen to see what she was driving, did you?" I asked.

"Yeah, it was a red Camaro, or something like that,"

"She must have moved it out of sight before I got here, then, because I didn't see anything. Did you notice the tags?" I asked.

"Uh. . . yeah. I don't remember the number, though," she said.

"Do you remember *any* of it? Even just the state would help," I said.

"No, but I think the license plate had a lighthouse on it," she said.

"That'd be Mississippi, then. I see those out on the interstate all the time. So I bet she's headed east," I said. It was a gamble, but it was the only clue we had.

We got in the truck and immediately headed out, knowing the chances were slim to none that we'd ever catch up with Layla. She had too much of a head start. I drove so fast I risked flipping the truck, but by the time we got to Linden I sighed and slowed down.

"It's a lost cause. She could've gone three or four different ways from here, if she even went this way at all," I said, admitting defeat.

We glumly turned around and went back to Goliad, driving a lot slower this time. I called Matthieu to pass along the information and tell him what happened, not that I expected it to help much. Even if Layla was really in Mississippi, she might move on at any time.

And in the meantime, I had worse problems to worry about.

The second I got out of bed the next morning, I knew something was different. It was hard to put my finger on what it was, exactly, but it was almost like having a cold, when my body was stiff and achy.

I felt a thin prickle of fear, and when I went to the bathroom to look in the mirror, that fear was confirmed. My hair was turning colors. It wasn't easy to tell yet unless you paid close attention; just a few strands of gray here and there. The stubble on my chin was much worse; nearly half the hairs were sugar-white. Not only that, but I was sure I saw faint lines around my eyes that hadn't been there yesterday, although that might simply be because I was still tired. I had a vivid memory of a thousand *Oil of Olay* commercials that promised to erase fine lines of aging, and I would have barked with laughter if I hadn't been so terrified at what it meant. James Fitch came to mind again, and I knew beyond a shadow of a doubt what lurked in my own future. In days, weeks; who knew?

I carefully plucked out all the gray hairs I could find and shaved away the salt-and-pepper stubble so Lisa wouldn't notice anything, and then washed out the sink so she wouldn't see it there, either.

She woke up while I was brushing my teeth, and silently came to put her arms around me from behind and kiss the nape of my neck. She must have felt the tension in my body, or sensed it some other kind of way, because almost immediately she looked up at me in the mirror.

"What's wrong, Cody?" she asked, in a tone that meant she knew perfectly well that *something* was. Even in the midst of my fear and distraction, I marveled all over again at how well she could read me sometimes. It was almost eerie.

"I don't guess you'd believe me if I said it was nothing, would you?" I asked, hoping it would make her smile. It didn't.

"Nope, not a chance," she said.

There was no help for it, and soon enough no hiding it either, so I gave in gracefully. I put her arms down so I could turn around, and stuck out my chin so she could see it in the light. Even shaved, it was easy to tell if anybody looked close enough.

"Look," I said simply.

She must have realized what it meant without needing to be told, because she put her arms around me again and put her head on my chest, and I soon felt the warmth of tears soaking through my t-shirt. I put my arms around her without saying a word.

"It doesn't matter," she finally said, hugging me tighter. Her words were muffled against my body, but I understood them.

"What do you mean?" I asked.

"I mean it doesn't matter. I love you, and I'm still going to marry you on Saturday even if it kills me," she said fiercely.

I couldn't say anything to that. All I could do was hug her a little tighter, and wonder what good thing I ever did to deserve someone who loved me so much.

"Lisa, there's got to be a way to undo this. Somehow, some way. I don't know what it is, yet, but I can't believe it's got to end like this," I finally said.

"Maybe the Guardian Stone will fix it. We could try that first," she said.

"Yeah, that's definitely the first thing. Or maybe we could find something in Matthieu's library, like he suggested," I said.

She let me go, and I quickly slipped a dry shirt over my head before grabbing my phone from the desk where I'd left it to charge the night before. Then I quickly punched in Matthieu's number.

And got his voicemail.

"So?" Lisa asked hopefully.

"Got his voicemail. I'll have to wait and let him call me back later. I didn't think about it before but I bet he's in class this morning," I said.

"Yeah, I keep forgetting that," Lisa said.

"Yeah, me too. But maybe he'll call back at lunch time," I said.

"Maybe so," she agreed.

"In the meantime, let's go pick up the crystal," I said.

So that's what we did, and I slipped it back around my neck the instant it was in my hands.

"Hopefully it works," I muttered as we left the store, and she could only squeeze my hand and agree.

Matthieu did call back at lunch time.

"You'll have to come to Natchitoches, if you want to find out anything else. I don't know if there's anything more in here about the Guardian Stones or Layla's magic or anything else that might help, but if anybody knows anything, this is where it'll probably be," he said almost immediately when I told him the news.

"What time?" I asked.

"Anytime after three o'clock is fine," he said.

"We'll be there about three-thirty, then," I agreed.

Lisa had overheard the entire conversation, of course, so there was no need for me to tell her what was going on. She quietly limped to the bathroom to change clothes and fix her hair, not even bothering to ask me if we were going or not. Her leg still bothered her sometimes, but it was getting better.

"Do you think we should take Marcus?" she asked when she got out.

"I was just thinking about that. All we're really doing is going over there to look at some old books. I'm not sure if he'd care anything about that or not, but we'll ask him," I said.

It turned out Marcus had had enough road running for a while, so me and Lisa ended up going alone that time. Natchitoches is only a little more than two hours' drive from Avinger, so we still had plenty of time to get there by three o'clock.

"I'm sorry you got dragged into all this," I said.

"No, don't be sorry. I made my choice with both eyes open. I got you, and that's enough to make me happy for the rest of my life," she said, and I smiled.

"You really think so, huh?" I asked.

"I know so," she said firmly.

The rest of the trip passed uneventfully, and not long after three o'clock we pulled into Matthieu's driveway.

"Well, let's go see what we see," I said, getting out. She followed, and we walked up to the front door holding hands. I pushed the doorbell, and chimes sounded from inside. After a few minutes Matthieu opened the door.

"I thought y'all would never get here. Come on in; I've already got some of the books laid out on the dining room table, but there are still a lot more to go through," he said.

"How's your leg?" Lisa asked, and he smiled.

"Better. It'll leave a scar, I'm sure, but nothing worse than that. What about you and Marcus?" he asked.

"Yeah, I'm mostly better. Him too, I think," she said.

"That's good. I was a little concerned about how things would turn out. Here are all the books I was able to find so far that have something to say about Guardian Stones, or sorcery, or anything similar. There's actually some method to all this disorder, believe it or not. My dad knows where everything is, if you give him a minute to think about it," Matthieu said, and then we got down to business.

"This is interesting," Lisa said after a while.

"What is it?" I asked.

"*This* book talks about attaching one of the Stones to a specific person, like Hannah did with Cody. It says you have to place the Stone in a spot of special significance both to you and to them. If it ever leaves that spot then it reverts to protecting whoever holds it," she said.

"That's good to know, I guess, but I don't see how it helps, much. We already knew the Stones could be attached to a single person," Matthieu pointed out.

We kept searching till we covered every book on the table and quite a few others we pulled from elsewhere. But in spite of hours of searching, that pitiful little tidbit was the only fresh information that we found all day. It hardly seemed worth it, and we left Natchitoches that night more discouraged than ever.

Chapter Thirty-Seven
Cody

"I have an idea," Lisa said on the way home that evening. It was dark by then, and we were both moodily staring at the lights of cars passing by on the interstate. She seemed unhappy, and I could hardly blame her.

"What is it?" I asked, tiredly.

"What if you asked for a dream tonight? So far you've only waited for them to come whenever they come. But it's like Brandon told me a while back; sometimes you have to ask," she suggested.

"Yeah, I hadn't thought about that," I admitted.

Therefore that night when we got home, that's what we did. I don't often pray on my knees, but that night I did, and so did Lisa even though I knew it must have hurt her leg. We put our foreheads together, and I spoke. I asked for wisdom and for courage, and for a true dream that might show me what to do. Then Lisa spoke and thanked God for His great glory and love. I've never believed in prayers of many words. I think God knows what we need before we even ask. To pray long is to think we can impress Him with what we say, like a lawyer in front of a judge.

After we were done I got up and helped Lisa to her feet, and then we went to bed. And that night, indeed, I dreamed.

It was nothing like any of the others, except that it was the same kind of vivid almost-real sort of vision. I found myself standing on the bank of a rocky river, full and clear, with a bright sun shining down and glinting off the ripples in the water. The grass was thick and green underfoot and the trees were just beginning to bud. And suddenly I knew this place, and would have gasped if I'd been awake. But as it was, I could only watch in mute horror.

There on the bank stood three teenagers, a girl and two boys, playing in the shallows of the river, while a slightly older man in dark sunglasses watched from a distance. Farther downstream I saw my father, not much older than I am now, fly fishing for trout. I saw my mother cooking hamburgers on a camp stove, and my own six-year-old self, thin and tow-headed, building stacks of rocks beside the table. I knew what was coming, and wished I could wake up.

Even worse, I knew with the sure and certain knowledge of dreams who those four people standing upstream from us were. Layla Garza and her three brothers; Andrew, Gabe, and Orem.

No one had been watching Layla at the time, but in my dream I saw her glance at the older man; Andrew. He nodded meaningfully at her, and she nodded back. Then she artfully pretended to slip and fall into the deep current, with a piercing scream that made everyone turn to look. The current snatched her away at once, and she didn't seem to know how to swim. No one else moved, but Daddy, poor, brave, selfless soul that he had been, never hesitated. He threw down his pole and kicked off his shoes and plunged into the water, swimming strongly to intercept the girl before she drowned. The current quickly carried both of them out of sight, and that had been the last time I'd ever seen him alive.

Until now. I seemed to hang above the river, and I saw my father reach the girl and struggle to pull her to shore. They came aground on a grassy bank, him crawling from exhaustion and Layla seemingly not much better. But then she grabbed a rock from the muddy ground and smashed the back of her rescuer's head while he wasn't looking. He collapsed to the ground, bleeding and knocked out cold, and I saw her smile. Then she rolled him over on his back and knelt down beside him. He was still breathing, and she kissed him on the lips long and deeply. She glanced around to make sure no one was near, and then she carefully and methodically dragged him back out to the edge of the current and shoved him in. She waited to make sure the river had him well and truly in its grasp, and then smiled in satisfaction before returning to the bank herself.

I wanted to scream and cry and curse, and I could do none of those things. Knowing that my father had died to save another person's life had been hard enough. Finding out he'd been killed by that same person was ten thousand times worse.

Layla was sitting on the bank sobbing her heart out by the time the first people came, and I had to listen while she told a moving story about how Daddy had pulled her to shore and saved her life but never made it out behind her. I hated the Garzas at that moment more than I've ever hated anybody or anything in my life, and I made a fist so tight it hurt even in my dream. I wished I could hit somebody, or break something, or maybe just weep.

He was her first, a quiet voice whispered in my mind, and I knew without asking what that meant. He was the first youth she'd drained of his life, and that must have been why she kissed him before tossing him back into the river to drown.

She liked the taste of him, and that's why she came after you in Alaska, the voice said.

The scene on the riverbank had played itself out by then, and in mercy my eyes were shielded from the sight when my father's body was pulled from the flooded Brazos nearly a mile downstream.

Why did I have to see this? I cried.

You had to know. You wouldn't have understood what you must do, if you had never seen, the voice answered.

What must I do? I asked, startled at the thought. I'd almost forgotten.

First, you must forgive her. You must forgive all of them. And then you must give her your Stone, and bring it here to this place, and leave it, the voice said.

I can't do that! I cried in horror. It was too much to ask; it was beyond anything I could ever have the strength to do. But the voice was silent, and would not argue.

She is my daughter also, it said, and that was the last thing I heard. I woke to find tears on my cheeks, and my heart more broken than it had been since that night in Alaska with Lisa. I was developing a real talent for crying lately, I thought to myself.

It was almost six thirty, and I decided there was no point in staying in bed any longer. I got up quietly, leaving Lisa asleep. Then I went to the living room to sit on the couch and try to pull myself together after what I'd seen and heard. I had no doubt it was a true dream; there was no way I would have imagined anything like that, even in my worst nightmares. I wouldn't have imagined being spoken to by God, either, for that matter.

I'm sure that's who it was, and that part awed and humbled me. The revelation of what had really happened to my father and what I'd been asked to do was no easier, but it was impossible to ignore. Forgiving the Garzas for all the wickedness they'd done was hard enough, but in some ways giving Layla the Guardian Stone was even worse. It seemed to be protecting me the way it was supposed to; at least, I felt no older than I had the day before. But without it I knew I'd quickly grow old, just like James Fitch. There was no doubt in my mind that I wouldn't live long enough to see my next birthday, at the rate I'd been going before I got the crystal back. It seemed like a complete victory for them, a careless tossing away of my whole life, a deliberate taking back of everything I'd promised Lisa and a dashing of every hope. I didn't know what to do.

Or, well, yes, I *did* know what to do, honestly. . . I just didn't like it and hadn't choked down my resistance quite yet, that's all.

As soon as I recognized the source of my trouble, I recognized the uselessness of it, also. When God asks for something, the only choice you've got is whether to refuse or whether to try to obey, and that's really no choice at all, if you're a believer.

Therefore I'd try to do what He'd asked of me, if I could. I guess that part was never really in doubt, after all. I remember reading once that few things are dearer to God's heart than a son or daughter who finds themselves forsaken and alone, who can see nothing but heartache as the result of obedience... and then obeys anyway. Well, I'd be a good son, and if that required throwing myself on a sharp sword, then so be it.

I didn't make the decision gladly, and I didn't make it without a residue of bitterness and fear which I don't doubt is a flaw in my nature. I'm not one of the martyrs, who could go into the flames with a smile on my face. Nowhere near.

I quietly got dressed and headed across the pasture towards the big house, my heart no more at ease than yesterday. Sometimes the truth is no comfort.

I made an effort to compose myself by the time I reached the back door, and when I got inside I found Mama and Marcus eating breakfast at the kitchen table. Bran was already gone to school, I suppose; he left pretty early.

"So, did you find out anything yesterday?" Marcus asked.

"Not much. But I did have a dream last night. A true one," I finished. As I expected, that got their full attention.

"What happened?" Marcus asked, leaning forward in his chair.

"I have to forgive the Garzas, and I have to give Layla the Guardian Stone," I said wearily. I didn't mention what I'd found out about Daddy; there was no need to darken Mama's heart with *that* news. I didn't say anything about having to take the Stone to Possum Kingdom, either, for fear she might guess too much.

"Are you sure that's what it means?" Mama finally asked.

"Yeah, I'm definitely sure," I said.

Maybe neither one of them knew what to say, because I finally smiled.

"But, on a more practical note, did y'all save me some food or did you eat it all?" I asked.

"There's some left on the stove," Mama said, and I helped myself. I left enough for Lisa, although there was no telling what time she might get up. She's a late sleeper sometimes when she gets the chance.

I ate my breakfast, and then went out to the barn to feed Buck and the other horses, since Marcus still couldn't do much yet. There weren't quite as many chores to be done in the wintertime, especially with the cows gone, but the few that there were couldn't be overlooked. Brandon helped a lot, but he couldn't do everything.

"Are you really giving her the Stone?" Marcus asked quietly, walking out to the barn with me.

"Yeah, I really am," I nodded.

"But you know if you do that, you won't be protected anymore," he pointed out.

"Yeah, I know," I agreed.

"Then why do it?" he asked.

"Mostly because I was told to. I'm sure there has to be a reason for that, even if I don't know for sure what it is," I said.

"What possible reason could there be?" he asked.

"I'm not sure. But I got to thinking, you know, maybe it'll stop her from hurting anybody else. She couldn't drain away people's life if she can't be affected by magic, could she? Maybe that's what Brandon meant about not being afraid to do something that seems insane and turning her greatest weapon against her," I said.

"Sounds logical, I guess," Marcus admitted.

"So then it'd be worth it, wouldn't it?" I asked.

"I reckon you're the only one who can decide that," he said, refusing to look at me.

"Marcus, we've been friends for a long time now, right?" I asked.

"Yeah," he agreed.

"Then don't be so down in the mouth. You never know what'll happen. Things might turn out better than you think," I said. I was speaking as much for my own benefit as for his, but that didn't make what I said any less true.

"I know," he said.

"Will you come with me, then?" I asked.

"Come where? You didn't say anything about needing to go anywhere," he said.

"To Possum Kingdom. I've got to put the Stone in the river, where Daddy died," I said, and for a second Marcus was speechless.

"Why *there*, of all places?" he demanded, when he got his voice back.

"I told you it's got to be put in a place that means something to both people, right?" I asked.

"Yeah, and I know what that place means to *you*, obviously. But what's it got to do with *her?*" he asked.

"You can't tell Mama, but she was the girl my father tried to rescue that day when he drowned. She knocked him out with a rock and let him die. He was her first victim, and that was the first place she ever practiced her sorcery. So that's where it has to end," I explained.

"I'm sorry," Marcus said, and I knew what he was talking about without having to ask.

"It's all right. He did it because he believed he was saving her. He's still a hero as far as I'm concerned," I said staunchly.

"I only meant. . . well, never mind. Yeah, of course I'll go. When are you leaving?" Marcus asked.

"In a little while, when Lisa gets up. There's no reason to wait," I said.

"No reason to wait for what?" Lisa asked, appearing in the archway of the barn.

"You're up early, baby," I said, smiling as I went to give her a kiss.

"Yeah, I guess so. I walked up to the house and Miss Josie said you were out here. She seemed upset so I wondered what was up," she explained.

"Did you eat anything?" I asked.

"Yeah, I had a biscuit and a piece of sausage. But I'm not worried about that right now. What did I miss?" she asked.

So I told her, recapping everything I'd already told Marcus, including my reasoning as to why it needed to be done. Then I waited to see what she'd say, because other than me, she was the one person most deeply affected by it all. When I was finished she looked at me solemnly.

"So what do you think?" I finally asked, when she didn't speak.

"I think even if I never loved you before, I would now," she said, and I laughed a little, embarrassed.

"Don't laugh; I was being serious," she scolded.

"I know you were. I'm sorry," I said.

"It's okay. But you're right, there's no reason to waste any time. Let's go while it's still early," she said.

Chapter Thirty-Eight
Lisa

We left in Cody's truck, without saying much to Miss Josie. There was room for three of us in the cab, if we squeezed a little bit.

"How far is it to Possum Kingdom?" I asked when we stopped at the light in Avinger.

"About four hours or so. Not far past Fort Worth," Cody said tightly. He was probably conflicted about having to visit the place, if I had to guess. Glad to strike a blow for justice, but dreading the memories he was sure to have to face. As far as I knew, he hadn't been back there since he was six years old.

"I wonder why it's called Possum Kingdom," I said out loud.

"You got me, there," Cody said.

"It's because they used to trap possums out there in the canyons. For the fur, you know," Marcus said.

"I didn't know they ever made anything out of possum fur. Seems like it'd be all thin and stringy and gray and ugly," I said.

"I don't know about that part. Maybe it was for people who needed some cheap fur and they didn't care if it was kinda ugly. I guess they could always dye it if they wanted to," Marcus said.

"How do you know all that, anyway?" I asked.

"I remember reading about it somewhere," he shrugged.

"You know, I thought about something just now," I said, turning to Cody again.

"What's that?" he asked.

"It said in that book that we have to make sure the Stone stays in the same place once we put it there. How can you make sure it'll do that, at the bottom of a river? Won't the current sweep it away?" I asked.

"Yeah, I already thought about that. We'll have to stop and get some epoxy cement or something like that, and glue it into a hole in the rock," he said.

We stopped at a hardware store in Mineral Wells to do that very thing, and bought two gallons of marine epoxy sealant and a small steel box to hold the crystal. Then, a little over thirty minutes later, we were there. Cody seemed ill at ease, and I could hardly blame him.

We approached the dam area slowly, passing by an ominous warning sign that told us the water was subject to sudden rise and we should wade or swim at our own risk. We parked near the picnic tables and got ready to begin.

The river was deserted; nothing unusual for a weekday in January, but that was all to the good. No snoopy eyes to see what we were up to. There was practically nothing but a trickle in the bottom of the stream bed, thin enough that we could have jumped across in places. That was because of the ongoing drought, which had shrunk the Brazos to almost nothing.

We all three climbed down the rocky bank onto the stream bed, glancing uneasily at the dam. The warning sign had said there would be a horn blast to warn people to get out, but we'd only have about two minutes before the water arrived. That's precious little time. But the dam looked dry and tranquil, and there didn't seem to be any immediate release planned.

"So where are we supposed to go?" Marcus asked.

"Downstream a little bit. As close as we can get to where she. . . " Cody began, and then left it at that, waving vaguely downriver with his left arm. We headed that way, stumbling sometimes over the rough limestone boulders that filled the streambed. It hurt my leg now and then, but I was determined not to whine about it.

I had a gallon of epoxy to carry, and Marcus had the gallon of hardener. Cody had the crystal inside its metal casket, a hammer, a tube of super glue, a five-gallon plastic bucket, and a pack of sandpaper.

It seemed to take forever, but it couldn't really have been very long before we arrived at a larger-than-normal boulder in a deeper-than-normal spot, and Cody stopped.

"This is the spot," he said.

We gathered around the slab of limestone, which was full of pits and crevices, and Cody selected one of these which let him slip the box inside the rock almost elbow-deep. He opened the box and took the crystal out, lifted it up to the sky, and prayed silently. I was almost certain I saw his lips move in the shape of Layla Garza's name, and then in a normal voice he spoke these words:

> *The Lord bless you and keep you,*
> *The Lord make his face to shine upon you,*
> *And be gracious unto you,*
> *The Lord lift up his countenance unto you,*
> *And give you peace.*

Then he kissed the Guardian Stone and put it in the box we'd bought for it, and shut the lid before stuffing it as deep inside the crack as he could reach.

"All right, let's seal it in," he said. Marcus already had the lid of his jug open, and Cody took the other jar from me and pried it open with the claw of his hammer. Then he quickly poured both of them into the bucket and stirred them vigorously.

When they were thoroughly mixed, Cody poured the entire concoction into the hole till it was full to overflowing. Then there was a thirty minute wait for it to harden until he could use the sandpaper. The idea was to smooth and soften the edges of the epoxy to make it look more or less like any other part of the rock, just in case the water was ever low again and some nosy explorer got curious.

"Where'd you get those words you said?" I asked, and he shrugged.

"It's the priestly blessing from Numbers. It's what my Grandma Hannah said when she attached the Stone to me. I tried to do everything exactly the way she did," he said.

"Do you think anybody'll find the Stone?" I asked.

"I don't see how they would. This place is almost always under water, unless it's during a hundred-year drought like this. And even if it was exposed, I doubt anybody would take the trouble to bust up enough rock and putty to find it. It's buried in there pretty deep. I just hope this works, and stops her from hurting anybody else," he said.

There was no way I could reassure him about that part, of course, so I didn't try. All I could do was squeeze his hand, and try not to notice the age in his eyes. After a while, the putty was hardened enough that he could start sanding it down. He did his best to make it even with the edge of the stone, to give the water as little of a crevice to work on as possible. We didn't want it eroding away the stone and moving the box; at least not till Layla Garza had lived out her life and was gone. What might happen to the Stone after that was anybody's guess.

He finished sanding and was ready to spread the superglue across the surface and coat it with dust to further camouflage it, and then we heard the sound we'd all been dreading ever since we first set foot on the riverbed. The horn at the dam sounded, faint and far behind us. Cody hurriedly finished spreading the glue with his fingers and threw sand on top, not caring if the job was perfect or if he got some on his hands. Marcus quickly started to pile the cans and trash into the bucket to take with us but Cody waved him down.

"Don't worry about that! Just leave it here and the river'll wash it away. Let's go!" he cried. Marcus grabbed the bucket and threw it across the empty channel, where it hit a boulder and scattered trash everywhere. Then we ran.

There was no place close by where we could get out of the channel. When the water level was high, then no doubt the bank could have been reached by a swimmer. But as it was, there were steep limestone banks on both sides which were almost impossible to climb. We had no choice but to run downstream, hoping for a place where the slope of the bank was gentler.

We almost made it. Two minutes can seem like two years when you're hobbling as fast as you can across loose rocks and boulders, praying to God you'll outrun a flood which is hot on your heels. We almost made it to a place where the bank was low and shelving, but not quite, because the water caught us right before we got to the tree line. Seconds later, all three of us were slogging through ice-cold water which quickly rose over our heads and swept us into the woods. That slowed the current a bit, but in a way it was even more dangerous since there were more things to hit or get trapped in.

"Climb that tree!" Cody yelled, and then took his own advice. There was a huge oak tree somewhat leaned over ahead of us, and when the water carried us beside it he grabbed hold of a low branch and pulled himself up. I was right behind him and he barely had time to turn around and grab my arm to help me up. Marcus managed it on his own, and together we climbed higher to be out of reach of the river. The water level was still rising fast and none of us knew when it might stop.

When we reached a point about twenty feet above the water, which was as far as we could climb. The trunk was broken off at that point, and the branches were too thin to hold us up. So there we sat amongst the leafless branches, huddled together and shivering in our soaked clothes but glad to be safe.

"Do you think it'll make it this high?" I asked, through chattering teeth. If you want to know how I felt, imagine getting dunked in ice water and then going outside on a breezy winter day. Not fun at all. Cody can go swimming amongst the icebergs in Prudhoe Bay all he wants to, but I'm no Polar Bear, I promise you.

"I don't think so. There's the water line, over there on those bushes. I don't think it'll get this high. All we have to do is wait till they stop releasing water and then we can walk out," Cody said. I hoped so; I'd never been so cold even in Alaska.

"How long do you think it'll be?" Marcus asked.

"Who knows? Probably a few hours, at least. All we can do is wait," Cody said.

So that's what we did, and a miserable few hours it certainly was, too. The water stopped rising when it reached a point about three or four feet below the place where we sat. Too close for comfort, but not close enough to be dangerous. After a long, long time, I noticed the level was gradually dropping. It was almost like watching a loaf of bread bake in the oven; you couldn't tell anything had changed unless you looked away for a while. But eventually it dropped to the point that it was no more than a sluggish flow.

"I think it's probably safe to climb down now, if y'all don't mind slogging through the water a little bit," Cody finally said.

"Sure, let's go," I agreed immediately. I was ready to walk through ten rivers if it got me out of that dadgummed tree.

We carefully climbed down, and found that the water was still waist deep, and in some places more. We had to swim across a particularly deep backwater, but when all was said and done we reached the shore with nothing worse than a fresh freezing. We were on the wrong side of the river, but nobody felt like swimming again.

"We'll have to walk down to the highway bridge and cross back over. It shouldn't be that far," Cody said.

It turned out to be less than half a mile, though that was far enough. The bridge itself was built of masonry arches, and I would have stopped to admire the prettiness of it if I hadn't been so tired, and so cold, and if my feet hadn't been so sore. My leg was hurting, too, but I hated to ask for help. We crossed the bridge, and then followed the road on the other side back up to where the truck was parked, just past the warning sign. I've never been so glad to see a heater in my life.

Cody didn't say a word about getting the seats wet; all three of us climbed in and turned the heat up full blast, and by the time we got back to Mineral Wells all three of us were toasty warm again.

Nobody seemed to be in much of a mood to talk, and after a while I put my head down on Cody's shoulder and closed my eyes. His clothes were still wet, but I didn't care.

"Do y'all think we should stop and get some cheap dry clothes?" he asked presently, when he saw a dollar store up ahead.

"It'd be nice," I admitted, and Marcus only shrugged. Cody pulled in to the parking lot, and soon enough we all had a cheap set of dry clothes, with the wet ones tossed in the truck bed. Cody covered the soaked seat with some bath towels, and after that I did fall asleep when we got back on the road. It had been a long day.

* * * * * * *

The next morning I woke up earlier than usual, and when I turned my head to look at Cody, I barely contained a gasp. He had hair in his ears, and his hands had dark spots on them, and his stubbly whiskers were white as snow, like an old man's. He looked fifteen or twenty years older than yesterday. Giving up the crystal had left him defenseless, it seemed.

I gazed at him in horror, and unwillingly tried to guess how much longer he might live like that. A week? Ten days? I didn't know if he'd keep aging that fast every day or if it would slow down at some point. But one thing was for certain; he wouldn't make it long. Not like that.

I thought of the day when he first walked into the Dairy Dip and swept me up in his arms with a laugh. So young, so handsome, so full of life, with his silly little grin and his blue, blue eyes. It seemed like a hundred years ago; all the more so when I saw him lying there looking like a man on the cusp of old age. I loved him so much, for so many different reasons, and now it seemed that I was about to lose him already.

I remembered my own words, about how I wouldn't be sorry even if a little time was all we ever had. They seemed prophetic now, and harsh. It's so easy to make promises, when nothing is at stake and you know they'll never be put to the test. Now I was staring Death in the face, and I wondered if I had the strength to keep my word. Jenny would have told me I deserved better. Maybe most people would have thought the same thing, even if they didn't come right out and say so.

Mama would have said that love with strings attached is worthless.

I reached out to run my hand along the side of his face and then through his short stubbly hair. Somewhere beneath that weather-beaten surface I could still see the ghost of the boy I'd known. I could *feel* him, with my heart if not with my hands, and I felt a flood of love mixed with sorrow. I kissed him gently on the lips, not hard enough to wake him, and then put my arms around him with my head on his chest, as if holding on to him fiercely enough might ward off the doom that was settling slowly but surely on us both. I closed my eyes, like a child who can't bear the sight of evil, and for a little while I could pretend that nothing had changed.

As I lay there, and as I so often had done in the past, I began to put some of my feelings into words, into verses that would express at least a little bit of how I felt and how much I loved him. And when I was done, the work read like this:

Cody

Sometimes at night I think I dream,
Of blossoms tossed by summer breeze,
While weaved amongst my flowing hair,
Beneath the rustling white-oak trees.

I watched you gather a blade of rye,
In June all soft and palest green,
To taste the sweet and loving earth,
So fresh and cool and misty-clean.

Your skin was warm as summer hay,
The sun had kissed all golden brown,
Your touch as soft as the breeze that day,
That curled your dampened hair around.

Oh, your love was all the world to me,
And the thought that you were mine,
More beautiful then than a shining star,
When only one is in the sky.

For who could ever take your place?
And who could touch my heart so deep?
And how could I ever count the ways,
Your love has meant so much to me?

Though storms may rage and dark may fall,
And heartache come for a year and a day,
I still feel the warmth of your hand in my own,
And your love washes sorrow forever away.

I tinkered with the words a bit, till the work pleased me. I thought I might have it printed on rose-paper and framed in a wooden frame, to give to him so he'd always know what he meant to me.

Thinking thus, I gradually drifted back to sleep, still holding him close while I could.

Chapter Thirty-Nine
Cody

"I wonder if I should quit my job," I asked at breakfast two days later. There wasn't much to wonder about, honestly; I'd never be able to get anything done at Prudhoe Bay in the shape I was in. I was in pretty low spirits about the whole thing; I only had about half the cash I needed to dig Goliad out of the hole. It helped, but it wasn't near enough.

"I'll go instead, if it comes to that," Marcus said staunchly.

"You're not up to it, either, Marcus," I said.

"No, but I will be. Give me a month or so and I'll be fine," he said. It was a noble offer, and I didn't know but what I might not have to take him up on it. I poked at my sausage and eggs, not sure what to say.

"You got a letter in the mail this morning, Cody," Mama said, filling in the silence.

"Really? Who from?" I asked.

"I don't know. I didn't open it, and there was no return address on there. Here it is, though," she said, getting up to fetch it from the mail holder on the countertop.

I took the letter, and there was indeed no return address anywhere on the envelope, but it was addressed to me and I did notice that it was postmarked from Athens, Georgia. I couldn't think of a soul I knew in that part of the world, but it didn't look like junk mail since the address was handwritten. I shrugged and tore it open.

It was from Layla.

There was only a single page, and it was nothing but a long, poisonous tirade of hatred and spite. She spent most of it mocking me, telling me she'd been having dreams about me lying dead in the moonlight and other cheerful things like that. I turned it over and found nothing on the back, and wondered why she bothered. If she was hoping to hurt my feelings then she failed miserably at that. I was unmoved by the whole thing, except maybe to pity her a little. Hate hurts the hater more than the hated, so all she was doing was heaping coals on her own head.

I shrugged it off and dismissed the whole thing.

"What did she say?" Lisa asked, as soon as I finished reading.

"Oh, nothing much. Just a bunch of insults and nastiness, about like you'd expect. Read it for yourself," I said, handing her the letter. She read it, and when she was done she turned to Brandon.

"Bran, do you remember the story about when the King of Babylon wouldn't tell anybody his dream, but Daniel knew what it was and interpreted it anyway?" she asked.

"Yeah, what about it?" he said.

"Do you think you could do something like that?" she asked.

"I don't know. I never thought about it. Why?" he asked.

"Because if Layla Garza's been having dreams, then they might tell us something, if you can read them," she said.

I hadn't thought of that, but it seemed highly unlikely. I could accept the idea that God might create such a thing as the Guardian Stones, but it was hard to see how such a stone would work for an evil person like Layla Garza. It didn't seem to make any sense.

But then on the other hand, it's certainly true that everybody serves God's purposes, whether they like it or not and no matter what they choose to do. They can choose willingly to serve Him like a son or daughter, or they can refuse and then He'll use them like a tool instead. So it was possible Layla had been used as a tool, since she wouldn't serve Him as a daughter. She could have been given the dreams He meant for her to have, to serve the purposes He meant for them to serve, regardless of what kind of person she was. That made sense, in a way.

But while I was thinking about all that, the conversation had moved on without me.

"I can try, but I'm not promising anything," Brandon said, shrugging.

"No, I'm not expecting you to. Just thought it might be worth asking," Lisa said.

"Maybe so," he said.

He put down his fork and started praying, his lips moving silently. When he looked up, he had that unfocused gleam in his eyes that he sometimes gets, and finally he spoke.

"I know what she dreamed, but you won't like it," he said.

"What is it?" I asked, grimly preparing myself for the worst.

"She dreamed you were dead beside a pool of water, on a cloudy night with only one bright star shining down through the clouds and reflecting in the pool," he said, and I think my heart stopped.

"What does it mean?" I asked. It seemed pretty dadgummed plain what it meant, but I had to ask. Bran looked uncomfortable, but he didn't answer me directly.

"Call Matthieu. Ask him to go outside to the brick wall that separates the front yard from the flower garden next to his house," he said.

"For what?" I asked. It wasn't remotely what I expected to hear.

"There's a ceramic troll about two feet high sitting in the corner where the house meets the fence, right next to the wrought iron gate. It's hollow and has a removable head. Tell him to look inside it," he said.

"What's in there?" I asked.

"A few years ago a boy had to climb over that fence, leaving on the path behind him a glass bottle full of water from a holy spring which had the power to heal any sickness or hurt. His reasons for breaking in don't matter; you can ask Matthieu if you want to know that whole story. He meant to slip the bottle through the bars of the gate once he reached the other side, but soon discovered that it was too big to fit. So he poured as much as he could into an empty Coke bottle from the trash, and then completely forgot about that *other* bottle which he left outside the wall. The gardener found it later, and since he was too lazy to carry it all the way to the trash, he just put it inside the troll so nobody would see it, and then forgot about it himself. No one has touched it ever since," he said.

"It's still full of holy water?" I asked, but Bran was already shaking his head.

"No, not full. There's only a very little bit left, and it's the last in all the world. Layla Garza's brother destroyed all the rest; Matthieu knows that story, too. But that one last bottle is the single star in your dream," he said.

"It's enough to cure me of being older than dirt, though, right?" I asked, with a sense of relief which I don't think you could possibly imagine.

"Well, yeah, it *would* be, Cody. But you can't drink it. There's something else you have to use it for instead," he said, and that instantly threw cold water all over the relief and happiness I'd been feeling a second ago.

"What's that?" I asked.

"Pour it in the Cadron Pool," he said.

"You mean the one back there in the woods behind Nebo?" I asked skeptically. I guess that was a silly thing to ask; I certainly didn't know of any *other* Cadron Pool. But Brandon's suggestion was so unreasonable and stupid that I had to make sure we were actually talking about the same thing.

"Yeah," he said, confirming it. For a second I was speechless.

"Why?" I finally asked, and he shrugged.

"That's what Layla's dream means. That last bit of water is the shining star that has to be put in the pool before you die. I can't say why; I just know that's what you're supposed to do," he said.

"You *know* this?" Lisa asked, and he simply nodded.

I don't like doing things on blind faith, when I don't know why. Which I suppose when you're dealing with a prophet is a character flaw. They're notorious for asking people to do things that don't make any sense, to test your faith and courage. The ones who trust them are blessed, and the ones who reject them are cursed. I've read all the stories often enough to know it. But trust me, when it's your own neck on the chopping block, it's a lot harder to believe. I knew that water could erase Layla's magic, and Bran was telling me to pour it out.

A year ago I don't know what I might have said or done, but I've learned many things about what it means to trust God at times when He asks things that seem impossible. So I called Matthieu, and even though he seemed skeptical at first, he did go look inside the troll. The bottle was there, just like Brandon had said, with about an inch of water left in the bottom. Nobody was inclined to doubt the rest of what he said, after that.

Two hours later, Matthieu arrived at Goliad with what was left of the water.

"Come on, let's go," I said, getting up from my chair as soon as he got there.

I had trouble walking very fast anymore, and I looked more like a man of eighty rather than the boy of twenty-two that I'd been less than a week ago, but I was still determined not to give in to helplessness until I had to. So it took us a while to walk all that way, but when we finally got there the place was just like I always remembered; black stones around a wide pool reflecting the deep blue sky. I stepped up to the edge and uncapped the bottle.

"Whatever You will, Lord, let it be," I murmured, and poured out the water into the pool. It made ripples that traveled across the surface of the pool to the far side and reflected back again till they stopped. Even the wind died down to nothing, and all the world seemed breathless with anticipation.

"Now wash," Brandon said, and I knew what he meant.

There are times and places when modesty is appropriate, and then there are other times when it's not. This was one of those times when it wouldn't have been proper at all. I took my clothes off and waded into the pool, which in spite of it being winter was no more than slightly chilly. The bottom was sandy, and when I reached the deepest point I took a deep breath and plunged all the way under.

When I came up again I heard simultaneous gasps from everybody except Brandon, and I saw so much joy on Lisa's face that I hardly knew what to make of it. As soon as I got to the edge of the pool she seized my hands and pulled me close, still dripping wet and buck naked, and her tears were mixed with laughter.

"You're cured, Coby; just like you were before," she whispered in my ear as she held me tight. But Brandon must have had very sharp ears.

"Even better than before. The curse is broken, too. This place is holy ground, now, and nothing evil can survive here," he said.

I don't know if cold can be considered evil or not, but it's certainly not nice, and I also realized that even if modesty hadn't been appropriate before, it certainly was now. I quickly grabbed my clothes and got dressed.

"What do you mean, this is holy ground?" I asked, while I was slipping my boots on.

"Both of you have sacrificed yourselves many times for the sake of Love. You've been faithful with small things, so now you've been entrusted with something greater," he said.

"This, you mean?" I asked, waving at the pool.

"Yes. God never repeats Himself, but He does love reflections. Far away, in a cavern green as emerald at the heart of the world, there's a fountain clear and cold, where the blessed of God may drink and erase for a little while the curse of the fall. This place is a mirror of that other and greater place, just as the spring whose water you poured out was also a mirror of it, and all of them are mirrors of God Himself, the Giver of all good things. People may come here to wash away whatever evil afflicts them, and it will be up to you and Lisa to guard it from now on," he said.

"Guard it?" I asked.

"There are people who would like nothing better than to crush this place and stamp out every memory of Heaven on earth. You can't allow that to happen here. It's yours to defend for as long as you live, and to use for the glory of God," he said.

"I never wanted to leave this place, anyway," I said, and clasped Lisa's hand.

"Me neither," she said.

They say the threads of fate are woven tighter than we can possibly imagine. I never really understood exactly what that meant, till then. So many seemingly unrelated things: Marcus and Lisa, finding Brandon in the swamp, Matthieu and the forgotten bottle of holy water, even Layla Garza; all of it was beginning to come together with a *click,* and who knew where it might all lead? The threads of fate are woven tightly, indeed.

I guess it's fitting, in a way, that the Cadron Pool should be a place where filthy and evil things are washed away forever. After all, it's written that long ago King Hezekiah cast the ashes of all the idols and evil things into the Cadron Valley in Jerusalem to make the land clean. Maybe that was a reflection, too.

I thought fleetingly of Moses on Mount Nebo, looking out across the Promised Land that he could never enter. I used to think my own life would turn out that way, once upon a time. But my prayers had been answered after all, and now I hardly knew what to think as I looked out on a future that seemed dazzling and deep. Whatever the years might bring, that was all right. I was content for now to enjoy the bright morning before the storm, if storm there had to be.

Chapter Forty
Lisa

When the day of the wedding came, it was worth all the work that went into it.

We found some white wooden lawn chairs to set up in the living room after pushing all the furniture out of the way, and Miss Josie found some white and blue ribbon to decorate with. It wasn't as fancy as some people have it, but to me it was everything I could have wished for.

I had a bouquet of white roses, and when I walked down that aisle to meet my beloved, I could truly say it was one of the happiest moments of my life. Even Jenny cried.

Halfway through, instead of lighting a candle, Cody surprised me by picking up a golden cup and holding it out to me.

"Will you drink with me, Princess?" he asked, with one of his little half-smiles. It hadn't been in the plans, but I knew immediately what he was talking about. So I smiled back and nodded before taking a sip. I didn't really think Tristan and Isolde had shared a cup of ginger ale punch, true, but I loved the symbolism, especially when I knew Cody understood it every bit as much as I did.

I think to be bonded with him at last in that way as in all others was one of the sweetest moments of my life, and it wasn't till then that I realized I was crying. But tears can be sweet sometimes, and there was no fear or shame in them.

He gently kissed me, and then it was done. I was reminded of that first kiss we shared at the fall dance in seventh grade, just as sweet in memory as this one was in reality.

"Now you have all there is of me," he said solemnly, and I smiled through what was left of my tears.

When the ceremony was over, Marcus and Cyrus played Paul Brandt's version of *I Do,* and we danced while everybody watched. I cried a little bit at that, too, because I don't think there's any song in the world more fitting for me and Cody. Then finally we ate brisket and cake and drank punch.

There wasn't time for us to go anywhere else before he had to leave, so we'd already decided to take our honeymoon when he got back home in August. He asked me where I wanted to go, and I promptly told him I didn't care as long as it wasn't Alaska or New Mexico. He laughed, and when he suggested Hawaii I was reminded for a second of that dream I had on the night when he first told me about the Curse. Maybe it was about to come true after all. I couldn't wait to see how it ended.

But all too soon it was time to put my daydreams away and let him go back to Alaska, to wait out the long seven months without him.

Just before he left, we drove the few miles to Autograph Rock, where we solemnly carved our names in stone below Blake and Josie McGrath.

"Love and peace," he murmured under his breath, in a voice so low I almost couldn't hear him.

"What are you talking about?" I asked, but he only smiled a little.

"Nothing, darlin'. Just thinking about something Daddy used to say, that's all," he said.

When we got back to Goliad, Miss Josie was standing on the porch waiting for us.

"I thought y'all would never get back! Look what came today!" she cried, holding out an envelope. Cody took it, and after reading the short note inside, he started to laugh.

"What's so wonderful?" I asked, confused, and Cody swept me up for a tight hug before he answered.

"This is what," he said, showing me the note.

Dear Cody and Lisa,

Congratulations on getting married. May God richly bless you both. In the meantime, please accept this as a token of our love and appreciation for all you've done in the fight against evil.

It was signed by John, Sarah, and Matthieu Doucet, and attached to the bottom of the note with a paperclip was a check for fifty thousand dollars. I almost fainted.

"You know what this means, don't you?" Cody asked, bringing me back to reality.

"What?" I asked.

"It means I'm not going anywhere, darlin'. Unpack that bag and tear up my ticket, cause I'm home for good," he said.

I did cry, then, but it was all I could do not to laugh at the same time. Sometimes things keep getting better and better until you almost can't believe they're real, but they are.

So we settled into the bunkhouse together, and for several weeks I redecorated, and repainted, and in the end I don't think I flatter myself too much when I say the place looked a hundred times better than it did when it was only a bachelor pad for a young buck with no sense of style at all. I love Cody to death, but he was and is a cowboy to the bitter end, and however much I love him I really didn't feel like living for the rest of my life in a house decked out in nothing but cowhide and bearskin.

My days were full and mostly happy, and if there was a current of leftover sadness underneath, well, I've come to believe that life is like that, sometimes. You may not always get everything you want, but I think you do always get what you need.

Spring came, with its showery days and green grass, when the whole world seems new. The pastures were full of bluebonnets as far as the eye could see, just like Cody had told me they would be. For a while I painted to my heart's content, trying to capture a little bit of all that fleeting beauty. I felt like I'd finally come home, at long last, and maybe even to have some of that pale and nourishing dirt in my own blood, just like Cody did. Blake McGrath's vision of a refuge for the hurting and a place of peace had come true for me, too.

The Mustangs started playing gigs again as soon as Marcus was up to it, and in March Cody surprised me by writing a song for me. The first time I ever had the slightest notion he was working on such a thing was the day when he first sang it, for a small crowd at Sufficient Grounds in Tyler, my favorite spot out of all the places they'd ever played. The patrons laughed and cheered when he stepped offstage to kiss me afterward, and even though it was kind of embarrassing to be made such a spectacle, I wouldn't have traded it for the world. Whenever I thought I loved him as much as humanly possible, he always managed to top it.

And then a few days ago I had a dream of my own, for the first and only time in my life, I think. It's not the one I asked for, to be sure, but maybe it's the one I needed to see.

I see, in my mind's eye, a boy of sixteen or so, with dark hair and a face that reminds me just a little of Cody's. It's a rainy night, in some warm place where palm trees grow, and he's working intently at a lab bench, all alone in a room full of gear I don't recognize. I'm not sure what he's doing, except that it's very, very important, and somehow I know that the fate of all mankind depends on what that one boy is doing that very night. He looks exhausted and close to despair, and I wish I could speak, to tell him not to give up.

And that's all. Just that one image, no context, no explanation, but somehow it means more to me than I could ever explain. Far in the future, he's some distant child of mine and Cody's. I know it in that strange and inexplicable way that you simply know things in a dream sometimes.

I don't doubt that it's true, and I admit it worries me a little, what may end up happening to them all in that far future time. But I have to believe that whatever may happen, things will work out as they should. Mama told me many times that now is all we ever have, that the past is gone and the future may never come. She would have said that God Himself has no future and no past, that all times for Him are right now, and that therefore if we want to be like Him and to get a small taste of what Heaven must be like, then the present is the only place we can do that. So I've been trying, hard as it is sometimes.

In May, I found out I was pregnant. My immediate reaction was to instantly start worrying about anything and everything that might go wrong, and for a while it was hard to be quite as happy as I felt like I ought to have been. I didn't even tell Cody for almost a month, irrationally afraid that if I got too excited something bad might happen. But gradually, as time went by, I put aside my fears and became more confident that things would be all right.

He came in smelling like peaches, on the day I finally told him. Yellow Freestones, to be exact; I've had a thorough education about the peculiarities of peaches since coming to Goliad. It was harvest time, and the scent had soaked into his clothes and even his hair, so strong it was almost like potpourri. It was a little odd, mixed with the scent of sunshine and sweat, but I wrapped my arms around him and took a deep breath of his t-shirt before he kissed me. He must have been eating fruit off the trees, because I could taste warm peach on his lips, too.

"Monkey kiss," I said, smiling.

"Yeah, couldn't resist. They're really good, fresh in the sun like that," he said.

"I bet," I said.

"Here, I brought you some," he said, handing me three of them wrapped up in his handkerchief.

"Well, so happens I have a surprise for you, too," I said.

"Oh, yeah? What's that?" he asked. I could tell he was completely clueless, and I drew it out a bit longer, relishing the suspense.

"Well. . . we're having a baby, Coby; aren't you happy?" I asked, enjoying the look of shocked surprise on his face.

"Oh, wow," he said, or something like that. Maybe he was too stunned to think of anything else, but it was a statement so bland that I couldn't help laughing.

"Is that really all you can think of to say?" I asked, still amused.

"Hey, you've had a lot longer to think about it than I have," he reminded me, and I relented.

"Yeah, true. I guess I ought to let you recover for a few minutes before I expect you to say anything. You *are* happy, though, right?" I said.

"Absolutely. Cross my heart and hope to eat Brussels sprouts. That's a fate worse than death, you know," he said. He took me in his arms and kissed me on the forehead without saying anything, and for a long time neither did I.

"It'll be born in January," I finally murmured.

"Cool. Maybe we'll have the same birthday. That'd be awesome, now wouldn't it?" he said.

Christopher Marlowe once said *Who ever loved, that loved not at first sight?* That's how it feels, sometimes. I feel like I've loved Cody ever since the day I was born, like we were made for each other stitch by stitch like a glove is made for a hand. He completes and fulfills me in ways I never knew I was lacking till I found him. I feel like God must have written us together into the story of the world on the day the universe was made. So many things could have kept us apart, and yet here we are.

I don't know what the future will bring, or how many sorrows and hurts it might throw at us. But I'm certain that as long as we're together, we can always overcome them. When I think about all the things we've already endured, it only makes me even more certain that nothing can ever come between us.

Cody loves me like the sun loves the green grass, like the rain loves a new-plowed field, like a burning fire that cleanses and leaves me pure. I love him like a yellow rose loves the summer heat, like a blue sea loves the blue sky, a reflection of glory that makes him whole.

There are times when love is so right that it can bring tears to the eyes for very sweetness, and all the poetry in the world could never be beautiful enough to capture it. Only the ones who are blessed enough to find it themselves can really understand.

I wish I'd known back in the old days, how much better the truth can be than even the most beautiful fairy tale. Cody and I have found it, at long last, in spite of everything, and I wouldn't trade that for any other treasure this world could offer. Life doesn't always turn out like a Scarlett Blaze romance, even though I know I once hoped it would.

Sometimes it's even better.

Epilogue
Cody

Goliad is full of life these days, in a way that it hasn't been ever since I can remember. The weather seems better this year, so hopefully there'll be no more drought to worry about. I keep busy in the fields and the pastures and the orchard, with farming and music and family, and even though the work is hard I love it.

Brandon is more help than I ever thought he'd be, especially with mechanical things. He can work on the tractor almost as well as I can these days. He's still enough of a kid to think I walk on water, though; I'm not sure exactly when the hostility got replaced by hero-worship, but it happened sometime.

I talk to the baby every night, which made Lisa laugh at first until she realized he'd stop kicking for a while to listen. Then she was all for it. So I tell him about life and love and red dirt bands and anything else under the sun. I know he won't remember, of course, but it's really kind of amazing how much you can socialize with a baby that small, if you only try.

Becoming a father makes you thoughtful about a lot of things you never paid much attention to before, and knowing there's another person who depends on you so completely is a humbling experience. I wouldn't trade it for anything, though. In fact, there's nothing else I know of which is more likely to inspire a man to greatness of heart, if there was ever a spark of it to be found in him to begin with.

I think a lot about what to do with Cadron Pool, because that's an awesome responsibility, too. The first thing we did was to track down as many of Layla's victims as we could, but that's been hard. She was always so anonymous about things, it's hard to know when or where she met people. James Fitch wouldn't believe me, not even after I drove all the way up to Nebraska to plead with him. I think that probably stung the most, but there was nothing I could do for him if he wouldn't listen. But there have been two so far that we *did* find and save; one from Missouri and another from Oregon. I hope we'll be able to find more; I'm certain there are plenty of them out there.

So that will be our life's work, it seems; to heal hurts and make things right, and Goliad will indeed be a refuge for the broken and a place of peace in ways I never even thought of before. I feel rich beyond my wildest imaginings, and I could never have dreamed of a life so sweet and full until suddenly it was there. God is awesome that way; a loving father who delights to give his children all the good things they ever wished for, and even more than they wished for. He may do it in a way which isn't quite what you expected at first, but He never forgets or overlooks.

I've also been thinking a lot about Layla Garza herself here lately, and what it might mean that she liked the taste of my father's life. My father was noble and his heart was always bound close to God, but there was nothing else to set him apart or make him special. So if Layla found that she liked the taste of that, if she learned to thirst for God even in the midst of all her wickedness, then maybe in time her heart might be broken with longing for what the world can never give, and she might, just possibly, become one of the saints herself. And if that's true, then Daddy really did give his life to save her, in a much deeper way than he or anybody else ever suspected. And for that I'm prouder of him than ever, and I wish I could tell him so. Maybe someday I will.

I had another dream last night, and I'm not sure if it was one of the true kind or not. I saw Lisa and me, standing in a field of bluebonnets, hand in hand. Three kids were playing around our feet, and the setting sun cast a golden glow on our faces. Was it real, or only wishes? God only knows.

But for now, I'm content to sit beside Lisa on the porch and pick my twelve-string, to watch the sun set on Mount Nebo, and to think about Love.

In Beauty be it finished, after all.

The End

Related Books

The Last Werewolf Hunter: *In this series you will find out many things about Matthieu Doucet, the Guardian Stones, Layla Garza and her brothers, and where the holy water that Cody poured into Cadron Pool came from, as well as information about Cody's ancestors and many other things.*

Tycho: *This book is the story of Cody and Lisa's grandson, Tycho McGrath, whom Lisa dreamed about near the end of Many Waters. The world is under serious threat of destruction, and only Tycho has the key to save it.*

Unclouded Day: *In this story you will learn all about how Brandon Stone came back from the dead when he was four years old to become a reader of dreams. You will find out why hymns make him cry and the whole history of the Fountain of Youth at the heart of the world.*

Music in this Book

His Life is an Open Book – The Lewis Family
Send the Fire – Traditional Hymn
Lord Have Mercy on a Country Boy – Don Williams
Unclouded Day – Traditional Hymn
Lily of the Valley – Traditional Hymn
I Do – Paul Brandt
Barefoot Blue Jean Night – Jake Owen
Leaning on the Everlasting Arms – Traditional Hymn
I Fought the Law – Buddy Holly
Dixie – Traditional
All Through the Night – Traditional

Author's Note

Many Waters has been an unusual piece of work for me. Even though romantic love has almost always played a part in all my stories, it's never been the central theme, as it is in this book.

But I felt that if I wanted to write about romance, then I wanted to explore the deeper issues of what true love really means and the ways that male-female interactions can be (although they aren't always) a reflection of God's relationship with humanity. That's a hard thing to write about.

Thus came the concept of magnanimity, or greatness of heart. Or, as Cody would have said, the casting away of self for love of another, the scorning of selfishness. This idea of unconditional love is woven throughout the entire story, from Cody's yearning to be (as he says) the sunshine and the rain to make little things grow strong, to Lisa's flat declaration that love with strings attached is worthless. This kind of self-sacrifice is the way Jesus behaved towards us, and therefore is the proper way that any man and woman should view one another, in an ideal world.

People are not perfect, of course. Cody allows himself to forget what he believes when confronted with the test of Lisa's cheating on him with Marcus, and Lisa herself fails to have the faith and trust she ought to have had when confronting Layla. But both of them live up to their ideals in time.

The title came from the Song of Solomon: *Many waters cannot quench love, neither can the floods drown it.* This is significant on many levels. On the simplest level, it refers to the fact that water plays a symbolic role in many parts of the book, from the bottle of holy water carried by Matthieu Doucet, to Cadron Pool, the Brazos River, the drought that so worries Cody, and others. On another level, the Scripture reference obviously implies that love is forever, and it obviously relates to Cody's father, but it also carries a strong message that the love of God is eternal in spite of all sorrows, and that He will take even the most horrible events and twist them into a blessing. It's a very profound lesson.

In fact there are many deep lessons in this book, for the perceptive reader. I like to think it provides a lot of food for thought.

The book also includes characters from several other books and actually picks up story-threads from three of them. Matthieu Doucet from *The Last Werewolf Hunter* is here and plays a very significant role, in fact, along with Layla Garza. Zach Trewick and Cameron Parker are alluded to, and their actions influence what happens in this book. The events of this book occur during the exact same time period as *Truesilver,* which is Book Four of *The Last Werewolf Hunter.* Not only that, but Brandon Stone from *Unclouded Day* has a large and critical part in this book, and even Tyke McGrath from *Tycho* is mentioned briefly. All these interlocking storylines meet and cross paths in *Many Waters,* which I suppose makes it in some ways the central story of everything. But I believe it works in such a way that the tale always feels natural, like it could never have happened otherwise. That's my hope, at least.

I'm not sure yet whether there might be a sequel to Cody and Lisa's story. I'm certain there will be one for Brandon, but we'll have to wait and see about the others. It'll probably depend in large part on how many people ask for one, so if you want to know more about Cody and Lisa or one of the other characters, please visit my website and let me know. I always take things like that into account when choosing my next project to work on.

But for now, I hope you enjoy this one.

William Woodall
June 21, 2013

Discussion Questions

1. Characters often see things in different ways. In what ways do you think the story might have differed, if Cody and Lisa's positions had been reversed? For example, do you think Cody would have reacted the same way, if Layla had ordered him to break up with Lisa?

2. Both Cody and Lisa have to struggle with personal issues as well as relationship difficulties. In what ways do you think their personal histories affected the way they related to each other?

3. Cody says that his dearest wish is to find his one and only true love and settle down to farm and have a family at Goliad, his ancestral home. Why do you think he had this wish?

4. Lisa has a love for symbolism which is partly expressed through painting and poetry, but also in the way that she talks about the world. Discuss some of the symbolism used in the book, such as Cody's high school ring or the cup used at the wedding.

5. Miss Josie never told Cody about the curse he was under or mentioned the Guardian Stone, even though she knew these things for years. Do you think it's ever all right not to tell someone certain things, even when it directly affects them? Give examples.

6. Some of the mysteries in the story are never explained, such as what happened to Layla, or the meaning of Lisa's dream. What do you think about these things? Explain what you think they mean.

7. Brandon says that God loves reflections. Explain what you think he meant by this and the ways it might apply in everyday life.

8. There were several times during the story when Cody and Lisa were forced to confront their deepest fears and have courage. What are some times when you or someone you know has had to do this?

9. Lisa says that love and beauty are linked forever in the soul of man, and this is why boys yearn after beautiful things. Explain what you think she meant by this. Do you believe this is true?

10. The "theme" of a story is the underlying message or messages about life the author is trying to convey. It is the lesson or moral of

the story, such as "Love conquers all". What do you think the overall theme of *Many Waters* might be? (There can be more than one.)

11. Cody says that he loves the way there's so much depth and richness to the world beyond what the eye first sees, and that a man could live his whole life awash in wonders, if he only knew. Discuss this idea. Explain what you think Cody meant, and give examples.

12. Jenny says that it's impossible for boys and girls to be just friends and no more. Do you agree with this statement? Give reasons for why you think as you do.

13. Cody says that greatness of heart (courage and self-sacrifice for the sake of love) is the most beautiful thing there is, because it's a reflection of God. How do you feel about this idea? Do you agree? Tell about someone you know who has displayed greatness of heart.

14. Cody also says that there's nothing dearer to God's heart than a son or daughter who sees nothing but heartache as the result of obedience, and then obeys anyway. Discuss this. Are there times when you've had to do something very difficult for God, which you didn't want to do? How did that experience turn out?

15. Lisa says that love with strings attached is worthless. Do you agree with this idea? Why or why not?

16. Brandon says there are people who would like to stamp out every memory of Heaven on earth. Why do you think anyone would want to do this? How would you respond to such a person?

17. Several times, Cody and Lisa discover that things are not what they seemed at first. Give examples from the text.

18. Cody says that God delights to give us all the good things we wish for, and even more than we wished for. Give examples of a time when God has richly blessed you beyond what you asked for.

Unclouded Day
By William Woodall

Brian Stone's life isn't easy. Abandoned by his father, abused by his alcoholic mother, and mocked by his classmates, his only treasures are his beloved little brother Brandon and his old guitar.

Then Brian finds a magical amulet in his attic, and things begin to change. Soon he has more power and wealth than he's ever dreamed of, and for a while all seems to be well.

But Brian's choice to trust in the power of magic is a terrible mistake which may cost him everything, and when tragedy strikes, his only hope is to seek out the Fountain at the Heart of the World, wherever *that* may be.

Unclouded Day is a tale of the glory of God's love; the life-giving Life, and the Beauty that makes beautiful.

* * * * * * *

"I would absolutely, without reservation, encourage you to read this wonderful novel, even if you aren't the fantasy genre type. It was a blessing."
-Sue Collier-Brannin, Reflections and Reviews

"There are so many nuggets of truth hidden in this book. It's about Heaven. It's about bad things happening for a reason. It's about deciding for yourself what matters most in life. It's a really good book!"
-Tattie Maggard, Christian Fiction Ebooks, Missouri

"William Woodall has the gift of writing , well, what I'd call young adult stories, though anyone could read this and be blessed,"
-Anna Rashbrook, England

Available now from your favorite retailer!

The Last Werewolf Hunter Series
By William Woodall

Zach Trewick always thought he'd become a writer someday, or maybe play baseball for the Texas Rangers. What he never imagined in his craziest dreams was that he'd find himself dodging bullets and crashing cars off mountainsides, let alone that he'd ever be expected to break the ancient werewolf curse which hangs over his family.

Even worse, his parents are determined to fight him tooth and nail to keep the Curse intact, his friends are not much help, and he's not quite sure his girlfriend isn't secretly trying to kill him. And that's just for starters.

But Zach is the last of the werewolf hunters, the long-foretold Curse-Breaker who can wipe out the wolves forever, and he's not the type to give up just because of a few minor setbacks. . .

* * * * * * *

"If you are looking for a story about a boy who learns valuable lessons about family, love, friendship and God this is the book for you. I recommend this book to a pre-teen or adult. I truly enjoyed this book."
-Rae, *My Book Addiction Reviews*

This author is an excellent writer who knows how to draw the reader into a story and make them feel it. The writing will resonate long after you lay the book down."
-Lynn O'Dell, *Red Adept Reviews*

"I found myself captivated with the story and could not stop reading until I reached the final page. Everything about this story is thought-provoking. Readers of all ages will appreciate this wonderfully told story,"
-Jancy Morgan Dunn, Kansas

"I love this story so much, I'm planning to buy it in its paperback form,"
-April, Southern California

Available now from your favorite retailer!

Tycho
By William Woodall

In the year 2154, sixteen year old Tycho McGrath is an advanced genetics student at the prestigious John Brooke Academy in Tampa. Life seems fairly dull, until he accidentally discovers that in less than a week, a recently designed bacterium known as the Orion Strain will almost certainly wipe out every human being on earth.

Tycho and his friends quickly form a desperate plan to steal an experimental spacecraft and flee to the partially-terraformed Moon, hoping to ride out the plague until it's safe to come home.

But the survivors of Earth soon discover that the Moon has its own dangers. Horrific storms, radiation poisoning, and mutant insects all lie in wait for the unwary, and worst of all, they must soon face the betrayal of one of their own.

* * * * * * *

"Reminiscent of Freedom's Landing, by Anne McCaffrey, Tycho combines the best of traditional space-exploration sci-fi with modern apocalyptic fiction. For any fans of hard science fiction, it doesn't get much better than this."
- Liz Ellor, OH2 Reviews

"Woodall tells an interesting sci-fi story, through the eyes of Tycho the young scientist,"
-David King, Missouri

"This story was awesome! What I liked best was when the characters jumped off the skyscraper-sized cliff without getting hurt. I also liked the giant vampire roaches. This is a must-read book if you like sci-fi."
-Scott Crawford, Georgia

Available now from your favorite retailer!

If you'd like to find out more about Cody and Lisa and the other people and places mentioned in this book, please visit:

**William Woodall's
Official Author Website**

www.williamwoodall.org

Here you will find:

Free short stories and sample chapters
Discussion questions for teachers and book clubs
Photos of characters and locations for each story
Musical soundtracks
Articles, Interviews, and Quotable Quotes
Contact Information
And much, much more!

Made in the USA
Charleston, SC
22 October 2013